Leporello

by the same author

The Good Republic

WILLIAM PALMER

Leporello

Secker & Warburg LONDON

First published in Great Britain 1992
by Martin Secker & Warburg Limited
Michelin House, 81 Fulham Road, London SW3 6RB

Copyright © William Palmer 1992

A CIP catalogue record for this book
is available from the British Library

ISBN 0 436 36049 7 (hardback)
ISBN 0 436 36050 0 (trade paperback)

The author has asserted his moral rights.

The author would like to thank
the Arts Council of Great Britain for the award
of a literary bursary during the writing of this book.

Typeset by DSC Corporation Limited, Cornwall, England
Printed and bound in England by Clays Ltd, St. Ives PLC

to Gill and Lucy

I remember the wife of a poet. Tall and slender with small breasts. A delicate inward-curving face, like a spoon, with a sallow glow lighting it – a spoonful of clear amber soup. A long fine nose. A tiny red mouth. I saw her at once as she came into the courtyard of the inn where we were staying.

This was – where was this? Somewhere to the north of Genoa. How can I remember the names of all these places? The people – that is different. They walk through this room tonight. I'm not cracked. I'm old.

The whole thing is a play, a game, a hoax, said my late master, my only true master, Don Giovanni. This room. Candle. The dark. The past. It all lights up. I sit here, and plain as day, the Don stands under the awning that runs along one side of the courtyard. He leans into the hugely fat wife of the landlord. Colossal woman, I tell you.

She looks lasciviously at everyone except her husband. When our carriage horses first cantered into the yard, her eyes went saucers at me – then cartwheels at the Don. Now the Don pulls away from her and she goes indoors, her haunches swaying as if each one held a young girl – he cannot help but please the ladies. We have been here one day.

He turns. The spoon-faced lady enters the courtyard.

She hesitates and gazes round at the confusion of doors and windows. My master crosses the yard swiftly. He bows. Close to her. That is the secret, he told me once, never to appear to doubt yourself; if you do, you are lost.

Madam . . . , he says in a soft insinuating voice that carries up to the balcony from where I watch.

She takes half a step back, startled. It might have been a hawk had landed at her feet.

He questions her.

She explains, with only a little more hesitation, that she is looking for her husband.

His name? the Don most delicately asks.

It is like looking down at a play.

His name? Oh, we soon find that out. We volunteer to send our servant to see if the gentleman is within. Meanwhile this is no

1

place for a lady to stay. The courtyard of this low inn. She may be observed. Her reputation. Perhaps, if she would permit, the discretion of the innkeeper's private quarters?

This way, signora ...

I can tell this a hundred times or more, a similar passage with a different woman, in a different scene. As I say, this one's husband was a poet.

For one of his kind he was quite a decent sort. My master took a liking to him in the week that ensued – without telling him that he had made his wife's acquaintance. But the fellow was a madman. A lukewarm madman. Before your eyes he would fall to writing on anything to hand: the leaves of the books he carried always with him; when they ran out, on his shirtsleeves, his own hands and wrists, scribbling, scribbling away. And all of it, my master told me, the saddest, most miserable stuff. The Don took him by the arm one night. Good Guercio, he says. Good Guercio ... I think that was his name. Or perhaps he just looked what it means. Squint-eyed. He had a habit of screwing up his eyes as we approached, then smiling as we drew near.

Good Guercio, says the Don, the mistake you make, the reason for the unhappiness in all your verses, is in thinking that all men are as unhappy as you. I assure you this is not the case. Take my servant here – Leporello. You are a happy man, are you not, Leporello?

I bow, but not too low. Only gentlemen bow low to each other; servants incline.

My servant, you will be surprised to learn, the Don goes on, can read and write – but not enough to make him unhappy. He is my secretary, my valet, my travelling companion, my right arm. He knows how to ride and if not how to fight, how to run away in the right direction. How to cook and sew; how to steal. How to nose out the best lodgings in a town and which house is the brothel and which the bishop's. Not at all the same thing. He knows when I am being cheated, and how to cheat in return. He knows, in short, how the world works.

At all of this I chuckle in the permitted way. By flattering me the Don flatters himself at having got such a good man.

They both look at me in silence for a moment as if admiring a statue. Then the Don continues:

Leporello's world is as foursquare and solid as this table, dear Guercio. He does not stand with fear and trembling under the weight of the universe. While you and I know – what was it Pascal said – the cold immensities of space – why, for Leporello, the stars he guides me by are simply fixed lamps, placed for his convenience. He does not worry how they got here and there in the heavens, or how or why they remain shining. What he calls *God* is what he sees. The lamps in the air shine through the mask on his God's face. You will have light and benign judgement at the Last, won't you, Leporello? And what will we have, Guercio? Extinction. Not even the knowledge of a dream.

The world, you see – the Don waved his hand to indicate me again – is made for stout, hearty men such as this. They don't give a damn what goes on in their minds as long as their bellies and bladders and, occasionally, their cocks, are full. Their women faithful. Or at least discreet. Is it not so? While you – he smiled at the poet – you address your Beatrices, your Lauras; the floating spiritual heart, the divine countenance seen for a moment at a window, the profile bent as *she* kneels in the transfigured cathedral; all else obliterated in this holy setting; prayer, God, the Virgin, responses, monstrances, candles, the sickening incense; all lost in your impious worship, in the pure nimbus which holds forehead, nose, lips, the delicate chin of the one you love. And do you know what goes on in the heads of these virgins, these first communicants? Tempests. Riots. They are on fire. Their heads reel in the embraces of brutes. They do not know you exist. They do not exist. Not as you see them.

They do, they do exist, the poet protested feebly.

While your most beautiful wife, if you will forgive me, but we are both gentlemen – while you neglect your most beautiful wife. She shines upon you – and what are you to her? The backside of the moon ... The Don could persuade himself, you see, that he genuinely cared for these husbands.

My wife is acting strangely, the poet murmured, so softly that I could hardly hear him. It is as if she hates me, he said.

Now, now, don't blub. What have I just told you? Why make life less than it is? said my master. The girls would rather see through their fine brown eyes a common soldier in his tight uniform, a brave rider bouncing in his saddle, a tumbler, an acrobat with every limb like a flicker of lightning, an actor with his pockmarks filled up with paint – rather any of these than a poor mewling bloody poet. You have to be strong, my dear fellow, to please the ladies. A bed breaker. And still you won't wear out their bottom furniture. Each one will exhaust you. They will rise up, smiling, saying, Come my love, just one more time. The littlest, whitest-faced, thinnest, most tremulous of them. Once more. One more time.

It's all very well for you, said the poet, at last stirred.

What had happened between the Don and the poet's wife?

How did the Don have her? How do you think? In the end there are not that many ways. What magic did he employ to seduce a virtuous wife he had met only a few moments before?

Whoever told you there was such a thing as a virtuous wife?

When I heard him invite her inside (from where I watched on the long balcony above), I made haste down the stairs and across the courtyard – I never knew when he might want my assistance. The ghost of his voice swam along the narrow, dark corridor . . . Your reputation, madam . . . The safety of the rooms of the innkeeper . . . She went before him, twisting and hesitating to his direction, while I concealed myself behind each corner, each twist and turn as they went inwards and upwards, towards the Don's room. Watching to see if she would panic at the last, being taken by this strange gentleman into the dark heart of a strange house. And then he was growing hot for her – the Don delighted in telling me later – at her tall, swaying figure going before him. Now she was at the door. He hurried forward to open it for her, stepped back gallantly to allow her to enter and looked back down to where I now stepped into view at the end of the corridor. If you will wait here, madam, he said. I will find my man and have him fetch your husband. Signor . . . ? Signor Guercio, came her low voice from the room. Then the Don came sauntering down to me, and whispered, A while, Leporello. Give me a while. He went

4

back to the room, carefully leaving the door ajar for modesty's sake . . .

Did I arrive back in time to hear the bed galloping like a fourwheel and two pair clattering at full tilt along a cobbled street, then the rattling, rattling, the final rallentando, shuddering to a dead halt, that I had heard so often before? No – this was a lady, not a chambermaid. There was only the low murmur of their voices.

I knocked. The door was flung open and the Don stood, a frank smile on his face. Behind him the woman stood up from the bed, her face colouring. Your husband, madam? the Don said. Ah, no, my man. Where is Signor Guercio?

I edged in. The gentleman was nowhere to be found, I said. I had searched all over, but it seemed he had left some time before.

In my trip downstairs I had slipped a coin to a boy to go to Signor Guercio and inform him that he was wanted urgently at home. I had seen him through the window grumbling, getting up from his table. I hid behind a wooden pillar as he walked by. His wife was supposed to meet him at the inn; she could not admit when she got home that she had been closeted with another gentleman for half an hour. At cross purposes they might fall to bickering. It all helped prepare the way for the Don.

Oh, what a pity, said the Don. But, madam, your time has not been completely wasted, I hope. Our talk has been quite the pleasantest time I have passed in your town.

She coloured again. Sir, she stammered. I thank you for your efforts. I think I must go now.

Of course, of course. My servant will escort you home.

No, no . . .

I insist. I hope that I might have the pleasure of meeting you again, perhaps with your husband . . . ?

Oh yes, with my husband . . . , she said, and she half-smiled at him and half-frowned at me.

And so I lead her back along the same passageways and into the yard. There really is no need, she says.

My master insists, I say, and as we go across the courtyard her step is sprightly, though she pulls up her shawl to cover her face.

5

And as we go through the streets, I try to go as slow as possible, and she seems not intent on hurrying home. Also, I see from the corner of my eye she seems about to speak several times, and then to draw back, until she hesitantly enquires, Your master . . . ?

Yes, Signora.

I heard of course of his coming to town. She is trying to hide the interest in her voice with the sort of blasé offhandedness these bored, provincial ladies affect. I suppose he is a great traveller . . . ?

Ah yes, I say. My master is a scholar and seeker after knowledge in all parts of the world. He is engaged on a great work of philosophy I cannot comprehend. I praise him, as I always do, the speech is well worn. There had never been a gentler, more perfect employer. A kindly man. A man of lofty ideals . . .

Really, she murmurs.

All too soon we are at her street. My house is just here, she says. I must thank you. She fiddles in her little bag for a *buonamano*. It is not necessary, I say. *I* insist this time, she says. And I accept her coin gratefully – it represents a small profit on that laid out for the boy at the inn. Signora, I say, if I may be so bold. If your husband should be at home – (it is time to be forward) – I do not wish your good name – perhaps the side door . . . ?

She looked puzzled for a moment, then nodded. There is nothing women like better than a pinch of intrigue.

So I delivered her to the side door. She slipped in, her mind, it is to be hoped, full of the Don's charming qualities.

As my master always said, it is not the first meeting, but the second when business is done.

Love? Ah, love. Let me tell you that that same afternoon he entertained the most willing fat landlady in the same bed the lady had sat on. While I was detailed to engage the attention of her husband, the landlord, and keep him behind his counter. We discussed the ladies of the town.

Take my wife, the landlord said, in a confidential tone, seeing I was a good sort. There, he said, is a woman without an ounce of passion in her whole great body. Now – he lowered his head and the sour wine of his breath made itself unwelcome to my nose –

do you blame me? he wheezed. I have a woman in the town who . . .

And next day – as I am now his bosom pal – as he tells me again of his mistress's accomplishments, my eyes are on the poet, in a corner, talking, his hands waving in excitement, getting tipsy with his idle friends, while the Don visits his house.

For the second meeting.

It was a couple of nights later that the poor poet told us how his wife was behaving with the most extraordinary coldness towards him. I could see how the Don smiled and took this as a compliment on his superior prowess, and it was then that he proffered the advice to the poet that I have already retailed to you.

We left this town shortly afterwards. As I say, I cannot remember its name. It was like a thousand others.

I make no excuse for him. I prefer to remember him as he was; not what he became. I judge the living by the dead – and find the living wanting. I have outlived my life. Now I read the death notices, look down on funerals going under the window; ask, How old was he? in that half-covetous, half-fearful way of a poor man asking the price of meat in the market.

But what of you, who write all this down for me? Who come peeking and poking into my life? Why do you sneak and snoop around the old, the nearly dead? Tut-tutting and rooting through this pile of rags.

What is this book of yours to be about? You will have no market for the truth I assure you. There is never a market for that.

The Don and his Women? Is that what you think will sell? Printed up by Monsieur Disparu, the Freemason, in his back shop, handed over a cartside by his mistress in the Saturday market for twenty sous a copy. The totally unbuttoned, every name named, Startling Revelations of the Ancien Régime, Rabelaisian Disclosures, Life of Sin Punished by the Merciful Intercession of God, Memoirs of an Utterly Worthless Man? Is that it? While you stand by, slyly, admiring the taste of the buyers, fondling and jingling your share of their coins in your pocket, next to your little water

7

spout? Well, if you think that, think again, young sir. I shall demand my reasonable cut from your endeavours – and more, depending on how you've dressed up or ballsed up my words.

No, the book is to be about Leporello. The Story of a Servant. God knows there are enough of us.

We see everything – and are invisible. When our masters die, we disappear from their lives; do not appear in their Lives. Look at the Bishop I serve now, in what must be my last post. When he dies who will think to ask his old servant what went on in even this house? What whisperings along midnight corridors; what intrigues, treacheries; what visitors, what holiness; what corruption? What strange creaks of beds, muffled bell ringings, letters sent, and letters burned? No, they will give His Grace a fine fat tomb in the cathedral and no one, gazing on his cold marble body, will ever know he was a man. And we servants, who could tell all, and more, go ignored; *our* births and deaths unrecorded, and whatever went on between might never have happened.

We fill the graveyards between the fine stone angels. Manure, fertiliser, slop, seepage; *That Bad Smell*. Still, I suppose it is better than being a soldier. I served once a general of the army, a great man whose face was on bronze medals, who after the battle of Quatre Bras pocketed a tidy sum from giving out the contract for the removal of bones and other debris from the field. Oh yes – it is quite a trade. Quite a trade. Friend and foe alike are bundled into the backs of carts and borne away, jollily jolting, mixing together as they never had the good fortune to in life, rubbing shoulders and everything else. They are brought to a yard. They are received with glee, as at a party. They relinquish their rags to the attendants, and are shown into – if there is any flesh left on them at all – a boiling vat. Here their fat, in a mad, whirling, hot dance, is reduced to candle tallow. The immaculate white bones are introduced to a fine upstanding bone-crushing machine. Bone-meal. Hurrah! Any gold from teeth, rings or other tomfoolery is usually absent from this unpretentious gathering – having long ago been removed from the bodies. Still, why should what is left not go to the aid the national economy? After all, they are no longer any use as soldiers or household providers; as lovers or fathers. Let's get on with my little crimes ...

PART I

The Iron Stove

1

I will tell you about my father's return. That's when my life began.

My father kept the inn, the *locanda* of our village. I was eleven or thereabouts; he had been away for some five years. Hard to tell how long. Or what was the day, or exact hour when he came back.

We had no clocks such as now infest the houses, except for the great one that stood in the castle on the hill, and that ran on and stopped and was started again and no one took any notice of it, except the servant who came to drink every night and told me of the clock's intricate brass gears and wheels, the painted silver moon in different phases that moved in a little starry heaven behind the gilded hands. What use is that, said a drinker, when we have the real moon? You could live in that village until you died and still know nothing but the sun and moon.

My master and I passed such places on our travels. He would look out of the carriage and say, Dear God, who lives here? How do they live? What do they live on? Or for? The earth goes round the sun – (which was news to me) – the moon goes round the earth, you and I travel in this coach, dear Leporello, travelling from this, embracing that, going forward with such high expectancy; all is movement, excitement, whirling of wheels, puffs of dust. And what do they do? They rot. They are born into misery. They live in despair. They couple. Rot. How do they stand it? And I shrug, ashamed to say that I come from just such a place. They live, sir, I say. They live. What else is there? Then we are past and he sits with his fingers drumming on the door sill, or puts his nose in some book, or falls asleep. He slept deeply – in snatches. Bed was not the place for rest. A great reader too, but on the road it would sometimes amuse him to ask me to tell him a story. I was ashamed of those things – they were what I had left behind in the rotting villages.

Tell me a fairy story, my master commands.

Once there was a dragon with seven heads . . .

Seven? Why always seven?

Because. A talking fish. An ogre with a human bride. A snake shedding gold coins for scales. A mirror that talks.

Tell me, Leporello. Tell me. I never heard such things as a child. You had all these wonders – I had only shepherds and shepherdesses sitting under trees in Arcadia.

Once there was a dragon with seven heads . . .

Her name was Bella. Aunt Bella. My father's sister, she kept the *locanda* while he was away.

It was a poor enough place with the ground floor making the wine shop and kitchen, a rickety open stair leading up to the one guest room, and on to the attic where Bella slept. I lay on a straw mattress by the kitchen oven. Guests? Like hummingbirds or elephants such creatures were rarely seen. But Bella did not lack for company. Each Saturday night when the place emptied out one of the men would linger behind. Bella would shoo me into the kitchen. I would hear her fasten the two narrow front doors, then her step on the stairs, and the man's heavier tread following.

My aunt never tired of informing me – as she twisted the hair on the nape of my neck – that I had taken my mother's life. How, in giving me existence, my mother forfeited her own. How – she told me over and over again – to look after her brother's child, she had given up the chance of a widowed farmer, two goats, and an olive grove. In remembrance of these, and for the good of my soul, she beat me every day. And as – with a kick here, and a cuff there – for my father, the worthless brute . . .

He came into the square one morning near noon, pulling his fortune clanking and rattling behind him. I didn't know him. A small, dark, square man, unshaven, his clothes patched and tattered. The companion he dragged along squealed and skittered and screeched against the stones. I rushed outside to see what it was. No one else greeted him. Most of the village had gone to the fields. The old women watched unseen from their dark doorways.

12

The sun burned white in a white sky. The square was empty. He was halfway across when he saw me. Giorgio, he cried, and dropped the handles of what he pulled and ran towards me, his coat flaring behind him. And that was odd, because no one had called me by my given name for as long as I could remember, but only by my nickname. Then I was caught up in this stranger's embrace and he said, Don't you know me, Giorgio? It is your father. Your father, silly boy. So he embraced me and I accepted him, though I still did not know him, because children take these things on trust, and I knew he could be no worse than Bella.

And Bella? She stood in the doorway and said simply, So you've come back, have you? And he said, Yes. And that was all after five years. He came inside and sat and ate ravenously and drank a bottle of wine. I sat and watched him in silence and awe. What went on in Bella's mind? Perhaps that this was an end to her easy, sluttish life. Then he got up and announced it was time to pull the stove inside.

I followed him outside. He took me up to the beast and explained, in high excitement, clutching my hand, running his hand across my hair, that this was a stove of the sort that travels with armies to bake their bread and boil their water. He pointed. Here, a hut on the top made the body. The chimney, the neck and head and tall black hat. Two iron doors, a hinged waistcoat. A small one below, the vitals, the fire chamber. The whole mounted on a chassis with wheels bound in iron. All the iron black, pitted with rust; the wood stained, muddied, gouged and scored. Ah, you could not know what it meant to him.

When I tried to move the stove I could shift it only a juddering inch or so at a time. My father got between the shafts and trundled it in, barking at me to move the tables back. He pushed the stove up beside the stone oven. When I told him that was the place where I slept, he said, No more, my boy. Those days are gone. You share my bed from now on.

He took the guest room. The stove squatted in the kitchen, proclaiming his sovereignty, and the dethronement of Bella. She was forbidden to beat me. I was only to wait on tables, to be prepared to be something in the world.

All this my father explained to me as we lay in his bed at night. The stream muttered and sang down the hill under the window as his voice rumbled in the dark until I slept and I was never quite sure what I had heard half-awake and what I had dreamt.

His language was as patched as his tattered coat with the way they spoke in the country to the North and the tongues of the great cities; it was sewn with Spanish swear-words he'd got from soldiers, and embroidered with bits of what he called French and German from even farther away.

He had been all things: a soldier, a deserter; labourer in vineyards and farms; a servant, a kept man; lastly, a baker. Blood, wine, love, and bread. He had brought the iron stove from Pomodoro. Covered in hay and bird shit in a stable. It had been there, he reckoned, ever since the Spanish chased the Austrians out twenty years before.

He had pulled it the sixty, seventy miles home – what did I know of distance? You never know where you are until you leave it behind. Pulling the iron stove home, he had pulled the world inside it.

He told me about this world in bed and as we walked up in the morning to that clump of wild trees and bushes where all the men and male children went to relieve themselves. The men greeting each other gravely, *Pietro, Tommaso, Luigi*, each going to his own spot. The sun would be coming up, lighting the castle and church on the hill while the little white-bellied birds flitted above, as we crouched in the ground mist, a head here, a head there, like shitting ghosts. And my father talked on, until somebody shouted, Eh, *oste*, we're at business here. Pipe down.

They are ignorant peasants, he said on the way back. One day you will go away, he said, pulling out the first bread of the day. You must go away before this place gets in your blood and you're not fit to go anywhere else. Do you want people to laugh at you?

I asked him why he had come back.

I wished to see my children. My place. Make my fortune. He laughed. In *this* place. A man should see his son.

14

He never told me why he had gone away. Not so that I could understand. Something to do with someone else's wife. He winked.

I would understand someday. Oh yes, no fear. He went and got himself a glass of wine.

As Bella went out with the washing basket to the stream, she said, The wine is for selling, not drinking.

He ignored her. It was not in our stars, he said, that we should be great men, to live in castles like the Baron. All that was arranged above. His gesture passed upwards, through Bella's bed, on up to Heaven.

But that was not to say things could not be bettered. I was to leave the village, leave and forget it ever existed. It was for a man to make his own way in the world while he was still young enough. He sighed. I was to trust no one. I should search out and attach myself to some great man as his servant. That way I would be safe and happy and not work myself to death and have to live in a hovel. The servants he had seen in the city, oh, they lived a grand, easy life. Find your man, said my father. If he fails you, then get another. The world, I must learn, is built for thieves.

The Baron in the castle up there – he pointed. There is never a penny turned, an olive picked, an ear of wheat cut, but that he has a bite of it. A great gentleman. A great thief. All servants steal. Small thieves who work for big thieves. It is the order of things; the many serve the few. How else would the world get on?

Then he looked me straight in the eye.

And what's this name they've given you, he said, this Leporello?

Everyone had a name that was not their given one. Bald-head. Flat-foot. Judgment-day. Crooked Wall Builder. Soup Sucker. Politesse. Head Cracker. Gambler. Hunchback. The Stomach That Walks Like A Man. Names for insult or flattery. And mine was given to me because, as a boy, I made the men in the *locanda* laugh. I learnt all their songs by heart, by hearing them every night. They stood me on a table, in my innocence, when Bella was not there, and I piped:

> Oh the Miller, the dusty, musty Miller
> The Miller that bears on his back
> He never goes to measure meal
> But his Maid, his Maid, but his Maid
> > holds open her sack.

> Oh the Baker, the handsome Baker
> The Baker that is so full of sin
> He never heats his Oven hot
> But he thrusts, he thrusts, but he
> > thrusts his Maiden in.

Stuff like that.

The place if anything got rougher after my father came back. The men had reined themselves in little enough for Bella, but she *was* a woman.

The room was empty most of the day, unless somebody was passing through the village. It filled up in the evening. They started with cards and dice; then the old songs over and over until they all fell out into the square, the last ones half the time fighting with knives or fists. You could tell when trouble was coming, for a man would start to pour wine with the left hand, leaving his knife hand free. Not every night, no, no. But enough. And though they boasted all the time, there was an etiquette to it that my father had forgotten. They did not like their poor bloody village being forever compared with the places and things he had seen; the fantastic cities, the beautiful women, elegant clothes, the carriages and great ships – all that was farther away to them than the moon that hung over the valley.

If any of their own kind had spoken that way he would have been bullied or laughed into silence. But father was the *oste*; he bought the wine and sold it; he treated with the Baron. He was halfway to them: the priests, soldiers, tax-gatherers, gentlemen, nobles ... All of those who could be cursed at behind their backs. Those in charge. He was an in-between to that other world. And when they met anyone from that world their faces would take on a sullen, cowed, stupid expression, their tongues lose all colour and force, their hands hang limply at their sides as if their strength had drained away.

So they drank the wine, and resented its provider. And he looked down on them.

You think we'll buy the bread from your black engine, *oste*, they said, but we won't. We can make our own. You won't get rich on us. Up there, in the hills, they call money the Devil's dung. The only wealth was in land, and the Baron owned that.

The land knew better than they. This year I'm talking about there had been a poor harvest and as it wore on towards winter their little stores of grain went down. My father had brought some gold back with him and could buy grain from the Baron. So, as the winter bit down, they were forced to get their bread, a cut of the wheel-sized loaves, from the iron stove.

My God it was a hard place in winter.

Mists hung in the square all day like ghosts, twisting and turning as the cold air moved them. Looking down over the broken wall at the end of the square you could not see the valley or river below; only the tallest trees poked their tops through the white mist. Behind the house the goats on the hillside came and went, their heads floating out of fog, their butts disappearing with a sad wag. The boys called their names anxiously, because at that time of year the wolves are the same colour as the grey air. If the sun broke through it shone pink on the tops of the mountains to the south, the mist shrank in the valley and hung along the river like a furry worm. Next day all was swallowed again.

The men came to drink still but lingered over their wine. They did not pay. They would settle up in the spring when things were going good again. They stared hard at my father, as if challenging him to take the silver out of their hard fists. He marked up their scores on the backs of a pack of playing cards. He could not write properly but had made up a code of marks and figures. It amused him to remember secretly the hunchback as the Jack of Spades; a notorious cuckold as the King of Hearts; to rate the other men as

17

one, two, three, four ... as the numbers on the cards. And this was another thing they held against him, as they saw him shuffling through the cards, another thing he had in common with priests and barons – that he accounted for their lives in mystical signs, that yet another man owned part of their labour, their souls, the next year of their lives.

Yes, a hard cold bitter place in winter. What is there for the men to do in the dark months? Nothing, but to send out their wives to cut and haul firewood. To sit in the smoky hovels with their three or four or seven children. Is it any wonder that they brood and their heads conjure adulteries, feuds, malign Fates. They go hunting but there is nothing to hunt. They imagine that their neighbours' wives are in love with them; that their wives are in love with the neighbours' husbands. And all this goes on only in their heads, for where, in this dank, cold, greyly weeping village, with its bare white and ochre walls, its scrubby hillsides of gorse and pale grass – where on earth could all this mad coupling go on? Nowhere but in their own heads and beds, making more children resentfully. More mouths to half-feed.

The snow came down from the mountains. The saint's blood in the reliquary under the statue of the Virgin in the church froze a dirty yellow. The square filled with snow that made the whitewashed walls look dim. Then the snow was criss-crossed with footsteps, melted in little islands by donkeys' droppings. Doors, swollen in summer, shrank again and snow blew under them instead of dust.

The stream at the back froze and in the morning had to be hacked at with a long knife. The earth at the edge of the stream stuck to the lumps of ice piled in the leather bucket; blades of bleached grass floated on top of the water as it heated to make the morning meal. At that, we were better fed than most in the village.

So was it to try and ingratiate himself that my father took me out one of those dreary winter days to visit a sister of my dead mother? We crossed the square and went up into the back end of the village.

It was the woman's confinement. Odd way of saying, when it

was the custom for all the relatives, male and female, to gather for a birth.

I was frightened. I did not know what to expect. Most of the women walked with their bellies rounded most of the year – until they had had enough of children and buried as many runts. But what happened between the women disappearing off the street and, a day or two later, reappearing in the doorways holding the new babies, I had no idea. A girl had shown me the cleft between her legs and told me solemn-faced that that was where babies came from. I had not believed her. Now I had the notion as we walked along a narrow alley that I would be asked to do something, to witness something appalling.

We got to the door. My father knocked. The door was opened and one of the women looked out. She stood aside without a word and we slipped in.

Six or seven men sat round the fire; along the wall the children sat in the shadows cast by the men.

The father-to-be, Cannelloro his name, said, Ah, the innkeeper. How well you are looking. And Leporello, how he is growing. Plenty to eat, eh? The other men snickered and turned their backs. They were drinking wine and after a moment or so Cannelloro rose up and grudgingly held out a cup to my father. Your best, *oste*. Don't drink it too fast. I still owe you for it. The men laughed again, looking slyly at one another. My father took a sip, then placed the mug on the table.

All this time I had been wondering where in this one room – there was no upper floor – they could be hiding the mother-to-be.

The bed had hangings round it, to keep out the mosquitoes in summer, the wind in winter. Behind a candle was lit and the light lay in thin yellow lines along the top of the hangings – they parted, a woman backed out, letting more light into the room. The enclosure of the bed, the white wall behind, made the candle-glow seem very bright. The sort of brightness in darkness that surrounds the Holy Family in the big gloomy paintings. Before the hangings fell back I had a glimpse of two more women bent over the bed, so you could not see what was in it.

The woman went back behind the hangings with a covered

basin in her hands. I wondered if the baby was in that and if they were now going to put it into the mother so it could be born. I could hear the women whispering. Along the wall, the children were silent. The men talked in low voices, ignoring us.

Bite, said a voice inside the hangings.

Muffled sounds. The creaking of the wooden bed. Breath, quickening and slackening. This went on and on. The hangings bulged out as the women moved behind. The men stopped speaking. The children stared at me. The eldest boy stuck out his tongue.

Why doesn't she get on with it? Cannelloro said suddenly.

What went on behind the hangings, went on. One of the women began to sing in a loud unmusical voice.

Ah, it has started at lasted, said Cannelloro.

We heard the bed writhe, the breathing pant and snort – but there was no screaming, no crying out to God in pain, no bringing down of curses on all men as I have heard since from women in this state.

The hangings moved in a sombre dance. Then the movement of the bed ceased. For a moment everything became still in the room, except the fire flickering. Then the cry of the baby – and this is a sound of joy everywhere, but here I do not know I have ever heard a more terrible sound, as if the infant wailed with horror to find himself in such a place.

Ragazzo, called one of the women. A boy.

Cannelloro, the husband, stood, and all the others did too, slapping him on the shoulders, congratulating his virility, wishing his son good fortune. The husband drew himself up, proud and grim at the same time, as all these peasants try to look. He had done his duty.

Bring me my son, he called.

There seemed to be some reluctance to draw back the hangings; a muttered conference was going on between the women.

Why does he have to wait so long? Bring me my son, Cannelloro demanded again.

At last they pulled back the hangings. The candlelight let loose seemed to shrink. The mother lay in the bed, her black hair falling across the bolster, her forehead glistening. She was taking from her mouth a piece of knotted cloth. That is why those women do not scream out. They bite on the cloth so as not to shout and bring shame on the household.

One of the women hurried forward with the baby wrapped in a shawl.

My father stepped forward to see, and as he did so, knocked over his mug. The wine ran, sinking into the wood. Some of the men crossed themselves, then the others, seeing what had happened, did the same.

Cannelloro had his back to us, busy with his son. It was only when he peeled down the shawl to show him off, turning him admiringly in his big hands, only then was seen the huge red birth stain circling the baby's body.

A curse. An abomination. They blamed my father and his spilt wine. The child? He died a month or so after, I think. Whether he was left to die, I do not know. It was a bad time for a sickly child, especially one marked by the Devil. Such a poor place as that, you need some luck just to keep going.

For nothing went right after that.

After the bad harvest, the winter. No grain arrived that spring. The far-away harvests had been bad too. The Baron announced to the surrounding country that some grain was available from his stores. At what price? Ah, the price. The Barons always fix the price. The size of the loaves my father baked shrank, and they were the same price. Because the price of grain went up. The loaves shrank again. Men and women and children went to the fields hungry and in more debt.

The spring rains were a trickle, like an old man peeing.

The sun burned. The wheat stopped growing. Its thin ears rattled. Hope revived when the saint's blood turned brown and tilted as the priest held up the phial. Prayers went fervently up into the still, thick air. The saint answered with a thunderstorm. Half a day's rain. Then no more. The stream at the back died. We took donkeys down to the river. The men set nets between the trees to catch more birds. The birds went away. Three men who had journeyed up north to the city to try to buy food came back, their panniers empty. The gates of the city were shut fast, they said, the people had shouted from the walls and told them to go home, that they could not afford to feed their own and had nothing to spare. There were many roaming the countryside looking for food and those who were lucky had got there long before.

So we were cut off, and ourselves sent away anyone who came pleading. The earth cracked and stood away from itself.

The pigs were killed off first because they live off what we leave, and there was precious little to leave. An orgy of roast pork and sausages after the terrible squealing as they were dragged to slaughter. The smell floated in the square for a week. Intoxicating. The goats, who can live on nothing, produced milk by alchemy from the parched hill. The carter brought nothing but a few rotted fish in the bottom of his wagon, then stopped coming altogether. Men filled their empty bellies with a little wine and fights grew more frequent.

Hey, *oste*, they would say with a sort of savage humour, saving your food for your own table, eh? But our stores too were dwindling.

A little grain came down from the castle. The mule who carried the sacks was muzzled so that he couldn't put his head back and bite at them. My father baked a few loaves and scrupulously sliced them and laid the slices out for the villagers. They came slouching in and took up their allotted rations without looking at him – but also without their usual curses. The Baron's bailiff stood in the doorway overseeing his master's charity.

Then there was no more of that bread. Strange soups of sorrel, roots, beans ... Have you ever been in a place that is hungry? Where the square itself seems to be a white, aching gut, the alleys emptying into it nothing but dust and shadow. The doors and windows gape like dry dark mouths, sucking at the air ... I had forgotten what it was like until talking about it now. People grew sullen and strange.

The children stopped playing in the square. The *locanda* was empty. No more drinking, singing, fighting. In these dreadful silences men begin looking for someone to blame.

Who do you think?

It was my task to take the donkey down into the valley for water each morning. The journey there and back was three hours' work; the stumbling down through the woods, and the slow haul up again. One morning as I led our sad animal along the side of the square, I was met, at the gap in the low wall, by a bunch of the village boys. They had been waiting for me and barred my way. I knew them all, of course. Now they looked at me as if I was a stranger. In a half-circle they crowded round, jostling me against the wall of the last house.

Fists jabbing but not quite punching, they informed me that my father was in league with demons, that he had cast a spell on Cannelloro's son by spilling wine at the moment of his birth, that he had caused the stream to stop running, the wheat to stop growing. He had dragged back the Devil in his black stove. I was a strong boy. I pushed my way through them, stern-faced, saying nothing. A brave one slapped the donkey on the flank as I tugged him forward and we went slithering down the stony path, the buckets swinging crazily on his sides. The boys jeered from the wall and swore they would meet me on the way back. But when I came back up again, the buckets slurping and full, they had gone. The square was as hot as Hell.

The boys had not dreamed this up on their own of course. It had been put in their heads by their fathers, resentful of their impotence. Because, between the four walls, it is the women who rule. The men may strut in the square, brag, admire their own manhood – they are great men amongst themselves. But the women know how to take their revenge. They have, after all, this endless capacity for labour – and labour. Their usefulness sustains them. In the days before my father came back I once heard Bella talking with a cousin, a dark pretty girl, just married, and, like all of them, sentenced to lose her looks soon. Her husband was a tall, handsome fellow well known for his boasting about the women he had had in the country around. And Bella, with all of her banked-down envy, said outright, Well then, how is it with him, with Montoncello, the ram . . . ? The girl shrugged, her mouth went down in a little grimace, and she said, Oh, you know, like all of them – *presto, presto*. My aunt laughed nastily. The girl laughed too, as if all her life was contained in that laugh, as if she knew that there was to be nothing better, that this was the best to be had; all that there was after this was the getting of children, and changing into a mother, into the shape and image of her own mother, and all the mothers before and after . . .

You see, the men were weak. They needed to believe that a devil came out of the stove.

Did my father have a woman? I never thought of it before – but where did he go the nights I woke on my own in bed with the moon slanting in through the window? No doubt in the village's eyes that he went out at night to couple with the Devil's elementals; with the bats and wolves and snakes who were his true companions. I would wake, feel the cooled shape of his absence in the bed, fall asleep, and dream his coming into the room, hear in the dream his sandals flap on the floorboards, the creak of the bed, half-dream the creak of the bed, his sigh as he lowered himself, divine the sweet-sour smell of him like nothing else on earth as he straightened himself, and half-wake as he sighed again and whispered, Are you asleep, Giorgio? – for he would never call me by that cant name of Leporello. Are you asleep? And I would not, could not answer, because like all children I was in that country where you divine in dreams the night world; the corner of your mouth gently weeps into the bolster, you are the innocent, the comforted; they are the guilty, returned, with the cares of the world creeping from their faces as they fall into sleep.

God knows we are flying away again.

The hunger?

A monthly dole of grain came down from the castle. It was never enough. And got less. The price was enough now to put my father in debt along with the rest of the village. One morning he took me aside and sewed a gold coin into each bottom corner of my jerkin. In case, he said, we should have to go away. Just we two. Say nothing to your aunt. Women can always look after themselves.

24

Did he know what was coming? Assuredly things got worse. The whole place whispered against us. We kept close to the *locanda*. One morning as I watched through the broken shutter, hidden in the shadow of the deep window, I saw the old man, Alberto, called Collo, or Scrag-End. He was something, great-uncle maybe – something to me. He came from an alley like a sick bird, his thin legs in old-fashioned plum breeches stuttering him forward – one step; ah, stop. Another step; halt. He took two or three of these steps into the empty square, fluffing the dust up with his toes. Then he stood still – it seemed for minutes, the hairs on the sides of his brown skull standing out like silver wires. He came shuffling on. Stopped. On again. At last he came to within a yard of the window. He stared straight towards me. I thought he could see me behind the shutter, but his eyes were so wide and mild in his long face that I almost laughed. He had a silly dazed grin on his face, like a drunk sharing in a joke he has not understood. He went down on his knees, slowly, his back straight. You would have thought he was sinking into the earth. But I could see the top of his head, rocking forward and back. Then he fell sideways. I leaned forward and peered down. He lay on the ground; his eyes were still open and his mouth still smiling. I stepped back, looking across the square. A man walked from a doorway. My father was coming down the steps from the floor above. As I opened my mouth to tell him what had happened, a shout came from outside: He came to you for bread, *oste*, He came to you for bread. Your own uncle and the door is barred. A woman began that slow howl they give over the dead.

That happened in the late morning. Just after noon – they had taken the old man away – a stone struck the shutter. The loose slat swung about. Silence.

Bar the door, said my father. He got up from the table where he had been tallying the backs of his cards and sipping steadily at a jug of wine. I will do the back, he said.

Bella was coming down.

I'm not stopping here, she said. She hurried past my father into the back. He shrugged and followed.

Go your own way, Bella, he shouted.

I heard the bolts on the back door shot open and then closed again.

The front, my boy, my father shouted from the kitchen. Bar the front! I fumbled the heavy wooden bar into the front door's iron hands.

A stone struck one door.

Oste. Oste. Where are you? We know you have food in there. Father came back. Stand away from there, he said. Are you afraid? Come here. Have some of this. He poured wine into a mug. He picked up his own and motioned me to drink.

I can still taste it; a sweet taste on top, a sour undertow. The front door rattled. The wooden bar jumped and fell back into place. The wine made me valiant and bewildered.

Through the shutter I saw that a crowd had gathered all at once in the square. Eyes appeared at the broken place.

We can see you, *oste*, guzzling. And your fat boy.

Fat boy. Fat pigs, they chanted. The door banged and rattled. A cry went up. There she is. Grab the bitch.

The eyes came back, hot and drilling into the dim room, a mouth, out of sight, saying, We've your precious sister out here, *oste*. Bella the sow.

Bella the sow. The mare, we heard them shout, the women's voices now as much as the men's, with cries of Witch, Whore – then Bella's harsh voice rose from the hubbub. Let me alone. It's not me. Not me, she cried out.

What are they doing? said father, white in the face. Open the door, Giorgio. We must put a stop to this madness.

She was his sister, after all.

When I did not move he strode past me, lifted the bar away and pulled the two narrow doors open.

All the village was out there, and directly in front of us, Bella. The women grabbed at her clothes while she flailed her arms around. She was a big, powerful woman. It's not me. Not me, she kept on shouting. Everything stopped when they saw my father standing in the doorway.

Before he could speak to gain anything from this one moment

26

of calm, Bella shouted, It's not me. I ran away. Not me – him.

Cannelloro, who had appointed himself head-man, said, Shut up you bitch. He looked round at the crowd. You all saw my son. He swung round and pointed at my father. Ever since he brought back that damned engine from the north we've had no luck. My son. The harvest. Old Collo today.

Old men die, said my father.

So do younger ones, said Cannelloro. They all began barking and baying again.

Give us the food you've hoarded, Cannelloro said.

I have no food, said my father.

He has, he has – he brings it from the black stove, Bella shouted. Ah, she was inspired, that one. She could not have said anything better for them. I could not stand it, she gabbled. I wanted to share with you, he would not let me. That's why he threw me out.

I thought you said you escaped, said my father. But now they had him by the arms and told him to shut up or he would be killed now. Bella went on:

. . . I crept back last night and through the window saw him fetch out of that oven – oh, all sorts – pasta, hare, clams, rice, *mariale* – pork – *soffritto* – pig's guts – garlic, tomatoes, *trota* – what's that? Trout. Peppers, aubergines, cow's milk, so many cheeses – and all this time her ugly black mouth was open and all this food seemed to come pouring out, and it was if it mounted in great piles in the square and as if there were demons descending to pop it into and pull it straightway out from their gaping mouths.

Get him away from the door, Cannelloro shouted. Pull out the Devil's engine. He was triumphant – burning with the first command of anything in his miserable life. Some of the men went into the *locanda*. I tried to get near to my father but now he was held in the press of the crowd and Bella was pointing at him and screaming, *Diavolo, Demonio*, and the women were chanting and crossing themselves against his evil eye and the men shouted for those who were bearing or nursing children to hurry away until only the men gripping my father were left and the children and women, old and young, were huddling in

27

the doorways across the square.

Run, boy, my father shouted. Run to the castle.

As I moved somebody's leg came out and I was sent sprawling and dazed against the wall. Stick there, said the leg, kicking me.

They pulled the iron stove into the square. With his new-found authority Cannelloro parted the men. My father's clothes were torn. Blood trickled down from his black hair onto his forehead and into the grooves of his cheeks. Two dark thimbles stood out of his nostrils.

Now.

They forced him to his knees at Cannelloro's sign.

Tell us how you make the food.

You are fools, he said. There is no food. Don't you understand. There is no food.

Show us. Cannelloro struck him across the face. One way, then the other, with the open palm of his hand.

My father's face came up and he saw me. We sometimes think – children, watching – that these things are a dream, a play put on for us. I stood, dreaming.

Again came my father's agonised shout, Run, Giorgio. Run to the castle. Get justice.

The food, Cannelloro demanded. He bent and spat in my father's face. If you do not tell us . . . He drew his hand across his throat . . . Understand?

You are fools. Ignorant . . . They pressed him forward by his arms and he groaned.

If you won't feed us from your oven, we will feed you to it, eh? said Cannelloro.

And the men all took up this chant, Feed him in. Feed the Devil. Feed the can. They ran him head down to the stove, Cannelloro opened the oven door. Then – God save me, I have tried to forget – it is so long ago, and yet here – they pitched him forward to the door. Run, he screamed. Giorgio, run. They stuffed him in the oven. Stuffed him in that oven.

And at last I began to run. But the thing that holds us back held me back. Perhaps twenty yards on I stopped, staring at them. They were all round the oven. The door had been shut and the stove sat there, dead, silent. Did my father hope to save himself, the only sane one there, by lying quiet? I stumbled on a few steps more, looking back over my shoulder, on again, and again stopped and looked back. What they did then I still cannot believe.

Cannelloro got between the shafts and began to push the stove. The wheels turned. Come on, he shouted to the others. Let's be rid of this and its master. They all began to push, and those who could not get a shoulder to it ran alongside, beating on it like a drum as it picked up speed down the incline of the square.

The stove smashed against the broken stones of the valley wall. In one movement Cannelloro lifted it so that it teetered on the wall. Then, with a mighty heave, he tipped, and it fell over the drop.

What did I do? Did I hear it rumbling and crashing down the cliff? Did I think it hung, caught on the poor bushes, tangled in the weak trees? That he was saved?

I screamed and my scream went up to Heaven or not so far. I cursed them as a child only can, because he has no voice or curses. Then I ran on up the hill, my tears streaming. A child is not a man. I was running up the hill to salvation. To turn back time. To whistle the stove up from the valley. To have the oven door swing open, my father to step forth, blithely smiling. Out of the magician's cabinet, the conjuror's smirk. It was all done to scare you, boy.

And there, at the first salvation, running to the priest's house, in the priest's window, the priest's white face like a white moon looked down on the square, and as he saw me and I ran nearer and nearer he crossed himself with one hand and with the other reached out and slammed his shutter to.

2

I see myself running in the street beside the priest's house. Hearing nothing now but the tearing of my own breath. I look back

29

once in terror, and run straight into a woman coming out of a door.

Giulietta, the priest's housekeeper. Whatever is going on down there? she says. Giorgio? Leporello, isn't it? Now I am crying. She hurries me into the house. In a narrow white passageway, Giulietta presses me against her skirts, hushing me. Shush, shush, little Giorgio, as I weep into her bosom. You are safe here. Safe here. You must save him, save him, I shout. We heard noises from the village . . . , she says. It's my father – they are killing him, I sob. And she calls to the priest and he comes, his face white, saying, What is the matter here? What is the matter? They are killing my father, I scream. And he dithers and hovers in his black robe. You must go, Giulietta says to him. Yes. Yes, he says. Reluctantly he goes out of the back door. I see him pass the window slowly, and think we are saved now.

Then we were in the kitchen. She comforted me. A great baby. At that moment she was my mother; all mothers. When she felt she could let me go, let my head lift from her breast, it was like being born again. She sat me against the kitchen wall and made up the fire and hung a pot over it. All this time, being busy, pretending to be busy, she looked back at me constantly, her bright face smiling. Not out of pity, but out of kindness.

She laid bowls and spoons on the table and poured broth into the bowl in front of me. When I heard the priest come in the front way, I started up. But she pushed me gently down and said, Eat, and went out, leaving the door open, as if her kindness was to hang in its gap. I heard her voice say something, then the priest murmur in return. She came back, closing the door. They are looking for your father, she said. His reverence says you are not to worry.

I stayed there the rest of the day. It seemed a terribly long day. But at last, in the manner of heartless children, I went to bed, led there in a dream by Giulietta.

I woke in a soft, billowy bed, with the sun falling across my face, and it all came back.

Giulietta stood at the foot of the bed in a yellow shift. She had slept beside me, and getting up had woken me.

30

I must find my father, I cried.

Lie there like a good boy, she said. She pulled a black dress over her shift. Lie there and rest. I will go and find out.

But I could not do that for more than a minute after she had gone. To my shame I found that she had undressed me. My clothes were folded at the foot of the bed. I got up and dressed. I couldn't think what else to do.

When Giulietta came back she told me that the stove lay smashed at the edge of the river. There was no sign of my father. And I thought, absurdly, that he still lived. That somehow he had survived that crushing fall. That he had been thrown off, into the river. Had floated down and down, the water laying him at last on the bank somewhere far away, but alive.

All this I gabbled out to Giulietta, and she said, That may be, Giorgio. Yes, that may be ... Miserable beasts. The Devil take them. Yes, he may live.

But I knew from the pity on her face that she thought it hopeless.

I was not to stir out of doors, she told me when we were in the kitchen. I was quite safe here, under the priest's protection, but I should not go out. My Aunt Bella was safe (God rot her). The *locanda* was wrecked. I could not go back if I wanted to.

So the rest of the day I pretended to help Giulietta, my thoughts veering between wild hope and despair. The priest had gone up to the castle.

That night, in Giulietta's bed, I dreamed that I was in the river, under the water, and my father's face looked down from the bank. Come here, little fish, he said, and his hand came down through the water to fetch me out. Then his face was under the water, the river flowed fast, the weeds streamed and his face grown pale floated up, his arms reached out and embraced me and began to pull me gently down. Come, Giorgio. Come, he said somewhere, but as his mouth opened only worms slipped out.

No, I shouted and woke with a shudder. To find myself held against Giulietta's strong curved warm body with her arms about me and she murmuring, There. There. Sleep now. You are safe.

Next morning Giulietta brought news from the village. Soldiers had arrived, sent down by the Baron after the priest's report. Later, about noon, I heard the ring of horses' hooves in the cobbled street. Giulietta wanted to close the shutter, but I looked out. There were two men on horseback, one pulling on a rope. The other end of the rope was round the neck of Cannelloro. He stumbled behind, his great bulk lunging forward at a half run as he was jerked by the rider, his massive face a stone mask. The footsoldiers, coming after, joked and prodded him on.

The next day Cannelloro was hanged.

Only then, by the curious custom they have in those places, could I go out in safety. In the tit-for-tat of death, I had lost my father, and the village Cannelloro. By their accounting, matters were equal. The earth had been opened up and smoothed over and we could all walk about on it again. Indeed, if anything, I was still in the wrong, for my father had been touched by the Devil, they thought, and his son was best avoided, his eyes not met.

That was fine by me. I stayed above their miserable village in the priest's house. In Giulietta's bed. Ah, what a marriage that would have made if only I'd been old enough.

Even so, she was unfaithful to my innocence. Two nights a week she would come to her room, while I lay in bed; undress to her shift, put away dress and sandals, kiss me, and say, Now go to sleep, dear Giorgio, and then she would pad away to the priest's room. I was not supposed to know this. She would excuse her conduct as if talking to herself: The poor man is so lonely. The priests have such a hard life in the service of God. Surely he can't begrudge them a little pleasure now and then.

A few weeks after my father's murder one of those old crones who infest the nooks and crannies of villages called on me with a message from Bella. She invited me back to the *locanda*, which had now been put to rights. Trade was starting to trickle in. As I well knew, Bella let me know, my father had made everything over to her the first time he went away, so there was no question of my inheriting anything, but if I cared to come back, I might work for my bed and board. I let the old woman messenger know that Bella might go and fuck herself, and she departed.

Now I was truly on my own. Week after week passed. What did the priest think of this cuckoo in his cosy nest? I ate his food. I drank his watered wine. But where could I go? I knew even then that my best chance of comfort lay in pleasing this man. I would be his servant. A little more gentility than was used in a tavern, that was all that was needed to serve at his table. But he did not seem to find me agreeable at first. He would not address me directly, but mutter and call out peevishly to Giulietta. Only when she was not there would he ask me to do or fetch something for him.

As time went on, I thought his voice warmed. I did not know that this was because he had decided that something had to be done about me.

One evening he asked me to come to his room.

It is a terribly lonely sight to see a table prepared every night for only one person. The dresser behind glowed with a century of polishing by priests' housekeepers. It held his books, his few pieces of plate and silver. On the top the Holy Virgin extended a pink arm from blue robes.

You are a common boy, Giorgio, he began. An innkeeper's son. He belched softly; he had just dined. One hand smoothed the black cloth over his belly, the other played with the cross at his breast; then they both met, fingers entwining, like crabs mating. What are we to do with you, boy? How old are you? Come nearer. Twelve? You think, twelve? A boy should start to think of his future. This is a poor place. We have hardly enough. I am a poor man. The people here are foolish and ignorant. They do not listen to God. This appalling business of your father. If you had not been given the protection of our Holy Mother – a moth thumped against the white muslin window screen – where would you be now? You cannot stay here forever, alas. You know that? You may sit down. On the stool there.

He sat forward and stared at me.

My position here as *padre* – as father to you all – I can have no favourites. Understand that. There is bad blood between you and the village. In the service of God . . .

He could not, looking back, have been all that old a man. What hair he had left was thick at the sides, turning to grey. His face was plump, the flesh hanging in bells along his jawline. And pale for those parts because of the broad-brimmed hat he wore always out of the house. His shoulders were broad, but sculpted from butter, soft and sloping. When he rose, talking half to me, half to himself, wondering what he was to do with me, he came round the table and I saw his grey stockings under his gown and the big toe on his left foot stuck out of a darn, the nail as thick and yellow and dirty as any peasant's. He circled the small room, passing behind me, and back to the dresser, where he stood fingering his knives and spoons, setting them in rows like soldiers. Well – you must do something, he said. Have you any wishes in the matter?

So plump, so nervous he was. With guileful innocence, I said hesitantly, Well, Father, I would … I would, if it were possible, like to be like you. A priest. I stared at him – an angel. After all, he had the only halfway comfortable life I had ever seen. Why not be like that? I did not think how such a man had ended up here, in this – God forgive me – godforsaken village. A lonely man with wine and Giulietta. The Baron's man. God's man. Another servant.

My answer amused him. He laughed. Forgive me, he said. Saints have come from less, I suppose. You see these. He pointed to his books. You would have to learn all these. Aquinas. Augustine. The Holy Fathers … You cannot even read. There is so much to learn … That's as maybe, I thought, but I had never seen him read one of these books. I had never seen him do anything except eat or doze or gossip with Giulietta. When I went in to clear away his evening plate – he always ate well, his food came down from the castle – he would be staring straight in front, the pent-in heat of the room suffocating.

He sat down again. He looked at me queerly. He almost smiled, then decided not to. He twisted his hands together.

It is a heavy thing to wish, my boy – to be a priest. You would have to work hard. You obviously could not stay here. His voice sounded relieved. You are a growing boy … My simple self nodded in piety. Yes, yes, he said. I will have to think of this. Go to bed now.

34

From then he was friendly to me. It was agreed that I was to leave at the first breaking of spring.

That winter I learned to read. The priest wrote me an alphabet on tiny squares of thick paper – on the back were fragments of his own handwriting. He taught me my letters; and then cut out more letters so that we could shuffle the slips into words. He produced, shyly and slyly, a translation of the Book of Genesis. He had made it, he said, for the children in his first posting as a priest, but had put it away on the orders of his superiors when they told him he had no licence for such daring. It surely can do no harm here, he muttered – and looked nervously about as if expecting a cardinal to lean in through the window and snatch it from his hand. You must learn from something, he said. This is the language you will meet when you go out in the world, in good society. He sighed for society.

I shuffled my little cards on the table, creating my Maker; Earth and Heaven. AND. AND. THE. THE. Light and Water. Grass and Fruit. Sun and Moon and Stars. Birds and Whales. Outside the real moon shone and the stars wheeled over the roof in their great, knowing circles.

I learned willingly, you must understand; for I saw this art as another tool to help me out of this place. I made good progress too. The priest one night took down the big black bible from his shelves and showed me these same passages in the language of the Church, disclosing the pages jealously, as if they were secrets only to be won by the initiate. This you will learn later, if you show a vocation, he said, and shut the book up. It struck me as odd that the same words should be set down in other words and asked him why. The good God did this to confound his sinful peoples, so that they would not understand one another, said the priest. But why? I persisted. It is God's will, he answered testily. You will come to understand these things one day.

I bowed my head and moved my letters.

I had no interest in books as such. It always struck me as comical how the Don would pore over these blocks of rag as if they were somehow the key to life. But if this was a skill a servant could use to get on, well then I would master it. The poor priest hoped to make me into another priest. Like all men without children – unless he had bastards I did not know of, a common occurrence with these men – he longed to meet and mould one who would grow into the man he had failed to be. Like the young men adopted as princes in the tales. If I had been his own child he would most likely have beaten or ignored me, but I was his prince. And of course I betrayed him.

I learned much there. Giulietta jealously guarded from me her tasks of washing the priest's black robes, the best for Saturday and Sunday, second best for the rest of the week, fumed with his sweat and the smell of incense; his purple stockings, his night shirts, his small clothes – the first I had seen. She changed the bed linen more often than I had ever seen decently done, beat the mattresses for vermin; cooked. I learned how to water wine, to lay his lonely table, to polish his bits of silver.

And to read, of course. When I came from a lesson with the priest once, Giulietta said, You are quite the scholar now, Giorgio. And another time, as I sat by the fire, she stopped for a moment, going out of the door, and said, Ah, how like your father you are coming to look, Giorgio, and she sighed deeply.

That puzzled me for many years.

In the winter my sleeves drifted up my arms until I began to look like a scarecrow in my jerkin. She made me a curious pair of breeches out of an old brick-coloured skirt of hers, and lengthened my sleeves.

The truth is that I was getting a trifle too big to lie with Giulietta. There was nowhere else though, was there? Now I woke and watched with curiosity as she undressed, where only a month or so before I had grunted down gratefully into sleep. It was wonderful to see her tall heavy form take off the shapeless skirt or dress and see her hands smooth down the shift over her great hips. One night, feigning sleep, I watched between my eyelashes her big shadowy form glide from the room. I followed, a minute after.

I stood in my shirt in the cold passageway outside the priest's bedroom door.

The bed creaked as she got in beside him. Their low voices. Rustles and muffled movements. Then the bed began to complain; slowly at first, then quicker and quicker it began to rock. A strange 'oof-oof' noise from the priest. A wail. The bed stopped. Rustlings came again through the thin wood of the door – it was a poor door.

Then their voices began speaking. So matter of fact – you would not know that anything of importance had passed between them. Their voices were low; the conversation short. In a little while the priest began to snore.

Of course I knew what they were doing. You always know, however innocent. But exactly what I could not envisage. I was ignorant of these transactions – compared with the other children of that village, who slept in the same bed, by the side or at the feet of their father and mother and went willy-nilly up and down with the two-backed humping as if they were all together in a boat at sea.

The next time she made her way to the priest's room, I followed again. They talked for longer this time. About me.

The priest said, Giulietta, I do not think it quite decent that the boy should continue to sleep in your bed any longer. Her voice, all sleepy and yawny, said, There is nowhere else, Father.

He is getting such a big fellow, said the priest. We could not have any ... any scandal. No, I do not think it quite decent now. He is a growing boy.

Yes, Father, he is, she said sadly.

We let him into the house from pity and for charity. I have taught him as best I can. It will soon be time for him to go.

Yes.

It was like hearing a father and mother talking.

The priest coughed. I shivered in the corridor. I will write a letter to the Abbot at P-. It may help him to a place as a servant. After that ... If he shows ... It is best that he go as soon as the weather permits. He cannot live on our charity forever. There is little enough as it is. Do not do that, Giulietta. You know it is useless. I'm not a young buck. It smarts.

Sorry, your reverence, said Giulietta, sounding genuinely

sorrowful. You aren't hurt? No, he said. It is just that after . . . No, do not get up, Giulietta. I think it best you stay tonight.

The bed creaked heavily.

Whatever your reverence wishes . . .

And in the morning we shall see . . .

Yes, your reverence. Let me cuddle you. That's it. That's better. It's a hard life for you gentlemen.

Indeed. Goodnight, Giulietta. I wish to sleep now.

That's it, your reverence. Sleep. Put your hand there. Leave your hand there if it makes you feel better.

I slept alone that night. And the next. And the next. Then the priest called me to his room again.

I have decided what is to be done with you, he said. I have written a letter to the Abbey at P-. I do not know if you will enter the Holy Order. It is a life only for the few. If you should show a vocation . . . Well, that is to be seen. I am sure they will find you some position. I will give you directions and a little money.

What, your reverence, is an abbey? I asked. It sounded a jolly place where you went to learn how to drink wine, say the Mass, and sleep with your housekeeper.

It is a place where men's faces are turned to God, said the priest. It is a great, cold, stony-hearted prison if you do not find Our Lord and Lady there – as is the world at large – but a fiery palace of love if they turn Their faces towards you.

Did you attend such a place? I asked. Why ever leave such a place?

His face went red.

Ah, Giorgio – I was unworthy, he stammered. Unworthy. I had not the wits nor spiritual strength to withstand certain temptations. At your age you would not understand – though I look at the people in the village and wonder if there is anything, from babe to grandfather, they do not know of temptation. We are all sinners, Giorgio.

How could a priest be a sinner?

Pour me a little wine, he said. Drinking, he gathered himself. He had not talked to anyone for such a long time that it seemed he was preparing for a feast.

38

Let me tell you, he began. The abbey looks like a fine, huge castle on its hill. You will be able to see it for miles before you come near. As you approach by winding ways the walls soar white and shining. You go on, and on, with it endlessly reappearing between hills and trees, and it never seems to be any nearer. It turns rosy in the setting sun, then at last you are under its shadow. It has turned black and forbidding, with only here and there a tiny glittering light high up. I came there at seventeen, full of devotion, of stories from the Book of Saints, longing to devote my life to Our Lord, Our Lady, my mind full of the sufferings of the saints. Oh, such men, who lived solitarily in caves and cells; who tortured themselves with needles and flails; changed their clothes never in twenty years, allowing the vermin to crawl over them; devouring their own excrement and drinking their own urine; who were so holy they could fly like angels about their churches, or rise from their deathbeds to hover over the holy processions – great men, Giorgio. Great men! And I was going to join them.

Oh, you could not imagine the awful beauty, the grandeur of that place. Within its walls was a veritable City of God. The novice quarters where I was lodged caught the sun as it came up. That then lit the huge round window of the chapel in summer. Hung in the West Door at Compline. It was the true enchantment, the only way we can be happy as men, Giorgio – in the service of God.

His face shone. He made the letter he was to give me sound like a pass to Paradise.

But he had stopped. His face clouded. When he went on, it was in a whisper.

I was there one year, he said. One year they give to a novice to test him. I failed. How can I say I failed? I have this after all. His voice rose again, his hand waved at the little room where we sat, the fire flickering low in that early spring night. How can I say I have failed, he asked the air bitterly, when all around me I have dirt and stupidity and witchcraft? Your people, Giorgio – they know nothing and want to know less. I am forced to speak their uncouth tongue because they will not understand mine. They worship snakes and trees, and tell each other stories of dragons and werewolves.

One year, he went on. One year to cross from the east to the west side of the Abbey. To the brothers' cells; those holy, honeyed cells. You see, I wished to stay there. The flesh, the impatience of the flesh was too much for me. Not enough simplicity. Whatever it is that needs the world too much – that is what I had. When we worked in the fields, I would snatch a look over at the monks, their fine faces cast down to the earth. I was impatient to join them, to have the secret of their serenity revealed to me. I knew this was a sin; that I should be thanking God that he had placed me here in the lowliest position of all, and not be envying the sweet, imperturbable brothers. But at night my body wrestled with my soul – the temptations of the flesh. My body itched intolerably. I longed to know the secret the brothers had found of casting off this hot, nagging load. Whatever it was, was there in the west side of the Abbey. I read and re-read the lives of the Martyrs hungrily; all their pains and tortures; their rackings, impalements, burnings, floggings, disembowelments, rapes, flayings, gougings, blindings, beheadings – from all of which they rose uncomplaining, their bodies unmarked, shining on white wings. I went out in the siesta and laid myself on a rock in the scorching sun until my eyes bled and my vision turned black. At night, I crept to a side chapel and spread myself crosswise, naked on the freezing cold stone. Oh, I was most holy. I was reckoned very holy. I suffered. I made myself suffer. I was put up in front of the other novices as the example they should all follow. But it was not enough. Self-knowledge is the greatest of all sins. I knew what I wanted.

One evening I stole away from the chapel as they all gathered for Vespers. I made my way through the deserted sacristy; the library, more silent than silence. Then crept along the side of the chapter house, and at last entered the innermost cloister. All around a small square garden doorless cells faced me.

Trembling on the threshold, I dared to enter one.

Oh, the little cell hummed like a bee; it sang of devotion; it was sweet with glory. A crucifix on one bare wall. The Madonna in a corner alcove. In the inner part, a low bed of boards, with a thin mattress, no coverings. As if placing myself in the palm of God, timidly I lay down and stretched myself ... What did I hope? To absorb the holiness of whoever had lain there? I stared up at the white ceiling, at the tiny cracks and brushstrokes of the white-washed plaster.

Oh, they were long hours they worked us. Was I tired? I closed my eyes, breathing in the balm of that place. It was very warm and close. The ceiling very cool. I opened my eyes and closed them again, basking in my devotion, thinking that *this*, this quietude and bliss, was my future – and I fell asleep.

Two of the brothers found me when they returned from supper. They heard snoring.

I was summoned before all the other novices. The Abbot himself stood in judgment over me. The cell I had breached was that of a very old brother who had died not a week before, after a life of particular holiness and self-denial. I was judged to have desecrated his cell with my licentious idleness. A hypocrite, I had cunningly sought out a cell I knew to be empty in a part of the Abbey where no one would think to look for me. I had probably done the same thing many times before, to avoid work or services. And some of my fellow novices, made jealous by my past preferment over them, now stepped obligingly forward and said, yes, they had noticed that I had been missing on this, on that occasion. That I had idled at tasks when I thought no one was looking. That I had confessed to this one that all my penances were a sham ...

I was sent away.

I could not go home. I entered a seminary here in the South where I was not known. A place like a barracks for common soldiers in a town set hard by a dark brown marsh. All summer the place was infested with flies and mosquitoes. My fellow students were pustular, pale and, where not actually stupid, a vicious, back-biting set of knaves full of thoughts of lechery and advancement. A bad place. Not one of learning; but of learning to get on, to press your foot firmly in the face of the fellow below you; of learning how to guide him in the most kindly way into the pitfall you have prepared. This was my true penance ...

Then the priest, so wrapped in his own memories, seemed to

remember that I was in the room. He straightened his back in the chair. He hooked his fingers firmly round his lolling glass.

He drank. His hand trembled. He looked down at the table.

I am a coward, Giorgio, he said. I closed the shutter on you. When I saw you running, I closed the shutter. God watches. The priest's eyes beseeched me to give him the answer he desired.

Yes, sir, I said. God watches.

Go to bed, Giorgio. Go to bed. He had tears in his eyes, I swear.

This was the first time I heard that life for a great man could be misery.

The day before the one fixed for my departure, the priest was called up to the castle. Someone was dying.

The dying took its time. I had hoped to see the priest, to get his blessing before I said goodbye, because in his own way he had been good to me. But night fell and he had still not returned. He had left the letter to the Abbey on his sideboard, saying, Do not worry. They will not remember me. But a word from a priest may help you ... Beside it was a tiny heap of silver coins.

Giulietta packed me bread and hard cheese – enough to last a man for a week. I was to leave at first light. Two days' walking would see me through the mountains and onto the high road. The priest had drawn me a rough map on the back of the sealed letter.

That night the wind got up, at first snuffling and sighing, then rattling the shutters. I was excited, jabbering across the kitchen table to Giulietta about my future. Until she said, You had better rest now, Giorgio. Go to bed now, there's a good boy.

I went to her room, undressed, put on my night shirt, and crept under the blanket. I lay, my mind rehearsing tomorrow's journey. Warming in the bed, I began to drift, and wolves' eyes gleamed from the bushes in the pass and huge mountains rose sheer on each side and my way was blocked by bandits twice the size of Cannelloro and Cannelloro himself swung like a pendulum on the end of a rope and his mouth opened and he groaned. Forgive me, Leporello. Forgive.

The door creaked open. I woke. Giulietta was in the room, her back to me, putting the latch on the door. She moved to the edge of the bed. Her clothes whispered in that shush-shush-you-must-be-quiet-and-not-wake-him way as she pulled her dress over her head. She cast off her shoes and rolled into bed.

She settled herself beside me, letting a draught of cold air under the blanket as she moved, defeating it at once with the warmth of her body.

Giulietta, I said thickly, mimicking sleep.

Now, now, Giorgio, sleep.

I thought you would sleep in his reverence's bed tonight?

No, no, she said, shocked. That would not be right. Not with him not there.

I jointed into the soft S of her body; my bottom on her padded knees, her breasts under the shift spread across more than the width of my back. Her arm encircled me strongly. Sleep, Giorgio. You will need your sleep.

And sleep I did. Until the dead of night when something woke me. I came from a dream where I was flying like a bird along the length of a valley on a white summer day. The trees were full and green and shining below; the river sparkled between their leaves; sleek-bellied fish, full and fat, idled in the water, a flick of the tail sent them scudding in and out of the waving shadows. Then the blackest, longest shadow passed across the whole valley and darkened and hid everything in which I had delighted. A clock in the castle stopped ticking and began to chime like thunder and I was falling, falling. And fell, shuddering to earth ...

Giulietta held me, fallen into her lap. There now. There. She stroked my hair. Don't dream so. The Devil waits for us in our dreams. And I, now more than half-awake, but pretending still to be sleepy, took her hand – knowing, not knowing what I did – and guided, pushed it down, overcoming its slight resistance, till it rested on the hard little rod that had grown down there.

Oh well, Giorgio. If you must, you must. And she rolled me round in one glorious movement and onto her and guided my new friend into her harbour. Where I went joyfully and was transported instantly into such delights ... My maiden voyage was all too short, but, ah well, you know ... She patted my hair gently, saying, Sweet boy, sweet boy, as my head rested between her breasts. And as I felt myself shrink and fall out of her, the door creaked open behind us, the light of a candle eased its way along the wall.

The priest's voice called softly, Giorgio. Giorgio – are you awake? The door creaked wider. I thought I would just look in . . . he said softly. His candlelight fell across the bed. I did not dare turn my head. Giulietta looked over my shoulder to the doorway. Her breath went on, slow and steady, under my weight. I swear I could hear the priest breathing too. Giulietta, he said in a strained voice, Come to my room. The candlelight wavered back across the wall and away. She pushed me off gently and got up and followed, padding softly down the passage.

I went from there in the morning, just before dawn. I left the letter and took the silver.

3

I went down the course of the river with the rising sun at my back. Which of my out-at-toes, thieving, roguish, scampish, bare-arse-tickled-with-a-thistle adventures do you wish to hear about first? How I lived by thieving what food there was in empty houses – their tenants being hard at work in the fields? How I raided the snares put out for rabbits and ran for my life from their owners?

A week after setting out, as my dream had foretold, I fell among bandits.

Two men suddenly stood in my path. I turned as casually as I could. Another man stood behind me. Both sides of the road banked steeply up in thick thorn bushes.

What can I do for you gentlemen? I asked, setting myself as well as I could.

When they had taken the priest's silver and kindly agreed not to cut my throat, after I had indicated where they might instead cut into my jerkin and release the two gold pieces my father had bequeathed me, I pleaded to be allowed to go along with them. There were three of them: Matteo, Luca and Antonino. They had been four, but the soldiers had got the other and he was no more. Matteo drew his finger across his throat and spat into the earth.

I said, Gentlemen, where I am to go now you have robbed me? The only place I have is with you. I told them the whole pitiful tale. Matteo said, It is plain you have suffered, lad. You may fetch and carry for us. Then, we'll see ...

The country I had wandered into was so much richer, greener, and plumper than the stone-hungry one I had left, that I thought I had come into another world. But if I thought that by signing up with the bandits I was in for a life of easy pickings, I was sorely disappointed.

Though the main road cut through the next valley and coaches and travellers were common, where was the good of that? The bandits had no powder for their ancient muskets; the coaches were well armed, and the odd man on muleback often poorer than ourselves. We could not rob the locals because we relied on their goodwill not to betray us. Their crimes to date did not seem so much greater than mine.

We moved camp often. Matteo said that an unprincipled and bloodthirsty troop of soldiers had been sent to clear the district of our kind. If we moved to another region, the bandits there would set upon us. Yes, I told them, in the hills where I came from they would literally eat us up. They nodded and looked thoughtful. Yes, yes, they said, we know that. For they had all come from such places. They were not evil men. They had simply done something to transgress the code of their village or, as I had, run away to find something better. I had thought they were all very much older than I was, real men – but after a few days I found they were not much more than boys themselves. Through hardship their faces had grown old before their years.

The one good purse we had was from a lone traveller; some sort of foreigner mad enough to roam the country on his own. Foolishly he put up a fight and Luca was obliged to club him. To Luca's infinite horror he found that the man's skull was paper-thin and that he had laid his brains out. That was the first man they had killed – and his purse was their downfall.

Because I was not known round there I was sent down into a village to buy food and, if I could find them, powder and ball. The people in that village served me surlily and I am sure they betrayed us. Perhaps I was followed out of the miserable hole, but I didn't notice. Perhaps the soldiers already knew where we were. Who knows? Our fate was the same. When I got back to camp the lads fell on the stuff I had brought. Matteo clapped me on the back, told me what a good job I had done, and sent me down to the brook to fetch water for the cook pot.

I lingered at the bottom of the hill where we were camped, squatting on my haunches, gazing at the water, and feeling aggrieved that after performing such a valuable and dangerous service for them I was still treated as an errand boy.

Thank God for resentment and youth – and God have mercy on their poor souls. For as I sat, staring down into the water, I heard distant shouts. I thought they were calling impatiently for me to come up. I sat on, chin on my arms. Let them wait until I was ready. At last the shouts ceased. I filled the leather bottles and made my way back up the wooded hillside.

As I came to the top there was no sound of the merry voices I expected. No curses or cat-calls as to what had delayed me so long. All was silence between the trees. In the clearing ashes were smeared across the earth from the fire they had built; the cook pot lay on its side. Then I saw my three companions, kneeling under the trees. I thought they were looking for something, the way their bodies were tilted forward. Luca seemed to have his head in a hole in the ground. Luca, I cried, all you'll find in there is a wasps' nest. What have you lost? None of them moved. I moved towards them and saw why. Out of luck, poor bastards. They were looking for their heads.

Each body bent forward to end with the neck in a pool of greasy-crimson grass and black, blood-sodden earth. Through the thin screen of trees I saw the file of soldiers riding away in a small cloud of dust. What must have been my companions' heads bounced in dark-stained canvas bags on the horses' flanks.

Oh, I tell you, all we know ends in madness and death.

What then? I made my way down to the coast, that's what then. We are coming to it – what you want to hear. The Don. How I met the Don. A woman led me to him, what else do you think? Well, a girl.

The sea led me to her.

I have traced my journey on one of the Don's maps. It looks such a little way. It took me two years.

On the way I was a shepherd, a bird-scarer, a grave-digger for a village touched by plague, a thief – from all these trades I ran away. When I came to the sea I naturally became a fisherman.

Now, all these trades came in useful in one way or another, as you will see. Except the fishing. That was nearly the death of me; it was such hard work for one thing. For another I could only get a place on the dirtiest, oldest craft, a disgrace to the fleet, owned by an old rascal who lived in a tumbledown shelter he had built himself on stilts, among the rocks at the seaweed-stinking end of the beach. He took to me at once. I stayed with him for one whole summer. It was time to move on when he became possessed of the idea that I had somehow become engaged to be married to his daughter.

Why he should have thought I would wish to share my life with this creature, when he would not even have her in the hovel with us, I do not know. A one-eyed girl who slept in a long low stone cairn just above the tide line, she lacked for any other suitor. (Though sometimes at night one of the old, wifeless fishermen might call on her, and you would hear muffled scrabbling and exclamations from her shelter.) She was called *A'Spugnalina* – the sponge. When her father began making noises about how a fine lad like me should get a wife, and she began to roll her one good eye lasciviously at me, I knew I must go. I wonder now what would have happened to my life if I had not delayed and gone on a last fishing trip.

The old man and a villainous cousin had been drinking all day. We set sail in the evening. The sky was a smoky yellow with grey rain cloud pressing up from the horizon.

47

I've been out in worse than this, said the old man when I expressed concern that a storm was coming. Are you a coward? he said in a slurred voice.

He is, said the cousin.

As we breasted the main current on the edge of the bay, the coloured cloud was directly overhead. Rain began to spike down. The wind got up. Before we knew it we had lost sight of the town and the coast was veiled. The sea chopped higher and higher. We shortened sail, clumsily and slowly. The waves drew back and advanced in glassy banks that shattered over the little craft. We rode and wallowed. The sail flapped like a mad bird or, suddenly filled to bursting, drove us wildly forward. I was no sailor. The tiller, which I was in charge of, either waggled uselessly as the bows went down, or almost broke my arm, pulling against me as the stern bottomed in foaming water. I must have done something wrong. I could do no other. The boat corkscrewed, the sail went straight up in the air, cracked like a whip, and soared away like a gull. Water swamped into the rotten well of the boat and we foundered – is that the right word? It is strange how we observe these things in an instant, and as though they are happening to someone else. God preserves some of us. God knows why. I remember little after that until I woke in the water. Had I gone under? Been knocked out? I woke, clutching a plank from the boat as a man might be found embracing his pillow after a nightmare. The sky above was starred; the sea rocked me like an awful, gentle mother. She guided me in sight of land. I had no fear of death. The young are immortal. I clung to the plank. It seemed to me, after what must have been hours, that I was drawing steadily nearer to the coast. Where else would a piece of wood want to go except back to the land?

I was tiring. The endlessly rocking sea took me in contrary motions, here and there; the coast seemed now to draw nearer – a tiny bit nearer – and then retreat by a good mile. I began to be angry with this endless to and fro. My anger was exchanged after a while for exhaustion; now I wished to give myself to the waves' motion, simply to rest on their bosom. I knew I must not sleep – but I must. A delicious warmth beckoned to me, begging me to lie down with it. This warmth, this light feeling, is the premonition of Death settling its wings about you. An invitation to sleep . . .

I slept.

In moonlight, on a sandy beach, I woke.

I was exhausted, bewildered, but alive. The sea murmured behind me; retiring gracefully after its delivery, taking with it my cross, my Saviour – the planks from the rotten boat that I had clung to. How long had I lain here?

The moon hung high above. I sat, coughed, shivered in my wet clothes, and looked about me.

The beach was narrow. In front of me a line of wind-sculpted trees on a rise of dunes pointed into the land. I thought I saw a glimpse of a building. I made my way through the trees, bending. At last I was clear of them and straightened my weary body.

The building I had seen was nothing more than one of those temples of the ancients come to ruin. In the moonlight was a field of white columns, standing on their own or joined by stones laid across their tops. A cloud swept across the moon – the ragged end of the storm, like a banner flying after a battle. The moon shone down again. The columns marched away, to end against the dark line of a wood. Some had fallen on their sides; in amongst these were pale boulders that looked like nothing so much as great doughy unbaked loaves. The wind blew warmer. I would rest and see what the morning might bring. Beside one of the fallen columns I scooped out a hollow trench and curled myself like a dog. The wind soughed and sighed in the trees, and in the ruins gave odd wheezes and snuffles as if the stones themselves breathed in and out. The last sound I heard, falling to sleep, was a dim, deep snort, like the moon farting.

So this is where the girl appears? In this antique setting? The Don would have had it so. He could make women appear out of air and stone and moonlight. Me? I woke from a deep sleep. Refreshed. I was young and strong. What was shipwreck to me? I

49

blinked at the sky. The dawn was making the little high white clouds pink. The columns stood out of a low ground mist. They had the colour of white honey. Some of the fallen stones I had seen indistinctly by night I could now see were statues of robed human figures; one lay with its nose broken against the earth, a blind eye regarding me. A lion lolled, shattered at its midriff, muzzle nuzzled in the dewy grass, haunches a quarter of a clock's turn from its massive shoulders and mane. I was in a land of stone giants, fallen and broken. Farther off, the white boulders rose out of the mist. I could have sworn that those shapes, scattered across the field in the night, had somehow drawn themselves together.

Then one began to move, to raise itself. Legs slowly unfolding, it got up, shook white flanks and snorted forks of steam from its nostrils. And what I had thought gods coming to life were huge white cattle. They heaved, steaming, free from the mist. They lowered their heads and moaned and stumbled mournfully about. And from being frightened at seeing stones move, I laughed out loud as one lumbered towards me, the bones sliding in its shoulders, the flesh slipping from side to side as if shifting a load. It halted a yard from me, a grey-pink tongue as thick as my shoulder lolled from the side of its mouth and it gave out a low, grieving howl. I clapped my hands in the beast's face and it stumbled round, front hooves slipping awkwardly on one of the fallen giants, and then cantered heavily away down the lane of white pillars. Hollo-oo, I shouted, half-mad. I capered in that fantastic ruined place, driving the beasts before me down the long aisle.

A mad boy? Of course. I was lucky to be alive. You must expect madness in the young. And the old. God save us from the young man who dreams of middle-age, of marriage to his first, plain girl.

My beasts lumbered unhappily in front of me.

Then I heard a shout. Julio? Juli-o?

Two men darted in and out of the pillars on the landward side. I stopped. The cattle did too, being uncertain stupid creatures. The men stepped out before me.

You are not Julio, said one, dressed as a gentleman.

No, signore, I answered, with a cheeky, sweeping bow. Leporello is my name.

4

So I began my association with the gentry. For the first of these two men was Signor Cavilloso, a local landowner; and the second, his servant, Enrico. It seemed that the boy Julio had run off. I took his job. Simple as that.

Now, if you discount the priest, I had never before lived with people who themselves appeared to do no work. Even the Baron in his castle had to preserve his position by strength and cunning and brute force. Signor Cavilloso, so little and white-handed, lived magically by the manipulation of account books and pieces of paper, and had people give him money or a share of their crops for farming his land, for no reason I could readily discern. It was all most mysterious and attractive.

He had a big farm house, the biggest I had seen to that time. It was shared with his wife, Amalia, a short, black-frocked, rotund woman with a fierce red face; his daughter, Eleonora, a spindly, pale girl of fourteen; and the two female servants, Placida and Marta. Marta was very old, a multiple widow. Placida, not so old, had buried only one husband. I was allowed after a while into their kitchen. When I expressed my wonder at the great hanging hams, bunches of onions, sticks of dried fish, casks of figs, cheeses and flasks of oil, the women laughed, and Enrico, who lounged in there half the day, waved his hands in disgust and cried, Southerners – animals. They don't know they're born.

And indeed it did seem that I had been born afresh. Washed ashore into some demi-paradise. At first. But everywhere and everyone disguises its true nature.

At the time of which I now speak, I had been there almost three years. I had advanced from herdboy to Enrico's assistant. Yard man, woodcutter, vine-tier, oil-presser, horse harnesser, stable cleaner – Enrico made sure to give me the dirtiest end of all these tasks. But the master had begun to take an interest in me. He was surprised to find that I could read and write. One morning a week he would invite me into the house, and let me enter up bills and receipts in his account books.

This was soft, easy work, though I felt uncomfortable some-times when Signor Cavilloso would stand behind me. He would put his thin hand on my shoulder and knead it gently, saying, Well done, Leporello. That is neat. That is nice.

Of course his man, Enrico, became jealous. As is the way of these things he became outwardly friendly to me in front of the signore. And, though in front of the other servants he was still his old bullying, piss-taking self, there was a moderation in these things, as if he knew I was a man to be watched, a potential rival.

At first I shared a bed in the stable-loft with Enrico. I soon discovered why Marta in the kitchen called him The Tree. As he slept an enormous iron-hard branch would grow out of his trunk, pushing at me, impelling me to the edge of the palliasse. Do you know what these huge ones are like? A lusty infant's arm holding an orange. I begged a mattress from the house and moved into the corner. He took no offence – it was another sign of my weakness. In any case, he was often absent at night, having a large circle of ladies in the district eager for his orange.

It was quite natural at my age that I should look round to suit myself with company. The kitchen women were plainly impossi-ble. The mistress, Signora Cavilloso? Enrico sniggered, Keep away, she'll eat you up. Eleonora? A thin girl before her time, the time of her time; unready, unavailable by her position, looking down from her window palely on the yard; the daughter of the boss. Anyway, at the time I am talking about she had been away a year at school in the great city to the north they called Pomodoro. I found a girl in the village a little way off who would have me. Then another. But all these were in some way spoken for. A dangerous business. Still, life goes on.

Let us get on with it. The time? The day?

Master and mistress had left the estate to go to Pomodoro. My master's brother had died. They had gone for the disposition of the estate, and to bring back Eleonora from her convent. Today was the day fixed for their return.

They had been away a month.

Signor Cavilloso came back in the first carriage, loaded to bursting with stuff looted from his brother's estate. Enrico and I were moving a massive travelling trunk, tremendously heavy, into the big bedroom when we heard the second coach, bearing Eleonora and her mother, clatter into the yard.

I joined Enrico at the window, standing back a little so that we would not be observed. The carriage was half white with dust; the poor bloody horse stood with his head drooping. Eleonora was the first to climb down. She was taller. Not a young girl any more – those holy convents bring a girl on without a doubt. In smart new clothes, a little creased and crumpled by travelling. She looked in an evil mood.

Old Marta hurried from the house with a bucket of water for the horse, a cloth over her arm to wipe him down.

Marta, Eleonora commanded, don't bother with that, for Heaven's sake. Get my things out, you stupid.

Now her mother came tumbling out, babbling at her to be quiet.

Eleonora cried, But Mother – they have been so jolted . . .

Marta had gone stolidly on to the head of the horse to give the poor creature his due refreshment.

Signora Cavilloso grabbed her daughter by the elbow, hissing words we could not hear, propelling her towards the house. Eleonora passed under us; as if sensing our presence, she tilted her head, her eyes black and furious. They went on into the house.

We heard her father's reedy voice in the hall say, Eleonora, whatever is the matter, child?

Seems the little bird has grown, said Enrico.

They came up the stairs, with Eleonora complaining, Look at me . . . Oh, my clothes . . . Oh, this place . . . It sounded then as if she burst into tears. Her mother's voice rose up again, scolding. A door slammed. Opened again. The two voices twisted together . . . Beasts. Peasants . . . How can you talk . . . Home . . . Stay there then . . . What do you . . . Oh, you stupid girl. Stay there . . . What can you . . . ? But Eleonora's question was left unanswered. The door was shut, quietly and deliberately this time, and the mistress came in to us.

What are you lazy clods doing here? she snapped.

Enrico pointed at the chest.

Well, move it then. Move it. I suppose you've grown idle while we've been away.

She was a tartar – and it sounded from her daughter as if she'd bred another. She went over to the window and bellowed down at Marta, The men will tend the horse. Get some food for me and the master. Sausage. Bread. She spun around. Have you two not finished yet? Go down. Go down. She drove us past her daughter's door. From inside the returned princess cried out, Marta, Marta. Where are my things . . . ?

In the kitchen Marta said that they had had their heads turned by the city. For once Placida agreed with her. God knows what ideas they have brought back, she said. I don't know about ideas, but that afternoon the mistress came down with a cloth bundle. New silver from Pomodoro; her eyes gleamed as she unwrapped knives, forks, spoons . . .

Everything must be new and different for the coming night. Superfine candles, long, thin and of a surpassing whiteness. Gentlemen's pricks, snorted Marta. Enrico started to laugh and she told him to shut up.

Placida said, You should know about such things. The talk in the village was that Marta had eight or nine living children by different men, and Heaven knows how many other infants ditched and buried. My men were men, said Marta. She brandished one of the candles. Better than these. My men were as thick as their arms. And off they went again arguing.

Your husband couldn't give you a mouse, Donna Placida, Marta cackled, her little old round face screwed up into wrinkles.

Rabbit-hole, said Placida.

Mouse-trap, said Marta.

That exchange of insults shut them up for a while. I looked at Marta and tried to imagine her as the beauty old men said she had been. She was round as a barrel, with lumps back and front of her under the perpetual black blouse, so that you could only tell by the way she faced which was bosom, which back-hump. Under her long skirts her legs were never seen, and by the way she

54

trundled over the kitchen flags they seemed to have been replaced by thick, uneven cart wheels.

Towards evening I was sitting idly at the table when the master came in. Marta had been telling us again of her cousin who had been born out of a wolf. Enrico had a candlestick in his hand, pretending to polish it. The pots bubbled busily.

The master hesitated in the doorway at the top of the steps. He was dressed in a new blue coat trimmed in silver. On his head was his short wig. He cleared his throat as if embarrassed, and called, Ah, Leporello, ah, could you come with me? Enrico leered. Placida turned her face away to hide a smile. Poor Signor Cavilloso was a figure of fun.

He led me upstairs and into their bedroom.

Let the women, ah, get on with it, my boy, he said in that same half-embarrassed way. He stood beside the great chest Enrico and I had carried upstairs.

Leporello, I wish you to do something for me tonight. He coughed again into his hand, and a little cloud of flour rose from his wig.

Yes, signore?

You are a good-looking young man . . .

Signore?

I . . . I wish to make some show in this neighbourhood. We have got out of the way of civilised people, my boy. My visit to the city has shown me that plainly. The change in our circumstances following my brother's death – may the Good Lord rest his soul – enables us – though I could not of course have wished it to have come in this way – enables us . . . well, let us just say that he has been provident with his estate. Much extra business will ensue, Leporello. Yes. Yes. It is important that my household reflects my new position. Yes. He plucked at his sleeve. He smoothed his fingers on his new yellow waistcoat. He looked like a plump bird.

Oh, I tell you, Leporello, the men of the city of Pomodoro are so well dressed. In fact, he said, I made the mistake of thinking that some of the servants were gentlemen!

From now on, Cavilloso said, they were to live like the

gentlefolk they were. For too long they had rotted like peasants in this house. Goats and fowl wandering into the kitchen, the hallway even – those days were to end.

I have therefore, he said, suggested to Donna Amalia that, well – see here, and he opened the trunk and took out a bundle of clothes.

He proceeded to hold up each item to be viewed.

A long brown coat with thin gold embroidered facings and pearl buttons.

A white shirt.

A pair of long grey stockings.

A pair of dark-green breeches.

A pair of buckled shoes.

He laid the clothes in turn on the bed, stepped back, pointed at them, and said, These are for you, Leporello. I wish you to dress in them. I wish you to be my servant.

I am your servant, signore.

You do not understand, he said. I mean a manservant. In the house. Not one of those lubberlouts like Enrico. I wish to make something of you, Leporello. Now – put them on. Put them on.

Now?

Yes. Oh, yes.

The little man seemed to be excited all at once. I was not used to taking off my clothes before I went to bed. And it hardly seemed right to undress in front of Signor Cavilloso.

Surely, lad, you're not shy. He had a big, silly grin on his face. His hands twisted in and out of themselves. Well then, he said. Go behind Donna Amalia's screen. He scooped up the clothes and piled them into my arms.

Behind the screen I took off my blouse and breeches and started to put on the new clothes. Reverently – I had never handled such fine things before.

I was aware of his hopping, expectant presence on the other side. I hurried, struggling with these strange garments.

Have you not finished yet? his voice came. Then he looked round the screen. There was greed in his eyes as he regarded me half-naked.

Oh, no, no. No. He giggled, and said, You have to put on the

56

stockings before the breeches. Take them off again. Come, come. Now that's it . . . his excited whisper talked to itself rather than me. Twisting away from his prying eyes, I pulled on the stockings and tied their garters. I felt like a girl. Then the breeches – presenting my handsome buttocks to him. I turned to face him, holding the breeches together with one hand.

You must tie those below the knee, he said. Let me assist . . . He fell to his knees in front of me. I took half a step back.

I . . . I can manage, signore.

He leaned forward, his hands reaching out, like a supplicant at a saint's statue. Buttons, he breathed. You will not be familiar . . . To my horror, I felt myself starting to be aroused in my manhood. His fingers trembled at the opening to my breeches. His hand came into contact with my swelling . . . Ah, Leporello –

His lips, pouting like a rosebud, sought my . . .

Now, now – what have we here? It was the voice of the mistress. Neither of us could have heard the door, and her steps across the room. Donna Amalia stood inside the screen.

What in Heaven's name are you at here? She said, hands on her considerable hips. What was it she saw, in the first gloom of evening, in the deeper shadow of the screen, past her husband's obscuring body? I was still naked from the waist up. What could she have seen? Her husband shuffled back on his knees, struggling to rise. The costume, my dear, he breathed, his cheeks puce as plums. The uniform. He stood. She glowered at him. Go downstairs, she said. Messing about here . . . Our guests are due. The boy should have been dressed hours ago.

The uniform . . . Leporello . . . unused . . . , he mumbled.

I will see to it. Such nonsense, she snorted. I told you it was all foolishness.

He retreated. Rounding the screen, he gave me back a look like a beaten dog.

I shall get him ready, she said.

My dear, he murmured.

Go about your business, she commanded. I heard him scuttle across to the door, closing it quietly behind him. Silence in the room. Her eyes glimmered like a dog in a different mood.

Now, what have we here? she said. If you are to be got up, let's make a proper job of it. Have you not seen buttons before? She advanced on me. She bent her head, but not before I had caught a whiff of her black breath.

But I have to admit, my master's late attentions had left me still in an excited state. You know? And as she bent, my little gentleman popped up and out of the plush breeches.

What have we here! she exclaimed. Quick as could be her fingers clutched me.

Ah, whatever curious sort of gentleman Signor Cavilloso might have been, he was still a gentleman. Assuredly his wife was no lady. I take that back in part – you would be surprised what I have seen ladies get up to. But she was no born lady. Her mother had married a Bourbon landowner by witchcraft, according to the women in the kitchen. So Amalia had a good dowry and could marry a man such as Cavilloso. But she was still half a peasant. The bottom half of her, at that.

She sank to the floorboards, pulling me forward by my no longer negligible gentleman, clutching up her skirts with the other hand, muttering and swearing in her mother's tongue. Perhaps fortunately, I could see none of her southern region as I fell forward onto the mountains of her breasts. She put me into her. Up and down, up and down, she commanded. There. Not there. Are you in? Where are you? Her black hair with its odd smell of bacon rose in my face as she tried to see what I was up to. She moved violently. I could not feel anything. Nothing. Supporting myself on my elbow, my free hand sought confirmation of my virility. Alas, I was out. I had wilted. What are you doing? she hissed. Get up. Get up. Her hands pushed against my chest with surprising force. Those women are strong, you know. Oh, oh, you are nothing but a boy, she said, struggling to her feet. Someone is coming, she said. Put yourself away.

It could not have taken more than a minute. Amazingly, as she smoothed down her skirts, she looked the mistress again in every particular, as if nothing at all had happened. Well, very little had.

She was right. Someone had come into the room. A diplomatic cough. It was Cavilloso. Is the boy ready now? he enquired.

We had to start all over again, she called out to him, then to me she said, Come, buttons do like this. And with brusque movements of her fingers she buttoned up my breeches. The shirt now, she commanded. The coat too.

We came out from behind the screen. I tell you, I could not look my master in the eye. I was sure my face was flaming.

There your servant is, said the mistress.

Oh my. Oh yes, he said. Pomodoro – quite.

Oh, he's pretty enough, she said.

Yes, yes. Most handsome, he said, circling round me. Let him see, my dear.

See? See what?

Himself. Let him see himself. He will christen the glass.

Um, she grunted. If you must.

He hurried across to the chest. She joined him, and they began taking things out and laying them on the floor as they delved down for something.

How could they behave like this? A little while earlier the master had made the most curious advances to me. And she – only moments after – had admitted me to the most unlikely part of her body. But then, as the Don observed, there is no creature so capable of opportune deceit, so capable of arousing, and then almost instantly disguising, its basest instincts, as the human animal. Clothed, perfumed – all animals, Leporello.

Laced, tied and buttoned, I watched them bent over the chest. At last they found what they were looking for. Cavilloso drew out a long, flat rectangle wrapped in sacking. My, it is heavy, he wheezed. They laid it on the bed and undid the twine.

What I had first thought was a picture was revealed as a looking glass in an ornate, gilded frame. The room was darkening. He set the glass against the wall by the window.

Step forward, Leporello.

For the first time in my life I saw myself whole. Not that fore-shortened view at the water's edge, or bits in the small panes of the farm windows, or the elephant nose and pointed head in the curved side of polished silver.

Ah, who was this handsome youth? You don't believe it? Smile away. You will come to it soon enough. Wrinkles, baldness, dim sight, deafness. Your cock at half-mast like a flag at a funeral. Cramps, back-aches, gout, swollen joints – all the robbers that wait round the dark corner, laying for you. A whole city of dark corners. Then I had a good figure, dark curly hair, brown eyes in the purest white – not this mustard. Broad at the shoulders, slim in the waist – no, not like a peasant or a farmer's boy – those boys look like wardrobes at eighteen – but a gentleman. Well, half a gentleman. A mock gentleman. A servant.

My master and mistress stood behind me.

Enough, she said. He will get a swollen head.

The master instructed me. I was to receive their guests. I was to stand behind his chair. To refill the glasses – though not too hastily. To remain silent.

None of your back-chat, she growled. And don't get your new clothes stained.

The night of their feast. Enrico stood in the kitchen, laughing at my new clothes, while the two women fussed and fingered my new glory. Running at last out of insults, Enrico said he had to go and look after the carriage horse which had been lamed on the journey home. I knew that he was off to the village to tell them of the latest follies of this house. When he had gone Marta went about her business in that darting way old women have. She regarded everything that Placida did as wrong. Every pot and plate and dish was in the wrong place, so that when Placida's back was turned at some task, Marta moved them about, and when Placida turned again her whole world had been disordered by the old woman and she shrieked and called to the saints to tell her why rabbits walk after they are dead and pots have legs, why saucepans can fly. The new clothes were forgotten as she screamed at Marta and Marta went on, waddling about the kitchen, unperturbed, a faint smile on her wrinkled mouth, muttering every now and then some tuneless song. I stood to the side and smoothed my hand down the brown coat, fingered the white blouse, lifted one leg forward, then the other, to admire the grey stockings, the yellow bows that tied my green breeches.

Leporello. Leporello! My master was calling me from the steps again. I went up to him. The guests are arriving, he said. You must admit the guests.

Be polite. Be dignified, he said over his shoulder as he hurried along the passageway to the hall. He darted across the hall and half hid himself behind the door of the room where they were to dine, waving me to the double front doors. They are here. Admit them. Admit them.

Piccata, the mill owner. A mountain of flesh, jovial, loud-voiced; cunning as a fat rat. His wife, tall and thin; a face with a bad smell under its nose. The premier family, below the nobility, in the area. No more after tonight.

They were surprised at the sight of me. They looked at me. I looked at them.

Announce, came the whisper. Announce who they are.

Signor Piccata. Signora Piccata, I shouted.

He and his lady bustled in and stood in the centre of the little hall. Cavilloso, Piccata bellowed. Where the devil are you? His head almost collided with the lamp hanging from the ceiling.

Close the door, came the ghostly voice.

As I did so, I saw Enrico leading their horse across the yard. He saluted me by sticking his middle finger in the air.

Take his hat.

Piccata had a broad hat in his hands. I reached out for it; he hesitated a moment, then laughed and threw it to me. His wife reared her nose up, as if to say, You are not taking my hat from my head.

Ah – the master emerged, greeting us with a pretence of surprise, rubbing his hands together as if he had come hot-foot from some urgent business deep in the house. My man, Leporello, he said, he is looking after you?

You mean your stable boy, said Piccata. Didn't recognise him at first. What's he all dolled up for? He laughed again and pinched my cheek hard. Like a bloody cherub, he said.

Leporello, conduct our guests into the dining chamber, said the master, coughing into his hand and blushing.

Say, *This way*, he whispered in my ear.

This way.

. . . *Signore. Signora* . . .

Signore . . .

But they had already swept through the open door. It was only a short step after all across the hall. In the room, it seemed that Signora Piccata's eyebrows had got stuck when she raised them, because they did not come down again as she looked around.

The women had worked hard. The table was covered with a fine white cloth with a gold edge. Two silver candleholders each had four of the new city candles. They did not spit and smoke like our homemade ones, but burned with a steady oval flame. A new wall-hanging, bright, unfaded by the sun, showed princes on horses, and hounds springing in pursuit of a hare. The glasses from Pomodoro glistened and winked. On the sideboard were bottles of wine, not the usual flask. The eyebrows took all this in. The nose sniffed – these people you must realise, like all friends in small, out of the way places, hated each other.

There was no sign yet of the mistress or Eleonora.

Basso, the lawyer, and his wife arrived in short order, accompanied with self-satisfied uncouthness by Enrico. – Good evening, Landowner. – Greetings to you, Miller. – Welcome, Lawyer. The women kissed each other with aversion. Signora Basso is my master's sister. Signora Piccata is a first cousin of my mistress.

Please be seated, said Cavilloso.

Had we not better wait for Padre Modesto? Signora Piccata enquired snakily.

Ah . . . My master's face was red again.

I'm here. I'm here, said the priest, running in just as they were saying this.

The master's chair is at the top of the table; the mistress's at the bottom, and there are three along each side. The priest makes for one at the top end where the wine is set. Signora Piccata graciously sits down beside him, saying loudly she did not know how anyone could have so many candles burning, the light quite blinded one. In the last chair on that side sits Signora Basso.

The two husbands sit opposite their wives. Basso puts his hand flat on the table and his long pock-marked face looks expressionlessly at his wife. She is still quite pretty and her mouth is set in a little, secret smile. Anyone not knowing would have said that the two men were married to each other's wives.

I was left not knowing what to do while all this settling of places was going on. Our womenfolk had still not come in.

Are we not to be joined by Amalia? said Signora Piccata.

Or dear little Eleonora? said Signora Basso.

Of course. Of course, said their husband and father. They are, I believe, changing.

Women, eh? Piccata rolled his eyes and his face wobbled with laughter. Basso frowned at his wife. His own wife.

It would be most unlike Amalia to hide herself away, Signora Piccata said.

Or Eleonora, said Signora Basso.

The two women smiled at each other.

I must commiserate . . . , Basso the lawyer began dolefully. He was obviously hoping for work from the expanded complications of the estate.

But he never got into his stride, because here were the ladies at last.

My, my, but they were splendid, resplendent, gorgeous, exotic creatures in the new clothes brought from the city. Never had anyone seen such great bell-like skirts, puffed out with so many petticoats; such low bodices – my mistress's huge breasts heave up like pumpkins; Eleonora's little white halved-pears with a sly shadowy line between them peep over . . . Oh, the cries and ahs of malicious admiration as they crowd through the door, swing into the room. Oh, the confusion as they try to get between chairs and table. They are quite the latest rage . . . These are nothing compared with . . . You should see . . . Impossible. They cannot sit down. They cannot reach the table without crushing and bending and breaking the frames of their dresses.

Leporello. Assist. Assist, says Cavilloso, agonised by the stupidity of his women.

I go to the mistress and hold back her chair, and then push it forward, pull it back again, as she huffs and puffs, hoisting her skirts and petticoats this way and that. It's all no good. What is to be done?

Stools, Piccata booms. Backs of the chairs, that's the problem.

They try again.

Stools – the only way, says Piccata again, grossly enjoying himself. Even his wife has allowed herself an unaccustomed smile, a crooked line that runs across the natural sourness of her face.

Then fetch stools. Fetch stools, boy, says Cavilloso to me. Take away the chairs. Take them away.

Then all is confusion, as chairs are taken out, the women in the big skirts sway and bob about, stools are brought from the kitchen, the table is juddered back and forth, and the women at last sit down.

The feast got under way. Marta and Placida brought in the dishes.

Rabbit pie.

Cheeses.

A capon.

Hare.

Sausages.

Fried cod.

Soffritto.

Melons – the eating of these was the nearest, I think, my mistress ever got to washing her face as she buried it in a half moon of gushing fruit.

The priest ate singlemindedly, without stop, his head bent over his plate, his fingers tearing away at flesh, fish, cheese, bread, as if feverishly going over and over his rosary.

Flushed with wine, my master got his composure back, and began to talk about the grand funeral given to his brother, the magnificence of the church, the colours on the holy statues; about all the grand people they had seen, the hugeness and richness of the city they had been honoured guests in; the harbour, the ships, the palaces . . .

64

And all the time, Piccata's wife broke in with the latest village gossip; news of the baron, of rents, sales; and Signora Basso kept eyeing the household's splendid new dress – for now, sanctioned by fashion and good money laid out, it had ceased to be ridiculous. Where did you get such wonderful stuffs, my dear, she asked Eleonora. The priest ate steadfastly on. My mistress wiped the grease off her fingers on her new white silk . . .

I stood as bidden behind Signor Cavilloso and my feet started to hurt in the new shoes. Then I saw Eleonora looking up at me, her dark eyes solemn, her expression mysterious and somehow wistfully dissatisfied.

Her eyes held mine for what seemed an age. Her mouth twitched into a tiny shy smile.

Leporello, my master commanded. More wine. More wine for the reverend father. Wake up, for Heaven's sake.

When I straightened up from filling the priest's glass, Eleonora had lowered her face again.

What could such a look mean?

Working in the house now I was able for the first time to study the habits of the family. My duties were light. The mistress had shown no interest in me since our unsatisfactory entanglement in the bedroom. She had, Enrico informed me, returned her attentions to himself and his enormous club. This surprised me, for coarse as she was, she was a gentlewoman of sorts and should, I thought, have confined her affections to the indoor servants at the lowest. I had though become Signor Cavilloso's pet. He inspected me each morning like a fussy sergeant-at-arms. Yes. Yes – touching my braided shoulders, lifting my chin with the tips of his fingers. Yes, very good. Look up, Leporello. Look up. Be proud of your position. You are an advertisement for the house of Cavilloso. He seemed always reluctant to stop touching me, his hands darting back and forth, nipping and tucking at my clothes. At last he would pull himself away to see to the rest of his estate. Glancing back as he went out, chirruping, Head up, head up, Leporello. That's a good boy.

And what of the daughter?

I have told you already how irritable, how unable to settle Eleonora had seemed since her return from school in Pomodoro. The whole family was infected with the airs of the city; recipes for new dishes they had eaten were foisted on Marta; the smart conversation they had overheard was retailed in an almost unintelligible mixture of dialect and Pomodoran. They thanked themselves for the good fortune they had inherited each time with a ritual sigh and signing of the breast for the dead benefactor. But it began to wear off soon enough from Mamma and Papa. The daughter continued to flounce about the house, banging doors, conducting endless screaming rows with her mother, or giving orders to Marta and Placida, which they conveniently and silently neglected to perform, until they were countermanded or senselessly renewed. Eleonora cursed them for their 'southern ways', their 'peasant idiocy'. Did she plague me in this way? No. I caught her eyes dwelling on me when they all dined together. The great hooped dresses had been put away; Eleonora wore her simple *adrienne* again. Her mother had reverted most comfortably to her thick black and plum coloured dress. Signor Cavilloso had given up his wig except on formal occasions; I stood behind his chair looking down at the little red spots raised on his scalp.

Talk of the great city dropped away. The master and mistress gabbled once more about land, neighbours, money, money ... Eleonora yawned. Sometimes, while they talked, as I turned from the sideboard, she would be staring at me. Instead of blushing and letting her eyes immediately and modestly fall again to the contemplation of her maidenly bosom, she would continue to stare frankly on at me, so that it was I who was forced to look away.

Until this time I had never thought of Eleonora as in any way attractive. Before she had gone to Pomodoro she had been only the master's little daughter; as straight and skinny as a pullet, with none of the curves of a woman. Now, excited by her obvious interest in me, I looked again and saw that she had filled out. If not much – it was enough. When she bent over to rummage in a cupboard her bottom assumed that satisfying tomato shape that

even the thinnest woman has. Attention flatters us, from wherever it comes. My uniform had made me vain and I could not
resist stealing into the master's bedroom to revisit my image in
the pier-glass. What a fine figure I must cut! How I was already
making my way in the world – here I was entertaining thoughts
of my master's daughter already!

The frank stares, the charming softening of her voice whenever
she had to address me, the allowing of her hand to rest on my
sleeve as I served her – all of this began to work on me to such a
degree that after two weeks of it I felt that matters must surely
soon come to some wicked, pleasurable, dangerous head.

Dangerous?

After all, I was getting on well in that place. The master had let
drop flattering half-promises about my future. For all this, I still
had to take off my smart livery in the flea-hopping, dung-smelling
stable loft I shared with Enrico. And Enrico was already resentful
of me because of all the rough work about the yard that had fallen
back on him. He lost no time telling me what he thought about
my future prospects.

High and mighty now, little rabbit? he sneered. Don't think
everyone hasn't seen you making eyes at our Eleonora. You think
one day you'll marry the Mastro's daughter, eh? You really think
that, do you, idiot? Well, I'll tell you – don't even think about
thinking that. Good, kind Signor Cavilloso would have you hung
by the balls from the church bell and ring you every hour as a
warning to others. Don't you know who these people are? They
are our masters. Why do you think she's been brought home?
They've pulled her out the convent to marry her off. Fatten her
up a bit – then it's off to market with her. We are stinking manure
under their feet. Watch your arse by all means from our master's
attentions. He won't think the worse of you for it in the end. But
touch his property? I'd advise you to fuck off while the going's
good. I wouldn't want to be the one to tell of your little romance
. . . You know what I mean?

This was the most considerable speech I had ever heard from
Enrico and though I put it down to jealousy of my success, he was
not entirely stupid. His speech ate into me and nibbled at my sleep.

So, for the next few days I was all cold civility and the most proper servant to Signorina Cavilloso. I avoided her floating hands. At first she looked puzzled. Then hurt and reproachful. Poor girl, I thought, to be denied the warm smile of her loved one. I allowed myself the luxury of feeling superior to these mighty people. We are very foolish when we are young. A day or two more passed. Her face put on its iron again. I felt sorry then that I had put a distance between us, because she had awakened something in me, but I thought, half gratefully, half reluctantly, that there was an end to it. What, of course, I hadn't reckoned with was what was going on in Eleonora's head the meanwhile. I was soon to find out.

Another role Signor Cavilloso liked me to play on their stage was that of his valet; beating the dust out of his clothes at night, sewing on buttons, or re-sewing loose threads – woman's work that I was too ashamed to take down to Placida or Marta in the kitchen, where I would also have to suffer the insults of Enrico lounging by the fire. Where's your sewing basket, girlie, he would call; or mutter in my ear, as he shouldered his way out, Bum-Boy, or Cock-Muff.

Anyway, this evening, Enrico was to drive the master and mistress to the Baron's estate. With his inheritance my master's stock had risen in the neighbourhood and aristocrats are ever on the watch for fresh money. The news in the kitchen was that Eleonora had pleaded a raging headache. She must have had one after her mother had finished screaming at her. So she stayed behind.

From their window I saw my master and mistress heave themselves into the perilously swaying little carriage. Enrico whipped up the horse and they clattered out of the yard. The house was quiet. I put away the clothes they had changed from. On the landing was a circle of white dust that had fallen when I prepared the signore's wig. In hungry times you might have been killed for the amount of flour that went to powder his head. I would have to go downstairs and fetch a broom. Going along the landing I was sure that Eleonora's door was closed. But when I came back up it stood a little way open.

Leporello? The voice from within was plaintive and faint. Leporello, is that you? Come in a moment, would you?

I pushed the door open. She sat on a straightbacked chair facing the window, one hand trailing, dangling a handkerchief on the floor. She turned her head; her eyes were red and puffed. Come in. Come in. Shut the door. Her face turned away again, and she dabbed at it with the handkerchief. Over here, she mumbled. Come to my side.

Signorina ... I ... I have ...

She sniffed once more into the handkerchief.

I did not quite close the door to. I knew I should not be in this room. If anyone had seen me enter and the door close after me – it would be the church tower, balls and clapper. I tiptoed across the room until I stood just behind her.

She blew her nose loudly and then looked up at me, infinite woe on her face.

Ah, Leporello, she said. Why are you making me suffer like this? Take my hands. Take them! I leaned my broom against the wall. Her hands were cold. Do you not know, Leporello, what I feel for you? Are you blind? Have you not seen the looks I have given you? The tender touches? She pressed my hands. She gazed up into my face and began to draw me down. As our lips were about to touch, she started away.

What was that? she whispered.

What?

A sound.

I listened intently but heard nothing.

Someone is coming.

We held our positions like a waxwork tableau.

Quick, she commanded, your broom.

My broom?

To the door quickly. Pretend to be sweeping.

I hastened to the door, banging it open noisily with my heel, all the while industriously hacking with the stiff bristles at the edge of the matting. I backed onto the landing with a great show of industry. There, it's done, I announced in a loud voice. Eleonora sat, head bowed, making a show of reading some piece of paper, a letter maybe. I straightened up.

There was no one on the landing. Or the stairs. From far off I could hear Placida's scolding voice.

There is no one there, I said softly. But her hands flapped. Go away. Go down. You must not be found here. Later . . .

Elated, and confused, I came down the stairs. Had the girl just made a declaration of love for me? Was it some joke? Was she mad? Was I? How was I to take what she had said? Standing in the entrance hall, I stared blindly ahead at the front doors.

What are you doing there, you great lump? Marta waddled vengefully across the stone flags. Have you no work to do? Sweep. Sweep away, she cackled, going out into the yard. One door banged against the other in the draught. I began half-heartedly to sweep back the dust that was blowing in.

Later, Eleonora had said. But when? She sat at table the next morning with her parents, her mouth drawn down in a tight line.

I do wish I knew what was the matter with our dear daughter, said Signora Cavilloso, a disagreeable expression on her face, as if she was gutting a fish as she spoke.

Something wrong? Signor Cavilloso munched his words with his food. Not ill are you, my dear?

I was talking, *cuore mio*, about Eleonora's temper, which you may or may not have noticed has not been of the sweetest since she came back with us. If you ask me that school has filled her with a load of nonsense.

As long as you feel all right, Eleonora. He dabbed at his mouth with his sleeve, looking in a concerned way at his daughter.

Yes, Papa. She lifted her head and her eyes locked briefly onto mine. By some instinct I took a nervous step forward. The movement caught Signora Cavilloso's eye.

Leporello, you're not here as a dancer. Serve, boy. Serve.

I picked up the flask that was an inch away from the master's elbow and trickled a little wine into his already three-quarter-full-glass.

No. Not for me, said the mistress when I offered her the bottle.

70

She wriggled triumphantly on her chair, confident that I had been put in my place. She had the true peasant's vindictive contempt for those they have risen above. The fact that I had once tumbled into the broad way of her fanny had evidently been forgotten, if not forgiven. Take those dishes into the kitchen, she commanded.

Poor Leporello, sighed Eleonora.

Poor Leporello! Why poor Leporello? Your father found him in a field.

Sh . . .

. . . among the cattle. Wasn't that right?

I left them to it and took the dishes off to Placida – who I found amusing herself by tickling Marta's whiskers with a feather while the old woman dozed by the kitchen fire.

Eleonora showed her hand the next morning. I had fixed a horse for Signor Cavilloso. He got up and settled himself with his usual Good Boy, Good Boy, and a sly look down so that I would not know whether the 'Good Boy' was for me or for the horse. He clattered off, stiff-backed, bouncing up and down in the saddle like a sack.

As Enrico was at some work in the fields that morning, I had to put the stable to rights. Work I had grown unused to: I found it hard going. And Enrico had left the place in a fine mess; harness slung everywhere, the horses not fed, the steps and wheels of the carriage caked in mud from their outing a week ago. The day I had gone into Eleonora's room.

Leporello, came a whisper behind me.

She was smiling at me from the yard. The light was behind her; her face glowed and her hair was a saint's halo. And standing there like that she was quite, not beautiful – but nice, quite nice. You know? Beyond her, I saw the kitchen window shutter pushed back and Placida throw a bucket of dirty water out into the yard. I beckoned to Eleonora to hurry inside.

Then it was all laid before me by her words, her pleas, her sighs . . .

I was so handsome, *bello*, so strong, *forte*, she had fallen in love

71

with me as soon as she came back from that dreadful convent – her words. I must excuse her conduct since her return. How it must have confused me. But she could not damp down her ardour for ever. I must have seen how she looked at me? What it cost her to invite me into her room? The wrench to her heart when our first sentimental conversation was so cruelly cut short? Oh dear, dear Leporello, what are we to do? she wailed.

What was I to do? She had scarcely been out of my thoughts of late, but the thought that I was to be called upon to do something had not occurred to me. In fact, it scared me. She was, you know, dangerous goods – good to think about, not so good to be caught with.

She knew, ah, she knew, my dear, that I too loved. Could I not see that we must, we must . . .

What?

Flee!

Flee? Where? With what? How? The cowardly questions jumbled about in my head. She was now in my arms, trembling.

Why, to the city. To Pomodoro. Horses. Disguises. Money.

It sounded like a French romance. We can do it, dear Leporello. Oh say you will – and you will be mine. Or what can I do? I cannot forever conceal my love. They will know. Then what will become of me? Of you? I shall be sent to the nunnery. But you, my poor, brave darling . . .

What indeed?

She had a plan, she said.

But before she could divulge it to me, there was shouting in the yard. Enrico had returned. Courage, *caro mio*, she whispered. From now on I shall have to appear cold to you. It's my plan. Trust my plan. Then, in a loud, hectoring voice, she demanded, My saddle – why have you not cleaned and polished it. I told you I wanted to ride. When my father comes back you will be beaten. You idle . . . and more of the same, most convincingly, almost too convincingly acted out. Enrico came lumbering across the yard and looked in, with that great, stupid grin on his face.

Out of my way oaf, she snapped as she swept past him.

Getting it in the neck, eh, little lover, said Enrico. His grin was like the moon turned on its side.

This all leads to the Don, I do assure you. The story is to show you to what variety of fool I belonged. Was I what is called 'in love' with the girl? I do not think so. I desired her, wanted her when she was near me – as we want any woman who shows the slightest interest in us. But when she was away from me, I felt only an unease, a sense of irritation almost. I had made no move towards her and yet here I was, being dragged along in some mad adventure she had dreamed up and which threatened to be the ruin of both of us. But it seemed she was going through with it, for there followed three days of studied coldness towards me on the part of Eleonora.

So, our little romance is over, said Signora Cavilloso. Our lovebirds have fallen out. I should think so too. The idea!

Eleonora looked steadfastly down at her book.

The country it seems is too boring for some, the old witch went on. The sooner they are married the better. That's enough to cool any woman off. She laughed with a horrible loudness. What do you say, husband?

Eh? Cavilloso looked up startled. He had been adding up a long line of figures on a slip of paper.

Go back to sleep, she said. It was quite amazing the way she spoke to him, but then all those women in the South are gorgons in the home. I am glad to see that the object of your affections has had the good sense not to join in your little games. She twisted round to glare at me. If I thought for one minute . . .

Mamma – how can you be so ridiculous, said Eleonora, and she laughed, in a way like her mother, but lighter, younger. Then, like her mother, she said witheringly, The idea . . .

Over the next few days the joke of Eleonora's infatuation with a servant began to pall even with Signora Cavilloso. It must have been Enrico who had told her of it, but no fresh evidence being forthcoming their limited wit came up with no fresh variations. And Eleonora carried her part with such skill that even I began to think I had dreamed her tearful avowals.

And the plan? How was that to be communicated to me? Even

if her mother had ceased twitting her about her infatuation I knew that she was watching Eleonora closely; suspicion once planted is hard to shake from the mind. Even so, the thought that Eleonora had been merely playing with me in some bored, malicious way troubled me as day after day passed and she made no attempt to approach me.

My answer came abruptly enough. Eleonora and her mother were to drive one day over to the Rannocchio estate. They were the owners of vineyards, olive groves, a disputed water-course, much land, many tenants – and a son. The talk in the kitchen was that Eleonora, for the sake of the water, and with the exchange of a few acres, was to be mated with the son.

Get ready to let your loved one go, said Placida. Land is land.

Anyway, here they come: Signora Cavilloso in a great black hat with peacock's feathers lolling crazily from the back; Eleonora modest as a nun about to be married to Christ. I open the door. Enrico waits on the box of the little carriage; he has been smartened up with an old cocked hat of my master's set insolently on his head.

As Eleonora squeezes past me in the doorway, though she has not the excuse of her mother's bulk, I feel her hand slide something into my pocket.

When they were gone I hurried to the stable and took out the piece of paper.

> Deerest lepporello you have heard the Worst. I am to be marrid
> to the clod Rannocchio the sun for our Loves sake this cannot
> bee My plan is this 2 horces saddled two nites hence it will be
> the New Moon so no wan will see a Saddlebag of Food and som
> Cloathes for you We must flie If we cannot escape I must confes
> All – [this was underlined three times] – and take our Chance –
> [underlined twice] – have Horces behind the oliv trees at
> Morganos farm the back at one oclock at Dark I will be wating
> My Love Do Not Fale Me

Between her writing and my limited learning the message was not easy to read. What was I to do? I pored over the note by the one candlestub in the stable loft.

It was obvious I had to go along with this madcap scheme. But if I did, what would my life be worth? And if I did not, the silly

74

girl, for revenge, or for whatever passes for love in a girl's heart – so conceited was I – would betray me. The criminal caught may plead some defence – the betrayed conspirator has none. And I considered this – did I wish to remain the rest of my life standing behind Signor Cavilloso's chair, at least for the rest of his life? My father had been killed for coming back. I would suffer the same fate by remaining. With Eleonora I could seek a new life. Set sail from the harbour of Pomodoro in one of those great ships my father had described so glowingly. He had said that they went across a great ocean to a place of enormous wealth and fabulous animals, where there were mountains of gold, lakes brimming with whales, bears higher than beech trees, wolves as big as horses, and men with eagles' heads. Centaurs with bows and arrows ... And if Eleonora failed me – well, she had so convinced me of my charms, she and the master's mirror, that I could easily find another.

I had made my mind up. I blew out the candle. My head whirled in the dark with my future.

It was almost ridiculously easy. Eleonora had chosen the night of our departure well. The morning before, Signor Cavilloso and Enrico were to set out on their quarter-day round of the estate collecting what rents they could, or signing up shares of the crops. Some of the farms were flung at a fair distance to the south. With any luck they would go there first and work their way back up, partaking of whatever hospitality they could scrounge from the tenants on the way. They would not return for two or three days and any hue and cry would be delayed for that long at least. With luck.

That evening, after they were gone, I saddled two horses. I took them down by the shaded path to the back of Morgano's farm. He would be no trouble; he was an old man, half deaf and blind who lived on his own, and on sufferance – a relative of the mistress. In a thick grove I tied the horses up where they had grass to crop.

The mistress, the master being gone, relaxed, as she was always ready to do, into the ways of her humble origins. I would not have to make up the dining table that night, she said, nor stand behind her in my monkey suit. She would eat in the kitchen, and Eleonora, who had sent down a message saying she was feeling unwell, would be served in her room. And not by you, Leporello, said the mistress, giving out that huge coarse laugh. Go down to the village tonight and get yourself one of the fat girls. Still laughing, she waddled off to the kitchen. I heard Placida's and Marta's voices rise in welcome; then the happy, malicious hubble-bubble that could be heard even through the closed door.

Going back to the stable-loft I took off my servant's uniform with regret. I liked the dandyish feeling the clothes gave me, the sense that they marked me out from the others in the household. I folded and packed them in a leather satchel I had taken from the master's wardrobe. I waited on my bed, feeling my bowels turn watery with a sudden fear of the whole enterprise. When it got dark I went back across the yard. I put my head through the open window to the kitchen. The three witches were still brewing gossip in their cooking pot.

I said, I am going to the village now, signora, if you please.

Go by all means, young man, she said. Don't wear it out. To their cackles and cat-calls I set off. As I went I looked back at the house. Eleonora's face, like a white heart framed in her black hair, stared out. She did not acknowledge my wave – half-hidden as it was in case they were watching me from the kitchen. Indeed, she did not appear to see me at all, but simply stared into the evening.

I picked up my satchel from the stable doorway and hurried out under the archway.

She came silently between the trees. I had fallen into a light sleep, wrapped in my cloak, sitting with my back against a tree. When I got up and tried to embrace her, murmuring, Eleonora, Eleonora, as I thought was expected of me, she wriggled free with a surprising vehemence in such a little body. No, no. We have no time for that. Then she added, as an afterthought, *caro mio*. For safety's sake, she said, we must travel as mistress and servant. I am a young widow – see. She pulled a veil over her face, and became instantly invisible in the dark grove. Remember, you are my servant, she warned. We must act that out at all times. She had now got up on her horse, and their black shape took the lead, out of the trees and rustling through canes to join the bed of a shallow stream that led gradually upwards. We got into the hills as the crescent moon dipped into the farther range of mountains.

We travelled all night; she going ahead indefatigably, not as if we were pursued, but as if she pressed forward to something not revealed to me. At last, I prevailed upon her to stop. The sky was beginning to lighten at its height. We rested overlooking a valley in which a silver river curled like a serpent. Spinneys and clumps of oak and beech stood apart, in which the first smoke-blue mist of morning hung, as though they were slowly and damply burning.

Eleonora, I said. That was the first time I had addressed her so and the word felt like a stone in my mouth. Eleonora, I repeated with more confidence. She huddled inside her cloak. Our romance so far had consisted solely of her tumultuous words and one embrace; now she was silent. I stood over her. She looked up at me.

My mother will have missed me by now, she said softly. Or perhaps they are still sleeping. Um? And I have spent the night out with a young man . . .

We have done nothing.

True, she said. She had an odd smile on her lips.

I looked away from her, down the valley, and I became aware of the terrible nearness of her father's estate, the knowledge that even now Signor Cavilloso and the monster Enrico might be turning for home, learning the news . . .

Oh, Eleonora, I said.

No, no – not here. She sprang to her feet. Do you not know what sweetness waited for tastes like?

I confessed to myself that I did not. We ate some salt pork and bread and mounted our horses again. Eleonora was composed. I have left a letter for my mother, she said. It says that I have left for the port of Bargigli on the east coast. There I am to take ship with you for Greece. Our love knows no frontiers or seas or barriers. That is what I have said.

Yes, I said. How far is it to this place of Bargigli?

Oh, we're not going there, she said. It is a trick. We shall go along the valley, turn north to the town of M- . . . – I can't remember all these names. It was a long time ago. There, she went on, we shall give it out loudly that we are bound for Bargigli. We shall go east a certain distance, then double back. It's quite simple. A trick, Leporello. A trick. You have heard of those surely?

Indeed I have.

There was a note of exasperation in her voice. She was not at all the swooning girl I thought I would have to take care of. She had taken charge. As we rode off, I again took up the place, a length behind, of her dutiful servant. Wondering when my reward would come. And when it did, if it would be worth it. When once, in the valley, I tried to canter up beside her, she said coldly, Any familiarity between us at this time would quite ruin our plan. Please, Leporello, who knows who may be watching. I dropped behind again.

At the end of the valley we hit upon the town.

I had never been in a bigger place to that date. Two churches. Graveyards with statues. A live fountain in the square. People milling in the streets instead of hiding. The black veiled lady – she lowered it again on the outskirts of the town – her faithful though wrongly sexed servant. Surely even a widow would travel with a maid? Not this one. In the courtyard of the best inn she astonished me by her bravura. She demanded a place to rest her horses and a room. All in the most imperious tones. She flourished gold from her purse in such a sly way that only I and the landlord noticed. Perhaps they could find somewhere to put up her man? Indeed, signora. So, once more, I was lodged in a stable-loft.

Next morning, from a bed of stinking straw, bitten by every bug known to Christendom or Hell, rehearsing my grievances to present to Eleonora on the road, I pushed her roughly into her saddle. We rode out of the town, down and down and down a terrible road from whose hillsides all trees had been ripped, whose fields seemed to be sunk into water. We headed east for more than a day, with the sun beating down, the country growing more barren around us. Then she reined in her horse – by this time I think I could have killed her. Now we turn west, she said excitedly. Oh, we shall fool them all.

To Pomodoro, I said.

To Caesaretto first, she cried, wheeling her horse, rising up and down in the saddle, and looking to the west in a sort of mad trance.

But Pomodoro?

Yes, yes, she said impatiently. But first, Caesaretto.

Then we were on our way. Bound, eventually, for the city. The ships. All I had promised myself. The golden forest. The diamond lake. But what was this place we must go to first?

Oh Leporello, trust me, she said. Trust me.

For two more days we rode, doglegging across country whenever she thought she spied riders in the distance. The horses and I were tired out – though Eleonora seemed possessed of more than human energy, so that the more we rode, the more intense her desire to press forward. At night when we stopped she fell into an instant and profound slumber, again delaying the consummation neither of us seemed to desire very greatly. On the third evening we reached the place she called Caesaretto.

Is this the city? I asked stupidly.

No, this is to be the palace ... only the palace! Look at it. You will never see its like again.

And I never shall. Seeming to cover the wide plain below us was the half-completed work of a great palace.

Dug deep into the earth were arches and vaulting columns that were to be the entrances and supports of cellars and crypts. Ground-works and half-built walls, and roofless rooms. One tall tower looked down on three stumps at the other edges of its quadrangle, as if it had eaten up all the materials that should have been theirs. And there, sweeping façades of windows, five, six storeys high, with the rooms behind declining, in various states of construction, like a ruin in reverse, winding itself backwards in time. And already apartments built on apartments, all finished it seemed, with winking glass under green tiled roofs, and here and there a soft candle burning to put off the night that was filling up the sandpits and hollow rooms. And all surrounded by carts, and strange engines, and swarmed over by men the size of ants. Beyond the palace, rising with the plain to the hills that ringed it, were laid out gardens, half-turfed, half brown with newly turned earth, crisscrossed with lozenges and deltas of paths, patched with shrubs and young, feathery trees.

But why have we come here? I asked. No one can live here yet. What have we to do with princes?

She looked at me coldly, then giggled. It was not what I had expected. Well, let's go then, I said abruptly, the sooner we have visited this place the sooner we can push on to Pomodoro.

She made no effort to remount her horse, but stood, chewing her red lower lip, gazing down at the plain. I suppose you do love me, Leporello? Her eyes rose, shining, to meet mine. Her fingers played with her horse's reins.

How could I answer her? Whatever the question meant, my answer was probably no. I still do not know what 'Love' means. It seems to be confined to the female sex in novels – except in other such unmanly creatures as poets and actors and such-like.

Ah. She sighed heavily. I know you do, poor boy. It is such a pity. I do not know how to say this to you. You have been such a help to me. A friend indeed. You have done much more than should ever have been asked of a servant.

What do you mean? I said. I don't understand what you are saying.

Ah – poor, faithful Leporello. I know ... I do know what you must suffer. And, if after what I have to tell you, you decide to leave my service, be sure I will do everything in my power to assist you to a new position.

The little bundle of novels she had brought back from the city had come in useful for composing such speeches. The gist of it all, as you will have long guessed, being far more intelligent than I, is that I had been gulled into her service; she had needed an accomplice, and now I had fulfilled the purpose. I had been of service – and what are servants for, after all?

Ah, Leporello, dear, good, faithful Leporello, she gushed on. If what I have done has upset you; if you had been led to expect . . . and have been denied, then I am truly sorry. My purpose in coming here – her hand waved at the uncompleted palace – was to meet a friend. A gentleman friend. A lady cannot travel about the countryside on her own. You were my protection, Leporello. A true knight. You have been chivalrous. I commend your behaviour. You have offered no insult to a lady. I can only . . .

What is to prevent me killing you here and now? The question rose to my lips, but I did not ask it. It was clear that whatever roles I had been assigned in the romance in her head did not include that of murderer.

I met the gentleman in Pomodoro, she babbled – where I was sent to complete my education. Though he is a nobleman, I could not possibly have prevailed on my parents to see him, or let them know that we had met clandestinely. But once I have joined him and we are betrothed, my parents will see the rightness of the match. They will not think of marrying me off to some poltroon. Then I can explain your part – and your total innocence in this affair, Leporello, she said sweetly.

How would it be, I thought, if I cut out your delicate tripes and hung you with them from this tree?

She was feeling in the folds of her skirt. It was all in the course of love, she said. You don't believe me? See, here is the letter I received at the beginning of this month.

Here. She held it out. You may read it. It contains nothing of an intimate nature.

So now I was her blushing little confidant, the maid who carries, and is allowed to read the messages between the lovers.

I did read:

My dear girl, I cannot say with what pleasure I received your
note. Forget you? How could I? How could you say such a
thing? By all means let us meet again. If, as you say, your family
will be at Pomodoro soon, you may find me most days at the
palace of Caesaretto just outside the city. I trust to your
discretion, and think it best you send me a letter to the address
overleaf before we meet.

I could not read the signature. But the letter hardly smacked of great passion.

I am glad to have been of some service, I said with as much hauteur as I could muster, handing the letter back. And now it seems my use is at an end, signorina. I hope you will excuse me if I take my leave.

Oh, but you cannot . . . You do not mean to go? There was a hint of panic in her voice now. How am I to enter that place alone? If I were to pay you . . .

I bowed stiffly in agreement.

Well then, she said, relieved, when we have reached the palace, or the city, if my . . . my friend is not here, and I am safely delivered to him, I will pay you ten gold pieces.

So, I said to myself, you are a thief too. You have raided your father's treasury. What is to prevent me from taking all of your gold here and now? It was not honour that made me honest, but the recognition that if I robbed the girl, I would be hunted down and most probably hung – while, if I delivered her to her 'friend', I would be rid of the little brat. I could fly on to the city and, parted from her, there was a good chance that my pursuit would be given up as a bad job.

You agree? she asked.

Yes, yes.

She was full of herself again then. We remounted and began to make our way down to the plain.

She rode on ahead, spurring her horse with such enthusiasm that he stumbled in the loose scree. I plodded along behind; a servant once more.

As we drew nearer, the palace, unfinished as it was, began to appear truly colossal. On each side of the road leading to it, rough tents and shacks made a miserable town where those who were making this magnificent structure were lodged. Even at dusk, their work went on. High on the walls, cranes like giant jackdaws, and huge drum winches, hoisted up and down pallets and buckets and sheets of marble; and men's outstretched arms plucked at them, swinging them dextrously through ragged gaps and smooth embrasures in the frontage, or dragged them along the platforms of scaffolding. As we came nearer still, the distant hum of noise sorted itself into the rumble of carts, striking of hammers, saws, the shouts of men from the scaffolding to those on the ground. Out of one of the last tents we passed, a black-faced man suddenly stuck his head. I had never seen such a one before. It could have been an imp or devil. I crossed myself and spurred my horse. The man opened his face into a brilliantly white toothed smile. More of these black men moved in the skeleton of the upper storey, toting with ease baskets of bricks; balancing long planks lightly on their massive shoulders. I learned later that they were galley slaves. The white men among them were criminals from the city jails, pressed to the work. But the craftsmen were all free men; carvers, carpenters, masons, painters, foremen, clerks.

We had ridden close and were slowed by a convoy of ox-carts loaded with stone and wood. The curved wings of the palace lay either side of us. Lanterns and torches were being lit. The carts turned aside, groaning heavily, were unloaded and rolled away lightly almost with joy. New piles of stone and wood were at once set upon to feed the great house. We rode onto the front courtyard. There was such a press and stir of men moving about us that in the excitement of watching them all thoughts of Eleonora's treachery vanished clear away ...

Now, my good man, what is your message?

A gentleman in a wide swagged coat, wearing a sword, a fine wig, and a cocked hat, had my horse by the bridle.

You have brought an answer from the city? he shouted.

Eh?

Are you a fool?

The truth is I could hardly understand a word he said. Eleonora raised her veil and spoke.

This is my servant, she said. We are not from the city. Kindly address me for the purpose of our visit.

It makes me blush now to remember how vulgar she sounded, before this palace, and this person evidently used to palaces and the strange, rare tongue spoken therein. But he was a true gentleman, sweeping his hat off and bowing in one fluid motion as if scything the ground with the brim.

Your pardon, signora. But – as you can see – there is no one at home. We are building the palace just as swiftly as we can, and it would help to the utmost the speed and utility of our movements if you could simply move your horses a little to one side. In short, madam, you are in our way.

He said this with the greatest politeness, while drawing my own horse to one side and signalling to a man to bring Eleonora's horse along also.

My business here, she said, trying to sound authoritative, with her voice faltering away, is with a gentleman . . .

Night falling fast there was something devilish about the façade, with torches burning about in empty window sockets; figures and their shadows moving about the scaffolding; the loads of marble and stone bobbing and rocking upwards.

. . . A gentleman, she repeated. I was told I would find him here. Don Giovanni di Tenario.

Ah – you should have said at once. I understand, signora. With a flick of his fingers the gentleman called up a boy. Show this lady to Don Giovanni. With another sweeping bow the man turned away.

The boy took the bridle of Eleonora's horse and led us under a high mock-arch made of wood. Men clambered about its rafters like monkeys in a tree, putting in the stones of the real arch. We came into a quadrangle. In the middle two men were handling into place a stone nymph, another connecting a pipe to the scallop shell in which she was to stand.

The boy asked us to dismount. Twitching a torch from a wall-bracket, he led us through a half-completed doorway and into a long dark corridor that stretched into the bowels of the building. Again I was astonished by the sheer size of it all. Walls, here and there punctuated by doorways and fireplaces but with no intervening ceilings, rose up as if to the stars which were now beginning to appear above.

We passed rooms full of rubble, rooms fully carpeted, rooms

with partly completed mosaics, rooms where figures stood under white sheets like vertical dead. As we penetrated deeper the torch glowed in the depths of rich wooden inlays, smeared greasily across marble, and danced high in the crystals of a chandelier that hung already in a great hall we crossed. We climbed a staircase, one side of which fell away like a gaping mouth, toothed with the ends of timber joists. We emerged on the next floor. The boy went deeper and deeper, turning suddenly a corner, so that the light flickered away and we were put into darkness and had to hurry forward, just in time to see the light fade again on the facing wall of yet another corner. We caught up with him crossing an open landing. There were no workers here; only a line of naked stone sentinels. The noise of building work had long died away. At last the boy came to a halt before two doors off their hinges, leaning either side of a high doorway.

The room we looked into was immeasurably tall, roofed only with brilliant stars. Some way down the room was a table lit with two candles. Behind the table stood two, no, three men – the last standing a little way off in the shadow. The room stretched away into darkness.

The boy halted us in the doorway. The two men lifted their faces.

Business for Don Giovanni, announced the boy, and we stepped forward.

Now you are going to ask me what was my first impression of the man? What am I to say. He was a man. He was, I would have said, somewhere in his early thirties – which was of course old to me. He wore no wig; his dark hair was drawn back from a broad brow. A powerful nose – the rudder of fortune. I have never met a great man without a good nose on him; the ladies reckon it shows pretty reliably what they can expect to find lower down. Fine, liquid eyes. But the mouth gross; the lips, though elegantly carved, almost as grotesquely full as those I had seen on the black men. A man of only average height, but seeming, as he came round the table and advanced towards us, to be taller, by the confidence, the straight-backedness of his gait. His sort of flowing strut – though with none of the martial swagger in it – was, rather, that of a man of energy and purpose. A man of none of that self-doubt which I have seen afflict other men – that uncertainty of breeding that wrecks their walks as they approach their superiors – none of the slight cringing which bends the back against its will. None of that.

The Don's body was well knit: square shoulders in his blue coat; strong calves in his white stockings. He came down the room in this easy motion as if he knew the world as his element; as the bird knows the air, or the fish water.

He halted close to Eleonora and bowed.

Signora. You are most welcome. Your visit is most welcome. How can I help you?

His voice was full, deep and musical.

You do not know me, sir, she said in anguish.

Your pardon, signora. Your face was obscured. Perhaps if you would draw your veil ... His smile did not falter, but if anything grew warmer as he inclined his head to one side.

I am Eleonora! She cried with dramatic impatience, clawing the veil back. I have come!

Eleonora. Ah, yes, he said conversationally. What brings you here, my dear?

The gentleman standing at the table threw down his pencil in disgust. It was plain that he had witnessed such interruptions to their work before. The man in the shadows watched without the amiably blank expression on his face changing.

Your letter, Eleonora squealed. You wrote me a letter.

Signorina, I murmured. Collect yourself. She was behaving very badly, I thought. It is a servant's duty to point this out from time to time. She ignored me.

You have forgotten me, she moaned.

Not so. Not so, my dear girl, the Don said softly as he drew closer to her. Perhaps if I might see the letter? He purred just like a leopard. I saw one once at Venice.

She took the paper from her pocket. He held it up to catch the light from the candles. He read it carefully, then folded it and stowed it in his coat pocket. Of course. Of course, he murmured. He took her hand and led her to the table. I followed faithfully, observing the near congress of his lips and her ear as he whispered away.

Mastro Vitellini, the architect of this great palace. Signorina . . . ? The Don cast charmingly for her name, introducing them.

. . . Cavilloso, said Eleonora. She was not angry now; her eyes shone, her lips were parted, showing her little white teeth. She looked like a bitch in heat.

Pleased . . . most pleased, Vitellini the architect muttered. Tapping his fingers on the papers strewn across the table, he bowed quickly and with some irritation to Eleonora. Now, my dear sir . . . , he said to the Don.

But Don Giovanni was intent on pleasing the lady, not some angry little builder. He said, Here on the table, see, Eleonora, a plan of the room we are in. And under that – he lifted the top sheet off – a plan of the whole palace. If you will permit me . . .

Don Giovanni, we *do* have work to finish. Vitellini tried to interrupt this charming tête-à-tête. What an excellent oil painting the scene would have made – Don Giovanni Exhibiting The Plans Of The Great Palace At Caesaretto To A Visiting Lady.

The architect looked on in vain as the Don pulled the plans this way and that, pointing out this room, this view, this wonderful hall. And here, where we stand, is to be the Experimental Chamber of His Excellency Don Carlo, the son of the Duke, he said. We share a passion for natural philosophy. Here we shall delve into the secrets of creation . . . The poor, stupid girl's eyes danced and glistened in the candlelight.

Don Giovanni, said the architect firmly. I must have the final dispositions of the cabinets for this room. His Excellency . . .

My dear Vitellini, it is too late. It is quite, quite dark now. It can wait till the morning. Listen, can you hear anything at all, signorina?

We all listened. There was absolute stillness.

All the workmen have finished for the night, said the Don. They are slaves and we are still working. No, Mastro Vitellini. Enough for today. He lifted his hands from the table and as if by magic the plans rolled themselves together in a loose scroll.

He transferred his hands to Eleonora's. The architect sighed and began to roll the plans up tighter against his chest. I saw the servant in the shadows; unmoved, unmoving.

Signorina, said the Don, you are far too young to pass for a widow. Why the disguise? I do not think you should be on your own now after dark, even with your man here. Where are you staying in the city? How did you come here? Your carriage . . . you have none? Well then you must surely share mine. Your family is in the city, I presume. Your servant may go ahead with your horses and say that you are under the protection of Don Giovanni di Tenario. Your father and mother must . . .

I am her father, sir.

The cry from behind was unmistakable. I turned. Our boy's torch had dwindled low, but there, in the doorway, a fresh torch illuminated the preposterous and travel-stained figure of my master, Signor Cavilloso. His excited squeak rose up to the stars.

And I her *mother*!

A more terrible sound. A more frightening figure pressing into the room. And backing them up, the huge looming frame of Enrico, a victorious leer on his face.

The hunting gun kept under his pallet in the stable-loft was trained on me. Signor Cavilloso had a sword in his right hand. This sword had hung in the hall of the farm ever since I could remember and had never, until now, been taken down.

Husband, do your duty! said Signora Cavilloso in awful tones.

Did he dare to hesitate?

On with it man, cried the virago.

Signor Cavilloso advanced one step.

Eleonora . . . , he began.

His wife snorted.

Eleonora. He started again. This time his voice was sterner. You have brought shame to our house, to your father, your mother. To go away with this . . . this *servant*. His finger wagged in the air accusingly, but he would not look at me. There is no excuse, can be no excuse for your conduct, he said.

The two parties faced each other; one by torchlight; the other by candle. Two more men had appeared in the doorway; tenants pressed into parent-daughter-lover pursuit.

I thought it time, for my own health, that I had a say.

But no, signore . . . , I began.

Be quiet, shrieked Signora Cavilloso. Brute! The idea!

Facing into Enrico's gun, I began to tremble, but went gamely on. Signorina Eleonora . . . (So quickly had she become my better again.)

You dare to use my daughter's name? The dear Amalia's breath spat into my face. We took you into our house, viper. My husband treated you as a son. Now you shall pay for your treachery.

Pay, Enrico echoed, smiling.

Signor Cavilloso flourished his elderly sword.

And here I was – with the quivering venomous woman glaring into my face, and Enrico's gun aimed at my guts. The Don spoke up.

Your pardon, signore. But may I ask who you are?

I am the girl's father, said Signor Cavilloso, plainly wishing he were not.

And I her mother, the hot mother struck in again. I advise you – whoever you are – to stand aside. This worm, this snake in the grass, this treacherous vermin . . .

Is this man your father, signorina? said the Don to Eleonora.

Yes. She began to cry.

This lady, your mother?

Alas, so, she sobbed.

Them I am afraid you must go with them, he said calmly.

Eleonora stared at him, stunned. But your letter. Your summons, she said breathlessly.

I answered your letter, my dear.

But when we *met*, she wailed. First. In Pomodoro. Last year. You swore. You did. That you would always love me. Would die for my love. We were to be married!

How many of you are in on this? the mother shouted, glaring wildly round. Come here my girl. At once. You are seduced by a servant. You fly straightways to another . . .

The architect, Vitellini, whom we had all forgotten, said

suddenly, Now come, my dear sirs – and madams – this is all very like a play. Could you not perform it elsewhere?

And who are *you*? Amalia demanded. The good lady was thoroughly confused.

All I ask is that you all go away from here, said the architect wearily.

Not without my daughter, the mother screeched.

With, without – but please go, he sighed.

The disputed daughter turned upon the Don. But you promised. Your letter . . . Love forever . . . The things you said. Did . . . She began to cry again.

Things are done, dear girl, said the Don patiently. Things are said at these times. His voice was low but carried down the room. You must go back, I'm afraid. You must see that.

What – what's that you're whispering, Eleonora? You knew this man before? In Pomodoro? At your convent? Come here at once, madam, her mother raged. At once.

And she reached out and grabbed her errant daughter by the wrist; Eleonora's free arm trailed back in supplication to the Don.

If you ask me, signora . . . , said Enrico, his gun still pointed unwaveringly at my stomach.

No one asked you, said Signor Cavilloso.

If you ask me, Enrico went on, it's this young sprat who's to blame for all this present bother. I've seen him looking at the young lady. He has talked about her at nights in the stable and said she was hot for him – begging your signora-ship's pardon – that he could have her any time.

Signore, I was tricked, I yelped at Signor Cavilloso.

I thought Enrico was going to shoot me where I stood.

Bring him, bring him, Enrico, the mother screamed, her face almost black with rage.

She pretended . . . She begged me, I begged.

You shall be whipped, you dirty little dog. Whipped until you bleed.

But as Enrico stepped towards me, the Don spoke.

Hold, hold, he said – quite equably. Are you this young man's parents too? If not, I fail to see what he has done wrong and on what grounds you can claim him. It seems to me, he went on blithely, that the girl tricked this unfortunate servant into accompanying her. What could he do but obey? He is a servant. But not a slave, after all. Are you?

For the first time, he addressed me.

No, sir, I answered, shaking my head.

Do you wish to go with these people? he asked.

No, sir! It was the most heartfelt thing I ever said.

Then die where you stand, shouted Enrico, and brought up the gun.

Everything happened so very fast then.

The Don's sword flickered like a bolt of lightning, cutting across Enrico's hand that supported the barrel. The gun discharged in a great shower of sparks, a thunderous report, and a cloud of acrid smoke. Then dropped with a clatter as Enrico clasped his whipped hand. Signor Cavilloso's sword came despairingly up, aiming at the Don. But the Don's sword, having deflected the gun, switched back at once, and without even deigning to parry the farmer's feeble thrust, instead flickered in the torchlight and buried itself elegantly in the good signore's throat. Signor Cavilloso – a man unused to fighting – looked surprised. His sword fell to the floor. He put his hand to his throat and said, My God. Dark blood came from between his fingers. He sank first onto his knees, then toppled forward. With one twitch his body contracted, then lay full length on the floor. The blood spread around his head and soaked into the uncovered boards.

For God's sake, said the architect impatiently, his view obscured by the Don.

Murder! screamed Signora Cavilloso.

Nonsense. The man is only nicked, said the Don, his sword now pointing at Enrico, who backed away, clasping his hand.

Signora Cavilloso, bent over her husband, beckoned the two tenants forward. They turned their master over. I was surprised to see such a red face grown so white. His neck was ringed with a crimson scarf not there before. They ripped open his shirt and one of them put his ear to the bush of his grey chest hair. After a moment he straightened and said, He's done for, signora. Cavilloso's eyes gazed unseeing up to the stars. The two men crossed themselves.

This one too, said the quiet, irritable voice of the architect behind us.

The bullet that I had thought harmlessly fired from Enrico's piece had found a home in the Don's poor servant. He, who had stood in the shadows, and had no part in our proceedings, was now the innocent victim of them. The man who had no word to say through all of this would never say another.

The Don marched away up the room, knelt and examined his servant. He came back down, grim-faced.

It seems that your idiot man has murdered mine, signora, he said to Amalia.

My husband, sir. My husband. She pointed at Cavilloso's body as if he was a poor beast slaughtered by accident, and spoke as if she was demanding recompense. A hard one, that.

No one asked you to come here, madam. A v-shaped vein stood out on the Don's forehead. Remove yourselves.

You have murdered . . . , she began.

Go, the Don bellowed. Take your miserable daughter, your bloody bodies. Go. Go! GO! His shouts boomed in the room. He looked more than half-mad, and for the first time Signora Cavilloso retreated a step back. I almost felt sorry for these poor people. Because that's what they appeared as now: Enrico wrapping his bloody hand in a rag; the two farmers taking up their landlord's carcass; the vengeful wife robbed of her vengeance; the sullied daughter weeping by her side.

Go! Go! the Don bellowed. Take your wounded and your dead and your daughters and go.

Don Giovanni, the architect protested, this is madness.

But the Don was possessed. Out, out, he shouted. If you are not all out of here in one minute I will kill you all. He began to strut up and down, between his dead servant and the back of the table, swishing his sword through the air, shouting again and again, Go! Go!

They bore the body of Signor Cavilloso through the doorway.

Eleonora, her hands covering, grinding into her face, stood sobbing in the middle of the room. Her mother pulled her to the doors – with all the time the poor girl wailing . . . Villain . . . heartless . . . re . . . venge . . . Revenge. And that was the last word that could be made out as she was dragged away, following her dead father. Revenge . . .

The old girl appeared in the doorway, an apparition of a witch in the guttering light of our boy's torch. You will hang for this, signore, she shouted.

Oh, I do not think so, said the Don. Now he was quite calm.

Then we heard them go away; the footsteps across the hollow-sounding boards, the shrieks and complaints; saw their torchlight swing crazily down the corridor, and suddenly be blotted out; and last of all, the last of Eleonora's shouts, growing fainter and fainter . . . Beasts . . . beast . . . Revenge . . . revenge . . . as the mother bore her daughter off to a nunnery, her husband to his grave.

When their tumult had died away, we too left the starlit room. The architect, Vitellini, went ahead with the torch. The Don went swaggering after, his hand on the hilt of his useful sword. I and the boy took up awkwardly the body of the dead servant. We processed through the silent palace.

The front courtyard that had been so busy was deserted, save for the piles of stone and brick and planks of timber. The scaffolding above was empty. The Don's coach waited in shadow a little way off, the coachman huddled in his cloak. There was no sign of the Cavilloso party. A candle burned in the half-completed wing. Singing and drunken shouts came from some distance off where torches flickered among the tents and shelters of the builders.

The architect exchanged a few muttered words with the Don, mounted his horse, and cantered away towards the camp.

On the Don's orders the boy and I loaded the body into the coach. The boy jumped down and stood clear and I was about to do the same when the Don said, No – you stay there. He clambered inside and settled himself on the seat beside me. To the city, he commanded the coachman, and off we set, away from the palace and onto the road that ran straight across the moonlit plain. On the seat opposite, the dead man was a dark hump covered with the cloak I had found there.

The first time I had ridden in a carriage. It did not seem proper to sit beside such a grand man. As we rolled along the events of the night began to appear in my mind, and to trouble me. The Don was silent. I saw his hands moving against the dark of his clothes. He was paring his nails with a small knife. We had been going along quite a time before I plucked up the courage to speak.

Please, sir – if you would, sir – let me down when we get within sight of this city . . . I shall be able to make my way . . .

Why on earth should you wish that? he asked in a kind, slightly amused voice.

I am afraid that the lady, the signora – you saw her, sir – her husband . . . They will surely pursue me.

Nonsense, he said. She has her daughter back. That was the purpose of their expedition. From what I know of these country women she will not mourn her husband very long.

The coach rocked, slowly crossing the wide plain. As we bumped over a stone, the cloak slipped from the servant's body. His grey face stared at us, the mouth open in surprise. The Don reached over and laid the cloak gently back.

Poor boy, he said. From the corner, pale in the darkness, his face regarded me, sizing me up. Well, he said at last, it seems I am at a loss for a servant. This poor fellow had only been with me for a few months. You were in the service of the preposterous gentleman I despatched? And took his daughter away from him? You must have been mad. And she spun you a line to get back to me? For the life of me, I cannot recall her . . . It's all rather like something in a novel, isn't it? Though I don't suppose you know what a novel is.

I had the impression he was laughing at me.

I can read – and write, sir, I answered smartly.

Really? A young man of accomplishments, he said. What are you going to do? A boy from the country will starve in our rich city. Now then, do you think you could be my servant? Do that poor fellow's job? I must have a good man, mind. How old are you?

I'm not sure, sir. I think seventeen. Or eighteen.

You look older. Give me your hands, he commanded. Well, they have not done so much work, have they? I suppose that shows you know how to get away with things. You can serve a gentleman at a pinch. With a little polishing. Your name?

I had two names, I told him. Giorgio from my father. And Leporello from my friends – and others.

Good, he said. Then I shall call you Leporello. And hope that we may be friends.

The plain was crossed. We entered a wood, passed through it, and emerged into bright moonlight to begin to crawl up a hill. The light was utterly extinguished as we plunged into a cleft. His voice came from the dark. Tell me about yourself.

Which I did. As I have told you. Or started to.

We went down and down. The wheels thundered in the ravine, thrumming and shouting until I thought I would have to cry out – when the noise died suddenly to a normal clattering and moonlight brushed over us again.

We descended more rapidly now, the trees falling back and villas beginning to show among them. Then we were in the city. High tenements engulfed us. There were lights in some windows and figures to be glimpsed in rooms – enough rooms I thought to hold the world. The road straightened and became smoother and we went along a broad avenue. Torches moved among the front pillars of great houses. Cloaked figures walked on the flagged piazzas which now lay regularly between the buildings. The smell of city and sea mingled. Out of the Don's window I saw shrouded masts of ships and fishing boats. A long mole thrust out into the bay; at its end stood a huge gloomy castle with one high tower whose dome gleamed fitfully red and dull gold as if reflecting fire.

I saw why. The coach changed direction and ran along the mole and out of my window I saw an awesome sight. In the distance, where the city dwindled down to the sea, a mountain rose up. From its pointed peak, lolled a cloud so huge that it seemed to fill half that quarter of the sky. Lit from underneath into a deep glowing crimson, shading to purple on its side, to lilac on the top where the moon stood above.

I turned to the Don.

There is a great fire somewhere over there, sir, I said.

He smiled. The coach was lit in dark velvety blood. The Devil's Mouth, my boy, he said, That's what these people call it. The Devil's Mouth.

We halted. We were at the entrance to the castle. A harsh challenging shout. A lantern was hoisted. A face peered into the carriage. Let us in, you dolt, said the Don easily.

The man lowered his lantern and shouted, Don Giovanni. We rolled forward under the stone arch. Behind us the massive doors ground and clanged shut like a trap.

PART II

Pomodoro

1

Little more than a year in his service and I was a half-polished young man, who could speak servant's French, the city's dialect, and the Don's tongue – the language the priest had taught me to read. We were still in the city nicknamed *Pomodoro* – after the gold dome on the castle tower. *Pomo d'oro*. Apple of gold. Or common tomato.

The Don had taken a pretty palazzo on the corner of one of the open squares that faced into the bay. Our front windows looked out at mole and castle. In the side window, distant, but somehow too near, stood the mountain, its cloud lessened to a long plume floating out over the sea. I did not like to look at it. By its occasional growls and rumbles, thunders and the glow that hung in its mouth some nights – I was sure the mountain meant us no good.

Our establishment was modest enough – at least viewed against the hordes of servants who infested the well-off houses in that city. Myself as a valet. An old woman who cooked and cleaned, winking lewdly at me, and making me frequent invitations to her body. Save her for your old age, said the Don when I complained. A boy in the kitchen. Ragoti, the coachman who had brought us from Caesaretto, in the mews below.

The smallness of his household was not due to lack of means. The Don's family had estates in the north to which he was heir. He was wealthy enough, it seemed. Every third Sunday in the month I would accompany him to the banking quarter; the Don would sign a piece of paper and receive a quantity of gold pieces and notes.

Not that I can say he was generous.

All servants cheat their masters, he told me, giving me money for the household. The better bargains I drove, the more I got to keep. I was expected to live off the land – as he did, in a manner of speaking. Sometimes, returning flushed from some particularly happy encounter he would toss me a coin. And there were times when money must be disbursed for some choice, extra service . . .

More of that. You may wait for that in its place.

Not all roses, I can tell you, even in the good days.

No, the Don's reason for needing only one good servant was that he did not wish to be observed in private. To be flattered, adored, noted in public places – well, that was no more than his due. But, in that most hugger-mugger of cites, he was a private man.

He rose early, and expected a fire laid in winter, the windows opened wide in summer. The big china bowl on the floor in the corner of his bedroom must be filled with cold water, his clothes for the day be put out on the chest. Rising naked from his bed he would make his toilet, washing himself all over – an act I had never seen done before. His body was compact, hard-muscled, with a great breadth of shoulder. His hair cut fairly short and curling. His member, that wondrous engine that had done such prodigious work, was no longer than most, but exceedingly stout, his knackers large even when the sack was tightened by the early morning cold.

Dressed, he breakfasted lightly. Later in the morning, he departed for the castle, to his work with the Duke. Why he should work when he had ready money I did not understand. Of those I had served before, the priest had God's work to do; Cavilloso had his farms to run; the fisherman fish to catch. The soldier finds a war; the poet someone to listen to him. But this class of rich men, who could be happily idle and yet worked, perplexed me. I thought that there must be a secret motive of self-advancement in anything a man undertook.

Well, he was gone to his work. I must tidy his rooms, but the rest of the morning, before his return, I could wander the city on my own account.

Ah, if I had thought this Pomodoro a huge, busy, awe-inspiring place when we arrived that very first night, what enchantment was revealed by day! Each day since the first I had taken delight in leaving my master's austere, white-walled rooms, descending the stairs, and emerging into the city.

There all life is turned out on the street, thronging and heaving like a great animal disporting itself. Houses of five, six storeys; palaces, churches, parks, piazzas, colonnades, alleyways; court-yards, mezzanines. On the innumerable streets hustling coaches, berlines, fiacres, pressing riders; calashes springing upon you, skirling away, their single horse straining forward, the gold-capped driver whipping it on, shouting, Make way, Make way! Soldiers, courtiers, courtesans, workmen, lawyers, priests – oh, a loaves and fishes of lawyers and priests – thieves, sailors, slaves, fishermen. Fiddlers, guitar players, blind men, beggars, cripples. Water sellers, ice sellers, flower sellers. Puppeteers, jugglers, acrobats, magicians, mountebanks. Orphanages for their off-spring. Cemeteries for their discarded bodies. Here gutters run with filth. There stone warriors on stone horses fling stone swords immortally into the blue sky. And all the time noise; a continuous humming made up of the rumbling of wheels, hus-tling footsteps, a myriad voices – as if you had a beehive placed over your head as you walked.

Talk and jabber and call and sing. The whores importune you raucously from their windows. Releasing sweetness in the air from the eggshells full of perfume they let fall on us gallants below. The good wives rend the air with their cat-like arguing from balcony to balcony, set so close together above the narrow street that they can reach across and tear at each other's hair or clothes.

Oh, and the air! The odour of the whores' sweet water; the smell of ordure; the stench belched forth from doorways, or up from the dark holes at the foot of cellar steps; the reek of the fishmarket, the sudden flood of warmth from hot meat. The odour, smell, stench, reek, flood of the people!

And in our rooms, when I regained them, the sweet salt balm off the sea . . .

Returned, I must sit and write my notes for my master before I forget, or muddle them. For this is part of my duty now, as instructed by the Don. When he is busy, I am to watch out for beautiful, pretty, or remarkable women; in the street, in the shops; walking, working, glimpsed through windows, on balconies, gossiping in doorways. To take the addresses of those at home; to follow those who are not and see where they go. The wives and daughters of noblemen; the consorts of officers; milliners' assistants, cooks, actresses, fisher-girls; matrons, nuns, courtesans. All but the old or irredeemably ugly. Because this was the Don's true work; the single-minded hunting down of the women of the city. Not a one must be missed; none can be excused.

For my part I must keep watch while he is at his work. Fine enough in fine weather to watch out for husbands, fathers, brothers and duennas, but when rain swept in from the sea and I had to huddle myself in a doorway, or idle like a beggar among the beggars sheltering in some rich man's portico – the work was no fun then, believe me. I could not even shelter in the Don's coach – for discretion's sake that would have been drawn a street or so off. Even here there were dangers. Many a poor woman must have been unjustly accused, by the gossip of neighbours, or a vengeful husband, because that famous vehicle had stood outside her door.

Tell me of one, you say?

I had been in his service a year, so a number between one and – what? You think that there is a limit to the number of women in any one city? Always there are those arriving and those departing from the fray. A thought to torture such a man as the Don, who must possess all, to know that there is no end to his quest, that he is chasing an infinity of generation . . .

I need my *aide-mémoire*.

In the chest.

What do you say – in a smaller town he could have possessed all? But what then? You cannot repeat a conquest. He had exhausted small towns. Nothing less than a city would do.

Yes, there. The Don's box. Open it. Under those shirts. At the bottom – I'll have to grub for it. A book. That's it. I have it here. This is what I kept for him. His tally book. The lists of love.

Now . . . here . . . This one . . .

Number one hundred and ninety-three . . . this numbering you must know was of my own devising, starting from One. Of the period before me, God knows how many there were.

One hundred and ninety-three – these spectacles are like staring through water.

Signora S- D-. That's her. Walks each afternoon on the Riva d. Schiavoni with a little lapdog. On a silken cord.

I had seen her the week before: an uncommonly handsome woman with high forehead, her hair a natural auburn dressed only in ribbons behind. Chin held up, clothes fashionable and rich; haughty, taking no notice of the world. But why is she unaccompanied? She is plainly married, but married women usually have a friend to gossip with, or a maid to carry their little packages. She walks just after noon, when the streets are thinner of people; the coffee-shops full, the households giving out odours of food and contentment, or simply food.

The hour of rest.

I wondered that I had not noticed her before. But with my manifold duties in other directions . . .

Today, she walks along the promenade but does not deign to look out across the bay. She quite charmingly waits and gently tugs and chides at her dog when he stops to piss, then goes on at a sauntering but not too slow pace. They walk, the dog and the lady, and she looks expressionlessly through the faces of interested men as they pass. She is not then a whore, or a bored wife out to be picked up. The dog is well trained. I lag a little way behind on the other side. Now she waits for a gap in a sudden flow of noontide coaches proceeding along the coast. She crosses and enters the square of St Joseph that spreads down from church steps to waterfront. All around us are tall houses where court gentlemen and lawyers have offices, with here and there the peeling façade of a warren of apartments for government clerks and scholars and copyists, musicians and poets and other such poor folk who need to live near the powerful . . .

She hesitates before one of these shabbier tenements. The dog sniffs at the door, gazes up at her – and she spurs him on with her toe, allowing him in consolation to nose along the gutter and idly pull her along, as if against her amused will. And, giving the dog this licence, she allows herself to glance slyly about.

Entranced it would seem to any innocent – if there was one such in that city – I gaze at the display of notices in an attorney's window, all the time the outermost corner of my eye keeping watch on her. Until she, satisfied that no one is observing her, bends swiftly, scoops up the startled long-legged little hound, and in the same single flowing movement steps back, pushes at the door she has just passed and is immediately vanished away, the door settling to, shadowy again, dumb to the sunlit street.

Now – what is this? Tick-tacking across the square, chest out, like a boat with the wind pushing its sail full to bursting, comes a tall, black-haired officer of the Guards with sky-blue tunic, orange shako, clacking boots, thwacking sword. A silly, curly-haired dandy, a fool, a fop, a ... He comes to the door, looks swiftly round. His eyes glide through me. I do not exist. Servant class – invisible man. He pushes at the door. It gives smoothly. Closes again. This door is eloquent in its dumbness; speaking of intrigue, the romance of strangers.

It was hot on that pavement. I looked up at the front of the house. Sure enough, after the time given for him to bound up the stairs two at a time, or even three in his eagerness – the sword lolloping behind – the time to embrace her, to swear undying love – after that short time I saw, as expected, the blue and gold embroidered cuffs emerge, the hands grasp the shutters and pull them roughly to ... I left them to their pleasures.

Evening was the time for my report. After the Don had bathed, taken some fruit, he sat down in his high-ceilinged parlour. The sun going down behind the city cast the shadow of our house almost to the quay's edge. This was his hour of amusement, when I told him what I had discovered during the day, and it sometimes amused the Don to tell me what had happened on the previous day with one of my recommended ladies, or to disclose what plans he had for another.

Alas, they did not always work out well.

He would say, That girl whose name you gave me, Leporello.

That maidservant or whatever. My God, how she stank! Like brimstone. And the place she took me to! Many more of her sort and I shall be hopping with fleas. Now, now, my dear fellow, you can do better than this.

I report on the lady with the lap-dog and her officer friend.

It must be love, said the Don. At that time of day. Tell me more, good fellow.

He was interested. That pleased me no end. It gave me satisfaction in my work. Few people realise the pleasure of serving someone well.

He instructed me to follow her and find out her background. It amused him to know odd facts about the ladies and to surprise them by the depths of his knowledge. For assuredly what woman could like anything more than to find herself the object of intense interest from such a man as the Don? . . . Ah, madam, I have followed you for days. Like a poor dog, starved of affection, but constant and loyal, I have trailed my devotion about the streets. I have stood below your window, watching your husband depart each evening, hoping for the merest glimpse of your divine shadow upon the blind . . . You have no blinds? It was the mist before my eyes . . . And so on, and so forth.

Such stuff, with all the time poor Leporello watching from the bushes, amazed at how a worm, a termite, a wiggling caterpillar could be taken in by such nonsense, let alone a grown woman. For hours I watched the Don's back, his arms moving in concert to the fine words. Ah, how I admired and envied him. That is why gentlemen are in their position and I in mine.

What else does it say here about one hundred and ninety-three? Husband a factor, a merchant. One of those who live on half per cents, on little shavings from other men's transactions. These gentlemen hang around ports in snuff-spotted waistcoats, noting every gleam on the water of an empty berth, watching with greed each incoming or outgoing vessel, their hearts alive with the poetry of lading bill, manifest, banker's draft. Such men always have bored wives. They are not one thing or the other, you see. Not tillers of earth, nor voyagers on water, sailors and suchlike, but creatures made of the paper they worship. So, she was married to one of those. I waited the next day until she came out of the tenement – a discreet interval after the pleased-looking officer had left. She set the dog on the pavement and led me to her home, which was near to the quays where the merchantmen put in. Her husband's office was below their living rooms. The merchant met her at the gate, bending forward and chucking the little dog under its twisting-away chin. But the dog went gaily enough before them, wagging its little backside into the house . . .

The Don listened intently, then laughed. Ah, they are always the best, that sort, he said. The temperamental ones are forever setting their husband's suspicions on edge, but the happy wives, the honest wives, ever willing, with a broad smile and a broad arse . . . We will have her, Leporello. Tick your book. See here – there I made the mark.

A small bribe to the landlord of the house in St Joseph's and I was able to view the room – intimating that my master was considering its suitability for a very private purpose. The landlord's eyes shone – more money can be made from those desiring a guilty privacy. The room was apt for its purpose, there being nothing in it but a bare mattress on a low bed and a tall empty wardrobe.

Excellent, said the Don. What more is needed?

I had observed the lady come to the house on Tuesday and Wednesday of each week. On her next Wednesday's turn about the town, the Don preceded her to the room – winking to the landlord, sighing, Ah, a surprise. Do not tell her I am here. And, pressing ten ducats in the man's hand – for he would spend where his prick was concerned – he was immediately accepted as the lady's new lover. Let into the room he waved the landlord imperiously away, then concealed himself in the wardrobe.

I was to allow the lady to go up, but wait in the street for the officer. In my hand a letter, forged by the Don, summoning the poor man to an urgent interview with the General commanding his barracks; on my face a solemn expression.

So, he came, swinging his arms, a smirk of expectation on his lips. I met him before he could reach the door.

Captain. Captain – your lordship, I panted as if had run a league. A thousand pardons. I have been searching all over town. His Excellency the General desired me to hand you this.

His look of surprise gave way to one of military contempt for a civilian. Up and down he examined me while his hand took the letter. What? What is this? he barked as he tore at the seal. His expression put on puzzlement, first, then petulance, then exasperation. He glanced up at the house, then back to the letter, then up again at his happy window. A slow reader.

Damn and damn, he said. He hesitated a moment. You could not say . . ., he began, and I knew that he wanted to go on with something like, You could not say you could not find me, could you? But his sense of honour, his code as an officer, his pride that was affronted at begging a favour from a servant forbade him. He sighed as a lover, and obeyed as a soldier. Stuffing the letter into his pocket, he said impatiently, Yes? Yes? What are you waiting for? There is no answer. Go on, off with you. You get no tip from me. With one last glare up to the balcony of delights, he stormed away across the square.

Yes, you see. I have written it here. L-, that is me, L- to lure away officer with letter. D.G. – Dei gratia, the Don – to take his place and await the lady. Then – this is in a different ink, written later – A successful conclusion. Has agreed to meet again . . .

I doubt if they did.

The pleasure, my master said, was in the siege and the first breach, not in the occupation. This one, he told me, had been easy to accomplish. The lady was already compromised, and, so, fatally weakened. When he had made his entrance from the wardrobe she was seated patiently on the bed. He had dropped to his knees . . . She must forgive him for his intrusion. She must not be alarmed. He was a gentleman. Her beauty, glimpsed but once, had driven him to distraction. He had taken the liberty of watching for her. Her lover was a good friend of his. He prayed that he might be given equal consideration . . . The lady was amused, he said.

But what, sir, I said, did you do with the dog?

This was a short, easy conquest. But the Don was also involved in longer-running campaigns. In these he could not of course hide from the women. They knew his true name. Where he lived. But these were easier, if not so amusing to organise. For the most part they were married women of a certain position, interested in love, but separated from that happy state by their husband's coldness or occupation elsewhere. Passionate women (as the Don said all women truly were), who, once roused, were hard to cool. And these women, cautious of their position in society, enjoyed their assignations, their blue hours, without ever allowing them to cause scandal or upset in their own homes.

And in the social round the Don was wonderfully discreet. Servants I met told me that he was popular with the husbands for his frank, manly ways, so that each chuckled at the Don's reported deeds, each poor deluded one confident that *he* at least was not the cuckold in question. The Don told me that he had attended gatherings at great houses where he had looked about him and seen that, at one time or another, he had possessed every woman there – and that all the husbands had greeted him warmly.

Then there were the women he did not have to pursue; those who sent him messages through their maidservants; lockets; locks of hair; whispers as he bent to kiss their hands. All served – and dispensed with almost immediately, as tending to attach themselves and imagine the Don in love with them – they had to be treated fairly harshly to dislodge them.

But the class of women he most desired were the virgins and the virtuous wives – few enough at any time, God knows. The innocent were his true quarry. How satisfying to lay siege to their tender defences; to mine under; to starve out while, as it were, holding feasts in front of the city by flaunting a stream of conquests, his terrible fame as a lover. To poison the wells of their true content. To burn the houses within their walls with incendiary words. To scale their walls, and take their devastated cities . . .

For, make no mistake, these, won after hard travail, were the source of all his troubles. The easy pleasures of the experienced are not for the innocent – they will have nothing less than Love – and if they cannot have that they will have its bedfellow, Hatred. And to win the bodies of such women he had first to win their hearts.

How much easier life would be, dear Leporello, he would sigh, if women had no hearts to bother them.

It surprised me when I first entered the Don's service that the house was not thronged with women. But he never entertained in his own bed. How much more comfortable that would have been. Why all this secrecy, intrigue, danger? Why was he not content, as any sensible man, to install a warm, loving woman in his bed – and then go roving? Or be like the English milord who kept a circle of beds round his own and visited each in turn on successive nights – by all accounts both he and the ladies being most satisfied. No, the Don's house was a refuge from his forays abroad. And what did he do in his refuge, when his cock was not pulling him like a stallion through the streets and boudoirs and brothels?

Take one warm May evening. The sun was sinking; in the side window, the tongue of smoke hung purple and lilac from the Devil's Mouth.

For the past few days the Don had grown lazy; rising late, eating a little too much, sending excuses to the castle why he could not attend the Duke, or the Duke's son. Worse, he showed little interest in the details I retailed of women I had observed. I took no offence – I had witnessed these passages before. He was genial, contemplative, gentle of manner. He asked after my welfare – not at all a common thing for him to do. Had I everything I needed? I must tell him if he was overworking me. He prayed I would not abuse my strength at his behest. The Don, praying? By experience I knew that this solicitude, this gentleness of manner, was a prelude to another outbreak of whoring, brawling, perhaps again killing . . .

All that afternoon he had sat reading by the window, not seeing any movement about him. Towards evening though he felt the need for company and sent me to bring Micali, the professor.

Tall, spare, patently poor by his shabby dress, Micali taught at the university and lodged in a slum above a common wine cellar. He hurried along ahead of me, his long white-yellow hair streaming behind like the flame of a candle.

He hurried because he was paid for his conversation by the hour.

They sat in the big corner room. As the sun sank the Don called for candles. I lit them with a taper from the kitchen fire. A jug of lemonade on the table between them.

Stay, Leporello, said the Don. You may learn something.

What did I learn? I sat in the corner. You learn patience as a servant. I can hear Micali's voice now . . .

. . . suredly as Vico says God is immanent in man and not a transcendental being. And his relation to God is that of the peasant who adores his King, is pressed by him, shakes him off. And empires grow and become corrupted and fall into barbarism. Man falls from the divine to the heroic to the human . . .

Then apparently, the whole thing starts again. And so round and round and round. Don't laugh. You think I didn't know the right words. Not all of them, but enough to know I didn't understand.

The Don said, And where are we now, Micali?

In the human, he said. The all too human, signore.

See, I know the words. I remember. Up here – yes, that's it. Write down in your little book, "He tapped the side of his head". That's it. No, I never read the books. I met some of my fellow servants who did. And where did it get them?

Yet by Vico's theory, said the Don, we should, after this, expect a return to the divine?

I do not think, my lord, we should find it very comfortable, said the professor.

And does not each man, in a way of speaking, said the Don, pass through all these stages; human, heroic, divine?

Each of us, said the professor, is caught like a fly in history's web.

History is what is past, said the Don, not something that surrounds us. You deny the existence of free will.

History, we must presume, presumed the professor, exists in

the future also – unless the world is coming to an end at the end of every present instant.

As Voltaire said, said the Don, we are free to act when we have the power to act . . .

I recognised that name, because the master was always at books by him. On they went, reeling the names of these dancing masters – Didro, Russo, Oom – they might as well have been dancing masters, for I had never heard of them, and neither have I heard their names since. Which just goes to show. Something.

But it shows what a memory I had, doesn't it?

The Don called me forward.

Leporello, he said, do you consider that you have free will?

I do what you ask, sir, I said.

That is not quite the question I asked, he said. I am not God. Say that I was removed from you – what would you do?

God forbid, my lord. I should get another position.

No, no, he said angrily. If you could order the course of your own life. Not as someone's servant. As a free spirit . . .

You mean as a bandit, sir?

No, not a bandit, he shouted.

A bandit is as sorely tied to his crime, said Micali, as a priest is to his virtue. They both try to struggle free.

I was steadfast. I believe, I said, that everything is written above. You can't change that, sirs . . .

I wasn't about to give in to their clever chat. *They* might put their immortal souls in danger. Not me. All that I have seen convinces me that all the talk in the world doesn't change one single thing; it doesn't stop the moon turning, nor the worms' march in the shroud, nor stop a fart that must come out. All, absolutely all, is written on the great scroll above.

It is all written on the great scroll above, sirs, I said. What God wants of us. And if we go against that . . .

Who, pray, unrolls this mighty scroll, Leporello? said the Don. Or is it turned by clockwork?

No, sir, I said. By God and all his angels.

He believes it, he said to Micali. He really does – in 'God and all his angels'.

What else should we believe, sir? I asked.

He looked at me, puzzled.

You presume too much on my patience, Leporello, he said. Go below. God knows there must be something for you to do. Clean my boots or something. Be a servant for once.

They began to talk about the equality of Man.

I went downstairs. A little later I thought I heard voices raised in anger. The wind was definitely changing with the Don. The good weather was at an end. We must look out for squalls.

How do I remember such discussions? I remember everything – I didn't say I *understood*, did I? These men, it appeared, committed the colossal and ridiculous error of refusing to believe in God. How could such clever men not think there was a God? That puzzled me. For all their fine talk and their books, they were lower than the merest Mussulman who at least has his Allah and Muhammad to guide his miserable life. It was puzzling also how God could permit such unbelief – perhaps it amused Him to see two men sitting in a room overlooking the sea, discussing His non-existence.

Night had fallen when Micali came down. Your master, he said as I helped him on with his shabby cloak, your master is a little strange this evening, Leporello. Do you not find him so? I shook my head, but the professor carried on regardless. I was reading a passage from my book, he said, when I glanced up and saw the Don was staring at me in a most odd way. As if I were made of glass or crystal and showed something through me which angered him terribly. Is he unwell?

As far as I know, never better, I assured him.

He should take a wife, said the professor.

He does, he does, I murmured to myself, letting him out by the side door. He scurried off into the night. Being a clever man he was too poor to afford a carriage.

Back inside, I heard my master bellowing for me: Leporello. Leporello. Where the devil are you?

He was in the bedroom. Some of his clothes had been flung

from the closet across the bed. He stood, buttoning his gold-coloured waistcoat, silhouetted against the window and the gleaming bay. My boots, he ordered. No wig. The broad-brimmed black hat. We are not going to court. My cloak.

I helped him on with all these, pursuing him with the cloak as he strode up and down, pulling the pleats of his cuffs to his satisfaction.

We are going out for a little amusement, he said. The good professor makes a rather dry appetiser to a feast – in fact, if he had gone droning on much longer, I would have flung him out of the window. You may accompany me, Leporello. Take one of my coats. You had better be covered in something halfway decent. Not the best. You know which.

He bustled down the stairs. I had to half-run to keep up with him.

Where are we going, my lord? I asked.

To the Abbess, he said. To see the nuns.

The Abbess's establishment was in that part of town where the houses of the well-to-do hid behind them warrens of slums – like a doorman's embroidered coat over a verminous shirt.

Tall merchants' houses. Lights burning within and shadows of people moving on the walls inside. The house we came to had all its shutters closed. Only the faintest wisp of sound from a fiddle playing somewhere upstairs betrayed that there was anyone inside.

The Don knocked at the door. We waited; the Don impatiently. At last the door was opened a crack. The Don pushed forward at once, and the doorkeeper, recognising him, stood aside. This was Orlando – well known in that area as The Wreck of Beauty. Thin, dressed in a long black coat; his white cravat like snow below his long face. It was said that he came from a noble family. And, to be fair, there was none of the servant about him; rather he was an impoverished gentleman inviting a guest into his home; tetchy at his fall from fortune perhaps, but not willing to show himself as an inferior.

We stood in a small, six-sided hall, with curtained doors in each side. One of them opened and out came the Abbess herself.

My, but she was a creation. Big, fat, shaped like a bell under a loose gown of cream silk. Her face was thickly powdered; her hair hennaed and piled high and hung at the sides and back with long curls of maroon and carrot-red, chestnut and carmine, like the tails of little animals.

Behind her, a room lit with many candles. Women standing, men sitting; four at a hand of cards; two more gravely discussing – what? Affairs of state? Love? One of them rested his hand on the backside of one of the women. She had her breasts bared, the nipples linked by a silver chain.

The Abbess carefully closed the door behind her. They did not like their visions to be seen, these folks – not without payment first.

My dear Don Giovanni, she fluted.

The Don kissed her hand. Come, kiss Madame the Abbess's hand, Leporello, he commanded. You are a gentleman tonight.

A cold hand with dirty nails. But if she seemed at first sight to be nothing but a foolish fat old woman, that was denied by the cold, hard stare her eyes gave me.

May I speak to you, my dear Don, she said. She drew him away from me, and whispered into his ear. Allow . . . the gentlemen . . . the Count of . . . Ambassador . . . Sir . . . is all I heard, and I have sharp ears. She was used to having just as much overheard as she wanted, that one.

The Don said, I do not intend going into the public room, so my man will not embarrass your guests. But I promised him amusement, and amusement he shall have. See he is treated well, madame.

And he was already on his way through another of these curtain-hidden doors in the six-sided hall. Inside this one a staircase rose straight up. The Abbess moved nimbly after him, stopping on the stairs only long enough to order Orlando to take care of me until she returned. Then they were gone.

Orlando led me through another of the doors. Behind, the passageway was a servants' run with whitewashed walls and no light except from the room ahead.

We came into the kitchen. At the end of the room, seated beside the stove there was the usual slatternly looking girl; idle, waiting for orders – for a whorehouse is like any other house; it needs its servants to work it, its mules to pull it from one day to the next.

How am I meant to amuse the Don's man? asked Orlando. It is a novel ordinance for me to have to entertain a *servant*. He looked with disdain at me. Sit down. He pointed to one of two chairs at the table in the middle of the stone floor. There is wine. But he made no attempt to push the flask towards me.

On the Don's word, I'd hoped for better from the evening than this.

The girl might as well have been invisible for all the notice Orlando took of her as he bent at the stove to light his pipe with a taper. He did not offer one to me. When he came back over, he knocked his knuckles on the table, saying testily, Wine, girl. Wine. Pour the wine for the Don's man.

And this was a cruelty far more than pure callousness of heart, or the wish to act the gentleman in a whorehouse kitchen, for I now saw that the girl could not rise or stand or walk. She was mounted on one of those trolleys that beggars and cripples use, revealed as she raised her skirts to push on the small wooden wheels. Revealed also were her legs, withered and twisted like thin brown sticks.

She rolled towards us.

Pretty, eh? said Orlando.

She poured his wine first.

Her face was quite pretty, as I remember – and that made things worse. Oh, yes – pity, pity, I felt – but almost at the same time a terrible thought came to me that *she* was the amusement the Don had arranged for me. To my everlasting shame – and, be sure, all these things are watched and recorded – I flinched from her as she steered round the table to bring the flask to my glass.

You like our little butterfly? said Orlando.

If the girl listened to the old man she didn't show it. I looked away. I heard her arrive in her corner. Across the table, Orlando leaned back, yawned, examined his fingernails, and said:

You need not worry. She's not for you. He gave a thin smile.

Relieved? You don't have to pretend in here, you know. This is a place where people can be themselves. Here dreams are fulfilled. There is no betrayal. No marriages to eat away desire. No growing old . . .

He was silent a moment, then he asked my name.

Leporello.

Then tell me, Leporello. He leaned forward. Tell me, he whispered, were you punished as a child? What form did your punishment take? The way he rolled that word – *punizione* – round his tongue . . .

My, my aunt beat me, I stammered. Like all children.

How? How? he insisted.

How what? I said. His face was very fierce.

How beaten? Were you tied? Gagged? Hooded? Never? Put away in dark cupboards? Walked upon? Shat upon? Chained like a dog? No? No?

No, sir! I was bewildered by his mad stare across the table. It seemed he was waiting for me to speak again, enjoying my embarrassment. At last I stammered, knowing at once that I had blundered: Wh . . . what then is your position in this house, sir?

Certainly not a servant, *sir*, he hissed. I am a gentleman born. A gentleman . . . a devotee . . . a follower . . . a slave – the willing slave of a lady. A noble tradition. Petrarch. Dante – you would not know these names. He looked bleakly at me.

Just then the Abbess came into the kitchen. Her voice shrilled, What are you doing here, little princes? Drinking up all my good wine? Is the Don's chocolate not done? Come on, slave – do you mean me to beat you?

The change in Orlando was dramatic. And ludicrous. He got to his feet, his head bent, body cringing, but his eyes bright.

I am most terribly sorry, my lady, he whispered. How can I repay the liberties I have taken?

I've no time for games, Orlando, she barked. Wine in 17 and a mess to clear in 3. I'll take that for the Don. Now come on, move.

And all this time he cringed and danced from foot to foot, saying, Oh yes, mistress. At once, mistress. Now. Now, mistress – whisking up tray and bottle and glasses, mop and bucket, all in

116

his two hands so that at last he looked like an overloaded clown in a play.

I began to laugh as the old man skittered through the door.

What do you find so funny, young man? the Abbess scolded. Your time will come.

As indeed it has.

And what are we to do with the Don's man, Lisa? She addressed the girl at the stove, who was making the chocolate. She got no answer, and went on, I promised the Don you wouldn't lack. And you shan't. Show him to Sophia's room, Lisa. The key is by the door. Make sure it's secured when you have admitted him.

Madam . . . , I began.

Young man, you are lucky. Don't protest. A lady. A real lady. Enjoy her. She laughed, picked up the Don's drink, and was gone.

Three shallow steps led out of the back of the kitchen and triangular blocks of wood had been placed on each to make a ramp for the girl's trolley. She ignored me when I offered to help and propelled herself up the ramp. At the top she took a candle from the wallbracket.

The corridor was lined with tall, closed cupboards and open shelves stacked with clean, folded linen. The smell was between a laundry and an apothecary's. At the end was a door. The key hung from a nail. Lisa took it down, unlocked the door and pushed it open, waving me to enter. Warily, I did. For a moment, in the light of Lisa's candle, I saw a girl, a woman, standing against the side wall. A mattress on a low cot. A cup, a dish, the remains of . . . and then the light slanted suddenly away. The door banged to. The key grated in the lock. And the rumble of Lisa's wheels dwindled quickly away down the corridor.

All I could hear now, in this room, in the pitch dark, was the rapid breathing of the young woman against the wall.

Signorina? I said hesitantly.

Signorina?

I did not know how else to address her. Surely matters in these places were not always arranged thus?

Don't be afraid, I said. I have been sent . . .

117

Sent? By whom? Her voice sounded very young and bravely assured. You have come to liberate me? You have come from Davidde? Ah, he has not forgotten me. You have a message? He has a plan?

Signorina, I asked, is there no light?

None, she said. The shutters are tight barred and cloaked. I have been locked in here for two days.

But why?

Her voice dropped. A punishment. Ah, sir – you *are* a friend of Davidde's?

I was totally flummoxed. Instead of being able to make out something, as most rooms afford some crack, some chink of light, my eyes continued to swim with specks and washes of purple and deep blue.

Was this some bizarre test, devised by my master – suddenly, with a flare, the scene would be illuminated? I had to be honest therefore.

I regret to say, signorina, that I do not know the gentleman to whom you refer. I heard only her indrawn breath, her long sigh of despair. Then silence. I thought with envy of the Don, rolling among cushions like a Turk, shone on by crystal lustres and lily-white candles, reflected a hundred times in golden mirrors, a hundred whores lowering themselves onto his hundred upraised weapons.

Then . . . , said the young woman.

I come as a guest of the Abbess, I said boldly, feeling that I must at least act the gentleman she thought I was.

Her skirts swished as she stepped back.

The next words came in a much lowered voice. I hope, sir, that you do not think of taking advantage of my unfortunate state. If you but knew . . .

Signorina – I do not *know* your state. As confidently as I could I took a step towards where I thought she stood. It may be that I have been misdirected to this room. But I was led to believe that . . .

That a lady awaited you here?

I said nothing.

118

No, there is no mistake, she said bitterly. And if you must have your way, there is little I can do to prevent you.

Of course, signorina. Of course. I could not after all forget that I was a servant and could not go barging ahead as a gentleman would.

There was a creaking sound. She had sat down on the bed. I advanced. My shin struck the edge of a stool and I swore. A thousand pardons . . . , I began. Here, she said; a cool hand guided me to sit beside her in the darkness. I kept hold of the hand, lightly. But she pulled it away. Only after a silence that seemed to last a long time did I dare to ask, a little forlornly, what she was doing in such a place.

Her name, she said, was Sophia P-. (Don't I know the rest of her name? It is like this in all the books. Be satisfied.)

She had found herself within this city – through circumstances she would explain – with no friends or fortune. She had not eaten properly for days and had had to sleep for some nights in any alcove or doorway, in the street. How did I get in this state? she said. I shall come to that. For all her trying to conceal herself from view, the keen eyes of that city had spied her out. One dawn she had been woken, sleeping against a tomb, by the gentle touch of a young woman. At first she had thought the woman was the daughter of some great house attempting to minister charity and had resisted her. But the young lady told her that she had suffered in a like manner and wished only to take her to a close, safe house where she would find food and comfort.

The house she was brought to was this one. It seemed a very heaven after the street. The woman known as the Abbess had made a great fuss of her, allowing her the luxury of a bath, drying and powdering Sophia herself with the most delicate attention, and allowing her to choose from a range of clothes the other girls laid before her. I asked, she said, if they were a religious order? You could say that, the Abbess had replied. One would have thought it almost, said Sophia, a kind convent – if there is such a thing.

The kindness had continued for a week, while she was confined to the Abbess's rooms at the top of the house – the one rule impressed upon her being that she was not to venture downstairs, and certainly not to leave the house.

All of this came to an end when one afternoon she was visited by the Abbess. Two of the friendliest, most handsome young women dressed her with especial care and took her down to a public room, there, it was said, to converse and mingle with gentlemen of the highest standing in the noble life of the city.

Surely you knew by then what sort of house this was? I said.

Yes. *No*, she answered. And there was in her voice an odd mixture of knowledge and innocence and defiance, for which, when I knew her later ... But I go on. Let Sophia go on.

For you see, she said, many more girls are ruined for love rather than vice. And it was love that had brought me low, not profligacy. How can one understand men? They worship us as virgin and mother, take us as wife and lover, and at the same time push us away, saying we are unclean, unfaithful; whores; ignorant children. Yet all the time there seems a madness in them, that there is nothing – no scruple, no moral, no doubt, that they will not ignore nor blithely overturn, nothing to which they will not stoop to gain possession of our bodies. Of one part of our body. The rest of it is forgotten. God might just as well have made us holes in the ground. Why encumber us with all this, this *other*; this heart, body, mind, when it seems only designed to delay, to interrupt men on the way to their true desire?

What was I to reply to all this? I sat like a priest, listening to her fervent voice. She had touched something in me. I cried out in virtuous protest, No, no – not all of my sex are like that. Did I? Men do not speak like books. I would like to think I spoke like one then. Whatever I said, or did not, she went on. I am here, she said quietly, because of what men call love – and for what men call love. Let me tell you. She seemed to gather herself in the dark. My father and mother wished me to marry a man of whom I had never heard. When I first saw him, and ever after, I felt nothing but revulsion. No doubt in other circumstances I could have regarded him as just another of my father's friends – if it was not that I was being asked to unite myself with him in the most intimate and holy of ways. When I said so to my mother she threw up her hands and told me not to talk such filth. Where had I learned such expressions? I would end in the madhouse.

Well, I haven't. Unless the whorehouse is a madhouse.

What was I to say? But, signorina, I said, how could love have brought you to this place . . . ?

There was a young man, she sighed. One day, looking down from my window, I saw him in the street below. This was at S-, on the coast, towards Rome. I was immediately taken with him. He was small, with the most elegant upright bearing. A dark, slender face, large eyes, a negligible mouth – how much we notice! It took only a sly mention to my maid to produce a report, dropped equally slyly, into my ears next morning, as she dressed my hair.

His name was Davidde. He was visiting his parents after his first year at the university. His family were Jews – traders. Why could I not have married this boy? Not because of his race. It was not unknown for us to intermarry; their good families with our good families. If I could have found a Rothschild now . . . But, no, as I say, my father had already picked out a husband for me.

This friend of his.

When my suitor came calling he sat heavily down, sweating with the effort of having climbed the one flight of stairs. A little hard of hearing, he would have to bend to catch what was said. So I would open my mouth maliciously and then gently close it again as if I had said something – my mother glaring at me from the corner – this big oaf of a lover leaning slowly backwards again, a puzzled look on his face, uncertain whether to smile or frown. I thought it all a joke. As soon as he left the house, I forgot him, and sat again in my window like a princess in her tower, hoping for a sight of my handsome little man.

Now I realise how foolish I was. How for all my arrogance and ridicule of my suitor, my parents were driving me towards their bargain – so must a proud beast feel when, petted and pampered, it is lured to the slaughter. But, while their negotiations went forward, I had through my maid arranged to meet Davidde. Oh, but how charming, how sweet, how clever he was. One night, my maid smuggled him into the house, and to him I gladly gave away

121

that virtue on which my father and his friend were trying to fix a price. That strangest of negotiable estate – which loses all its value as soon as used.

The result of my sacrifice was to be the very opposite of that intended, however. From his sweet awkwardness it was plain, and he admitted it, that he was an innocent too until that time. But instead of our union binding the gentle boy to me, why, it seemed as if I had only performed some sort of initiatory rite for him – here Sophia's voice grew indignant. He made excuses not to see me. My maid returned with my messages unopened. She had great delight in telling me that Davidde had been seen paying court to another young woman, visiting her house openly, with the consent of the parents. A marriage was expected. She had been told by a servant that Davidde had a mistress too. An older woman. No, no – I refused to listen – he *must* love me. I shut myself away and refused utterly to see my father's friend. It was thought that I had gone mad. Perhaps I had. I was possessed; the image of Davidde perpetually in my eye. When I heard he had left town to return to this city, I followed after him – leaving my reputation, and my virtue, behind. I waylaid him at his lodgings. He rejected me out of hand, in the coldest, most heartless way, making plain to me that I had never been more than . . . her voice shook . . . more than you see before you now.

I couldn't see a thing.

But I'll not be a whore for any man, she said fiercely.

She could not then have been more than seventeen.

Remarkable, said the Don as we walked in the dawn light, but did the girl do nothing but talk?

A dung cart swayed away from the front of the Opera House at the end of the piazza, heading for the country.

Could I tell the Don how I had sat respectfully at her side while, upstairs, he screwed a round half dozen whores? While he sweated and thrashed in their salty caves, her voice in the dark told me how she had been confined to that cell for refusing the first gentleman presented to her. I saw then that the giving of

Sophia to a servant was a further humiliation for the girl – and I felt angrier at *that*, that I had been slighted, than at all of her pathetic tale. How could I tell him that, when the Abbess at last unlocked the door and let the light in, Sophia had fallen asleep, chastely, and to my discomfort, in my arms, and I was relieved to jump up and put her aside, the very picture of the interrupted lover.

Ah, sense at last, said the Abbess. And, to my shame, I swaggered out, without looking back at Sophia, to wait for the Don in the street.

I did not reply to his question.

Well? he insisted, swinging along.

I tell you, sir. She is a prisoner.

My God, he swore. He halted and laughed. I do believe you've fallen for the little tart. He strode on before I could open my mouth. For I did intend to. Whoever he was. Don or no Don.

Really, he said, if the girl chooses not to think of herself as a whore, that is her prerogative. But this flummery she has given you about *seduction* and *lost love* – his voice minced along in imitation of a girl's. Well, again, she may choose to believe it. I would advise you not to. I have a long experience in these matters and have found that it is nearly always the case that the girl takes the lead in these first affairs. How would an innocent youth know what to do? It's not so easy, you know, when both know nothing – the woman has to help out. No, Leporello – this story is told a thousand times a day over the world – in the brothel it is a constant refrain. But – he considered – if she is as sweet as you say, perhaps I will take a look . . .

And there, trotting along at his heels, any mad dream I might have had of rescuing fair Sophia from her bondage faded almost clean away. If I did the impossible thing, she would only be his after all.

The sun had risen behind the city; our shadows pointed to home; sliding in the cobbles, darkening flagstones, aslant on kerb and wall.

I could not let it alone though.

But, sir – she will be forced . . .

Nonsense. He cut me off. In a month, he said, she will be a fully-fledged whore and not know you from Adam. If she is sensible, she will have a pleasant life. When she starts to get too old for the house the Abbess will look out for some fat widower who will do what you have done – fall in love with her. But whereas for you it would be a disaster, this old man will be happy. What is more important, she will be made respectable. Not that she won't be happy too, in the way women are when they get older – counting his money and wondering how she could ever have been so foolish as to believe in love.

Still I made a last feeble attempt to save her.

But, master, I said. These houses. Disease . . . She said that one girl at least was poxed . . . Surely, sir . . .

Will you shut up about this wretched girl? He stopped and turned on me. His voice, which had been light and bantering, was now cold and hard. He stood like a stone statue against the sun.

Do not presume against my good nature, boy, he said. Your life may be inscribed by your good God on his scroll, but that scroll may also say that I shall crush you or run you through as you stand. Well, well – his voice relented a little . . . *my* free will says that you shall be spared this time. But no more talk of Poxes or Tartars or Penalties of Venus. You think I don't know these things? That my nose is going to drop off? Eh? Eh? He butted his head forward at me. Go on, he said. Take it. Go on. Take my nose, between your finger and thumb.

No, sir. No, no . . .

Come, don't be bashful. I insist.

I took the great rock, the promontory, the eagle's beak between my fingers fearfully. How solid, how inflexible, obdurate and adamant was his rudder of Fate.

Dow you cab say you leab be hobe by the dose, he mimicked. He pulled free, laughing. Come, come, Leporello. Cheer yourself. Be a man. There are as many women as there are fish in the sea . . .

And see . . . he whispered.

We had come to the corner leading to the promenade. On the next corner was our palazzo. Outside it, against the kerb, a small black carriage had pulled up, its back to us.

Master? I said.

A woman. His eyes were alight.

How do you know?

A beauty, my senses tell me. He might almost have been talking to himself.

Your eyes see through wood? I said.

For a woman, he murmured.

Just then the carriage door opened. He pulled me back into a doorway, then encouraged me to peep out. A lady got down from the step, advanced firmly across the pavement and knocked on our front door.

She is fair? whispered the Don.

I nodded.

Go on ahead, Leporello, he instructed me. Admit her to the side room. I shall follow and present myself in a little while. Go now. Go.

What shall I say to her . . . but he pushed me out of the doorway. Go!

Isabella, yes – that was her name. Isabella could be reckoned to have been the start, or at least the first of all our disasters. She and the other one – I'll come to her by and by.

Isabella.

What's that you say? What are you asking? Is she the one known as Elvira in the opera? What opera? What are you talking about? I know no operas. Another nonsense, the stage. The Don told me that people had been writing plays and stories and poems about his ancestors for centuries. That I was called Sganarelle by some Frenchman two hundred years ago. That the women had other fancy names. That he himself, in these plays and other efforts, was variously Don Juan or Giovanni or John. That the family was doomed to produce a Giovanni or Juan or John at the rate of at least one a century. That – he hoped – he was the last of a deplorable line and that in future they would have to find someone else to incompetently impersonate. And you say my *real* name is given to the servant in this opera? Now there's an extraordinary thing. Who did this? Who wrote this taradiddle?

What? What name?

Moser? Mosar? Never heard of him. Though, now, shaking my head, it does ring a little bell somewhere. It will come back when it wants. If it wants. So he put me on the stage did he? As if I were a made-up painted actor, all powder and noise; a few windy shouts thrown out at people talking among themselves . . . I have only ever seen it from the side of the stage, while the Don beavered away at some actress or other. Some of the servants had to stand in the back of the box while the family sat watching. A terribly wearisome task. Standing up for hours listening to that doo-dah.

Isabella?

Ah yes.

I hurried down the pavement. The lady stood at the door and rapped again.

My lady . . . , I panted, as if I had been running far and fast. Allow . . .

She was, I should say, twenty-three or -four years of age. Her eyes were large and black, her nose easily long enough to look down, her mouth two tiny cherries pressed together. Are you a servant of this house? she asked, looking from the door to me, and back to the door.

I had that honour, I informed her. I bowed. Out of the corner of my eye I saw the Don's coat tail flick out of sight round the corner.

The name of your master? she enquired in a harsh voice.

Don Giovanni.

Ah, she breathed. Her little white teeth bit into the bottom cherry.

Signora . . . ? I put on concern.

She recovered herself. Admit me, she commanded. Announce my presence to your master.

Your name . . . ?

He will know me when he sees me.

That seemed final enough.

I fumbled the large key out of my breeches pocket. My master sleeps at this hour, I said, softly easing the door open. If you would enter.

126

She flounced in. I went to take her shawl, but she clutched on to the fringe. She shuddered, though not with cold. I ushered her into the small, right-side drawing-room where the boy should have made a fire. He had, but it was low in the grate. I poked it into a sort of life and fetched the strange lady a stool. I chattered loudly, offering to get her coffee, whatever she desired. Please call your master forthwith, was all she said.

Certainly. At once – I made as long a circuit as I could of the little square room.

She muttered something I could not catch.

I beg your pardon?

Call your master, she said. Her voice was as cold as a dead man's heart.

I went to the door. I had but laid my hand on the door knob when the door was jerked open from the other side.

The Don stood, as if just woken. He was dressed in a long blue dressing-gown that showed his strong brown ankles, the Turkish slippers on his feet.

Leporello, why did you not tell me we had company? And such delightful company. He turned to the lady, bowed low, and, when he straightened up, said, Great God – Isabella!

It *is* you. She hissed like a kettle. This is your nest of deceit.

He took a step back, an odd smirk on his face.

Monster! Villain! Her little bosom heaved.

Lady – calm yourself, said the Don. Leporello . . .

I never discovered what he wanted me to do, for on she charged:

Calm! How may I be calm? Her voice cracked in the air like a whip. You fawned your way into my home, my heart, with your endearments, your oaths of undying love, your sighs, your . . . Does this servant have to be here?

I tried to look like a piece of dumb furniture. I must have succeeded, for on she went again:

Here is the ring you gave me. She held up her right hand. That I showed to all. My father was so proud, my mother in love with the sun and stars she thought shone from you . . . On the eve of our marriage my maid bore to me news that you had left the city.

127

I did not believe her – could not – nor those who came after. The next morning, I was an animal in a cage. The town's eyes pried between the lattices of the garden, tried to pierce the shutters – hoping for a glimpse of the abandoned bride. And all that long day, Don Giovanni, I was like a bowl that is slowly being emptied by the sun. For as water dries away, so hope dries too, until there is nothing left but sickness and shame. And their mirth . . .

The way it came out was just like a printed book. I was moved, I must say. Not having the Don's knowledge of the duplicity of the world, I did not know that people can rehearse and work up their despairs and frustrations so that their plaints achieve a life of their own, and become like, eh? . . . well like a brass water bowl, scoured and brightened, with the sun working round in it all day like a hot, burning button . . .

Believe me, Isabella, said the Don, stepping forward, his arms wide in supplication, There were reasons – secret reasons – why I could not communicate with you. Is that not true, Leporello?

Is what not true? I thought.

Sir? I do not recall . . . perhaps I was not in your service when this lady . . .

He stared at me. Why? Why were you not with me? his eyes demanded angrily. Why, his look demanded, can you not be in the place and time where I want you? He was like a spoiled child angry at a plaything for being in the wrong place, though he must have put it there himself.

Reasons? *Reasons*? Hah, Isabella hahed, drawing herself up on her already drawn-up self, like the hunchback handing his hunch up to an angel so that he can climb unimpeded into Heaven, where the hunch is straightway slapped back on – for whoever said that God was to straighten us, or make us beautiful? You are what you are.

I swore then, sir, she cried, that I would track you down. And you swore . . . and here she began to cry.

Now, madam. You are upset, the Don said reasonably. There is no need to become melodramatic. These things happen between men and women.

These things? She glared at him. Betrayal. Seduction. Abandonment. You, sir, swore, everlasting devotion. In return you were permitted . . . in return . . . She sobbed into her handkerchief.

The Don looked on with distaste. And yet he hesitated, then beckoned me to his side. For heaven's sake, Leporello, he muttered. You must attend to this. There is nothing to be gained from my staying. It will only serve to set the lady off the more. See. We both watched her, mopping at her eyes and nose. This has happened before, he said. It always ends the same.

But sir, I protested.

Get rid of her, he commanded.

But what am I to do, sir? To say?

He looked at me with a kind of confused contempt. What? he snapped. Tell her the truth. What kind of man I am. Read to her from your book. Tell her I am a mortal.

My hand reached by instinct to the pocket where I kept the book. The one got out of the chest. Remember? Good. Pay attention.

Whatever you see fit, he said. He released my arm, and hurried out, shutting the door behind him.

Her eyes stared at me over the bunched, sodden handkerchief. Where has Don Giovanni gone? she gasped.

The Don is not well. I coughed into my hand as if to lend truth to the meagre lie.

I heard you talking. What is this book? What truth does it give? In her enquiry there was a pathetic undertone, as if she hoped this book would give her a reason for the Don's perfidy; one that would excuse his past conduct.

Book? Everyone knows that books don't tell the truth, madam, I said. Why else should people make them up?

I saw you touch your pocket, she said. Her eyes were bright. The tears had miraculously dried.

It is nothing . . .

What is it? What is it? she said eagerly, and stepped towards me.

Well, he had told me to tell her the truth – and, truth to tell, I rather liked to have the lady in my power. The Don had sown a doubt in my mind that Sophia was wholly deserving of my sympathy. This one would not escape so lightly.

It is a list, I said airily, drawing the book out.

A list of what? she asked.

I shrugged my shoulders.

A list of the ladies the Don has, ah, befriended, I said. At least, since I have been his servant.

(For, before that time another book altogether would be required – and that one is not written. Which, come to think of it, beats all the libraries and books in the world into a cocked hat – a thousand times better than those actually put down are the living books that a man breathes, his blood flows; that he dreams and eats and fucks . . .)

Give it to me, she demanded.

Take my word, madam . . .

What do you think I am, she said haughtily, that I should take the word of a *servant*?

That touched me to the quick. For all my rough handling by the Don, it would never have occurred to him to insult me thus.

I opened the book. Listen, I said. Perhaps you will understand. I struck a pose – the poet, actor, orator – and began to read:

One hundred and twenty-one. The yellow haired. A butcher's wife . . .

What?

Another? My fingers tickled the pages for more fine fish. Eighty-eight. Two sisters. Twins. Lately from the convent. About to be shipped to Sicily as virgins. Hasten. Hasten.

You are mad, she cried.

One hundred and seventy-two . . .

She ran to the door.

Only daughter, I read out. Virtual prisoner. Kept up to raise the price for her virtue. Looks wistfully down into street . . .

I shall go to the Duke. To the King. Your master is a monster.

. . . from high window at rear . . .

I pursued her into the hallway.

She clapped her hands to her ears. I will not hear. I will not, she shouted.

Another – household of elderly aunt and father only. Father

gambles. Way through sentimental Aunt ... Virgin of sixteen summers ...

Isabella scrabbled at the street door handle.

There are many, many others, I said blithely. If you wish to stay.

She had pulled the door open, and fled through. A moment later I heard the carriage clatter away.

Bravo. Bravo. The Don sat on the stairs in his dressing-gown and gravely applauded me. He appeared fresh, his face flushed, his eyes sparkling. You are learning, he said, and threw me a whole gold piece.

2

But the coming of Isabella into our lives did seem to bring about a subtle and uneasy change. Sometimes as I watched the outside of a lady's house for the Don, I felt as if I too were being watched, as if alleys and shadowy porticoes and street corners had suddenly grown eyes to watch our conduct. Then too, the summer heat became oppressive. In June the winds died entirely; the smoke furled on the mountain-top like a monstrous rose. I was glad when the time came at the end of the month for us to leave for Caesaretto, the Duke's summer palace – its building now near completed.

What of the Duke?

He was a big man, with the body of a bull reared on its hind legs. His head was massive, with all of the features – cheeks, eyes, lips – puffed redly out. Eyebrows were set in surprise; his nose being a plum, or deflated prick. He was no great dresser; happiest in a drab green or brown country coat. On state occasions, when he had to appear in his yellow and blue silks, he looked like a beast in a circus.

Yes – a bear, he lumbered through the pretty rooms of Caesaretto. More at home in the cavernous, gloomy chambers of the Castel d'Oro, where he could roar and pace, and have the walls echo him.

For he had a voice like thunder and bellowed as coarsely as any beggar or peasant. He spoke the court language too – though whether a Tuscan could have understood him I don't know. Cunning – but without education. His elder brother having turned out to be an imbecile, their father, the old Duke, had ordered that no heavy weight of learning should encumber the new heir's mind. So the present Duke had grown straight and vigorous, as men who lack acquaintance with books do. He would have been at this time in about his forty-fifth year. Married at sixteen, he had had since a succession of plain, plump mistresses taken from the lower parts of the city. His mistresses must have borne him many a lusty, honest bastard.

His wife bore him one son, neither lusty nor honest, but definitely a bastard.

Carlo. I'll come to him in a moment.

Anyway, there we were on the road to Caesaretto. We had left the shade of walnut and cedar behind to enter on the open plain under a burning sun. The Don ordered Ragoti to whip up the horses as two coaches had already passed us, and the Don could not allow that. Soon we were weaving in and out of a clutch of other coaches – to shouts of abuse from their drivers.

The nobility were gathering towards Caesaretto for the summer. The finest and best. The noblest . . .

. . . the clods of your country, said the Don, throwing a piece of orange peel out of the window.

Is it not strange – he addressed the view, for though he allowed me to ride inside when we were alone, he rarely spoke directly to me, but as if talking to someone absent – Is it not strange that such a beautiful, ornate structure as this palace (its huge magnificence had at that moment swung from the distance into our sight) should be constructed by such a wormy, soft man as Vitellini. It will last and delight for centuries, while generations of these guests will age, their cheeks and breasts and balls droop and ache. They will rot in the grave while their children grow and decay among marble. The works of man, thank God, outlive him.

Truly, I ventured, these things are strong, sir. Marble and stone. But none as strong as a man's immortal soul.

132

He stared at me in surprise. You would be saved, Leporello, when all the world is lost?

We all have souls, sir, I said.

Perhaps. And perhaps some more than others. Wait until you meet the Duke's son. You may reconsider.

I had seen Carlo, the son, riding in his father's tall glass coach. And at the castle, the odd times I went with the Don. I remember Carlo's pale triangular face with its very red lips as the door closed confidentially on them. For the Don had been appointed – or in some mysterious way had appointed himself – to act as companion and mentor to Carlo.

Alas, like many sons of strong men, this Carlo was anything but robust. Some malign spirit must have whistled up his mother's womb to have produced this green stick from such a great oak. In any poorer household, in the natural way of things, such a runt would have perished very early on – but surrounded by warmth, clean linen, rich milk, and the best, highest-hatted doctors, this one scraped through.

Now Carlo was a pale thin youth of twenty-one. A peasant at his age would be a weathered, married man, a father twice over – so I say 'youth' advisedly of Carlo, for he had a long, girlish face – a soft face, but not foolish; rather foxy and cunning in its mild expression. A milk-sop, but a vicious-looking one, you might say.

(Am I going on too far? Spoiling the story? After all, though we have not met him yet I am telling you what to expect of Carlo. Hardly fair on him – you should make your own mind up. *What?*

Go on?

I intend to. In my own way ...)

What do you mean, my lord? I asked the Don. The Duke's son must have a soul. Without one he could not have been born. And if he had been born with one and it had left him before his death – a thing I cannot understand – why, he would be nothing more than a heap of skin and bones and fine clothes on the floor.

(For, assuredly, how should our bodies know how to behave if there were no soul to order them?)

Very good, Leporello, said the Don. Remember me to take you to the university one afternoon. There are gentlemen you would swear death had entered before they had a chance to give up their souls; who have never met a common man; who would think him the most extraordinary creature they had met in all their paper travels. Well then, for your sake, we shall give the Duke's son a soul. A soul with strange tastes.

I had heard of the tastes of Carlo; and rumours of the places he frequented, in poor disguise. For you know that in every city there exists another city – in fact, many other cities, so that the citizens of one may not know of the existence of another and another and another though they live cheek by jowl with them – and would hardly credit the existence of these other cities, even if led on a rein through them.

There is the city of the rich. Of the poor. Of the merchant. The beggar. The child. The dog. The horse and his carriage. Of lawyer. Madman. Whore and soldier. Scholar. Peasant. Of thief and murderer – and, worse, in the city under the city – of jailer, torturer, executioner.

It was whispered – only whispered, because they had their police and informers all over the place – that the Duke's son liked best of all to visit those cities where hope is given up – the prison, Bedlam, the charnel-house; the dungeons where his father's enemies were kept; the walls running with water; the naked prisoners going mad if they were lucky; or strong men who kept their wits and lost all else. It was Carlo's pleasure to witness the *Tortura Acre*, that delight our wise ancestors brought back from the Crusades, whereby a man is hung up by his arms from cords, weights are attached to his feet, and added to progressively, so that dislocation of his bones is followed by the slow tearing of sinew and muscle. This took place, I am told, in dungeons beneath the innocent, sunlit Via S–; where that lady walked her dog in the afternoon.

Carlo had had a succession of tutors to aid his education. Most left soon after they arrived. Why did they go? Well, Carlo, unable, in that city of light and learning, to visit vital terrors on these poor scholars, submitted them to other, more or less innocent torments. These ranged from the prank of introducing live lizards into the tutors' beds – one lost a toe; another the end of his manhood – to drugging an elderly – German, I think he was – who was then taken from his bed in the early morning, stripped naked, to wake in broad daylight, hung in a cage like a bald monkey in the piazza before the cathedral. Yet another was conducted genially on a tour of the dungeons by Carlo, then locked as a jest in one of the cells. For all I know he may still be there. There were those whose linen was set afire; those shot at; spat upon; screamed at, their faces torn by Carlo's long nails. All who could flee did so, as I say – at least it was assumed they had all fled – one or two mysteriously disappeared, no doubt casualties of Carlo's more robust whimsies.

Why was the boy not locked in a madhouse? Whatever he thought secretly of his weakling son, the Duke would not hear a word against the boy from anyone. He shut their warnings out – in his heart he must have feared that the insanity that afflicted his own brother had made a knight's move through his loins and infected this son.

When all those in the city eligible to teach this brat had been used up, tutors were recruited from other cities; then other countries. As the notoriety of the young man spread so did the Duke have to search farther and farther afield, until at last no one could be found willing to take the job. Then the Don came to the city.

Of course, a gentleman of his standing was welcome to the Duke's court at once. The last tutor had just left the city, riding a mule backwards, his legs tied under it, and when no other was forthcoming the Don was prevailed upon to act as companion to the wretched little tosspot.

But if the boy was vicious, he was not wholly stupid. He had – it could hardly be helped – picked up from his army of tutors smatterings of knowledge, oddments of learning to join the fantastic stew in his head. He affected, or perhaps had a genuine interest in, matters of art and natural philosophy. He shared the Don's blasphemies, and the pair were rumoured to be wizards, meddlers with knowledge, disturbers of nature, and nuisances to God.

Why did the Don wait on such a monster? It amused him. He had to do something – you can't be at fucking all day long. Just as it amused Carlo to play cruel jokes, or watch poor prisoners suffer, so it amused the Don to introduce the young man to the more wholesome pleasures of the gaming rooms and cathouses – cats and catamites ...

As we rode along then, I said to the Don:

Will the Duke's son be at the palace, sir?

I hope so, he said, yawning,

Emboldened, I went on, They say he is a most peculiar young man, sir.

The Don looked coldly across at me. His eyes turned to the land rocking past us. Two thousand years ago, he said, Don Carlo would have been the son of a Roman Emperor. No. He corrected himself, At his age he would have been the Emperor, because he would have poisoned his father. He sighed. Of course, that was before the birth of Our Lord, Jesus Christ, so it did not really matter what people did to each other. Doesn't the Church tell us they are all damned anyway, Leporello?

I don't know about that, sir, I said. They were nothing to do with me. It's as simple as this – if you go round poisoning your father you're going to end up in trouble whenever you live. I suppose if they didn't have our God and Holy Mother you can't entirely blame them for carrying on like that. Without God, how would we know we were sinners at all, sir?

He laughed. You are hardly a white soul yourself, my boy. I suppose you think me a great sinner?

Not a *great* sinner, sir, I said.

He was insulted by this. He protested.

I have killed. Seduced other men's wives. Abandoned innocent girls.

All through passion, I assured him. You may still repent, confess and be saved.

We were drawing near to the palace, rolling past columns with the stone heads of beasts looking down on us.

You are insolent, Leporello, he said. And a great fool.

Yes, sir, I said.

In the courtyard into which we drove servants and coachmen bustled about, unloading baggage from empty coaches. Of the gentlemen and ladies who had recently arrived in them there was no sign. Even when we mounted the front steps and entered the first great hall I saw only one couple in the distance. The huge palace had swallowed the rest of them easily up.

As we went between pillars and tapestries and mirrors in which we and all these wonders were repeated, the couple ahead of us parted, the man disappearing through a mirror-laden door, which, swinging open for a moment, showed us advancing. The lady sauntered up the hall towards us.

Ah, said the Don. He knew her – or wished to know her.

Where are you going? he said to me as we drew nearer to the lady.

With you, sir, I replied.

Oh no you are not. Impertinent fellow. Go about your business.

What business is that, sir?

Your business as a servant. Give Ragoti a hand with my box. Find our rooms. Make sure that the bugs have left the beds. Put water in the bowls . . . Do I have to tell you everything? Go.

I stopped and he went on to the lady, hunting his way up another warm valley.

This was the part of the job I found most disagreeable. The working part. Fine to walk about and act the gentleman in the Don's cast-off clothing. To be told to go and get our things out of the coach was almost an insult. A servant should never be seen *carrying* anything. It lowers him in the eyes of his fellows. Especially in a grand place like this.

I went back to the coach and gave the Don's orders to Ragoti, making believe that he had the most part of the work. He spat in the dust at my feet and began to lead our horses away to the stables on the side of the courtyard. I went with him. Some of the palace servants were hanging about under an archway and I made a great show of ordering Ragoti to do what he was already doing. Bugger off, shit-face, he murmured. I left his side, and with a lordly wave of my hand, shouted, Carry on, Ragoti. There's a good fellow.

He carried on. I resigned myself to the work costing me and whistled a couple of the stableboys. I gave them two soldi; then made a brave show, walking boldly back to the steps at the front of the palace and ascending, the two boys grunting behind me under the weight of the Don's travelling chest.

At such moments I could feel a little of what the Don lived every instant of his life – that I was a person of some consequence, one who would excite notice . . .

As we gained the top of the steps, a voice said in my ear, Excuse me, cockchafer. Where are you off to?

There's no fooling a fellow servant. A tall, barrel-chested footman stepped in front of me. The boys let the box down on the marble floor.

I am the valet of Don Giovanni di Tenario, I announced. If you would direct me to the rooms set aside for his party.

He looked me up and down, and said, You had better follow me. No doubt you are not used to a house of this size.

The boys picked up the box again and we started in procession. A fine young dandy, I paraded between footman and boys. As we went, I exchanged frank glances with fine ladies, and hard stares with gentlemen. Make way for Don Giorgio. Don Leporello. That sounded right. But as I swaggered from one corridor to another the footman in front of me, without turning his head, hissed:

Cast down your eyes – your looks are impertinent.

Have you got eyes in your arse? I muttered back.

About to fall into a servant's quarrel – and what happened next? As we came to yet another junction of corridors, who should sweep round the corner – almost colliding with the footman – who but dear Eleonora.

It took me a few seconds to recognise her as she halted to blister the red-faced footman with her tongue. Two years had grown her from that scrawny girl to the appearance of a great lady. Her hair was up in a hoop; her face white with powder except for one black beauty spot below her mouth. Her bodice was a rich silk with pearl buttons and she now had something to swell it out. A diamond winked at her throat. I would not have known her then but that her angry face beneath the white mask gave me such a searching, suspicious glare. Of hatred and fear in equal measure. It seemed to say. Do I know you? I know you. You know me. Don't you dare to acknowledge me. How dare you ignore me. A pretty little maid scurried after her; she looked half worried to death.

We went on our way. They went on their way. But not before I had winked at the maid and she had given me a quick grateful smile. I knew I could get to know more of her. And of what brought Eleonora here.

While the masters feast at night, their servants feast too. Their world lives behind the wood panels, marbles and rich hangings – a world of narrow, whitewashed runs, of kitchens, laundries, closets; a rookery of attics under the eaves; places of strong smells; dirty linen, cheeses, bodies, chamberpots, food cooking; the noises of plates clashing, of farts, belches, shouts, jests, curses, and the endless chitter-chatter of maids like starlings among the pots and pans.

And as those gilded, painted, silk-dressed figures above move about each other in their intricate, genteel dances – like the tiny manikins over the face of some fine-looking clock, their servants are the dark, oil-stained mechanism, its harsh ticking made softer by the thick, rich wood casing. As *they* cram their mouths full with Périgord pies, red fish, blue fish, pâtés, fried chicken, boiled chicken, baked eggs, boiled eggs, sweetmeats, cakes, creams, ices; while they sluice their gullets with black and piss-yellow wine, brandy, coffee, chocolate, I do not think they even dream of the world behind their walls, above the topmost ceiling, below the lowest floor they tread on. Ah, if they only knew how their servants ape them. How our kitchens are arranged in orders of distinction like a court. How we conspire to share the lives of our masters. How dirty fingers pick as much as they dare from the surface of the rich dishes before they are served. How their wine is watered; their shoes scuffed so that the maid or valet can point out, with a rueful shake of the head, how impossible it would be to pass in society with such worn things – so that the servant inherits a perfectly good pair. So too with loosening the threads of shirts and gowns – that then can be sewn up and put on an underling's back. How servants linger in corridors listening to their masters' calls for attention, or the ringing of a bell, waiting until another, weaker-willed, feels compelled to answer the call. How the most intimate conversations are listened to, the postures of love studied through keyhole or cracked panel. How often their daughters are seduced by idle young servants. How their love affairs and finances are the common tittle-tattle from kitchen to kitchen, from stable to stable.

Me? I was up to none of these tricks with the Don. I was the servant of one master – his one true servant. I had nothing but contempt for these idle footmen and thieving butlers and greedy pantryboys. The maids were another matter . . . When we had arrived at Caesaretto I had straightway recognised this insolent footman as a rogue. As we progressed through the palace I was damned if I was going to allow him to station me in some high garret cot, or volunteer me to carry dishes from the kitchen. Reaching the Don's rooms I made a slow play of unlocking and beginning to unpack the box while the footman waited impatiently in the doorway. At last, as I went slowly back and forth from the closet, hanging the Don's clothes, he said, Come, come. I shall show you to your quarters.

I said coldly, My master, Don Giovanni, the friend of the Duke, and the companion of his son, Don Carlo, requires me to be in constant attendance upon him. He does not allow me to leave his quarters at night.

On my mentioning his master, the Duke, he considered, licking his upper lip with his tongue. With an attempt at a sneer, he asked, Where shall you sleep then?

I had already noted the sofa in the dressing antechamber. There, I said, pointing to it.

To rub it in, I added, I presume that the senior servants dine at their own table in your kitchen?

They did. He did.

Then please keep me a place, I said, and went on with my duties, ignoring him.

He went off, as proud-backed as he could manage. I knew he was off to make enquiries about my master, and I knew that he would then keep me a place at his table.

Yes, most pleasant, I thought, looking round the rooms. The golden light of late afternoon filled them. Through the open window came sounds of the courtyard below. I lay down on the sofa. Time for rest. Like a dog I could doze and wake instantly at the sound of the Don's step. Then I would help him dress, see him down to his conversations, his flirtings, his feasting. That would be the time for me to go to the kitchen to eat – and to search out Eleonora's little maid.

I lay and thought of Sophia and her tale. I felt angry at myself for telling the Don of this one among all others, and angry at the thought of him possessing her. And that puzzled me because that was his right and how could I think of having a lady, even if she was in a whorehouse? And from there I drifted into a dream, where the Abbess was just that and Sophia was a poor novice confined against her will, as girls often were, and for her troubles was locked away in one of the punishment cells, those Christian places that had *Requiescat in pace* or some such wicked jest above the door. And somehow I was there, at her rescue, and she lay on her bed and her white robe rode up and showed her plump white legs and more and she turned her face slowly to me and it was no longer Sophia but the little maid who smiled at me and then she had Eleonora's wicked face, she scowled, and The Wreck of Beauty clapped my arms behind my back and what he began to do to me did not bear dreaming of ... and my master entered the other room.

I sprang up. He had not noticed me sleeping. He was in a good mood and hummed a song. One for your book, Leporello, he said cheerfully, and as he changed out of his clothes he told me of his afternoon.

The woman he had left me for in the hall was the wife of one of the Duke's counsellors. He knew her from the city and had offered to accompany her to the gardens, where she was to meet and walk with her woman friend.

But on the way I wondered if she would care to see Don Carlo's latest pet, he said. This was a brown bear some Northerner had brought as a present for the Duke last year. It had its own house in a wood to the north side of the palace.

She was intrigued. She could only spare a few minutes – to see the rough brute rattle its chains when goaded with a stick; to draw back in ladylike alarm when it reared on its hind legs, and roared and clawed the air . . . Ladies need a reason to be given them to go anywhere, even if it is not the true reason in their hearts. And what could befall her with a gentleman such as the Don to accompany her?

By the palace there is a wood, and in the wood there is a house, and in the house there is a bear . . . and close by, its door set in an artificially raised hill, was the ice-house serving the palace.

And so, after frightening her with the terrible creature and then comforting her, he had suggested that a visit to the ice-house might allow her to calm herself and perhaps she might partake of a glass of ice water, which was a sovereign remedy for all nervous conditions. Especially on such a hot day . . . He had led her, her hand holding tightly to his arm, to the door of the ice-house. Which, opened, led down by a bricklined tunnel lit by flambeaux – because it was always night inside the little hill. He knew there was no water to be had. The ice reservoir was simply a huge brick cylinder let down into the cold earth where ice would keep through the hottest season. An iron rail circled the brick well. They stopped to lean and look over. A ladder led down to the blocks of ice; at its foot lay straw and baskets and cutters – the Don had met a servant carrying ice up to the palace on their way to the bear, and so had known the place was probably empty.

The cold radiating up to them had made the lady shudder. The Don gallantly removed his coat and gently placed it round her, saying as he smoothed it over her shoulders, Pardon, madam, in such a soft voice that she hardly noticed his hands slip inside the front of the coat and settle on her breasts. Ah then, the whispered avowals of love as the flambeau flickers above in the brick dome . . . their shadows dance on the shining ice . . . her petticoats rustle upwards . . . What a hot coming they had of it – the heat of their bodies, the surrounding cold being, the Don said, the chief value of this encounter. The familiar does, alas, breed contempt, he sighed.

But there was an added frisson of danger – as the lady, in her transports, had begun to catch her breath and groan, the Don, kindly adjusting his stroke to her mood, heard from behind them the unmistakable sound of a pebble turned underfoot, and steps scurrying away up the tunnel. He stopped. The lady, thinking that he was tiring, had pulled him to her crying, More, more, and he had obliged.

Leporello, I swear someone was observing us. He was thoughtful for a moment, then shrugged and said, I hope they learned something of value.

You think you were followed, my lord? I said. I told of him of my sight of Eleonora, and my worries as to what she was doing in this place. That she had vowed to revenge her ... her father's death. I had to hurry to correct myself before I said that her purpose might be to revenge her seduction and rejection. Perhaps it was that lady, I said.

The Don said merely, Who is this Eleonora? What is her father to me, alive or dead?

He had genuinely forgotten. I retold the events in this half-built palace a year before.

Oh, that chit, he said. She will be no bother. He looked around the room. Get me some water to shave, there's a good fellow.

A simple request, this getting of water? I had to walk half a league, thinking how odd, and how the mark of a gentleman, that so large a part of my life and memory should claim so meagre a part of my master's. When I filled the basin with water and got back it was tepid and the Don rejected it. I retraced my path and came back with the basin above a tray of hot coals that, as I came along, burnt into my fingertips. Then he complained that this heated up the room too much. But all quite genially for once. After I had shaved him, he went to sleep for an hour. I woke him as the sun, about to set, shone straight into our windows. He washed in the shaving water and perfumed himself.

And you, he said, as he dressed for the night ahead, They are serving you well? You are near, I trust?

In the room to the side, I said. On the sofa ...

Yes, yes, he said. Just so that you are close enough to be called. And do not come until you *are* called.

He leaned over my shoulder as I entered the bare details of his latest encounter in my book.

Ice-house. Cold. Followed? Number 253.

With the sun going behind the hills and the gardens grey, we went down.

All the earls and counts and barons and landlords and their ladies were assembled in the public rooms. We walked grandly through one, then another, with the Don gravely acknowledging the deep bows, inclinations, nods, and merest tilting of heads as we approached the innermost hall. At its end, at the top of a broad flight of stairs, Don Carlo sat curled in the crimson plush of a great chair, like a babe in its mother's womb. He caressed his knees. His eyes shifted about, now on the old man who stood halfway down the steps, addressing him, now away again, searching the crowd below. The old man wore an old-fashioned long wig, inadequately powdered, and spoke earnestly, inaudibly, and interminably. Carlo ignored him, twisting instead to talk to the man who stood just behind his throne. A tall, well-built sergeant of the Guards; moustachioed, marble-eyed, ruddy-faced – he looked at the soft life around him with grave, unblinking contempt, as soldiers do.

In one corner of the vast room, two tumblers tumbled. No one took any notice of them. In another corner, Martelli, the poet, a thick clutch of papers in his hand, harangued the air, his free arm waving as if warding off a flight of bats. No one listened. There was a great babble and bubble of greetings and cross-conversations as old friends met again after a pleasant year spent away from each other. Who was dead; whose daughters married; whose estates bought; sold; what scandal among neighbours; the greed of peasants; the unholiness of priests ... When is the Duke expected? How pale his son is ... Who is that fine-looking man at his side? *No!* Who is the old man going on and on? The Count of F-? I thought he was *dead*.

Through this babble the Don advanced, drawing admiring glances after him as a great sleek fish draws minnows in its trail.

On seeing him, Carlo – I can hardly say *leapt* from his chair – rather he slid from his throne to his feet. Don Giovanni. Where have you been? he chided, embracing the Don. Desiderio – a chair for the Don. The big soldier moved solemnly, bearing with great fortitude the name that Don Carlo had given to him.

All this time the old Count had continued his mumbled speech. He now ceased, bowed low to the Duke's son, and retired slowly backwards down the steps, assured that his petition had been heard. A chair was brought for the Don. I took up my station behind it.

It's been so dull here, Carlo chattered. My father has made me look after all these awful people. I looked for you to come yesterday, and the day before that.

A thousand apologies, Excellency . . . , said the Don, then he leaned across the arms of the chairs, his voice lowered so I could catch no more than a mellow hum, punctuated by little excited jets from Carlo of, What? . . . really . . . how big? . . . where? . . . we must, my dear . . . Carlo suddenly fixed his large bright eyes on me.

A pretty lad, your servant, he said.

Pretty enough, Excellency. But, poor boy . . . and here the Don whispered in Carlo's ear. Desiderio glared at me. Carlo pulled away from the Don and examined me again, this time with a look of distaste.

Make yourself scarce, Leporello, said the Don. Go and find some food or something.

Yes, away with you. Away, squawked Don Carlo, waving his hand at me.

Later, angrily, I asked the Don straight out what he had said to the Duke's son.

He laughed. I told him you suffered from piles of an extremely large and venomous nature. Be grateful, he said as I pulled a face. I have saved your backside from a fate far worse than that.

I went through the first blind door in the wall I could find and made my way along mazy passages to the kitchens.

A huge, high-ceilinged place rich in noise and reeks. Here, the servants ate at long, heavy tables, laid out in a T shape. Raised at the top was the high table where the most august servants of the household ruled. In the centre place, lord of all, the steward of Caesaretto, with fine linen before him, a silver goblet, devoured his master's finest food, condescending to talk now and then to one or another of the great men on either side of him. Ranged away from these gods, in descending order of grandeur, were the butlers and footmen and valets and grooms and housekeepers and maids who worked in the palace, or had been brought there by the guests. And all these – there must have been more than a hundred at dinner at that time – were only those not at work immediately in the house above or estate around. The working servants ran in and out with commands from upstairs; along the walls the cooks laboured and sweated before the ovens, bawling and cursing at maids and scullions for more of this, less of that.

Ah but those servants did not stint themselves. They dined off a buffet of chicken wings and rabbits' legs, dried fish, thick cheese rinds, bruised fruit, squashed figs, soups and stews of left-overs from the feast above – and in amongst them, grabbing at what they could get, the children of the lords and ladies above were shouldered aside and ignored by their underlings, while under the tables hounds gobbled at droppings, and cats pawed at tit-bits.

On my way to claim a seat – and the better food, near the top of the table, I happened to see Eleonora's maid.

Poor thing – how bewildered and alone she sat. She had not succeeded in winning much to eat in the battle for life along the table, just a piece of bread which she was trying to break with her fingers. No one was taking any notice of her. I quickly marched across the floor, took a plate from a pile on the board and proceeded to fill it from the array the cooks were laying out for those above. For Don Giovanni di Tenario, I announced grandly – and took it over to the little maid, together with a goblet of wine.

How grateful she was to see a friendly face, and fill her empty stomach. And such a handsome face, and such a finely dressed young man – for I had swiftly ejected the creature who sat beside her. He went grumbling further down the table.

She remembered me from the corridor. She had thought me a proper gentleman, she said – with no hint of mockery, rather a naive charm.

Ah, she was a pretty thing! I soon had her story out of her.

What in God's name was her name? Call her Maria. It seems such an injustice that the unworthy should be so clearly remembered and this one good soul lost for want of a name. Just so it is with those in Hell, whose names live forever – the legions of the good shine nameless in Heaven.

Maria was a simple country girl, new to this work as a lady's maid, and terrified by the palace. What passed in the country did not pass here. Besides which she was cruelly . . . she hesitated, knowing she was being disloyal . . . cruelly and spitefully used by her wilful mistress . . . Do not cry here, I said. You will be even more cruelly used by the servants if they see your weakness. I made her take a pull at the wine, and gently and artfully pressed her to tell me all.

She had been in the service of Baron B-, whose estate was some thirty leagues north of Pomodoro. She had heard of this great city, but only half-believed in its true existence. She had never thought to live to see it – or quite believed that there could be such a place outside of a fairy-tale. The Baron's was a quiet sleepy estate; the usual thing – a small, run-down castle on a hill, a village, a church, and farms and vineyards around. Her master and mistress were solid country types who never travelled. They had one son, Ottavio.

(What's that? Your blessed opera again? The husband of Donna Anna? Well, do let me get on with *my* tale. My tale within a tale within a tale).

Two years ago they had received a letter, which was a rare enough thing in itself, announcing that distant cousins were travelling their way and might they pay a visit? From a Signora Cavilloso. As they were on the road, already firmly on their way, there was no way of saying yea or nay to their coming. And when they had once arrived, the terrible mother and her daughter, accompanied by a great hulk of a fellow . . .

Enrico? I said.

Enrico, said Maria. But how would you know ... ?

Go on, I said.

Why, once there, they showed no inclination to depart. It was plain to the servants that the Cavillosos had come for a purpose and until that was accomplished would not depart. Eleonora put herself in Ottavio's way at every opportunity. With her terrible mother's connivance, the young man was soon tied and brought to heel. It was easily done. The Cavilloso family was rich. Signor Cavilloso was recently dead – a tragic affair – the mother still in mourning – a new head of the house was required.

What did they say of Signor Cavilloso's death? I asked.

Why nothing, she said. Not until later. Then ...

No, no – go on with your story in order, I said.

Well, the courtship had proceeded with such an indecent haste that the servants thought that Eleonora must be pregnant. The marriage was conducted in the fly-blown village church and not in some great cathedral as was thought proper. And then, instead of bride and groom departing to see the bride's estate, they remained in the castle, and the clod Enrico was sent back to manage the estate.

(I marvelled to think that they trusted its running to that great lout – then I remembered his possession of Signora Cavilloso, and the cunning which served him in place of intelligence, and began to see the rude sense of it. For how many times have we seen men of crude force, vulgar men make fortunes, prosper as generals, and now even, in this modern age, act as rulers of men and found dynasties ... ?)

Onwards. Winter followed summer and it seemed that Eleonora and her mother wished to hide themselves away forever in this backwater, though the servants heard Ottavio insisting that it was now his right to visit the Cavilloso estates. He who had been such a nice young man had grown wilful and impatient since marriage, said Maria.

Since money ... , I said.

Yes. Perhaps it was that, she agreed. She had once gone into Eleonora's room when she was closeted with her mother, and had heard Eleonora say, Well, now I have him, what can he do? I don't want to rot in this hole forever. They had stopped talking abruptly when she came in, and the old lady had cornered her after and asked if she had heard what was being said. She quite terrified the poor girl. Come the spring and it was announced that the young people and the mother were to leave for the Cavilloso estate and that they had asked for Maria to accompany them as maid. She had not wanted to go, but what choice had she?

It was in the kitchen I knew so well; inhabited, Maria said, by an old dragon of a woman – I recognised her description of the immortal Marta – that she had first heard the story of Signor Cavilloso's death retold with great delight. How Eleonora had been abducted – abducted herself more like, growled Marta – by a young coxcomb of a servant. How the Signore had pursued them, only to be murdered by the servant and some accomplice faraway in the wicked land to the north. How Eleonora had been brought home, protesting her virtue was intact. But of course the engagement to the local landowner Rannucchio's son had been instantly called off. There was no question of accepting goods that were even rumoured to be damaged, however wealthy the girl's estate. That was why they had had to fetch a husband from so far away.

And what of Ottavio, that husband? Ah, there is always some kind soul wanting to pour good news into our ears. And nothing could be kept secret in those places for long.

The house heard a fearful row coming from their room. Ottavio got the truth out of Eleonora. The truth? A truth. Eleonora admitted that a great gentlemen had made her acquaintance when she was attending the convent in Pomodoro. He had promised her marriage, had said that he would approach her father. Then one night he had crept unbidden into the convent by some secret way, gained her room, and attempted her virtue. She had fought him off and roused the sisters. The Don had fled. But such was his wicked perfidy that he had insinuated a servant into her father's house. This youth had taken advantage of her parents' absence to carry her off, with a knife at her throat, to the palace of Caesaretto. It was only her father's arrival that saved her a second time from dreadful rape. And he, poor brave Papa, had paid for his courage with his life.

149

You swear this is true? shouted the tearful Ottavio. That you were pure when you married me?

By our Holy Mother and all the saints, I swear so, was Eleonora's sobbed reply.

Oh dear, Eleonora, I thought, with that answer you have consigned yourself to Hell. The palace kitchen buzzed and shouted about us, but we might as well have been in a confessional.

But how did you hear all this? I asked Maria.

She blushed. I listened outside, she whispered.

Ah, then you are a true servant, I said.

And what then?

Ottavio swore that they must be avenged on this *gentleman*. His name? Ottavio insisted. Don Giovanni, Eleonora whimpered.

Did Ottavio believe his wife? Did he think back to their wedding night and wonder if he had been tricked? Money has put a patch over many a tattered maidenhead. If he did, he kept such thoughts to himself. Perhaps he imagined they gave him some power over her. But Eleonora was a cunning girl. She knew that the money was hers still, that her husband could, in time, be made pliant once more. And so she agreed willingly to vengeance. For her father's sake, if not hers, she declared. For the sake of all those other poor girls this wicked man had attempted to dishonour. They would go to Pomodoro and track him down . . .

When did they come to the city? I asked.

A month ago, said Maria. Since then strange people have come to the house at all times of the day and night to make report.

Of this Don Giovanni? I asked.

I think so. And then last week a beautiful, dark lady called and they were as thick as thieves together. Now we have come to this place. I don't know if the man they seek is here.

He is, I said. Let's talk of more pleasant things . . .

I was worried at the trouble Eleonora might cause. The other woman sounded like Isabella – no, not your damned Annas and Elviras. What were they cooking up between them? Had their agents been following us? But yet, I reasoned further, what could two silly women do against my great master? I decided I had done my duty and that it was now time to delve into the more intimate secrets of the delightful Maria.

Soon, I shall have to attend my master, I said, putting on a worried expression. I do not like to leave you alone with all these rude grooms, and worse. You are bound to have some insult offered you.

She looked around her. But what shall I do then? she asked.

Perhaps you would allow me to accompany you to your mistress's room? I suggested. This palace is large and full of false turns . . .

Ah, would you? I would be most grateful. Are you sure?

And with other such timid touches in her speech she rose and I escorted her from the kitchen – to the accompaniment of a barrage of obscene farewells from that rough end of the table, to which I gave the finger, behind my back, so the gentle girl would not be alarmed.

When we gained the public corridors I told Maria to hasten as if she were on some errand for her mistress. But we passed no one; the public rooms we went through were in darkness, or lit with just one or two candles to show the way. I took advantage of this, for as we passed from one dark room to another I pretended to trip, held on to Maria and she stumbled into my arms. Leaning against one leaf of tall double doors, her soft body against mine, we kissed as well as any gentlefolk. So sweet – I can taste her country mouth now. Then, she pulled away, softly enough to be sure, and said, Oh, Master . . . I do not know your name . . . I must go to my mistress now . . .

You don't know where you are, I whispered. How are you to find your way on your own?

At this she grew a little nervous. I made a show of relenting. Don't worry, I said, taking her warm little hand in my warmer paw. This way, I said. I shall show you to your door. Of course, I had already found out where Eleonora had pitched her tent. Farther to the west than the Don's rooms, so that as we passed his doors, I pointed negligently to them and said that was where I slept. Did her pace quicken or slow? I was at some loss to know how best to proceed. We were past both doors before I could summon the courage to ask her to step in, and I had to pin my hopes on Maria allowing me entrance to her own bedchamber. If she slept, that is, by her mistress.

In the most distant part of the palace, we came to Eleonora's apartment. Maria gave a little squeal of disappointment on trying the door. It is locked, she said. Oh, how am I to get in before my mistress returns? Oh, how she will scold me. How she will beat me!

Now, now, I said, comforting her. I told her that they would be talking and eating and dancing for hours yet upstairs. I would take her back through the palace, she could seek out her mistress and humbly ask for the keys to set the rooms to rights.

Mollified, she allowed me to kiss her again. This time there was passion and urgency in her mouth. She clung to me, until I broke away. You are a kind man, she said.

I took her hand again and led her back the way we had come. Outside the Don's rooms I halted, and told her that I had to call in for something.

With no resistance on her part, I drew her into the small dressing-room.

Wait here, I said, grateful that the shutter was closed and that the dark would not make her any less nervous and in need of comfort. I went into the Don's room. The moon shone brightly in through the tall windows. I laid out clothes and other necessaries against the Don's return. Satisfied that my work was almost at an end for the day, I went back into the dressing room. Maria – how can I say? – *flowed* into my arms. Intertwined, I guided her backwards to the sofa. As we sat heavily down, my free hand fumbled urgently, loosed my breeches, and released, like a bird from a cage, my stirring, sturdy, not-so-little poker. Her mouth was glued to mine, her eyes closed. The same hand stole under the hem of her simple dress and petticoats, caressed her soft knee, and from there stole to the end of her linen stocking ... all the time lifting her garments with my arm. Ah, she was not as innocent as she seemed, for as I let her fall back on the cushions, she rolled expertly under me, seized my burning cock and guided me into the sweetest, hottest, most recep-

152

tive honeypot I ever hope to meet with in my life. O Darkness. Summer –

I moved, swooning, in the tightest, smoothest, most velvety passage, My God, that my ecstasy came in such a hurry that I feared to have disappointed her. But no, she continued to embrace and kiss me so strongly, breathing so deeply that I thought she would suck the breath out of me, and I became armed again even as I came out of her. Oh, again, again, my sweet, she moaned. But somehow, in her shifting to accommodate me once more, I slipped from her, and in that brief moment of sense in recovering my position and whispering, My love, my love – I heard the catch of the Don's outer door click open.

He had come back much earlier than I expected. There was a murmur of voices – a lady was with him. The maid and I clung to each other, and all passion was cold and I could feel the spirit steal swiftly from my other man. The maid whispered in my ear, like a warm tickling fingertip, I must . . . I must go. She slipped from under me and into the dark pool of the room. A moment later the other door to the corridor opened a crack, she slid out, it closed again, and I was left alone, breeches awry, stomach down on the sofa, peering at my master in the moonlit room ahead.

Thankfully the Don did not light his candles. The lady had followed him into the room. They stood close to each other. The Don, bowing his head, kissed both of her hands, slowly and solemnly.

Sir, we are quite safe here? the lady asks.

Quite safe, my dear lady, says the Don.

My husband? Her voice very precise and businesslike.

It is my experience, says the Don, that His Excellency, Don Carlo, never allows anyone to leave his card game before at least one o'clock.

He began to undress her.

No easy matter, but the Don was experienced. First, the outer gown. With this one it was a puffed-sleeve, furbelowed thing tied at the back with two bows. The Don's fingers were at these.

Ah, but you are wicked, sir, I heard her say, very low.

The bows parted. He drew the short sleeves down, making her

153

shoulders and arms bare. With one tug, the gown, gathered over the petticoats at her hips, lies round her feet.

Pardon, madam, said the Don.

Now she was in only petticoats and bodice. The laces of one bow after another fall slack to the Don's fingers. When they are all loosed, he draws the bodice away from her bosom.

Ah, my lady, he whispers.

For she's bare from the waist up. And I can see, past the Don's dark coat-back, the outline of one glorious tit, and the scallop-shaped bruises where the stays of her bodice have bitten into the flesh.

My dear, he murmured and kissed both of her breasts.

Now she is bending, rising, bending again, as one, two, three, the petticoats come over her head. I see the lovely curve of her legs in their white stockings. The Don's fingers busied themselves with the laces that held up the padded frames on each of her hips. The frames drooped, came away, and were laid on the bed. The big dark rings round her nipples stared back at me like eyes, I swear. The Don reached up into her underskirt and unrolled first one then the other of her stockings. And last he drew down over her hips the white underskirt and she was quite naked, her skin the colour of milk in the moonlight.

The Don stood back and I saw all of her. My eyes went straight down to her black triangle; the delta where all men sail, drift, drown, sojourn, bask, fish, storm, pump, wallow, die, suffer endless joys that end – in short her tuft, her reeking sweetness, her fishy paradise – and saw more, or as much as I could of that shadowy cleft as the Don laid her at the edge of the bed and her legs parted. Then no more, as the Don covered her, reaching inside his breeches for his weapon (he being fully clothed still).

He ran into her course. Another dialogue ensued. One of grunts, groans, moans, entreaties; mumblements and murmurations – what is this wine you have given me? – of whimpers and exultations, cries and sighs. The conversation took place between the Don's thrusting back, and the white columns spread either side. A two-backed, four-legged beast at war with itself. More. More. More, she cried. And Now. Now. And with a harsh cry, the

154

Don ground to a halt.

He lay on her a moment or two, then rolled off, clutching her to him, affording me the briefest glimpse between her sprawled thighs. They lay for a while, cooing and clipping. Then her hand travelled south to where his resting soldier lay outside its tent. She took a delicate hold. She dandled the fat sausage in her fingers until it stirred. The Don began to raise himself on the bed, but the lady pushed him firmly and gently back. She kneeled and straddled him with her legs, her arse presented to his face. Her breasts dangled as she bent over him and lifted his pillar and slid her lips over the big bell-shaped end, rolling it in her mouth like some impossibly sweet fruit. Her lips closed round its shaft, and up and down her head bent, as she sucked at it, her fingers all the time working at the shaft below.

I must admit that I had become intolerably aroused by the sight and sound of her sucking, whispering mouth about his cock, and as she went on and on, my poor spout spurted feebly against my will and against the sofa.

The Don was made of sterner stuff. On she went with her sucking and sighing and fingering. The side of his hand moved like a saw between her legs.

All at once she tore herself away from him, twisted and pulled him on top of her – and into her.

I was sated. Disgusted with myself for the state I had got in – but what was I to do? The Don barged and rammed, rutted and butted, shoved and slashed. The bed seemed to take on some life of its own, leaping and beating its head against the wall, till I thought the Don would ride clear through the wall and they would go, bucketing across the countryside.

I dared not move. There was a sullen ache and wetness under me. Soon I would become aroused again. Oh, let it come to an end, I prayed, and buried my head in the cushions to deaden the din of Love.

It came to a stop at last. I lifted my head. The Don stood, buttoning his breeches. The lady sat on the edge of the bed, pulling on her stockings. Now she got up to tie her garters; black bush showing so large on such a small white body she might have been any servant girl.

If you would be so kind, sir, she addresses the Don. Tie me behind. They clap the padded frames back to her hips. Then, with the Don gravely tying and knotting and assembling, she is put together again. Underskirt. Bodice. Petticoats . . .

A moment sir. She steps into her high-heeled shoes. The Don waits with the rich, brocaded outer gown. Her arms are raised to permit its lowering over her head. Now their four hands place and lace and pat and tug and pinch pleats and creases, bows, ribbons and furbelows and folds and falderals, and all the prinks and teases, creases and pieces, eyes and hooks, tucks and channels of her silky armour.

Then their four hands are at her hair, putting back curls and strands that have sprung out of place in their late exertions. And in all this the Don is as attentive as the best of ladies' maids.

She is ready. She asks for a glass and he brings one. Her moonlit face looks at her moonlit face. A finger pats at her lip, smoothing powder down where it has been smeared away . . .

The Don stood, as I say, like a maid at her side, assisting her to become what she had been. She handed him back the glass.

I think, sir, she said, we had better rejoin the company. My husband . . . They went out of sight, behind the connecting wall.

Ah, perhaps even his beloved cards . . . , I heard the Don say. The outer door opened.

He will have lost as usual, she said.

Perhaps I may relieve him at the table before he . . . , said the Don, and the rest of the exchange was cut off by the door closing.

How civilised this discourse after their passion. And how extraordinary, how dazzling – even by moonlight – that the gentry should have bodies just like ours. My mind full of their late passion, I let them have enough time to get clear. Then I got up, cleaned myself, and lit the candles in both rooms with my tinder, remade the bed, went a long journey to fill his water jug, found out his tooth powder, about which he was very particular, his hairbrushes, his morning linen – all as if I had never seen – or done – anything but my duty in these rooms.

3

Leporello – you are very quiet. I hope you are not worrying about the girl at the Abbess's? I do not want you made unhappy on her account. I have said I will help her. Matters are in hand ...

Our horses trotted side by side on the open plain, behind those of Don Carlo and Sergeant Desiderio. The Don was in that mood where he loved to dispense advice.

An unhappy servant is an unsatisfactory one, neglecting his master's needs for his own, he said. You have the makings of a good servant. The bumpkin you were ... Why, look at you now. You could pass as a gentleman – in the country. No, I will do something for the girl. Quite what ... he mused for a moment. I wondered if he had seen her. He had revisited the Abbess I knew, though without me. But then he laughed and said, But why worry about a lady twenty miles off when the palace is stuffed with little maids?

I said rather huffily that he need not concern himself. I had struck up an acquaintance already. I did not tell him that Maria was Eleonora's maid. Secrets are the only power a servant has.

I see, he said. Here I am lecturing you on the unsuitability of one attachment, and that hardly cold, you begin another. He reined back and stared hard at me. I hope that you are not *in love*, Leporello.

He frowned. The word is a grand one, he announced, but much misused. You cannot too soon forget that word in casual dealings with women. Only a little copulation has to do with love. And not all love has to do with copulation. He looked pleased with himself at saying this, and surprised that he had thought of it. I shall have to remember that, he said proudly. You will be no good to a woman, Leporello, if you are forever falling in and out of love with her. You will grow too excited and too cold by turns. The whole fine edge of the affair will be lost.

He warmed to his fatherly task.

What women seek is not *you*, he explained, but themselves. They wish their low opinions of themselves to be confounded;

their high confirmed. So the man must be a perfect mirror to their expectations. Often they do not wish to be seduced; only to be recognised as worthy of seduction. That is enough for them. Of course, the Don added immodestly, you have to be the *required* seducer. Then it is easy.

Our horses walked slowly together. The sun was hot. His eyes were alive; he raised a hand from his reins to address the white heavens.

You see, it is not that I pursue women. But I cannot bear to think that one has escaped me. It is Woman I adore – her sameness, her variousness – of voice, hair, eyes, breasts, odours; their most hidden secret. The wonderful fecundity – their condition – that spreads these marvellous creatures across the earth; into every city, village, house. Flocks and tribes and hosts and whole nations of women. I ache for each woman I pass in the carriage; each one I glimpse in a window; who dwell in cities I have not and never shall visit. Who I shall never know, for there is not time enough in all the world and our miserable short lives. For each who has to lie beside some spindle-shanked, limp-cocked, half-cocked, cold-buttocked poltroon of a husband. Or suffocates each Sunday night under the lardy bulk of some red-faced, hulking barber or butcher as he executes his after-Mass rights. For the girl who frets at her virginity on a narrow bed. The nun who diddles herself to miserable sleep. The sisters who lie, flaming, together. For the jolly widow and the spinster with little green eyes and a terrible heat between her legs. For all, all of them, Leporello, I feel the same desire. Make no mistake. It is not just the caressing, the ramming of them. They desire, they thirst also. For no woman, no man can ever be happy if they are under an obligation to another.

My God – the hypocrisy of husbands.

I am called a libertine – I am a liberator. I unshackle women. I kill the tyrants in their hearts. If they then elect me as a fresh tyrant – am I to blame? I ride up, easily, as we are riding now, to the castles of marriage and virginity, dissatisfaction, or simple boredom, still my horse, and say, Here I am. I am not known to you. You have nothing to fear. Come, jump up. Ride just a little way. And then *Love* comes to spoil all . . .

Don Carlo's voice chided us from where he and his companion had reined in some distance ahead. Come, come, Don Giovanni – he had a high nasal voice like that – You are falling behind. Ride up! Ride up!

So we spurred on and joined up with them. Carlo was ordered by his father to ride each day for his health. And Don Giovanni, the Duke's friend, was here to enforce the prescript in the Duke's absence. Well, Carlo had to do *something* with his day. Our masters, you see, who do not have the making of a living and its work to fill up each day, must find some other pastimes. They sleep when others are awake; they dress, eat, undress, re-dress, eat again, rest, make love – depending on their age or inclination – dress again, eat again, talk, hear music, undress, sleep. So they consume each day. And in the city there are love affairs, opera, theatre, parades, festivals, the Mass.

Oh, and making money. And a few use, and confuse, their brains in a fretting way to think who they are and why they are and if they are loved by some contrary woman. I told you of Carlo's interest in natural philosophy. It seems he had heard from the Don that in the foggy North, in France, and in the even farther-off grey island of England, gentlemen were busy turning stables and attics into what they called *experimental rooms*, where they presumed to study Creation. The Don had encouraged him to send abroad for all they needed to stock such a magician's cave, or alchemist's hell-hole. I saw the place that morning before we set out for our ride.

We had presented ourselves outside Carlo's door. The Don knocked quietly. It was opened by Desiderio, dressed in stockings and breeches only, his powerful torso covered by a pelt of black hair. Admitting the Don with a deep bow, he glared at me, and shut the door, and I was left in the corridor. A few moments later I heard the mumble of voices and laughter. Coffee was taken in. At last they came out, with Carlo, dressed for the ride, saying, I must just see. Come along. The four of us proceeded down the corridors, Carlo with clicking little steps leading. Some way along Desiderio branched off to go the stables.

A moment, said Carlo and disappeared into one of those small dark closets the size of a confessional, to shit.

The Don and I went on and entered a long, high room.

Remember, little Leporello – this room? the Don asked. Your bunch of country bumpkins? This was where I despatched one of them.

And indeed this was the very same room; now with shelves running the length of two walls, the ceiling white and gold, the sun slanting through east-facing windows at the end. The room where Signor Cavilloso had died. But there was no sign of that. The world fills up without us.

The shelves were lined with many stoppered and corked bottles and pots of porcelain and glass, shaped square and round, six-sided, or like stone eggs. On one long table three large glass vessels were connected by their beaks in a conversation of swans. On another a great bowl was three-quarter filled with a purple liquid; around it were ranged smaller glasses holding vilely brilliant yellow, aquamarine, blue and red liquids. In them grew strange plants of crystal, or curious furry ice.

On a third table against the wall stood an iron column to the top of which, like an inverted bottle, was screwed a large glass globe. A wooden pump-handle stuck out from the side of the column.

The Don was amused at my wonder.

Come – look through this, he said.

Before one of the tall windows was a long brass tube pivoted on a wooden tripod. A spy-glass – but of such a size. Look through, he commanded. I obliged him by dropping down on one knee and applying my eye to the small glassed end. All I saw was a disc of bright blue sky, edged all round as if with a rainbow. As I moved, the tube tilted. The branches of a walnut tree presented themselves as if I had climbed in amongst them. The Don nudged the instrument. A lady's face yawned into mine. She stared straight at me – I might have been standing an inch in front of her nose. Away, said the Don. A lady's small face looked down into the courtyard from a window in the opposite wing of the palace.

A telescope is not used to examine women, the Don said,

chuckling, but the Heavens. If you could make one of sufficient power you could perhaps see the ladies of other planets; the amorous negresses of Venus; the phlegmatic elephants of Jupiter. How would you like that? Even so, with this – he patted the tube – you may see two or three times the number of stars the sharpest eye can make out.

I did not ask him why stars should be put there if we could not see them with our natural eyes. What ships can navigate by stars that cannot be seen?

Now here, said the Don, beckoning me over. He moved to one of the tables and peered into yet another tube; a short one this time, encased in leather, pointed down. Something else you have never seen, he said.

I stooped to look into this other device. A gorgon, a hellish centaur, a creature of the most horrible description confronted me. With scaled eyes, armoured horns, a crab's claws for a mouth that opened and closed in a slow pulsing motion. I pulled away. What is that, sir? I said. It is a monster.

From the bottom of the tube he removed a thin wood slide with a round of glass in its middle. He held it up in front of my eyes. In the centre was a tiny insect in a bubble of water. A louse, he said. Only a louse. The dragons that roam the crotches of beggars – and the scalps of lords.

I said that if the good God had meant us to be frightened by the appearance of such things he would have made them the size of horses.

You are absurd, said the Don. Before he could enjoy himself by demonstrating my absurdity further, Carlo came into the room.

He tripped up to us, rubbing his hands in glee. Have you seen it? he asked eagerly. The atmospheric pump?

I have indeed, Excellency, said the Don. They went to the globe on the table by the wall.

I had it shipped from England. The experiment – we can now perform it. Carlo hopped like a flea in his excitement at his new toy. He darted forward and pulled a wicker cage from behind the iron stand. In the cage were two mice. One sat in a corner cleaning its face with its front paws, the other stood upright, its body spreadeagled against the bars, its pink claws clutching them, for all the world like a tiny pink-bellied man.

I have been impatient for your coming, said Carlo petulantly.

The Don murmured, A thousand apologies.

Carlo said, Yes, yes – well you are here now. And before we ride we will do this – yes?

Of course, of course, said the Don, and the two men bent over the cage, the standing mouse gazing up at them with its bright unwinking eyes.

Your man . . . , Carlo said.

The Don turned to me. Hop on the table, Leporello, he commanded.

I clambered up.

Take hold of the globe, the Don said, and twist it towards the windows. You will find it unscrews.

I did, and held it awkwardly in my arms. It was of thick glass and heavy. Big enough to hold perhaps two gallons of water.

I embraced the globe and unscrewed it. On the top was a small valve. At the screwed end a leather washer with a small hole in the centre, covered with a fine brass grating. I squinted down the iron column; what looked like a cannon's ram-rod plugged the greased inside.

The Don gave me my orders. Leporello, tip your finger through the end and tilt back the mesh. I did. The grating flopped open on a hinge.

They rummaged in the cage.

Oh, Don Giovanni – too revolting, Carlo squealed. You must hold them.

Both? the Don asked.

Yes, yes.

The Don lifted the two mice up by their tails. He beckoned to me to lower the globe towards him. He put in first one, then the other of the mice. Upright, he said; the grating will fall to so they cannot escape. Screw it back on and step down.

The mice skittered about the base, their tiny claws slithering and skating on the glass wall.

Work the pump-handle, said the Don.

162

Were they going to drown the mice?

I pumped away, but no water entered. The mice went busily on, reaching up the sides, searching for a foothold; only to slide and tumble down again, falling over each other.

I stopped for a moment. Carlo cried, On. Carry on. There. You see. There they go.

I pumped away. The mice stopped scrabbling. One ran a little longer, going nowhere fast against the curved glass, but then both lay panting on their sides on the brass grating. Their legs twitched and contracted. They became convulsed. One pissed uncontrollably upwards in a thin hard stream.

Then they were still.

Magic. Of a kind.

Carlo said, You see, Don Giovanni. It works. How splendid. Now, if we got together creatures of different sizes and weights we could see how long each takes to die. And how much of the atmosphere we must draw out.

He was most excited.

It proves . . . it proves . . . , he said

. . . that the experiment works? said the Don.

Precisely, said Carlo.

Your Excellency would need to fit a gauge to measure the displacement required, said the Don.

We must write up the results – I must – in a learned paper, said Carlo.

I am sure the university would be only too pleased to issue such a work, Excellency, said the Don.

The Duke's son gazed in wonder at his toy. It is a pity, though, he said, that the apparatus is so constricted in size. With a larger globe we could use larger animals.

Indeed, said the Don.

Carlo gabbled on . . . Why, it might be possible to prepare a room, a sort of atmospheric cell, with a pump attached to an outside wall, the whole properly sealed, into which a man could be placed, with no apprehension of his fate – and the air then to be slowly withdrawn.

A splendid idea, said the Don.

Of course – Carlo's eyes were bright – some sort of concealed window would have to be provided, in order to witness the progression . . .

That would be essential, the Don murmured.

Carlo looked round, but the excitement ebbed out of his face when he saw there was nothing spare to kill.

We must obtain birds, he said decisively. The Englishman, you say, used birds?

Doves, said the Don. He tapped one hand slowly and patiently on the side of his coat.

White doves . . . , said Carlo dreamily.

But his dream was interrupted. Desiderio stood in the doorway. He announced that the horses were ready.

And now, I suppose, I must go on this tiresome ride, said Carlo, then he brightened up. Perhaps the servants might catch some birds on the way.

On the plain – unlikely, said the Don. But we may buy them caged in the old town of Caesaretto, Excellency.

We'll ride that way then. Come along. Come along.

We rode between the low hills along the road to the old town. We heard music before we reached the outermost house. As we went up the narrow street, Carlo thought it would be amusing to see what the people were at. We went on past a house whose threshold was littered with flower petals. Following the trail, the music growing louder, we came into the main square.

There was a wedding feast going on. The village band stood on the church steps; a fiddle, a clarinet, and a boy beating time on a tabor.

Household tables of all shapes and sizes had been dragged to form a rough circle. Inside it young men and women were dancing. In the centre of their dance, the bride – her hair braided with flowers, face flushed – stood stock still, as if she could not move in her white and silver dress. The groom at her side was in an embroidered coat that was too tight for him. His face was smug with the promise of delights to come.

We clattered across and reined in close to the tables. As we came up the music died away. The clarinet player wiped his lips with a red handkerchief. The fiddler tapped his bow against his boot. The drummer beat a short tattoo. The dancers settled to a halt. The dust at their feet was speckled white with salt to keep the Devil out. The looks they gave us might have done for that as well. In the country well-dressed, well-mounted strangers are almost always bringers of trouble. Their eyes, now downcast, had weighed us up as soldiers or bandits or tax-collectors to fear. Or, perhaps, rich, stupid travellers from the North, foreigners it would be their pleasure to fleece.

Carlo rose up in his stirrups – not such a great height – though the Don was the grandest looking of us all and might have been taken for the boss. Carlo's voice fluttered a little way into the air.

I am Don Carlo, he informed them. The son of your good master, the Duke of D-. Resume your feast. He plumped down in his saddle again.

The silence of a good time halted in mid-flow. Their faces were without expression. Then a girl giggled. A baby began to wail. The clarinet player moistened his lips and put his instrument to his mouth. Tooted once. Then he pulled it out again and looked across at a fat man in a blue, pearl-buttoned coat. The fat man rolled towards us through the dancers.

Excellencies, Excellencies, he babbled. You are most welcome. He touched his brow with his fingers and bowed low to each of us in turn. Dismount please, Excellencies. Dismount. Take wine with us. Break bread. You do us too much honour. He sounded as if he had never been happy before. We dismounted, and he went ahead of us through the tables, shooing people off their stools to make room.

He was the mayor, the head man, the chief of the families, and he insisted on pouring wine for all of us himself. The Don took a sip but was more busy searching about with his eyes in that way I knew too well.

There were some pretty girls in those villages and you could wish to make their acquaintance – until you caught the evil eye the mother cast at you; the nudge to the boozing father to tell him that he had virtue to defend. But much must be endured from noblemen and when the Don went after the country girls their mothers had to grin and bear it. God knows what fantastic dreams they had of a great match for their darlings.

The fawning mayor was revealed by the Don's genial questioning to be the bride's father. Would you excuse me, gentlemen? he said. I was to have directed the dancing. May we continue . . . ? Ah, it seemed his heart would break to leave us.

Carlo waved his permission. The mayor waddled up the church steps, and put up his hand.

Il Quadriglio, he shouted. *A spasso*.

The clarinet began to noodle quiet, the fiddle to whisper hoarse; the boy tapped slow on his drum.

The men went into a circle round the women, the women made another inside that. The men began to walk clockwise; and the women like time running back; slowly, slowly round the newly-weds.

Carlo sat and watched them with a glaze of amusement. Desiderio, po-faced as ever, stood in attendance behind him. I tucked myself among the old men on another table. Best to keep out of the way.

And what of the Don?

Why, when the music began, what was he to do but join it? He stepped deftly between the circling men, more lingeringly through the walking women, and arrived in front of the bride.

He held out his hands in humble submission, inviting hers. A wonderful, puzzled look came over her face. She slowly raised her hands and touched his fingertips. He took a step sideways, and drew her gently into the circle of women, stepped sideways again, and took up a place among the men.

There was an *Ah* from the seated women, and clapping in appreciation of such a *signore* joining the dance. The old men at my table looked on with as much expression as lizards basking in the sun.

The groom stood in the middle of all this, angry hands on his hips, not knowing what to do, watching his wife walk and smile at the Don as they passed.

Arm in Arm, the fat mayor called. The music grew louder and quicker. Each man turned and linked arms with the woman inside, and turned one complete revolution so that now the women were outside, the men in. They began to walk again, but brisker now. The instruments quickened again, doubling the time. The dance began in earnest. A man takes the left hand of the nearest woman passing, whirls her into his place and puts himself in hers. Then he seizes the right hand of the woman who now passes on the inner circle – flung there by the man in front – and whirls her back to the outer – get that? So in and out they circle and chase and all is mix-up and order, mix-up and order, with the Don acquitting himself marvellously as he moves in and out, and the bride swirls with her eyes alight from one man to another – while her husband red-faced pursues her, clutching at hand after hand with every woman but never quite catching up with his own.

So they go madly round and round, with the music faster and faster; the clarinet squeaking and baying, the fiddler sawing the air in half. Fat women drop out coughing with laughter; the middle-aged men go puce competing with the young.

Then all of a sudden the music stops.

Everyone is panting and laughing and falling about. The bride-groom plunges through the broken lines to reach his sweetheart – whom he looks fit to murder – and who by some miracle of chance of the sort I've seen too much, has finished the dance beside the Don, and is leaning into him, her white teeth smiling, her face high, fanning herself with a handkerchief.

And, *Bis! Bis!* shouts the Don. Again! Again!

The lines reform merrily. The groom inserts himself roughly in front of the Don. Walk, shouts the mayor. But the formality of just *walking* irks them this time. They want to get on with it. The fiddle and the clarinet sound are tied down, tugging to be let loose from this melancholy pace.

Arm in Arm, comes the next call.

And the dance begins again; wilder this time. The music doubles and redoubles. The dancers whirl and twist, laugh and squeal. The girls' skirts lift so you can see right up their bare legs.

They go round and round, round and round, faster and faster, and just as the groom is about to catch up with his wife and seize her hand – why, by some magic, the Don checks, reverses the flow of the dance, turning the men so that they go back against the clock, the women with it, again faster and faster – and the groom is once more left floundering, pop-eyed with anger, in the centre of the salted floor.

Then he has darted suddenly into the fray and dragged out his woman, his spouse, his promised spout. He screams at the dancers to stop – and you can hear that, and his wife laughing, because the dance suddenly has stopped. The music flourishing to a halt, the dancers fall against each other; the women breathless and bubbling; the men gabbling and boasting how fast they have gone. And, to each other, whose breasts or bums they were lucky enough to touch in the heat of the moment. Oh that there should be more weddings – but not mine, O Lord, not yet, they say.

Carlo was laughing, tears on his cheeks, but you knew that he was laughing at these folk, not with them. The Don, with a kiss of his hand, bade farewell to his partner. The villagers came, limping and gabbling, back to the table, looking for refreshment after their exertions. Which left just the groom in the open, hissing furiously into his bride's ear – who now contrived to look properly contrite and chastened, though the lively glance she shot the Don from under her black brows betrayed her true feelings. For all women love a good time – and know that there are precious few after marriage.

The bride's father came round us, pouring lemonade from a pitcher. He clapped the Don on the back, apologised for his temerity, then poured forth a great volume of compliments as to how gallant the grand signore was, how graceful, how fiery the dancing of the lord. The honour, your honour . . .

Meanwhile, the groom had withdrawn his bride to the farthest table on the other side and sat her down between a ferocious lady who looked like his mother, and a very old, even more ferocious one who looked like his grandmother. He was pinning his little butterfly well down.

They served us royally with food and drink. All reserve had

168

been lost with the Don joining their dance. Carlo earned a few strange looks whenever he addressed his faithful Desiderio – and the girls who admired the handsome figure of the Sergeant got little enough encouragement from those iron eyes and bristling moustachios.

When we had eaten, Carlo raised his hand. Desiderio called for silence. When they had it, Carlo spoke.

I have had a wonderful idea, he announced. There is to be a ball tonight at the palace. Your village is invited. This wedding feast will be completed at the palace. Desiderio – you will ride back now and tell my steward to expect more guests. You, he pointed at the mayor, will give the numbers of your people here to the Sergeant. Oh yes. It will be fine, fine. He was full of enthusiasm for his new idea. He said to the Don how amusing it would be to see these peasants mixing with their guests. Really, it would be quite like a painting. Of centaurs and fauns in a palace. Perhaps they could get – and he mentioned some damn painter – to run something up on those lines . . .

The mayor was waiting patiently.

All of us? said the mayor. You want all of us?

All, said Carlo grandly. All of you are my father's subjects, therefore all shall share his hospitality.

Ah, said the mayor, and went away to interpret the news to the other tables who might not have heard or understood Carlo's piping.

He came back. We are most grateful, your lordship, he began. But . . .

Carlo glared at him. I don't want Buts, he snapped. You are invited. The Duke will look ill upon anyone who does not accept his invitation.

But, how shall we go there? the mayor asked.

Carlo said, You have horses, haven't you? Carts? Carriages? Oh – what do peasants have, Don Giovanni?

Mules, said the Don. Perhaps horses.

There you are then, said Carlo to the mayor. Those who can ride, ride. The rest can walk.

The mayor gave the slightest shrug of the shoulders and turned back to his people. But, I must say, if he was not overjoyed at the prospect of a journey of several leagues under the afternoon sun, the rest of them seemed happy enough at the news. All except the bridegroom, that is, who was stirred only enough to deliver some fresh, sour-faced tirade into his bride's pretty ear.

Desiderio rode away.

The dancing began again. Now it was in an altogether more leisurely, late-afternoon style, with the older folks sitting out. As did the Don. For the bride and her party had disappeared; though the mayor still hovered about our gentlemen as if he expected them to order his head off at any moment.

The afternoon dwindled. Shadows lengthened across the square and the murderous heat abated. Carlo decided it was time to move. The caravan that had assembled in the square began to move, following our horses down the village streets, between the hills, onto the plain.

Directly behind us, in the mayor's own dilapidated calash drawn by a skin-and-bone piebald, sat bride and groom, still dressed in their wedding clothes. Then came the second carriage, an ancient berline stuffed with mayor and mother and grand-mother; the other father, mother and grandmother. Then an ox-drawn cart full of old folks and children, like a parable. An-other with the musicians, who had been joined by a bagpipe and a mandolin and a woman singing as if she was at a funeral. And after them the tail of walking peasants. Some of the young men held aloft flags of their village, and the groom's village, looking like an army on the march. And as we went on, the musicians' ox-cart and the walkers dropped farther and farther behind, their notes bleating and piping in the breeze, the woman wailing, until all we could hear were distant drum beats and shouts for us to wait for them. Wait for them ...

The hills fell off behind. We entered the grounds of the palace while the palace itself still lay at a league's distance. We waited for the stragglers to catch up. We had kept the palace in our view all the way across the plain without it seeming to get any larger – now, though it was still some distance off, it was awesomely massive. The villagers coming up fell silent, the music stuttered to a halt; their flags drooped. Passing through gardens; between lawns, carved hedges, marble fountains, the statues of nymphs whose breasts spurted water, the peasants were as properly chastened and overawed as Carlo's horrible little smile expected them to be.

As we drew near the palace, amused faces watched us from the upper windows. The wedding finery of the peasants faded to gimcrack, shabby stuff. As if sensing this, and resenting it, the Don halted, turned in his saddle and addressed them. Now, he shouted, Good people – sing up! Raise your flags. Lift up your heads. This is your feast. You were here before this palace – and your children will be here when it is gone. Let them hear you!

And on they rolled, their faces clearer, some ancient song welling from them in their own tongue. The young men ran on ahead, waving their flags and banners. The music struck up. The Don spurred on. He might have been a victorious general coming to raise a siege from a city; the hero, the victor. And so it must have seemed to Carlo, because he leaned over and spoke vehemently to the Don, his face angry, though I couldn't hear the words. I cantered up to them. The ball, Excellency, remember the ball, I heard Don Giovanni say. Carlo smiled again then, no doubt thinking the Don had some trick up his sleeve to amuse him. Come, Don Carlo, said my Don. I will race you to the stables.

Leporello, he called back to me, Look after the village people. Then he was off on the chase with Don Carlo – hot enough, but politic – I saw him pull his horse right before the stable arch – to let the Duke's son pass under first to win their race.

What – the bride and groom in the village wedding were called Zerlina and Masetto? What? Why bother telling me that? Ah, your blasted opera again. These are *real* things I am telling you, not make-believe. Call them Zerlina and Masetto by all means, if it makes you happy. I can't remember their real names anyway. If I ever knew them.

When the villagers had all arrived they were assembled together in the stable yard, awaiting our master's pleasure. I was one of those who took wine and food out to them. But it was as if by uprooting them, the feast had lost its savour.

Some of them were for going home, muttering why had they allowed themselves to be led away; considering that now they had obeyed the mad, girlish signore, why they could just not go? But Carlo had ordered the stable gates to be shut and Desiderio stood on the back of a cart to announce that they were there to enjoy themselves at His Excellency's behest – to be let go when His Excellency considered they had enjoyed themselves sufficiently.

Going up to my own master, I glanced down through the stair windows into the yard. Bride and groom sat stiff as brocaded dolls on the chairs that had been brought out for them. The musicians had begun playing again, but all I could hear through the window glass was a mournful cheeping like a bird shut in that globe.

As soon as I reached our rooms, I had to go again to the kitchen to fetch hot water for the Don to wash. He undressed to his breeches and began to wash his upper body. It was in these moments, when he was naked, or tired, that I was permitted to address him freely, to act the confidant. Almost, I dared to think, as his friend.

You know the maid I was telling you about, I said as I rubbed his back with a rough cloth.

What maid? he said, and, There. There. Rub there.

She is the lady Eleonora's, I said as casually as I was able. I told you, I saw her yesterday. (I never could keep a secret for long.) It was being in that room where he had fucked a lady, and I had watched and next door had done likewise, that gave me a fellow feeling. And I wanted him to know that I was looking out for his interests. As well as my own.

He pointed at his back where I was to scrub. All he said was, Oh, that preposterous girl.

My clean shirt, he demanded.

I went into the dressing room and from there said, I don't know about that, sir, but from what the maid told me, the lady is up to no good. I must warn you ... As I strolled back in, he glared at me.

Warn me? Warn me? Of what terrific danger must you warn me now, Leporello?

Why, my lord . . . I swear he terrified me when his face hardened up like that. Why, I said, the lady has sworn vengeance on you. She has been making enquiries . . .

He laughed in my face. Not another of them, he said. Vengeance! *Enquiries*! Whatever next?

What is your advice then, Leporello? he asked. Before I make love to a woman, to question her thoroughly? In writing if possible, with answers in her own hand so that they cannot be gainsaid? To ask her why and on what conditions she loves me? To notate sighs, entreaties – the moment of bliss itself? How long the affair is to last? How we shall each conduct ourselves afterwards? What reservations she has, knowing my reputation? I tell you – Questions. Conditions. Reservations – She will answer, *None. None. None.* You are free to leave me, my love, if that is what you truly want . . . Then it is tears and You said . . . You promised . . . And you say I have *two* of them on my track? Time to worry when they raise up a host and come marching upon me. No – I think I shall ride out the ladies' storms, Leporello – with the aid of your invaluable advice of course.

He said this with such intolerable sarcasm that my heart withered and if my eyes could have pierced him he would have fallen dead on the spot. He didn't.

Besides, he said, it encourages the others. You say this Eleonora is married now? Perhaps I might take another look at her. He leaned on my shoulder as he tugged at his stocking heel.

His tone was calm and even again. I had gone too far and he had slapped me down. These times of liberty, when confidences can be exchanged between master and servant, must be conducted to a strict code. I had overstepped the mark. The forms must be observed or the whole thing comes tumbling down. Only when he was dying was I able to speak with complete freedom and insolence to him. And that was a victory not worth the having.

Am I to see the maid again, sir? I enquired, putting on timidity. It is like angling a fish out of the water, playing your master. The enquiries . . . , I said.

Find out if you must, he said airily. It's as well to know what mischief is about.

There – we were back to normal. It was like a young marriage back then – all up and down, if you know what I mean. The Don looked at himself in the glass and said, plucking at the shirt, No, this won't do. Let us apply ourselves, my dear, to the matter of this evening. Don Carlo has invited our friends from the hills. We must make an effort to welcome them. He eyed me for a moment. Now, he said, what do you say that I go as the servant and you as the gentleman. Yes, yes. He didn't wait for my answer, being very pleased with his own. Yes, you shall go as master. Eh? I want to see this pretty maid of Eleonora's. And for you, Leporello – perhaps we shall provide you with a great lady. A Baroness. At least, a *Contessina*.

This is too grand. He tossed the silk shirt back to me. Bring me some of your own clothes, he said. Soon he was dressed in a plain white shirt, a blue and gold waistcoat, brown breeches, white stockings, leather pumps. Is this the plainest wear you have? he complained. I had to say yes, and remind him that most of it was his cast-off clothing. Ah well, he sighed, I shall have to pass as best I can as a peasant. He tousled his hair, and had me tie it at the back in a tight short queue. He rubbed at his eyebrows until they stood out in fierce brushes. He looked more like a bandit dressed for Sunday than a servant.

Then I was made into a gentlemen. He allowed me the pick of his clothes and though I chose modestly I could not help but come out the very appearance of a dashing young signore; an officer perhaps, back from a long campaign, which would explain my sun-blackened skin, the coarse heavy hands that came out of the Don's lace cuffs. I was topped off with a freshly powdered peruke with a crimson bow on its tail. He stood back, laughed, and said that all in all I looked as fine a gentleman as you could meet in a week's march.

At least in these corridors, he said as we came from the room. Swagger, my lord. Swagger.

My God, who should be the first person we meet? Here comes little Maria, the maid. She scurried past me without a glance, but her eyes lifted and brightened at the sight of my 'servant'. I felt affronted – and betrayed. *Così fan tutte* ... Damn her. I took her and now could leave her. Could I ever make my heart as cold as my master's? I tried to put her from my mind and swaggered on. A gentleman and his lady came out of a door and started towards me. The man inclined his head in a quizzical nod, as if not sure who I was, the lady smiled as we passed. I had survived my first encounter. I felt a foot taller and as if I had been given new eyes or that the world had been angled away from the one I normally walked in. To convey my delight at this new world to Don Giovanni, I turned my head. Sir, I began – and he had gone. The corridor was empty except for that couple going away. I was piqued at missing my 'servant' so soon. The rascal had set off in pursuit as soon as he had seen Maria. Was no one to be safe from him? By stepping into his world, I had allowed him to step into my mine. It is hard, though it has to be endured, that our masters own both worlds. We like to think them separate, but in truth, all is theirs; there is nothing under the sun that belongs to a servant.

Still, the hour was mine, even if by a trick. Let me go on to my destiny. I squared my gentleman's shoulders – roomily enough in the Don's coat – and strode on.

Each corridor gave into another a little wider, a little busier, until at last I came out into a hall and to the foot of a great staircase that flowed up and up like a frozen river fall. The people on the stairs were dressed gorgeously for evening. The light was beginning to fail through the tall windows and servants were lighting candles and lamps, and two footmen on two high stepladders lit the great chandelier above the landing. Their hands holding tapers moved busily in and out of the tinkling brilliant lustres. I joined the flow of grand folk moving up the stairs, my head high, glancing and glaring boldly about me. But my nerve almost failed when I came to the top. In the chamber ahead, among the throng, I saw Eleonora. She was talking to, or rather, addressing a short young man who had fair hair and no great distinction. I gathered myself, and sailed on, getting as near to them as I dared.

While the young man was replying to whatever she had just said, she was looking about her in a darting, insatiable way, like a bird pecking the earth for food and not wishing to miss a single morsel. When he had finished talking it was plain by the way she took his arm absent-mindedly that he was not merely a casual acquaintance, but indeed the Baron's son, Ottavio, whom she had married.

I made my way through the crush and babble. Waded through the stench of powder and perfume. The odd reek of sweat was almost welcome. Which of these tightly-laced, brocaded, stiff-coiffed women had the Don had last night? It was impossible, in this State room, to imagine any of them in the animal motions of love. And which of the corseted, ribboned, dress-coated, smiling plump men was the cuckolded husband?

Talking of cuckolds – for you can call a man who has married an *experienced* girl a cuckold at one remove – I was now close to Eleonora and her husband. I hung at the back of them listening.

If I see him . . . The blackguard! said the brave young man, separated from his foe.

I told you, Ottavio . . .

What's that? *Another* name in your opera? Well, I never – the man who wrote it must have heard of us after all. But I'm not responsible for that, am I?

I told you, Ottavio . . . She spoke severely. You will not make a scene. Her voice dropped. I edged nearer. I thought we agreed; it is not my honour that is at question, but the memory of my dear father. She crossed herself. We shall do it my way . . . If you wish me to be pleasant to you . . . He did. He did. His eyes watered, his mouth watered. He licked his lips.

She gripped his arm. They are moving in for the dancing, she said.

And indeed there was movement at the end of the room and the leaves of two high doors were being folded back. Eleonora and her husband moved forward in my direction. I was trapped and could not move away fast enough in the crush. I dreaded her discovery of me. I feared I had betrayed myself when she caught my eyes. But no – she smiled, that mysterious seductive smile that a woman can exchange across a room with a complete stranger. And the amazing thing is that this communication always re-

mains secret, unnoticed by the complacent accompanying husband or lover. Truly all these women live secret lives, as the Don
said. I turned my gaze hurriedly away. She had not recognised
me. I had difficulty for a moment in recognising myself. As we all
moved forward I was pushed past a square column with mirrors
on all its sides. Who was that good-looking, faintly familiar young
man dressed in the Don's good clothes, his face a version of mine,
but made to appear squarer and more mature under the wig – ah,
who is that fine fellow, I said to myself. No wonder she smiled at
you.

I let them press on ahead. She did not look back at me. A woman
does not like to have her smiles ignored; she has given a small
piece of her soul away. No second chance is given.

I wondered what the Don would have done. What he *had* done.
For assuredly, at some time in Eleonora's stay at the convent in
Pomodoro, before she was brought home to the farm, the Don had
fallen like an eagle on that smile – and how much more innocent-
seeming, fresh and fetching it must have been that short time ago.
And what was the Don doing now? With Maria? Bursting out of
my breeches, that's what. Into her ...

Sophia, whom he had promised to search out in the brothel;
Maria who was with him now; Eleonora, who had duped me and
been discarded by him ... were all my women to be had by the
Don? I wished *Spugnalina* in her noisome beach den of stones on
him. Let him try his wiles on her!

I was still his servant. It was my duty to keep near to Eleonora
and her husband. From what Maria had told me, Eleonora had
had little choice but to come here, if she was not to admit the truth
of her past. And it was plain that this fool Ottavio planned to
somehow confront the Don. I could not imagine a duel, or an
assassination – Ottavio was not the man for the first, and I doubt
he had the cunning for the second. They had mentioned Isabella.
Spies. Enquiries. It smelt of conspiracy. There was always enough
of that.

But, back to the dance.

We pressed through the doors and dispersed into a huge
ballroom. It was on three levels; a mezzanine set with lines of

chairs for those too feeble or disinclined to dance to look down on those who did; a promenade, set with mirrors and tables and alcoves and pillars and giant vases and trailing plants and oh, all sorts of contrivances and hidey-holes for little intrigues; from here steps led down into the long, red-calked pit of the dance-floor itself.

There was music; but no dancers.

The musicians were from the Opera in the city, closed at the start of the hottest season. They were set on the promenade, at the edge of the dance floor, like anglers sat to catch the fish swimming below them. Heaped in a pyramid, with fiddles at the bottom, clarinets, horns, trumpets in shorter and shorter rows, and at the top a kettledrum. The wall behind them was mirrored from top to bottom, so that another band sat back to back with them. Fat tall candles of the sort little virgin communicants love to fondle in church rose between the crimson and silver uniforms and the tall scarlet feathers in their hats looked on fire. How they did not catch fire I couldn't say, because hot as it was, it must have been infernally more so for them – and hotter still as they began, after a minute's rest, again to saw and mewl, toot and rumble in some slow minuet, their notes so lethargic and half-spirited that they got lost among the conversation of the crowd. Still no one took the floor. Protocol demanded that everyone wait for the Duke. Or the Duke's son. Or the next one down. Or the next. They could have waited forever if you think about it. If you thought about it.

But he did not appear. People consulted their watches – though they all had different times, coming from so many different places. Whispers and muffled laughter as some malicious spirits wondered if Don Carlo would take the floor himself. If Desiderio would partner him. And which would wear the gown? – the opinion in that coming down in favour of Carlo's youth and against the Sergeant's moustachios.

So while the band sweated and its strains crept and wandered about the room, I moved boldly through the press, looking for Eleonora. For the moment I had lost her.

In all the mirrors the men and women were pictured over and over, as if they would go on forever. Among all the pale powdered faces I searched for my own, admiring it more each time I found it.

Ah, you are – are you not? Donna Julia's son? An elderly hawk-nosed woman had stepped in front of me and accused me rapidly thus, and without waiting for me to answer, rattled on: I was so sorry to hear of the fate of your poor Papa.

You come from E-? I said, giving the name of my village.

What? Her nose wrinkled in that look of disgust these people put on – oh, quite unconciously, inbred as it must be – whenever something is mentioned with which they are not familiar. Which is quite a lot. Anything, that is to say, not to do with the amount of gold and land they have, the number of tenants, the exact age and state of health of their wealthier relatives.

My village? This woman would have been as likely to have known the backside of the moon.

Your father. I was talking about your father, she said. His illness. I believe . . .

That he was a baker, madam, I said. And that he was put into a barrel and thrown over a cliff. That of the ruffians who did it one only was hanged – though the others will meet him in Hell.

It was worth it to see the affronted confusion in her face. Don Giorgio, I announced, at your service, and went on my way.

Extraordinary! Her shocked voice pursued me.

But I was safe, for just at this moment, when the old hag might have come after and discovered me, the orchestra struck up a series of dreary fanfares, of a vaguely royal, hunterly fashion.

With an ancient lady hung on one wrist like a dead hawk, Carlo entered the ballroom. After him came Desiderio, enormous; grave.

On either side heads tilted; the deeper the bow, the deeper the debt. The old woman let fly, Carlo sat down overlooking the dancing pit and signalled to the orchestra to play again. His hooked finger commanded Desiderio to bend over him and Carlo whispered in his ear. Desiderio straightened and boomed in his great voice, You may dance. His Excellency says let the dancing begin.

The music welled up again. Lines formed and re-formed on the red floor. But the dancing was poor stuff. A polite and ball-less version of the village dance. When it should have been fast and furious it never rose above a sedate flurry. The gentlemen raised their arms, the ladies pattered like mice beneath them. I saw Eleonora among the dancers; elegant, quite elegant. Her husband betrayed in his lumpy movements that the only dancing he had done before was in a farmyard. It was hot. Servants were bringing round glasses of iced water and slices of melon. Would the one who served me know me for what I truly was? But no – his eyes fixed on my waistcoat buttons and rose no higher. The world for those house lackeys consists of a headless gentry, for they never have the temerity to look their masters in the face and deal honestly with him as I did with mine.

What happened to the peasants, you ask?

I had begun to wonder that too – and to feel myself exposed as the dancing floor filled and the promenade grew dangerously empty about me. Had Desiderio spotted me? I saw him look my way twice, his bold dead eyes unblinking. The second time he bent and murmured in his master's ear. About me or not – Carlo did not deign to look my way. And when he despatched Desiderio from the room on some errand, the bold Sergeant passed by me without showing the slightest interest. A few moments later he appeared in the doorway again and a sign passed between them.

Carlo stood and put up a hand to command silence. A new round of dances had begun, but the music fell quickly away. The dancers looked up at Don Carlo.

My friends; we have a pleasant surprise for you . . . , he began.

At the other end of the room Desiderio bellowed an order. All the people in the pit craned to see what was happening. The old stirred in their chairs on the mezzanine.

. . . I have invited . . . Carlo squeaked, but the rest of his speech was drowned in the sea of noise that came swamping into the room; the wave, the eruption of peasants.

They had spent the afternoon well. They had recovered their spirits. They were roaring drunk.

They carried Zerlina on their shoulders, still in her wedding

180

dress, through now thoroughly rumpled and her hair tossing in front of her eyes. Masetto in his wedding suit strutted in front, a wine bottle in his hand. And they were accompanied – their rears brought up, as it were – by the hideous, ferocious wailing of the *Zampogna*. What you would call *cornamusa*. Bagpipes. Following; the piper, the fiddler, the clarinet player, and the boy banging lustily on his tabor. And all the peasants rosy and brown and hawknosed and savage-faced like wolves. Drunk, as I say, and spilling like wine among the pillars and vases, and filling the mirrors full of life. Once in, the doors banged shut behind them. Their instruments with a final mad flurry wheezed into silence. They gawped in awe down at the dancers, and up at the gold ceiling with an angel blowing out wind in each corner, and fish-bummed women and Uncle Neptune in the middle glaring down at them. For to be sure they had been led here by the back way, and what they had seen of the palace so far could not hold a candle to this sumptuous room.

And, right in the middle of them, a red kerchief round his throat, my shirt that had been his shirt tight across his chest and shoulders, the very picture of the sturdy bandit: the Don.

No trouble with recognising *him*. Cheers and clapping came from the dancers as first one then another saw him among this rabble, and passed the reassuring news to each other. For it must be admitted, these gentlefolk had been a little startled and perhaps even frightened at the uncouth clamour, the sight of this horde, the discord of such ... such ... in this place. But when they saw that a gentleman, a signore was among the revellers, and appeared to be their leader, well that was all right then, wasn't it? And as they looked harder they thought they saw others they knew. Wasn't that the Marquis of O-. The Count of Um ... ? Um? Such convincing disguises!

As the two parties examined each other, the orchestra sat looking put out. They did not know whether to play or not. It could not have been pleasant for their trained ears to put up with such caterwauling. They put their pieces up to their mouths, flexed their bowing arms, ready to acquit themselves nobly again.

Don Giovanni herded the peasants towards the dancing pit.

Masetto shambled forward, loathing written on his face. Zerlina smiled serenely.

... How successful those costumes ... How like *real* peasants they look ... Where did they get those materials? The plaudits echoed from mouth to mouth ... How amusing ... But who were these masqueraders?

Ah, the sweet and unsweet confusion as the peasants mingled with their masters. The band begins to play once more. The palace guests once more twist and turn with their studied grace. The peasants lumber and stumble about, not knowing what on earth this music and these steps are asking them to do. Until some of those who had drunk deeply all afternoon but retained some native wit, began to ape their dancing masters; at first clumsily, colliding with the satin shoulders and laced hems of the ladies, then more wildly, bumping the gentlemen out of their way.

And, ah, what amusement at first at these merry antics. What sometime irritation, disgust, consternation, and then fear in the fainter-hearted as whoops and cries come from these fierce inter-lopers. Voices are raised; the careful modulation of a landlord and brothel-owning Count against the rough, thick dialect of a goat-herd. They can't make each other understand, face to face in the swirling mêlée; they exchange obscene gestures; the finger, the fist, the pulled earlobe, the horns.

But, my lord, came a despairing voice as the first reel ended, these are no ladies and gentlemen. And the realisation that what they had thought a masquerade was in reality an invasion by real, stinking peasants spread to even the most obtuse dancer, then to those on the promenade, and was whispered along the ancient ears on the mezzanine.

They are ladies and gentlemen if I say they are ladies and gentlemen, Carlo shouted, his face clouded with anger. Excel-lency ..., another voice protested.

Be quiet, Carlo fairly screamed. You are all my father's subjects. Does a father have favourite sons? Now, dance with your neigh-bours, or I'll have you dancing on the end of a rope. Signor Aprile, he shouted across to the bandmaster – for the band had again faltered to a stop at this latest interruption. Signor Aprile, have you run out of music? I'll send you some decent musicians. You there, he called down to the village musicians squatting in one corner of the dance pit. Go and join the orchestra of the Opera. Signor Bagpipe. Prince Fiddle. Go. Carlo turned his attention back to the band. You – move up there, he shouted. Come along. Make room for these fine players. Horror on their faces, the musicians bunched along and the village players perched on the ends of the lower benches.

Maestro Aprile, let these others play for us. Your fellows may join in if they choose. If they can. Carlo rose from his chair and went to the edge of the pit to address Don Giovanni. Let us have the dances we had this afternoon, he called. Where is that little man?

His face sweating, the village mayor came round the back of Don Giovanni like a pet dog.

You know how these things go, said Carlo. Instruct our guests.

The mayor bowed and begged Don Giovanni's help. He didn't like to order the gentry about, you see. And some of those began to leave the floor, until Carlo yelled from his chair that all must keep their places. All. So that ladies must link arms with fat brown field women, and bankers join hands with goatboys.

But among those who had escaped the floor and were now safe on the promenade were Eleonora and her Ottavio. She stared down, and I saw her nudge her husband and point out the Don. Ottavio started forward, the little hero, but she caught his arm, speaking rapidly, her eyes angry. She seemed to be telling him to wait. That their hour would come.

Now the circles had formed. The Don was in line next to Zerlina, her husband, Masetto, once more juggled out of position, so that he fretted three places behind the Don and was opposite a countess who was trying to pretend she was in another country entirely.

The mayor stood in front of the orchestra and clapped his hands.

A *spasso*, he shouted.

The village players started slowly. The circles of men and women began their parade. How unearthly and uncouth their simple music sounded in that glittering room. As soon as the Don passed under me he smiled up. Join us, signore. Join us. But I shook my head, took a step back, and blushed at once for disobeying him. But he was away.

As the walkers made one full round, some of the gentlemen and ladies began to fall into the step needed. A few of the Opera musicians noodled along *sotto voce*, half-ashamed it seemed to join fullbloodedly in with music they must have heard half their lives in the villages and small towns they came from.

When the call *A braccino* came, there was much reluctant linking of arms and wrinkling of noses. But some of the gentlemen were quite taken with the common girls – and some of the ladies with the sun-blackened young men with their blue-black hair. A spring crept into the steps. The music went faster and louder and louder as more and more of the Opera players joined in and the music whirled the dancers faster and faster and into and out of each other arms.

And chief of course among the dancers was the Don, the white bride on his bared arm. Oh, but he would have her. And Masetto, a heavy clumsy dog trying to course a hare, chased and chased them through the rout, but could never quite overtake their switching and sliding and gliding away.

Now the whole band was playing – but not drowning the wild wails of the *zampogna*. Carlo beat a mad tattoo out of time on the arms of his chair. The Don sang out, *Bis, bis*, again, again, whenever the dance threatened to slack. *Viva la Libertà*. Did I hear that? Or do I imagine that from later – but this dance was indeed the very emblem of the Don's dangerous ideas about liberty that he picked up from his Freemason friends. Perhaps all that did come later, but he would often refer to this bacchanal as his very ideal of Revolution. Revolution! Well, they certainly revolved. Again, he shouted, and the society span like a top. Round the pit they went, faster and faster. Until someone dizzied, stumbled and fell and half the dancers tumbled into him, and the other half, coming the other way, crashed into them and suddenly there was a grand mêlée of silks and linen and worsted and corduroy, and bare calves and white-stockinged legs, petticoats up, hair down, legs waving in the air, such injudicious, delicious sights as a breast spilled here, a flash of white thigh there. Only the Don, somehow miraculously dodging the ruck, stood triumphantly above them, holding Zerlina by the hand. Somewhere under the writhing mass was Masetto, the husband. All the people on the promenade were laughing and crowding to the edge of the pit to see their friends trying to struggle up out of the mess.

The band stopped playing. The bagpipe wheezed to mirthful death. The clarinet gave a bird's bright peep. The Don was posed for flight, his foot placed on the first step up from the pit, drawing Zerlina on, and she holding back with what looked like only a token resistance, when ...

What in God's name is going on here? a voice bellowed.

The Duke had arrived.

4

It seems, said the Don, that a whole gaggle of nuns and priests and lawyers and spies have been sent for from the far corners of this tiny world and that it will take them until Friday to assemble. Close your mouth, Leporello. Are you bored?

I was. It was now Monday. We had been shut in these rooms for all of the hot Sunday. The Don did not attend Mass in the private chapel, as all guests were required to, because the Duke's chaplain had sent word forbidding him. It is very hard, said the Don sarcastically, to be denied entry to somewhere you had no intention of entering. I've mentioned this priest, I think. He was the same one who had been shocked over dinner by the Don's freethinking conversation. The same for whom the Don had arranged discreet meetings with various ladies in a room at the Castel d'Oro, for which I had to steal the key. This good priest was to be part of the tribunal set up to try the Don.

What happened in the ballroom when the Duke came? Ah, what a to-do.

I remember the Don standing in the middle of the dance pit,

alone as the others drew back. (I watched discreetly from round a pillar.) He looked massively well-humoured that night, like a God amused as their thunderbolts – Isabella's, Eleonora's, Ottavio's, even humble Masetto's – hurtled into the red ground around him. Isabella had arrived with the Duke. Stately, pale, shaking, her finger pointed at the Don like a spear. As for the Duke, it did not seem that he was so much put out at the near orgy he found in his palace as by this parade of voices and their accusations of seductions, spurnings, stealing of hearts, blasphemy, murder . . . until at last he cried, Enough! in a terrible voice.

He had heard all this, and more, he said. The most serious charges had been laid against the Don, he must be given a chance to answer them in a civilised fashion. The Duke set Friday for the hearing; by which time both parties must be ready. Meanwhile, the Don was to be furnished with copies of the affidavits sworn against him, and a list of the witnesses who would give their evidence in person, so that he might prepare a defence.

There were cries from the Ottavio–Isabella lobby that this was too much – such a monster should be banished forthwith. Silence, the Duke roared. If the Don is guilty let him be punished. But the judgment will be mine. And this ball is over. Carlo, I wish to see you . . .

Carlo, looking very much younger suddenly, squirmed, attempting to smile. Desiderio had disappeared.

The peasants were rounded up and hurried off, with Masetto snarling and twitching his face at the imperturbable Zerlina. The ladies and gentlemen melted away, as the ice in the great silver tureens of lemonade had, leaving only a fine rainbowed scum bowing and kow-towing to the Duke . . .

A servant had come to our rooms this morning bearing the documents in the case of Don Giovanni. These were spread around his bed. Every now and then, with a, Now listen to this, Leporello, he would read aloud some passage.

'Observed proceeding to meeting of the Freemasons. Entered furtively' – I was never furtive in my life. My God, the cheek – 'Entered furtively house of the radical Z-. Name of Rousseau heard spoken in the same terms as God by all present in their oaths . . . '

As I could attest, my master did think such people as this Rousseau and Diderot greater than any God. You see – I do know the true names. Never underestimate the common man, dear student. I could surprise you with my knowledge.

'He put his hand beneath my skirt and swore that he loved me, that he would die . . . ' Who the hell is this? said the Don. Some poor little maid they put up to swear I am a monster of lust . . . 'Pressed me against the wall and said he would kill me if I did not submit . . . ' More likely she would kill me . 'He came into my room through the window. I thought it was the Devil'. There are quite a few of these, he said, 'His eyes glowed like coals in the dark'. Ah, who would be at the expense of candles. Impious thoughts. Sleeping husbands. Foolish virgins.

'He suborned my mistress saying that he knew ways to make her young. How if she lay with him on a certain night under the stars as they were and the moon risen she would lose twenty years and he could love her twenty more . . . '

Moon. Stars. Magic – what defence need I put up against such rubbish, said the Don. A thousand men in any city might be faced with the same. But now this – 'Don preached equality of all men. Death to tyrants. Argued for the hanging of priests and princes' – there is the danger. Sedition. Rebellion. The Duke could not care less how many farmers I have spitted on my sword – or their daughters. All these tarts they bring against me, Leporello – who cares if what they say is true or not. But the other charges are grave. I must have enemies, he said, and seemed astonished at the thought. And here they are, he said. The list of witnesses. As he read, his face darkened. They have been busy, he murmured. There are some here capable of hanging me. Some of these account themselves as my friends.

He swore and threw the papers on the bed.

This is too tiresome, he said. The Duke is not the man to pay attention to tittle-tattle like this. Then he thought again for a while, and said slowly, No, these will not be the only accusations. There will be worse to come on Friday, unannounced, and they will be enough to hang me, no doubt. He smiled up at me from the bed. Then you, poor boy, will be forced to take a new position. And where will you find a master as forbearing as me, eh?

Hang you, sir? I was aghast.

Not yet. Not yet, he assured me with a laugh. Go and ask Don Carlo if he will be good enough to visit me here. He should come. His father rode out on the hunt this morning and will not be back until late.

Carlo hurried into the room, wailing, Ah, my dear, what is to happen to you?

Nothing, Your Excellency, as far as I know, said the Don. Just silly women chattering. But it is remarkably tedious to be confined to this room. Do you think you might allow me to walk about the palace – discreetly? If you have the power to grant such a thing? Carlo, chastened by whatever awful harangue he had had from his father, was evidently resentful. Power? he said loftily. Of course I have the power to grant that. Anything I wish. He tried to make his soft little vicious face stern. Yes, you may move freely, Don Giovanni. Within the confines of the palace.

A thousand thanks, Your Excellency, said the Don.

Carlo was silent for a moment, then stammered, As long, as long of course, as you keep away from the State quarters. My father, you understand.

Your father is out of humour with me, alas, said the Don. I would not wish to do anything to cause him further displeasure.

My father has never liked my friends, said Carlo darkly.

I am sure that is not so, said the Don.

There was the Englishman, Mister Leslie.

Most unfortunate, sighed the Don. Then, allowing Carlo to dwell in memories a moment, the Don spoke again.

It seems I may have to quit society for a time. Or even perhaps leave the city altogether ...

Oh, surely not, said Carlo.

Perhaps, perhaps, said the Don. He looked at his protégé.

However, it was my intention to mount a little entertainment

188

for my friends in this place – the gentlemen only, you understand. As I did for Your Excellency last year. But with all this ridiculous storm about my head ...

Carlo's eyes gleamed. An entertainment? Yes, why yes – if it was kept discreetly to a few ...

I don't know what the Don had arranged last year for the Duke's son. Though I had been involved in rounding up the company of stableboys, whores, two cockerels and a magician, I had not been allowed to witness their proceedings. The Don had told me that I was too young for such disgusting sights; that for his own part, after having seen every type of such show, in a dozen cities, it now amused him more to watch the audience at these occasions. They, he assured me, were far more diverting a spectacle than the poor, hired performers.

It would have to be a little broader in its appeal, he said to Carlo. Not all of the gentlemen here would appreciate the more specialised pleasures of the city.

Carlo was excited. Yes, yes, he agreed fervently. But the boys ...

You have some quite, ah, suitable-looking boys in your stables.

Carlo looked disappointed.

Or perhaps you would allow me to send my servant to town, and bring some choicer buds? the Don said.

Carlo brightened. Yes, most certainly. But, discreetly, Don Giovanni. Discreetly. My father ... He was terrified of the old man.

I thought we might use the theatre in the palace, the Don continued. A select audience. I will make a list of the guests and my servant will bring you a copy.

Carlo giggled and said, You are sure these are men that can be trusted?

I would trust them with my life, said the Don.

My father has a meeting in the city with the *Annone* on Thursday. Could it be done that night?

It leaves me little time, said the Don, with a heavy, mock sigh. But then, perhaps I have very little time left. Your father returns to hang me on Friday.

189

Carlo hastened to say that this was impossible, but something in his manner suggested that he might derive pleasure from witnessing the execution. Even of a friend. Perhaps especially of a friend.

They agreed on Thursday. Don Carlo was to have the theatre made ready. Don Giovanni to provide the actors. And the piece.

I was sent into the next room while they discussed matters of a more personal nature. I heard my name mentioned several times – as, Leporello can do that. And, Leave that to Leporello. And, Leporello is a good rider . . . My God, my mind reeled. If this entertainment was what I thought, what part in it were they planning for me? They talked and laughed. I was sent for wine, but soon after I came back Desiderio arrived on an errand from the Duke and took Carlo away.

At the door Carlo turned and said, The experiments, we will have time for them, Don Giovanni? I was so looking forward to the death of the doves.

How could I disappoint Your Excellency? said the Don. We shall have time to kill many creatures, I am sure.

Ah, I am so glad, Carlo breathed. And went off in the custody of his loving Sergeant.

Now, said the Don, let us pick the distinguished audience for my entertainment. Bring your book, Leporello.

Which book, sir? I said.

The book, idiot, he said. Let's see which of the little men match up with this. He held up the list of witnesses he had had from the Duke. If they can name names, so can I, he said.

I did as he asked, and he settled down contentedly, tearing up slips of paper, and inscribing notes on them. When I brought the Don his evening meal and coffee he was still scribbling away. He said he wanted to be alone, but I was to remain near. I went into the dressing-room and slept. Like a dog, as I said. And like a dog you had to catch your sleep when you could with such a master. He got on with his writings. Or perhaps he slept too – he had to sleep sometime. It was deep night outside the window when he next called me into him.

He had pushed his papers aside and stood looking out at the

night. Lights were burning in the opposite wing, perhaps the sedate music was playing once more: in our part of the palace there was only silence.

He turned away from the window and looked at me. I've never been trumped yet, Leporello, he said. I have resolved – or it has been resolved for me – that we shall have to leave this place. It will do us good to travel. I have been here too long. Too much time for troubles to mount up and breed. Still, we'll have some fun with them first. And what shall we do with tonight, eh? Something to amuse us?

My heart sank. We were in enough trouble as it was. He said, You know, you looked well in my best clothes, Leporello. Quite the gentleman. And when I took your part – I didn't realise what a fine time you servants have. The food you eat. The things you say about your masters. But I didn't waste my moments in your existence. While you were at the dancing, I was at your work. If you can call it that. What a garrulous, gabbing lot you servants are. If I had been dressed as a gentleman I'd have had to bribe half the country for the secrets I was given gratis. And, before I joined the peasants, I went in search of your choice beauty again. I must admit I spent a few pleasant moments with her earlier – but there has been no opportunity for any union between our souls . . .

To myself I cursed Maria and the Don and the whole deceitful race of men and women.

Alas, I could not find her, he said. But you know where she and Eleonora are lodged, don't you? Your nose can take us there. And on the way we'll find out where Isabella is hiding herself.

Oh, no sir, what are we letting ourselves in for now? I couldn't help saying.

What's the matter?

Surely we have enough trouble with that lady, I said.

We? Trouble? Not nearly enough, he said.

He insisted we go as master and servant transposed again. He was already in only shirt and breeches; I was made to put on his long court coat once more, and we set out.

I asked a footman to show us the way to Donna Isabella's door. When we came near, in a corridor dimly lit by one tiny lantern at the far end, he pointed to the door, and asked, Shall I knock, sir? Who shall I announce? My 'servant' took his arm, halting him, and said, We are Don Giovanni. We shall announce ourselves. The footman shook himself free and looked at me as if to say, What sort of servants do you country gentleman employ? That's all right. Perfectly all right, I blustered. And he went away, stopping at the corner of the two corridors to look back at us again.

Now to the business in hand, the Don whispered, as we stood before the door.

What business would that be, sir? I asked, knowing full well it could only be mischief or worse.

Surely you wish to enjoy the fruits of your position? said the Don.

What fruits would those be, sir? I enquired.

My dear boy, the love of a woman of high position.

Not more women, I groaned.

More women? Of course, more women. They are the air that we breathe. The holy spirit.

I crossed myself. But Donna Isabella . . . , I began.

Keep your voice down, he said.

But she has complained of you to the Duke. Forgive me master, but what use is it you making love to her?

Not me – you. You are dressed for the part.

This is madness, I whispered, You. Me. She has no love for either of us.

He drew in his breath irritably. Ah, when will you understand women, Leporello, he said. It *grieves* Isabella's heart to do these things to me; but her pride, her conscience, her family – her city indeed – demand that she wag her tongue this way. Why did she travel here alone? Not simply to take her revenge. She still has hopes of me, Leporello. I'll wager on that. Perhaps she has hopes of saving my soul – and a little of my body too into the bargain.

But why me, sir? I pleaded.

It is a game. An amusement. Don't you have any spark of curiosity in you? I want to watch me at work. And then there is the little maid. After you have settled I can steal away. She's the sort of honest girl who would be afraid of a grand gentleman –

her mother has told her what to expect of *their* attentions. But as a valet ... I must have her, Leporello, or my breeches will burst. Then heaven knows which way my desires might stray.

The Don loomed darkly before me, his face a few inches from mine.

I backed away in alarm. Not me, sir. What can you mean ... ?

His leering face broke into a laugh. So you are not so innocent, he said. You must have been a pretty youth indeed, Leporello, to know so much. Now – knock on the door. And remember you are Don Giovanni. The great, the irresistible, the potent Turk, Don Giovanni.

But sir. How do I ... ?

Knock. I will speak for you. And stand off from the light. Draw your collar up.

Trust me, he whispered from the alcove in which he was concealing himself.

My God, what a hope.

I knocked; a timid servant's knock.

Louder, the Don commanded.

I knocked again. Almost at once a voice from inside – a weak, tearful voice that one would never have thought could have issued from the proud Isabella – demanded to know who was there, what was wanted?

I opened my mouth, but the Don's deep strong voice spoke first.

Isabella. Isabella. It is Don Giovanni. Giovanni ...

There was an awful silence. Then – G ... Go away. How dare you? What do you want?

Isabella. My mouth moved after his words. Barred from you by the cruelty of this closed door how may I implore your pardon? I repent. I have been temporarily mad. I adore you, dear Isabella.

There was no answer. Another terrible silence. Then the key scraped in the lock. The door opened a little.

Turn down your lamp, my dear, or douse your candle. I do not wish you to see the pain that repentance has etched upon my face. And you – ah, dear God – have you been weeping? Turn down your light, so that only Heaven may look upon us.

A patter of retreating footsteps. The candle inside was blown out.

You . . . you may come in, the small voice said.

My feet stuttered. The Don's hand propelled me forward.

I will leave the door open, my love, in care for your honour.

The Don's voice followed me like a warm wind into the room.

You cared little for that two years ago. Her voice, though with a catch in it, had grown a little stronger. Two long, suffering years. If I could think for just one moment that you truly mean what you say . . .

I do. I do, my angel.

(The rogue must have been right by the door post, smiling in the shadows.)

I stood in the room, what light there was from the corridor at my back. Isabella's white face floated in the darkness.

Ah, if you knew how many tears you have wrung from me, she said. How many nights have passed without sleep. How I . . . I dreamed that we were married. That you came to me that day in your wedding clothes and we . . . and then . . . we . . . I dreamed the very colour and pattern of the carpet of the room in which we slept . . .

Do not torture yourself with these remembrances, said the Don softly.

You will stay? You won't go again?

Never. I swear.

Why did the Don, a man who would kill for his honour, lie so readily? Because it was to a woman. A man's word between men is his bond of honour. My master detested lies, hypocrisy, and double-dealing. But a woman is a campaign. A war.

Then . . .

My own . . . For she was in my arms and our lips met before I knew what was happening. And that was very nice – not that her mouth was any different from that of a maid, but in that they all taste a little different from each other, or why should we fall in love with one rather than another? Only the lips were somewhat thin, and I never cared much for that.

She broke away from me. There is someone there, she said. At the door. I saw the shape of a head.

It was plainly impossible for me to rely on the Don's voice now.

Impossible, I said, muffling my voice in his coat collar.

Look outside for me, she pleaded. Perhaps we are watched. After what I have set in train ...

I gladly made for the door.

As I lurched out into the passage, the Don, with a soft *pfff* of breath, blew out the lamp at the end. And the swaying light of a lantern appeared at the other end of the corridor. The way was cut off. In my panic I bolted back into Isabella's room. Do not light your candle, I said, closing the door. Someone is coming. All this in a haughty, ridiculous impersonation of the Don.

I have no fear, she declared boldly. My God, these women; contrary, their feelings forever in a spin, they never go in the direction you want. It's like pissing in a whirlwind trying to argue with them.

Please be quiet, I begged, and leaned against the door, listening.

In the corridor a rough voice said loudly, Halt. Who is that?

And who is that? The Don's voice.

I am Masetto. From the village of Caesaretto.

Ah – but I know you, said the Don, as if recognising him for the first time. Your wife danced with my master this afternoon.

And who may your master be? snarled the bear.

Don Giovanni, said Don Giovanni with pride.

That's the wretch I seek. Where is he? I have no quarrel with you – but you must tell me. Poor Masetto sounded half-insane with rage.

What is it? Where are you? Isabella whispered. What game is this?

Please, be quiet. I must hear.

What is wrong with your voice? She was close to me again. There is something ... I am going to light my candle

My love – we shall be discovered, I growled.

If I could only find the tinderbox. She scrabbled blindly about behind me.

I applied my ear to the door again. I *must* escape.

A pistol, I heard the Don say. You mean to shoot him?

He must die, said the terrible Masetto. It is the law.

Then follow me, said the Don, sounding most light-hearted. I will lead you to my wicked master. About time the devil was taught a lesson. Why, let me tell you . . . The voices faded away down the corridor.

And – God – what was that? A star in the room? A spark. Another. Soon there would be light. I felt around for the door knob. Some demon had moved it.

Now, Don Giovanni . . . , Isabella said.

Candlelight glowed on the wall.

Ah, there was the handle. I pulled open the door.

You are not leaving? she cried.

I must, I cried, sweeping my hand in the air in a tragic gesture – as I had seen the players do – and made my escape.

My escape!

What a nightmare.

Almost at once, as I closed the door I heard a groan from one end of the corridor, and from the other a low babble of voices. A dim flickering of candles neared the corner. Then a veritable thicket of bobbing, burning candles presented themselves, coming towards me; and under them, the faces of Ottavio, Eleonora, the village bride – what was her name? – ah, Zerlina. And with them two or three servants, in whose hands swords and knives glittered.

Then came a cry of, Seize him, seize him, from behind me. Masetto stumbled out of the darkness. His coat was torn. A black worm of blood oozed from his nostril to his upper lip.

Which way could I go? As I hesitated both horrible parties drew nearer to me along the corridor. Every moment the light grew stronger. I tried to hide my face in shadow.

But Masetto came hobbling on, and as he did, Zerlina broke from the ranks of Ottavio's party and dashed past me. She embraced her husband with many sobs and avowals of love, and demands to know what had happened to him. He allowed her to support him as he limped along, though not without him spitting, Your fault, your fault, out of the side of his mouth at her. They would make a fine couple.

I buried my face in the coat collar. The two avenging factions arrived on either side of me at almost the same moment.

Masetto raised an accusing paw. You are Don Giovanni. Outside this room I met your servant, who tricked me into going with him, saying he would lead me to you. He took me up there – he pointed to the lightless end of the corridor – and beat me. Before I could see what he was about. Or he would have rued the day . . . And, without a doubt, Masetto must have come off worst from the encounter, or the other man was surely dead. And you – he flung Zerlina off his arm – you're the cause of all this, he bellowed. Fresh from the altar, from the eyes of the Virgin looking down on you, you went off with this man.

I tried to look the libertine, while still turning my face from their light.

Ottavio spoke next, in a most pompous tone, It seems, signore, that not content with the catalogue of crimes you have already committed against decency and the laws of this State – he'd obviously been rehearsing this – you now add to your offences by setting your servant on this poor man and attempting to ravish his bride.

Strike him for me, sir. Strike him for me, came Masetto's hoarse entreaty. He still knew his place, you see.

Let me pass, I bellowed into the collar, hoping to bluff my way out.

Hold him. For the first time Eleonora spoke. In that voice of glass and ice.

I don't have to tell you that by this time I was scared. I was close to shitting myself.

Don Giovanni! There came a despairing wail through the door at my back. I clung to the handle to keep it shut.

Take heart, dear lady, said Ottavio loudly, we have the villain here. Remain inside your room. But though he fingered the hilt of his sword, his fingers were nervous. He must have heard of the Don's prowess with that weapon – if not the other – from Eleonora.

But then came a malicious cry from Masetto of, Don't kill him, sir. Beat him. And without more ado the ruffian rushed on me, his great fists pressed together in one mighty club, and delivered such a blow on my shoulder. God send us – the pain. I thought my arm had come off.

Yes. Beat. Beat, cried Eleonora. Ah, the bitch was excited now.

Come men, said Ottavio. This man is to be thrashed. Another blow from Masetto felled me to my knees.

Good sirs, for Christ's sake, stop, I yelled.

The door, released by me, opened; out came Isabella.

Oh murder, murder, she shrieked.

The assassins drew back. Eleonora rushed to Isabella's side. They were all in it together, these women. Go back, Donna Isabella, said her friend. We have him. You are safe.

Good sirs, I wailed, I am not the Don.

Coward. Bastard. Worm. Then who the hell are you? Masetto demanded. He thrust his fingers into my hair and pulled my head back. Ottavio thrust his candle forward.

It's that little bastard Leporello, said Eleonora. She laughed. That's not the Don.

Leporello? said Ottavio.

The Don's servant. His accomplice, Eleonora said.

Am I to be deceived again? Isabella moaned.

There, there, my dear, Eleonora comforted her. He shall be beaten. Twice. Once for his master and once for himself.

But the Don made me do it, I protested from my painful pose.

Be quiet, scum, said Masetto. His fingers tightened in my hair. I thought each hair must be popping out, one by one. Tears, for myself, for my hair, for my pain, sprang to my eyes.

You mean to say, said Ottavio, in a new, determined voice, now that he knew that he had only *me* to deal with, You mean to say that you – a servant – impersonated your master to gain entrance to this lady's bedchamber?

No, no, the Don ... (Where in God's name was my protector, my master, while this injustice was being visited on me? Stuffing my girl.) It is all the Don, I whimpered.

Oh villains. I see it all, Isabella sobbed. Let me see him punished.

Yes indeed, madam, Ottavio said. But he took a step back. He could not now soil his hands on a mere servant. You two men. And you. What is your name?

Masetto, your exaltedship, said Masetto. He leered into my face, raising his fist. The two servants drew near, expecting to make a treat of me.

Masetto, you shall be rewarded for your part in discovering this subterfuge, Ottavio announced. Now, lay on, my men. Lay on.

Oh stay, sir, I cried out, attempting at the same time to struggle up off my knees. The Don, you would not know such a master, I gabbled. He ordered me to come here. And here – I slapped my pockets – A letter. He gave me a letter. To give to Donna Eleonora . . .

(Anything to get out of this damn mess.)

My wife? Ottavio's voice was sharp and anxious. What letter? Let him up. The letter, the letter, he demanded.

Here. I brought out a piece of paper from the Don's pocket. God knows what it was. Bring your light nearer, I said.

Ottavio leaned over me, thrusting forward greedily.

As he did, I swept out with my arm, knocking the candle from his grasp, and fetching Masetto a good one in the mouth. His teeth hurt me, but he squealed. Your letter, I shouted. I dropped the paper and ran.

It took me an eternity, twisting and turning in the dim or black corridors to find our rooms. And where do you think the Don had just got back from?

What has happened to you, dear boy, he said. Look at my coat. My God, can't I trust you with anything . . . ?

To hell with it.

Why hadn't they pursued me? Perhaps they did for a while. But remember, they were only guests, as we were, and hardly made of the same mettle as the Don and perhaps they got lost after a while in the great vaulted and burrowed palace. After all, they had their day waiting for them. Their day of indictments and confrontations; the Don's come-uppance come round at last.

Well, *he* retired quite merry at the outcome. I sat up half the night on watch, dozed fitfully, and woke to find a guard placed outside. We stayed in the rooms until noon, when the Duke summoned the Don.

The Don dressed resplendently; insisting that I too dress in the best he could spare me – but now as his servant rather than a counterfeit gentleman. Be sure, as a servant your days of grandeur are few and snatched out of the ordinary. You own nothing – not even your soul. That is a malleable item in most people, but in service your very thoughts are at the beck and call of your master. A servant is nothing apart from his master. He develops a dual character; part parody of his master, part parody of himself. The original character of the servant dwindles as the years pass, until he has been almost wholly absorbed by his master and functions as no more than an extra limb or organ to that unregarding monster.

How we strut in our master's cast-off clothes, boast of the size of his household; how jealously we guard our position in it and scheme to grow closer to our masters, so that we may shut out the light from shining on others. For the closer you are allowed to come, the higher your position in the household. The mistress is first, steward second, valet next, and so all the way down to the old pensioner who holds the door, the slip of a kitchen girl warming her toes by the fire. And all this, I suppose, is waste and vanity, but not more than the rest of the world, which is only a series of households under God. Do not our masters serve Dukes and Kings themselves? And do not higher servants have lower servants to spurn? And they, in their turn, can spit on beggars. It was true, as my father had told me, that our position in life is fixed by our stars, by our Fortune, and we may as well accept it, for great misery comes from those who would overthrow such order as there is.

These thoughts come to me now, as I remember walking with the Don, and the terror I felt at meeting with the Duke. I fully expected to be hung, or at the least to be taken away decked in chains to provide another poor inmate for Carlo to visit in the Pomodoro dungeons. To console myself, I asked how I could be blamed for carrying out the Don's instructions? Servant and master are one, surely. How can the hand be blamed for doing what the mind tells it?

Why should I have worried? I'm still here, aren't I?

At my age all terrors are idle. Except one.

As soon as we came into the room the Duke got up out of his chair and began pacing energetically to and fro in front of us, talking nineteen to the dozen.

I really cannot spare the time to deal with all this, my good sir. It's not as if it was just the ladies who have laid complaints against you, but now I have a horde of people besieging me, all stirred up by these damned women. Agents out all over the city, sifting the dirt you have left behind you. Spies and dirty monks invited by the coachload. My dear Don Giovanni, this was designed to be a place of rest and retreat, where I could get a little peace and quiet. Now it is overrun by harridans shrieking your name, by cuckolds and shamed fathers after your blood. Well? Well? He ceased his pacing and glared at the Don.

I hardly know, Excellency, what to say, said the Don suavely . I have read the documents and affidavits you so kindly sent me. I am confident in my defence against them. In essence, what do the charges against me amount to?

The Duke charged into the Don's sweet reason. That you can't control your cock, sir, he trumpeted. That you are led by the nose by it.

Which is an odd way of putting it.

The Duke said, This lady, Donna Isabella – she is the daughter of the cousin of the Duke of –, who is a close friend of the King of –, who trades with my King, who is my master. These are people not to be trifled with, Don Giovanni. If I had known that you would drag all this trouble behind you when you came to me . . . We all like a woman, but you really should examine their connections. At least of those connected to me.

Excellency. The Don's voice was humble.

And what was all this business last night? asked the Duke.

Last night . . . ? The Don's face put on a puzzled air, and he looked at me as if I could somehow explain what, if anything, had happened last night.

It seems, said the Duke, that a fresh insult was offered to Donna Isabella. Whether or not – the story is like a bloody opera – all candles, hysterical women, beatings, serenades, servants running around in disguise . . .

(I stood against the wall, trying to look like one of the statues.)

A misunderstanding, the Don murmured.

Well, they insist that you be punished, said the Duke. Now, don't try to fool me. He waved the Don down. I welcomed you here and was grateful to you for keeping my son out of mischief. I thought you had a bit more about you than most men. It seems you have quite a bit more about you. For the first time the Duke laughed. Then remembered to frown again. But I will not be in bad odour with my princes, Don Giovanni, because of what you give their women. We have – come here. The Duke beckoned to a man dressed in lawyer's cloth, who had stood silent and unobserved through all this. The lawyer or whatever he was came forward, a sheaf of papers laid across his outstretched hands.

The Duke picked up first one then another of the papers. You see, we have here more of them, he said. Depositions, accusations, indictments, anonymous denunciations – what you will. Not one of them has a good word to say about you – or if they did, they have neglected to furnish me with them.

I do not ask for recommendations, said the Don.

The Duke slapped the papers on the lawyer's pile again. This girl – what's her name? – seems to have been the one to have set things alight. Says you murdered her father. Hardly sounds right. What was it – a duel?

I was not aware of anything dishonourable on my part, said the Don. The man had a sword. And his man a gun pointed at my head.

Enough said, said the Duke. (All these things being easily explainable between gentlemen.) He waved the lawyer away and went and sat back in his chair. He yawned. I have to go back to the city tomorrow and would appreciate this matter being cleared up without recourse to any lengthy proceedings. Many people want rid of you. Now – we can have all these read and call all of these damn fool witnesses and spies and adjourn to the city if there is a case to answer and try you there and hang you there, if need be. It will take a great deal of our time . . .

The Duke left the rest of his sentence hanging, as the Don would be, in mid-air.

I would not dream of putting you to that trouble, your Excellency, said the Don. I have just one request.

Of course, my dear sir, said the Duke, equable now that the gentlemanly thing was to be done, that his time was not to be wasted further.

I had arranged, said the Don, to present a small entertainment in the palace. I had hoped Your Excellency might join us. On Thursday evening?

I shall be in the city, Don Giovanni. And for me to appear . . . No. But by all means go ahead. But mind – Thursday, Friday – it leaves you little time. You have my meaning?

I understand, the Don murmured sweetly. It only remains for me to thank you for all your past kindnesses, Your Excellency.

Yes, yes. Well, now, Matters of State to attend to. Good of you to be so reasonable, Don Giovanni. He nodded his head in amiable dismissal.

Your Excellency is too . . . All sweetness and charm, the Don bowed himself backwards out of the room, pulling me along on an invisible string. Outside his countenance changed. To be dismissed so. Like a footman, he said bitterly. Well, we shall make a good exit, Leporello. A good exit.

Don Giovanni sat at the table in his window for the rest of the afternoon, writing letters and working at his other papers.

He asked me to take two of the letters down to Ragoti, our coachman, and tell him where to deliver them in the city. I read the superscriptions. One was to the Abbess at the brothel. The other to a Signor Ambrogetti, an actor.

I found Ragoti in the stableyard, playing dice with the boys left over from the village party. Too idle to return home, they'd chosen to stay and add themselves to the palace staff. I roused him up and gave him his instructions. He spat into the ground at my feet, but ambled off for a horse, and a little while later I saw him canter off towards the city. When I went back up the Don was again with Carlo. I could hear the young man giggling as the Don read something to him in a loud, mock-heroic voice.

Ragoti returned in the late evening and came to the Don's room to report.

Had he found the Abbess in?

Yes, he said.

Could she do what was asked?

She asks five hundred soldi.

The letter promised to pay her, said the Don. But not that much. And Ambrogetti, the actor?

The coachman regretted, milord, he hadn't found the actor. But he had left the letter at the theatre for him.

Ragoti looked pleased at his own cleverness. The Don did not and called him an idiot. His instructions were to give the letter by hand to the actor. Fool, imbecile, he fumed.

Do you not think, sir, I humbly suggested, that the theatre will forward the letter to Signor Ambrogetti's lodgings.

Oh, in time. In time, the Don said. It could lay in some pigeon-hole all summer or be lost. This is too much. Leporello.

Yes sir. I jumped up, the bright as a button servant, beside the oafish Ragoti. The Don told me that I must go to the city, find Ambrogetti and bring him back without fail. I followed the coach-man down and watched him resentfully saddle a horse for me. Then I set off westwards into the dying sun.

It was dark when I got to the city. I first went to the Teatro del Fondo and hammered and hammered on its tall locked doors till a little port opened high up and a dusty old voice asked what was wanted? There were no plays. All the gentry were out of the city.

Cutting him short, with the chinking of money, I quickly recovered the letter and got Signor Ambrogetti's address.

My, the places where these actors really live – they who sit on stage in make-believe palaces, wearing the most gorgeous silks and jewels. I had seen this man acting at the grandest theatre, though it was said he was past his best, long past his youth, and that soon he would be pressed down or out of the company, yet he had what my master called a stumbling grandeur. To find out that he lived like everyone else in a tenement with children tumbling in the hallway came as a shock. I mounted through the warm stinks of food and excrement to the top, where Ambrogetti lived, perched in a loft like a great, bald owl.

For that is what he looked like as I knocked and he answered, looking down at me from his height, his massive body blocking out the doorway. Who? Who? he intoned. A drunk owl. There was a bottle open on the table and empties gathered round each leg like hungry families.

He didn't invite me to take a drink. He sat down and huffed and puffed over the letter. Quite impossible, he said, even for his good friend the Don. Why there was a mighty tragedy he must rehearse for; a journey to Rome; a multiplicity – ah, how he lingered over that word – of parts he had under consideration. When I showed him the purse of gold the Don had sent, his tone changed at once. He dressed rapidly and put on an auburn, tight-curled wig over his baldness, and then another, a white peruke, on top of that. Then he kept going to and fro into dim corners of the room to turn over this or that pile of costumes or properties, coming back to consult the Don's letter every now and then, and then lurching off again on a forage. At last he had everything packed into a long carpetbag – and then there we are, on the road to Caesaretto, though now it is night, with my grey pony tied behind the small black chaise bearing the huge blubbery emperor, King, ghost, or whatever he is being fetched to play.

By the time we got back it was late. The Don allowed me retire to my couch in the outer room, while he and the actor went on talking and turning over the Don's writings. I went to sleep to the rumble of their voices. In the morning they were still at it and I went out to deliver messages to the servants of the men the Don had chosen to invite to his entertainment. The rumour that something was about to happen to the Don had seized good and hard in the palace by now. There was to be a trial; the cause of it some scandal too awful to be told beforehand, and to which everyone was only too willing to put in his or her fourpenn'orth. The Don had seduced the Duke's wife. Had offended the Archbishop by propounding Freemasonry and worse heresies. Had committed buggery. Bestialism. Was a wizard. Had the legs of a goat. The member of a stallion. Could pierce through stone. It was difficult to know which of the things that used to amuse them in gossip they found worse now. Soon the Don would be punished for his blasphemy and lechery, said some of the men, smacking their lips in anticipation of feeding on the corpse. Others, whose wives had been visited by the two wronged women, Isabella and Eleonora, feared that they might be among the husbands to be named when the Don was brought to book. So they hastened to accuse him of every other crime they could think of; rather to be seen as public-minded citizens than jealous cuckolds. They would all, husbands and wives, sleep easier in their beds if this gentleman left the city.

All this I gathered from their servants; hunting them out most of the day, one passing me to another. Whenever their masters caught sight of me and were told who I was, they informed me gravely of their undying devotion to the Don. Their determination to defend him. Yes, they would be only too pleased to attend the Don's entertainment. *Always such an amusing fellow.* Leaving them, with a bow, I discreetly ticked off their names in the Don's book.

And when I mounted through the palace once more and looked down from the windows, I saw these people taking their walks in the garden below, stopping every now and then in huddles, looking up, pointing to the Don's windows. How little they knew, these good gentlemen, but how much tortured in their thoughts and suspicions they must have been as they walked with their ladies.

The Don's windows were open to summer. The birds sang blithely; fountains tinkled and tiddled and plashed below; behind me the Don talked in an easy, deep voice to the actor, his pen scratching, then stopping as he passed the actor a sheet of paper and the two men read to each other, putting on odd voices; booming male; piping female – the two of them laughing at each other's jokes – the actor's laugh dutifully following the Don's.

I said once, said the Don, that it was impossible to imagine any sin that would get a man banished from Pomodoro. The good citizens have committed all the known ones, and most possible permutations on them, so you'd think they'd welcome any fresh ideas.

The actor laughed, rumbling in his booming, fraudulent voice, Ah-ha, you do not mean that, sir. By God, you're a character, sir.

The Don called to me. Hey, Leporello. What is going on out there in the bright world of my enemies?

They are just walking in the gardens, sir, I said. Walking and talking.

So the afternoon passed, with the Don and the actor piecing together their drama. In the evening Carlo arrived in high spirits to tell them that his father had left for the city and would not return until Friday, and all three of them fell to plotting the entertainment, which was to take place the next night, Thursday, on the eve of the hearing.

When they had gone that night, the Don at last went to bed. He woke refreshed and summoned me with a cheerful shout. I was to get the big trunk and the other boxes packed, but to leave them in our rooms until night fell, when Ragoti was to take them down while we were at the theatre. He was to have the carriage ready at the unlit entrance in the stableyard at midnight – for this was to be our last happy day at the palace. And there, I've told you enough for now. Let's pass on to the night. That's what you really want to hear about. The entertainment. The escape.

The scene is the little theatre at the rear of the palace. On the first floor: a long narrow room, with galleries running its two long sides, at the end the stage, and its arch showing cherubs and nymphs, and Neptune in his cockleshell chariot drawn by plunging horses; all gaily painted in pink flesh and blue sky and green sea and yellow manes and a gilded trident. There are no windows, but lamps along the walls and three small chandeliers, though tonight the Don has had them all put out, except a pair of candles at the door, so that the stage gives out a warm, mellow glow. And on the stage the Don stalks about, ordering two servants to manhandle two sofas into the positions he desires, to do this, do that, the orders all most purposefully and energetically given, while Carlo follows him to and fro, tweaking at him in his weak voice, What *is* the show, Don Giovanni? Will there be boys? Will it be a real show tonight? A *real* show?

All my shows are real, says the Don magisterially.

Through a servant, I had heard that some of the wives had got wind of this evening's entertainment and had enquired if they might accompany their husbands. The men had insisted, saying contradictorily, No, no – it is that rogue Don Giovanni. It is a serious matter. Not fit for your ears ... Now, what was not fit for their ears that the Don had not already whispered to them?

The two servants had hauled up a backcloth representing the mountain outside the city. A tawdry, garish painting of the beast spewing out huge tongues of red and yellow flame, with tiny faces gazing terrified towards it. The Mouth of Hell indeed. I followed the men round and saw them place four pots about the size of small wine casks in a line some way behind the cloth. The Don came round and told them to fix fuses to them, but keep all lights away. They are our grand finale, he said to Carlo. I thought they resembled bombs. The Don caught my worried look and said, laughing, Simply fireworks, Leporello. I'm not going to blow the place up. The men sprinkled sand thickly on the boards around to save sparks from catching.

At the very back of the stage, beside a paper and cloth palm tree, were three boys. Two, bare to the waist, stood idly about, while the third knelt before the actor I had brought from the city. He was painting the boy's torso and face bright red with a small brush dipped in a large pot and laid on with a perhaps too caressing hand. Carlo stood and watched, his eyes eating up the boys.

I heard women's voices gabbling brightly in the front. Ah, the ladies, said the Don. We went round the backcloth again, and there, mounting the side steps onto the stage, were four beautiful young women, dressed in fine white shifts which brushed the boards. As one stepped forward a footlight shone through her shift's delicate stuff and I saw that she wore nothing underneath and I could see the whole beautiful shape of her slim legs, the delicious rounds of her thighs, the delectable curving of her hips ... My God, I can see her now, in this one miserable candle light.

Come up. Come up. The Don kissed each on the hand, and they seemed thoroughly familiar with him. He ordered one of the servants to fetch wine and food for his guests.

Who are the ladies? I enquired innocently as the Don swung back across the stage and came up to me.

What – you don't recognise them? My little nieces? He laughed. Why, fool – these girls are sent from the Abbess. But there should be five. Where is the other?

Below in the carriage, sir, they chorused. As there is no part for her.

I stared at them, wondering how women so much *used* could look so young and virginal. In their white dresses they might have been queueing for their First Communion.

The Don's eyes were amused as he watched me staring at the women.

You contacted as many of your fellow servants as you could, Leporello? he asked. You told them eleven o'clock?

Why yes, sir, I said.

And for them to be discreet?

Oh yes, sir.

Good, then it will have been blabbed all over the palace by now. What are they talking about down there?

About you, sir. Nothing but you.

He was well pleased at this, and taking me by the shoulder with a friendly hand he led me backstage. Now for your part, Leporello ...

The boys, two now with glistening red-painted bodies, and all in puffed-out red satin breeches, stood watching the last boy being daubed. My heart sank. Surely the Don did not want me to be painted as well. Or perhaps he had some more humiliating guise for me?

But ... I will say no more of what he told me, or our further preparations – the women getting up from where they had sat eating and drinking on the two sofas, the Don handing them slips of paper. No, no more. It will give our play away. We must keep our secrets of illusion to ourselves, we men of the theatre ...

By the time appointed the little theatre is rapidly filling. Gentlemen unable to gain a seat mill at the back, their heads bobbing black against the light from the corridor. Others lean over the rail of the galleries and chat or call to their acquaintance below. Half a dozen musicians pressed up against the foot of the stage are playing some dreary minuet. The footlights show the stage empty but for the two sofas. Behind the backcloth a lantern has been hoisted to shine through, making the red flame at the top of the mountain glow like a huge coal. I watch all this from the side edge of the cloth so I can see forward into the dark auditorium; or onto the stage; or backstage, where the red boys play dice.

The Don chats quietly to the whores. The actor paces up and down, mouthing silently from a sheaf of papers. He has dressed himself gloriously and preposterously out of his carpetbag as a man of high fashion, a sword at his side, a blue and gold embroidered mask covering the upper part of his face; his lips made up in a red, slightly smeared, licentious smirk ...

There is a babble of intense conversation from the audience. Trembling, I, *I*, make my entrance and announce –

THE TERRIBLE TRAGEDY OF DON JUAN OF SEVILLE.

Some of the gentlemen laugh. Others complain, We have not come here to watch a *play*. A voice enquires loudly, Where is *our* Don Juan? Nervously I pull out the scroll of paper the Don has given me.

> Masters and Lords, Common-men and Kings.
> You are summoned here to see such things
> The stout heart should know, the honest mouth will tell,
> How that great man, Don Juan, was took to Hell.

These are the lines as I remember them; I'm no poet. The Don had made them up from the coarse vulgar stuff in the shows of this play performed at streetcorners in the city.

I read on:

> This paper you see, is one which is writ
> With all true tales of his wiles and wit;
> What cannot be said, we will honestly show,
> What cannot be shown, we will tell to you.
> But if your wife you trust, and think this a sin,
> Please to withdraw, or let the play begin,
> And take your chance that your name be not herein . . .

At which I turned the scroll with its long list of scribbled names towards them. There was again laughter, but it was uneasy, as if each one of them feared that by not joining in he might be thought a cuckold.

I withdrew.

The play began.

The actor strutted onto the stage. Now I realise that he is meant to represent Don Giovanni. Is this how the Don sees himself? His breeches bulge enormously at the crotch.

He booms:

> True rogues are most desired by others' wives,
> I visit two – and must avoid their husband's knives.

He advances to the front of the stage, his rouged cheeks cushioning his mask, mouthing more nonsense, his lecherous mouth chewing and mewing and ogling at the words. Two of the whores come on. Each sits down on a sofa. They get up at the same time. Raising hands to shield eyes, in dumb-show they look down from imaginary windows into a non-existent street. Whoever they are looking for, they fail to see the huge form of the actor with his back to them. This is how they do things in the playhouse.

Now the two women abandon their airy windows. They show signs – sighs, hands to fevered brows – that they are languishing for love. They lie themselves moping down on their sofas.

The masked 'Don' stands proud, his hand on his upthrust sword pommel. Without moving his body, his head goes round, his eyes flicker as he catches sight of first one couched beauty, then, his head moving slowly all the way round, of the second. His face returns to gaze in utter silence at the gentlemen gathered below, and his big red mouth smiles, spreading like a wound across his face, his eyes glittering through the mask, his right fist rising in *that* gesture.

Then, all amorous briskness, he twists round and takes a couple of steps – it was only a small stage – towards the first sofa. He halts, raises one hand, knocks on air, and thumps down twice on the boards with his heel.

Ah, our beauty stirs languorously on the bed, her eyes open slowly, they are afire – then her face drops, she mouths –

My husband!

But the false Don whispers, like distant thunder:

> No, no, my darling; have no such fear;
> It is your own, your lover is here!

The young lady jumps up from her couch, takes a step forward, unlatches the airy door. The 'Don' strides into her wall-less room, in its phantasmal house, in this transparent city.

> Now I bring you passion, fire and love;
> Come fly to my heart, my little dove.

And she does – with a pretty billowing of her white gown. They embrace; big man, black clothes; small woman, white. There are no more words for the time being. He holds her a moment longer, then lays her down on the couch. She draws her legs up, plants her feet on the couch, her knees tenting her shift. And we can see – *they* can see – Ah, now; wait, no – yes – no – almost all the way up her exposed thighs. The mock Don reaches down and pulls apart the pleats of his baggy breeches. And out pops the most enormous pink and purple mock cock ever seen. On a spring or somesuch, I suppose. It leaps and bobs as he advances on the delighted female. This was in none of the street plays. The Don's addition to the text.

She takes it between her hands and strokes it, and addresses the great engine daintily with her lips. Then she lies back, and moans and writhes about so that her shift rides up again, but further this time, and at last the gentlemen can see all. Together, they sound like a dragon snorting and licking its lips. And for me, stuck behind that poxy curtain? A glimpse of her black bush. The 'Don' takes another step forward and cuts off *their* view. Oh, the cries of outrage, mixed with, Go to sir. Ah, now sir. Make her squirm, sir, as they see him close upon her. The great actor lowers himself down, the prodigious size of his stage member making him look like a three-legged stool. Of course, he didn't penetrate her with this monstrous weapon. As he dibs and drives and delves, the pump-handle wobbles and bobbles and slides on her tum. And though she moans and groans and wriggles and wiggles, I can see from my vantage point that her face turns to stone under him, glows again in delight only when in the candlelight. For all this was for the benefit of the audience, who truly thought they were watching the act of love.

His task performed to her seeming satisfaction the 'Don' raises himself up off her. She sits up. She reaches out her arms in supplication. But the great lover only bows, packs back his mighty tool, half-turns to face the assembly and announces:

> No, no my dear; I must now fly.
> Footsteps I hear – your husband drawing nigh . . .

And she reads aloud, in a sweet, loud voice, from a piece of paper taken from under the bolster on the sofa:

> Without your love, I shall surely die.

The 'Don' smirks, swishes his cloak about him, opens the door which isn't there, closes it; steps out of the house made of nothing.

What of the other lady?

Why, she is waiting patiently for her lover, of course. While all this humping and bumping has been going on a few feet from her, she has remained posed in a pitiful longing.

The whole action is repeated. Approach to door. Knocking at

it. The starting of the woman. Her joy in her visitor. But this time the business at hand is more robust.

By now I had been joined at the side of the stage by one of the red-painted boys, and another of the whores. She smiled at me. I was going to speak, but she put a finger to her lips and pointed to the stage, as if saying, No, that's the business going on at the moment, not ours.

On the stage the preliminaries to love were rushed through. Then the same pantomime. The breeches pulled open. The pink and purple *salame* with its sculpted head like a Commendatore's helmet. This time more variations are played. She presents her bare behind – ah, here there are cries of rapture from our men. It's clear a good number of them prefer the servants' entrance to the pillared and pedimented front way. After all, in most villages it serves to keep the number of children down. She displays herself to the admiring 'Don' in a variety of poses. A regular contortionist, so that you don't quite know where her head has gone; or how her tongue got *there*. The boy at my side watched goggle-eyed, a bump in his breeches. Poor boy – he would be tired in the morning. The white-gowned whore behind him yawned and scratched her backside.

I must say I feel invigorated – however little – by the memory of those lovely girls. I feel the murmur, the rumour of a twitch, the briefest tremor of youth returning to my loins. With the envy of age I should now regard these exhibitions as shameful and disgusting, but the white flesh glows in this room and warms me.

And, after all, weren't we – the boys and whores on the stage and behind – all pure in comparison with those whose eyes watched from the dark?

What was happening now? The 'Don' putting his truncheon back in his breeches. The woman standing, smoothing her shift. On the side of the stage opposite to me, the other two red boys giggled and nudged each other.

But the 'Don' has heard more footsteps. He cocks his hand to his ear dramatically. Says, again, that he must fly. He kisses the lady on the cheek. There are cries of Shame. Shame, from our audience. Again. Again. Is that all? Some people are never satisfied.

The two ladies flutter demurely off, one to each side.

The actor faces the audience, raising one arm in a gesture of sorrow; of farewell to pleasure.

> Alas – *he says* – those beauties have vanished quite away.
> But – hist – what tender sounds make here their way?

The third whore brushed past me and tripped onto the stage. She has papers in her hand, which she waves in the 'Don's' face. His mouth immediately puts on a haughty, contemptuous expression. The girl begins to gabble, reading from one of the papers:

> Ha, you know me, wretch. Alone and wronged,
> How many the month and day that I have longed,
> Journeying from my tainted home,
> That I might send thee to thy well-deservéd doom . . .

There is laughter at this. The 'Don' rears back in stage horror. Then, from the other wing, the last of the whores walks on. She stands at the other side of the Don and recites like a child:

> My name is Donna Eleonora;
> My husband known as the Great Snorer –
> But when this great Don so gaily leapt
> Into my bed, I *never* slept . . .

They laughed at that, as they all knew by now of Eleonora's part in accusing the Don. But again the laughter was uneasy. I heard Ottavio's name called out. The laughter became crueller as he was spied at the back of the audience and their eyes sought him.

The two whores on either side of the actor now turn to him and recite these lines together:

> On this cruel Don, who will seduce, betray,
> We seek our due revenge without delay.

They trip merrily each to a sofa. From under the bolsters they produce short wooden daggers. They proceed to fall upon the 'Don' and make a great show of thrusting and stabbing at him, while he writhes and cries out in anguish, Ah, I am murdered. Murdered! By the contrivance of a bladder filled with pig's blood bursting beneath his shirt, a great blotch of bright red shortly stains his white linen. Groping and moaning, he makes a staggering progress from one point of the compass to another across the stage. The women pursue, continuing to rain enthusiastically murderous blows upon his coat. Exeunt – fleeing, pursuing.

The stage is empty.

The gentlemen, who had been entertained by the sight of murder, were silent a moment. Then a cry of, Where is the Devil? rose, and another of, Is that all? No play this. I heard Don Carlo's high disappointed voice say, Gentlemen, it is not over. I hope it is not over.

The Don has come out on stage. The real Don this time. No mask, no trace of blood on his shirt, his face calm; powdered a dead white.

He spoke gravely:

> Now that the Don indeed has died,
> All wives are sad; all husbands satisfied.

He paused for fully half a minute, then pulled out a paper from his pocket and read to them what follows. He had written it that afternoon. How I give it is in no way as fine as the speech he actually made. But here, I will stand and read and let time shudder away and let you imagine in my frail old self the brave figure of the Don in candlelight . . .

Don Carlo, gentlemen – the question is – what is to be done with the Don?

In the play I have been murdered by two ladies who consider themselves wronged by me – played by the delectable nymphs many of you will recognise as being from Signora S-'s establishment in the city. Or perhaps you know of better whorehouses?

(They didn't know whether to laugh or not now.)

I am accused by some here – and some elsewhere – of being a libertine; a despoiler of virgins, a *disturber* of marriages. A mocker at God and Creation. Of all your fondest beliefs indeed; that there is a God, that your wives are faithful, your daughters virtuous. I'm accused of witchcraft; perhaps because of the speed with which I fly from bed to bed. But there's no sorcery, gentlemen. No wings or broomsticks at midnight. I *want* them – that is enough. There is nothing a woman desires more than to be wanted. Not to be *had* – that's the tax I impose, that they willingly or not so willingly pay. It is, of course, important that they are flattered by the quality of the man desiring them. He should be blessed with at least one, or a combination, of these virtues: good looks, quick wits, energy, charm, a silver tongue, an indefatigable weapon, position . . . and desire. It is unfortunate for my rivals that I possess most of these. If the ladies don't like one, they can pick and choose among the others. But above all else is desire. One must simply want more than anything else in this world or heaven the woman who presents herself. If I tell a good wife that she is a great beauty, she will not believe me in her soul – but she will wish above all else that she may believe what I say. In love she is blinded by her own radiance, which is only reflected by my eyes, my tongue, my hands, my . . . You understand. And my reputation is that I cannot be satisfied, so that when I assure her that now, at last, in this one, I have found my ideal . . . Well, the rest follows. I recognise my virtues, gentlemen. And my vices.

What of the play? a voice shouted.

The Don sighed, and went on.

The trouble is, you live by calculation. Estates, wives, children all are acquired by acts of calculation. You make marriages for money, and you make children to inherit that money. You make love in a brothel, and your wives take it where they can find it. From your friends. From novels. From me. I am simply life, good sir, knocking at your door.

Vile adulterer! Was that Ottavio crying out?

I do not *force* your wives. The Don's voice grew angry here.

If they wish for something other than your flatulent arses jammed against them in bed, your sour-wine breath across their pillows, is that my fault? You employ them as objects of desire in your hot youth, to bear your sons, to keep your houses, to nag, to detest you – where is *their* life in all of this?

Large, burly Count G - stepped forward to the foot of the stage.

Our wives? What the Devil do you mean by *our wives*? he demanded of the Don. Is this the play, or do you really mean to insult our honour in this way? We'll have no more of it.

Oh, just a play, good sir, said the Don sweetly. A play. Let us continue.

He stepped back and beckoned me onto the stage. Now this is when – in the play as given on the street – the servant steps forward to read the list of his master's conquests. This was the part he had chosen for me to play. I wore a harlequin's mask, tied on my face by the deft warm fingers of one of the whores. Trembling, head bowed, I teetered on.

Read, Arlecchino, read, the Don commanded.

The paper rustled in my fingers, my eyes refused to focus for a second, then I began, stutteringly:

> Here, from the list of his conquests, I'll tell
> Of all the fine ladies who succumbed to his spell.
> The frisks, the frolics, the wanton games;
> Here is a list of all their names …

But as I read on, to my surprise, my voice, from a near whisper, began to ring out loud and full. Such is the intoxication of the stage.

> Signora A -,
> Countess B -,
> The little baker's lady, C -;
> The wives of the fat Chamberlain,
> The banker D -, the Duke of E -,
> With all these fair ladies he has lain.
> The squinting Colonel, the limping Count,
> – their beautiful daughters have made him their mount.

Some of the gentlemen, in their foolishness, laughed immoderately, recognising the names of friends and enemies in this doggerel, and glanced round, searching for their faces, to enjoy their discomfiture to the full. But as I read on, and more and more of them were named, until the uncuckolded were in the minority, then their mood changed. The laughter trailed away, shouts of protest rang out, and a sullen mob of them pressed forward to the stage. They frightened me; my voice shrank again; I faltered, staring down at their angry faces. The Don stepped forward, putting a hand on my arm, and saying, Enough, Leporello. Enough.

Count G- had elected himself speaker for the mob. He raised his hand for quiet.

Don Giovanni, he bellowed. What do you mean by this? You have gravely insulted gentlemen here. You have shown us a lewd exhibition and now drag the names of our wives into your midden.

The Don looked coolly down. Forgive me, he said. I thought you were all enjoying our show. It is after all only what you practice in the whorehouse. I have seen you at it. Ah, but your own women are pure, aren't they? My God, then where do all the loose wives come from? *Someone* is having them ...

Why, by all that is holy. Spluttering, the Count began an assault direct on the stage, attempting to clamber up when ...

When he was interrupted by the most tremendous knocking on the doors at the back of the hall.

The leaves of the doors were flung back. The figure that entered, a great helmet on his head, candle flames reflected wavering in the shiny breastplate of his armour, seemed as tall as two men. He halted in the doorway, outlined by the corridor light, and spoke in a mighty, hollow voice:

> *Impious* man! I am the ghost
> Of all you wronged – the host
> Of husbands, fathers, brothers of the pure,
> Who lie profaned, the victims of your dreadful lure.

He stepped forward. One of the country cousins cried out, It is the Statue from the play. The crowd parted before the figure. Now as he came nearer to the stage light I could see the fearsome mask, painted like that of a stone statue indeed, with its stone lips parted in a snarl round the black hole that served for a mouth.

I must admit I had not been expecting this apparition and feared it. I huddled behind the curtain.

But the Don, as cool as ever, simply said:

Ah, welcome Sir. You're rather late.
Tell me – before these gentlemen decide – what is to be my fate?

The spectre raised his arm, his mailed finger pointing at the Don.

As causer of all this past and present woe,
To Hell thou must go!

To Hell. To Hell, the cry was taken up. To be silenced almost at once as the pots at the back of the stage flared into fountains of emerald, sapphire, blood-red, and lightning-white; as a door hinged in the mountain on the backcloth swung wide, and through it could be seen the four whores at the top of a ramp, their white gowns suffused with shifting, fiery colours, their hands held out in invitation. And the three crimson-bodied imps of boys ran across the stage and seized hold of the Don.

In the brilliant light streaming through the mountain door boys and man struggled, the Don's face wearing a look of amused terror. The spectre mounted the steps at the side onto the stage, intoning, To Hell, to hell, in his deep bass thunder. They dragged the Don towards damnation. The spectre followed. The door in the mountain flapped to behind them.

There was a stench of sulphur now as smoke began to fill the stage. Creeping under the backdrop, it rolled into the theatre and set men coughing and cursing. The last I saw of Count G-, he was pressing a handkerchief to his mouth and shaking his fist at the stage. The last I heard was Don Carlo shouting, This was not as arranged, Don Giovanni. Not as arranged!

I felt a tug at my sleeve. One of the imps grinned up at me. This way, Master Leporello. Come quickly. I stumbled after the little rogue, through the smoke and fumes, past the fireworks farting out their sparks.

Then it's down the narrow back stair, down, down, following the boy. We tumble out into the stableyard. Two carriages. From one a whore grins and waves to me as it starts away. The other carriage is ours.

The master is inside, a look of triumph on his face, a girl leaning on his arm. In the opposite seat, the actor, helmet and mask on his lap, wipes his huge face with a handkerchief smeared with paint and sweat. Ride with Ragoti, the Don shouts, as I go to hoist myself inside . . . Before I could, the coach jolted. Bastard, I shouted at Ragoti. I barely had time to cling on to the back as they rolled forward.

The red boys, half-naked under the flambeaux of the yard, pursued our coach as they realised they were being left behind, crying piteously, Take us, dear sirs. For the love of God, take us. A shower of bright coins flew from the coach window and they scrabbled among them as they bounced and chinked on the cobbles. I turned as we swept under the arch, just remembering to lower my head before it was struck off by the jutting bottom of the keystone.

My, that was a warm night.

I hung on for my life as we flew out of the yard, careered through the gardens and wheeled, sparking, on to the road to Pomodoro.

There was a bright high moon that showed the whole plain behind us and the mountains folded into their shadows. As we slowed I was able to claw my way to a safer position on the box and look forward over the bucketing coach. In the sky ahead, even at this distance, the red glow from the mountain above Pomodoro was unusually bright, suffusing the cloud above. The Gods had taken the backcloth from our play and hung it over the city.

We were going at such a pace that we soon outstripped the whores' coach. They hung out of the side and cheered and waved as we passed, and laughed at my predicament on the box. I gave them a mad salute with my free hand, and we left the kind, warm, laughing faces leaning out of their black coach behind, its horses plodding and dwindling smaller and smaller as we raced on, until they were lost to sight.

Who was the one inside with the Don?

We bowled over the plain, the light from the mountain growing brighter; the cloud of smoke billowing up and up and out so that it leaned across the plain like a giant's hand. I was glad when we entered the woods, the road ahead lit by shafts of the friendly moon. Then there was no more moon. Looking up through the tree-tops I saw the huge, morose, rust-coloured cloud had blotted it out. As the trees thinned their trunks were lit by the red flame-light. I had heard tales of the mountain's terrible shows, but it had been quiet all our stay in the city, and I wondered that it could glow so and penetrate through the depths of a forest. We came out on the hills above the city.

The Don shouted for the coach to be halted and put his head out. What I had taken for the loud rumbling of the carriage wheels did not stop when we did. From the mountain across the bay came a grinding, a humming, a roaring, as if a great wind was rising though all was still about us. The mountain top was now covered by a glowing and glowering cloud which now and then gave a glimpse of its fiery mouth. There was then a great clap of sound as if a cannon had been discharged and the mountain top spewed out a stream, a pissing of glowing stones; another, mightier, crack, and white-hot and red and yellow stones were flung higher, like rockets, and curled back, their light dying, into the smoke. Again the beast roared and cannonades of stones and long licks of flame spurted up.

My God, the Don shouted – the actor's head appeared beside his – This beats our show, Ambrogetti.

The actor frowned and withdrew his head, jealous at his Creator upstaging him.

Drive on, the Don commanded.

We went down. The city was bathed all in red – or reds, rather. Ruddy, bloody, flushed, blushing, wine-stained, pink as flesh, with the shadows between tenements deep maroon gashes; a murderer and his prey. The sea, his bloody path. The cloud over the sea had grown into an enormous, billowing, violet and carmine beast's belly. As we descended the hill, floats of black and white ash as big as coins, small stones and black coals rained in the air and pattered on the coach top. I pulled a corner of the weatherproof sheet tied across the boxes over my head as best I could. Peering out and up I saw faces looking towards the mountain through shutters held just ajar. Some braver spirits leaned out on their balconies, shielding themselves with parasols. As we got lower in the town all the shutters were banged tight to, and the few people caught out on the streets scurried between doorways for cover against a fine thick downfall of grey ash mixed with the heavier stones. A cinder stung like the Devil on the back of my hand where I held the tarpaulin up.

We were on to the promenade. Under the wall the harbour was spotted with small boats putting out – the wise fleeing, or gallants setting out for a better view of this mad fireworks from the bay. The coach ran on to the mole. Men, women and children ran beside us, shielding their heads with bundles of clothing. Cinders and clinkers and hot coals dropped all about us; we were like mice under the grate of a huge fire that someone was poking from above. We stopped near the landing stage.

A barque stood in.

The Don jumped down as I did. He spoke to the girl inside and told her to remain there for the moment. Leporello – I didn't know you were there, he said in some surprise. Get down our things. Ragoti, lend a hand. Signor Ambrogetti climbed out and stood looking back at the city, dismay on his face.

My costumes ... the theatre ... he said. If there is a fire ...

Sir, you may go to them directly, said the Don, taking him by the arm. First, take this for your services tonight. He pulled out his purse. Ambrogetti blinked and extended his palm, his anxiety for the moment allayed. There, the Don said, and counted out gold. Sell the coach and horses and give the proceeds to the Abbess. She can take what I owe her. I will write for the rest. See you do all this, mind – I still have friends in this city.

Ambrogetti, with a huff of insult, flung his cloak dramatically over his shoulder and said, Sir, you may trust an actor, *surely*? Then he thrust the money deep in his pocket and hurried away up the mole towards the city. For Art is stronger with these gentlemen than Life itself.

Take the bags down to the ship, Leporello, the Don ordered. Going along with the big chest between me and Ragoti, I looked back and saw the Don handing the girl down from the carriage as if they had arrived at a ball.

There was a crowd at the top of the landing steps. A loud argument between those trying to board the ship and the captain and two of his men denying them passage. We dumped the chest and hurried back for the bags.

My hair was singed and my coat. The Don had a hat. The girl a hood. They were talking urgently, close together. The young lady accompanies me, the Don said, breaking free. He paid Ragoti off then, assuring him he was a rascal, but that no doubt he would find another master soon. For one dreadful moment I thought that I was to be cast off too, but then he said, Stir yourself, Leporello – we are for that ship.

The mob at the top of the landing steps glared resentfully as we came up to them. The castle reared terrible and black. On the other side the ship's masts rose. Seamen clambered in the rigging, freeing the sails. The Don, his woman in tow, pushed through the crowd. A last suitor was bargaining angrily with the captain for passage, but that stout man barred the way down, saying, No, no. I have told you. We have a full complement. I can take no more on board.

Captain B-, said the Don, presenting himself, You had my letter?

Letter? The captain said impatiently.

I am on an important embassy for His Excellency, the Duke. This lady – he brought her forward – is the good Duke's niece. We came to lay our belongings on board for your voyage in the morning. We find all this . . .

I intend to put out now, said the Captain. I've no wish to see my vessel burn in the harbour.

It seems that we are just in time, said the Don. Perhaps your men will assist mine with our belongings?

The captain hesitated a moment. But the Don's bold stare outfaced him. Come on then. Come on, said the captain. But no more. No more. He turned and went down to his ship. And so, to much complaint from the waiting mob, we went aboard.

Not before time, for immediately the captain gave his orders and the long-boats began to pull us slowly away. What little cover the deck afforded was already crammed and the Don despatched me to find a cabin. You know how, dear boy, he said.

Most of them were full already, the inhabitants congratulating themselves on their good fortune. Only a tiny single-berth was empty. Almost. I put out into the passageway the grip that lay on the bed and distributed the bags I had brought down with me across the floor to establish my ownership. When the old gentleman who owned the grip came back a few moments later, I parroted grandly the Don's lines. On the Duke's business. Important persons. Niece of Duke. Donna whatever-her-name is. He went off without complaint, his back bowed, like an old mole in his black coat – one to whom life is done. I bolted the door, hearing others moving along the passage looking for shelter. The ship creaked and wallowed as the boats turned her to the wind. When I was reasonably sure things had settled down, and that no one would work my trick on me, I went up on deck.

The long-boats had cast us off; the wind just filling the sails as we tacked across the bay. The distant promenade was lined with people. The fishing boats stood already some distance off, and from the shore cries mixed with curses for them to come back carried across the water. The pale walls of the waterfront palazzos glowed first red and then a ghostly pink. Higher in the city fires had started. Beyond, the hills cast back an awful light. Over all, the monstrous sombre cloud grew out of the mountain.

I found the Don at the rail, the lady clutching his arm, pressing herself to him. His eyes were bright; he seemed enchanted by the terrible vision. Coals hissed in the sea and fell onto the deck. He was not perturbed.

I have found a cabin, I said. Poky little place, but the best I could do. Come quickly, sir. Or it may be taken.

I wanted to get below as soon as ever I could.

It seems, he said, that the damnation which was to have been mine has been visited on the city instead. Poor folk. Poor folk.

The cries of the poor folk could no longer be distinguished. The ship leaned into the wind and surged forward.

My dears, let's go below, said the Don. And see what snug little palace my Leporello has found.

We were at sea for three full nights. For two of the days the pall of smoke and cloud mingled in the sky behind us; and for three evenings we had the most parti-coloured sunsets I have ever seen, which the Don called beautiful. Then the horizon cut off all but a smudged band of grey-blue.

I slept in the hold, along with the other servants, and the gentlefolk who had not been able to obtain cabins. The passage was smooth enough. I bought wine and bread off the crew and took them to the Don each morning. He opened the door and I could see the girl in the tumbled single berth, her face to the wall, the bedsheet drawn up.

She is not a good sailor, whispered the Don.

There was something mysterious and not altogether pleasant in his expression, as if he knew a secret I did not and took a delight in keeping it from me. Get some water, Leporello. I must wash. And you and I must shave. He fingered the stubble on my face. What a pair of brigands we must look, he said softly.

I did not see the lady fully until we lay in harbour and they came up on deck. A fine city we had put into; doubly fine to me for the pure blue sky above it, its white staring buildings, and a blessed lack of fiery mountains.

She was in a neat plain gown with her hair tied back. From her clothes you might have taken her for a superior servant but for an elegance of manner, partly her own and part reflected from the Don, who was in his best pale blue coat, a little rumpled. She did not look sick from the voyage. She smiled most charmingly at me, but didn't speak. I began to wonder if she was indeed the Duke's niece – and what trouble that would bring.

The bags carried ashore, I asked for the largest inn – it is easier to disprove what you are shown than asking for the *best* inn. You will only be taken to some rat-infested hole owned by the carter's uncle. Arriving, I took two large rooms overlooking the harbour for the Don, and a small one along the corridor for myself. I was most polite and gentle-voiced with the chambermaid. I thought I might make her acquaintance a good deal better. I told her what a great and wealthy and particular man my master was. This always shows the servant to better advantage.

When they arrived I was whistling and happy, putting out his things from the big chest. He seemed most amused by my good humour. What had I done to be made fun of?

He drew me aside, saying that the lady would like to change and refresh herself and that we should step out onto the balcony.

This looks to be a grand place, sir, I said.

Yes. He leaned on the balustrade, and turned his face to me. Again, his expression was quizzical and amused. Do you not know her? he said.

Know her, sir?

Your friend from the Abbess's house, he said. Sophia.

And just at that her voice called out, low and sweet, asking the Don for something, and I knew her at once. Her voice I knew.

I told you I would rescue her, my boy, he said, laughing. And very glad I am that I did.

Would I have known her if he had not told me? I had only seen her the once, for a moment, in that dark room. I knew her now right enough, her voice talking to the Don, who had gone back into the room. Here, Leporello, he called. He introduced me gravely to her. Signorina T-. My man, Leporello. She desires to be your friend, Leporello, as you are mine. Shake hands. Was she joining in some game to bait me? But no, her expression was so frank, her smile so winning that I knew that she had not recognised me.

And so it proved. She treated me with the proper courtesy due to a servant. There was no sense that she had known me before. And I had to ruefully admit, despite my jealousy and anger at the

Don for twitting me with her presence, that she was a different woman from the one I had held and comforted, a woman now rather than a girl, so that that memory became strange in my mind, as if it had never truly happened.

Where the difference lay I could not catch hold of. She was a lady – and his mistress. She was not shy, or tearful. She was modest and charming and quick-witted. Was that the Don's doing. Had he, to put it coarsely, fucked her into this sweet sensibility? And though at first he took great delight in parading her before his servant's eyes, he knew – and I did too – that I could not tell her who I was – where I had met her before; in what circumstances. So the joke grew hollow and was dropped. And perhaps he felt, as I did, that it was unworthy of him. She was a lady, after all, not a whore.

When the Don went out, she would talk to me. About the Don. Our travels. I was used to this with his ladies, and knew how to give a good account of both of us. She did not recognise *my* voice. After a while I was glad she did not. She was happy, and I was reasonably so. She was set free, and set back in the society to which she belonged. What good would it do any of us if I revealed myself to her? I would become ridiculous in my own eyes. I was happy that she took me as a friend – as far as that was possible. It amused me also to hear her account of her own short life and how much she managed to omit in telling it to a servant, rather than to someone she imagined a gentleman.

For why should I wish to spoil our time in this city? For a week or two we lived happily as Man – or two men and a woman – is allowed to. I had gained access to the chambermaid; who every time she jumped into bed, crossed herself first and asked the Holy Mother to forgive her. The Don was closeted with Sophia for most of the morning. They walked out in the late afternoon to watch the local nobility parade in their carriages to the harbour, where they would get down and stroll about and flirt with each other's ladies.

The Don became quickly known to them. It was impossible for such a man to remain invisible in any place for long.

I too went down to the harbour, to a wine shop where my fellow servants drank, to get up the town's gossip and lord it as best I could. I was drinking there one afternoon when the barque that had brought us came back from its round trip to Pomodoro. I went down to her, taking a bottle with me, to pay for the latest news.

The mountain is quieter, they said; though still seething with anger. A good quarter of the city is burnt or damaged by fire, but that has been doused now. The mountain has laid an inch-thick scum on the bay. The Duke has taken personal charge, and opened his treasury and warehouses to the stricken. Any more? No more. Wait another few days. There will be another ship.

There was, and it brought more news. The seaman said the city was returned to its usual life; when all the dust was swept and carted away you would not know it had suffered at all. Except – the mountain had turned white with ash and looked like a ghost under the moon. And that the Duke had ordered the arrest of a terrible monster, the great Don Giovanni, for sorcery, blasphemy and sedition. The Don was reported to have fled Pomodoro on the night of the eruption, after he had called for a revolt against the Duke and murdered a priest. He was travelling with a harem of nuns.

And swallows the blood of Christian babes, no doubt, I muttered.

The seaman looked at me queerly. I should not be surprised, he said. Do you know him?

No, no, I protested. No cock crowed. Every day brings bad news for someone.

He helped himself to more wine from my bottle. They say the Don and his crew took the packet over here, he went on. All the captains have been ordered to watch for him. Upset quite a few folk, it seems. I once saw a man done up for only writing against the Duke. They tore his tongue out at the roots and lopped off his hands. Though this Don is a gentleman and will get off lighter, I suppose. But he had a servant with him. You're a servant, aren't you? he said, with a sudden acute lifting of his eyes to look into mine.

To Signor Ambrogetti. The great actor, I said too hurriedly. I got up and put the cork in my bottle with a thwack of my palm.

Thought I hadn't seen you before, he said, getting up also.

I must go, I said.

He shrugged and went over to another table and bent over it, talking rapidly to some other sailors. He was informing on me, surely. I swaggered out, and then ran, as a mouse runs for its hole, back to the inn.

The Don and Sophia were out. They did not come back until late evening. My lord, I said to him as soon as he came in. Later, Leporello – he waved his hand at me – later. He followed Sophia into the inner room. I stood on the balcony while he went about his business and looked down into the harbour and saw it swarming with spies and traitors, inquisitors and informers, torturers and executioners. Ah, I was a coward in those days, when it comes down to it.

Master and mistress still did not emerge.

Evening shadows rose in the streets below. The sun exchanged its dying light for that of the full moon in the large room. Their door was still shut. I hovered and hovered, moved things aimlessly about, sat in a chair, got up. I weighed up how fast I could pack the chest – then the door was flung open and the Don appeared. Leporello, he said, all I can hear as we try to rest is you moving about like a dog in here. For God's sake, go to bed. And he stepped back and shut the door.

I went to my room with a heavy heart. I left the door open, to listen for the steps of soldiers coming to take him. At last I fell asleep. I was woken by the Don, shaking my shoulder. It was just before dawn. Leporello. Leporello. Am I your servant to wake *you*. I started up, Ah, sir ... I said, and started to gabble out all I had heard of the warrant out for him. That the Duke knew we were on this island ...

You are a good soul, Leporello. He smiled down at me. I know this. I know. I have friends in this city as in every other. The corvette due this morning carries men to take me back. It is time to move. I have packed the one chest. Carry your things in a bundle. You are coming with me? I am afraid that if they can't have me, they may very well take you.

I meant to warn you, sir ... I struggled into my breeches. I was disgusted to think that he had had to pack while his servant slept.

Hurry, he said gently. I can't carry the bloody chest down by myself.

We went back into his room. In the next room Sophia slept on. I pointed to her door, enquiringly. We shall travel lighter without Donna Sophia, he said. I have come to like her . . . I have left her a letter. And some gold. Come – lift up that end – let us go quietly before she wakes.

The truth is, Leporello, I never felt so much attached to a woman in my life, he said as we rode out of the city. It is an annoyance, he continued, that I have to leave her *regretfully*. Usually we flee from them, don't we?

He had arranged for a fishing boat to take us off the island. The fishermen had no love for the Duke or anyone else set in authority over them. Whatever the Don had done, it must be good if it was against the men in uniforms and carriages; and so he was, like them, outside of the law.

I missed Sophia's company. The Don's stay with her had been the closest to a home, an *establishment*, we had set up. A servant likes stability about him.

We sat on coiled ropes in the fishing boat. The Don said, What Leporello, does a man do when he has died and been dragged down to Hell? And then is granted a further lease on life? It's a problem that did not trouble my ancestor in all those wretched plays. He sinned; paid, and satisfied consciences all round. But what to do now, my boy?

I said, They pursue you now, sir – but they surely will not pursue you forever . . .

Well, they do *now*. They must have something to chase after. The Duke has no hatred for me. But he is surrounded by fools and consults fools, who are advised by worse fools. This is known as government. To quieten their cares, and to make his own life tolerable, he must pursue me. I am an itch they must scratch and to make them comfortable makes the Duke comfortable. While I am fresh in their minds they will talk me up and think me up until

I am a great devil. If I was caught now they would take me back and hang me. The Duke would sit on that day in some distant part of his castle and think what a grand companion I had been, and regret my passing, but feel relief that I was gone, and that my going had made his courtiers happy. Once we are out of his domain we will be forgotten.

But I worried and moped, and lying beside him in the belly of that boat, I said, Wasn't that a terrible thing though sir, the destruction of their city. It is as if God willed it. Perhaps, I said wistfully, they will all have been swallowed up. It must have been a wicked place for God to have treated it so.

A judgment of God? He laughed. You think God cares who puts what of his body where, or where what? Dear Leporello, in that case we should both ignite upon the spot. And every other poor sinner and lover. Only the holy, celibate souls be left. If your God worried so much about the conduct of the sexes he would have peopled the world with alabaster statues. Fortunately, the priests have had the clever idea of cooping all those in the churches and letting the rest of us get on with it.

He sighed and lay back. Look up at the morning, my boy, he said. How beautiful. Be glad of it.

We arrived at the next island at noon. I half expected to see the harbour wall ringed with soldiers; but we were travelling faster than our bad news. The Don reproved me. I am always ahead of my fate, he said airily.

Losing no time, we found a ship to take us to G-; which I found a city of men dressed in black, of stinking, close air and many beggars. The Don, having had no connection for over a week, was bursting and spent three days rampaging in the brothels; using the rooms I took for us only to wash and change in, before charging forth once more.

So our travels began.

PART III

The Stone Guest

1

The Don sits in the opposite corner of the coach, wrapped in a great fur like a bear. I have swathed myself in two blankets. I shiver and doze; doze and shiver.

This thought of Pascal's, the Don announces in his sudden way (as flakes of snow flurry between us through the open window), that the body is merely the corrupt and corrupting carrier of the mind. Such an idea is offensive to the world; it obliterates. As this snow (he waves his hand to the window) covers the world in its obscuring whiteness; obliterating men and women; all beauty; sublime Nature; the animals, seas, blanks out the heavens even. All is reduced to four blank white walls, and a blank white sheet of paper. The man is worse than a eunuch. At least those poor creatures do not renounce the world voluntarily.

He tosses the book on to the seat and blows across his hands, then draws on the thick gloves he removed to turn the pages. This Monsieur Pascal has obsessed and angered him all the way of our journey. He picks the book up, puts it down again; picks it up . . . the rigmarole with the gloves off and on, off and on, each time. How he could read on that nightmare of a journey I do not know, but the Don did just that, rehearsing his arguments with a dead Frenchman, his angry refutation, to the carriage; to his ignorant servant.

But the Don was right about the snow. It had fallen thick two days before, but he had insisted on setting out, hiring a carriage for twice the normal price. On the way out of that town, the tollkeeper had come out of his cabin and said that he hoped to see us again, though it was plain from his face that he had no real prospect of that pleasure. The horses had pulled us like a sled sometimes; at others like a bucking boat. Ever and again we had to get down, put our shoulders to the wheels and, we, more than the straining beasts, hoist the carriage on its way. Back inside, and going on in that intolerably slow, jolting progress, the Don would grow impatient and shout to the coachman, How much further? How much longer? And the coachman would sing back, Not much further, Excellency. Nearly there, your worship.

The sun that had shone early that morning and spurred the Don forward had been squeezed thinner and thinner and then swallowed quite away inside the grey-yellow sky. Its faint warmth had served only to melt the very top of the snow in the ruts and channels and by this mid-afternoon the crusts have frozen hard as stone.

I draw the blankets about me in new folds, trying vainly to increase their warmth, and look, like a poor mute dog protesting with his eyes against some punishment, across at my master.

He has been ill lately and should not have been travelling at all. But he is barely human at times. He must be as cold as his poor servant, but will not show it. We are getting too old for this game. The Don has passed his fortieth birthday; I am near thirty. With no wife, no home; only a little money saved – in secret, against the Don's depredations. He stares fixedly out of the window; when he leans forward – to follow the passage of some miserable bird across the monotonous sky – the crown of his head shows through his thick black hair, and silver wires glint in the remaining mass. His face has grown heavier and deep lines are scored in his cheeks and from nose to mouth. His eyelids have thickened and his eyes often trouble him with some irritation he has picked up and cannot shake off. He is still a mightily handsome man; but his whole body is heavier and slower; in repose it is sometimes as if the quicksilver of his youth has turned to stone.

And what of me? After nearly a decade in his service, I am a thorough gentleman's gentleman, as the English say. I have been schooled in the best, if not the most conventional, academy in the world and consider myself a good few cuts above those other servants I meet. Away from the Don's sight, I can swagger as well as any Paris valet. At least, I could in the early days. Now, I am ashamed to say, my clothes have grown a little shabby. The Don has not passed me any cast-offs for a long time now, our affairs having got into some disorder. Under his fur, he is wearing the uniform of a soldier. What, a common soldier? you say. No. A general. Well, a general in prospect. We are on our way – if we ever get there – to offer our services to an emperor.

Now we have stopped utterly. A thick tree branch, brought down by the weight of snow, lies across the road. We help the coachman to drag it aside and cast it into the snow-filled ditch. We climb back into our ice-house and resume our awful way.

How did we get in this case? What became of us? Last thing you heard we had escaped the flames of Hell. Twice. What then? What then . . .

What happened to Sophia? And Eleonora? Isabella? The Duke and Carlo? All the others? Surely, you say, they played some part hereafter, as they do in novels, endlessly twisting and entwining themselves in our lives? But, in life, whatever threads bind our lives together are visible only to God – and he is no novelist.

We had journeyed in the whole of Europe and seen great men and little men – and I could not readily tell the difference. We visited his hero, the philosopher Voltaire. I don't know what they said. All I remember is my master coming out of a room, with a tiny spry old man who looked like a bright monkey. No teeth and mischievous glittering eyes like a very ancient little boy. I crossed myself and avoided those eyes.

Another time we attended an orgy given by servants – I smuggling my master in. This proved a grave disappointment. The donkey brought to mount a cook turned mulish, shat upon the floor, and ran amok.

What did we live on? The romances and plays never tell you about such mundane matters. His ready money soon went. We would hole up in some place on credit while he wrote to his bankers. After whatever delay – of weeks or months – a fresh letter of credit would arrive. But this was hardly enough to keep the Don. As I have said, he was never a free spender, but in every new city or town we came to, he would have to have a good house or apartment, if only to expunge the remembrance of all the dirty infested inns we had stayed in on the way to this new place. He would take on two, three mistresses, try the girls in the whorehouses. Keep a good carriage. A man, he said, would have to be a complete fool if he could not live beyond his means. His name demanded a certain standard of life – and his name ran ahead of us, sparking the ladies; putting the men on their guard. But if it was a name earned by his indefatigable exploits in the bedchamber, it was also a name known to be attached to property, to estates. A name quickly made known to those harder, wiser heads who wed plain wives and lend money, not time or hearts. So, as the Don accumulated maidenheads and adulteries, multiplied bastards and abortions, so he also heaped up a pretty pile of mortgages on his inheritance.

Along with the records of his amours I kept his accounts. My service with the late Signor Cavilloso had fitted me for the task. When I pointed out that his outgoings were far more than the occasional credits could ever afford, he flew into a rage and stormed out of the room. A while later he came back in – I was brushing his clothes. He stood, with the shy, sly smile that he used to charm, and said, My future, Leporello? My future – what is that? as if he had never contemplated it before.

But I thought that at his age it was high time to give some thought for his future. Servants like to see their masters settled. I was tired of endless travel. I dreamed of a house, a wife for each of us, a life of sensible toil. But every time I struck up a liaison with a woman, I would no sooner fix up another meeting and return high-hearted to our rooms, than he would cry out, Pack, Leporello. We are going to A-, or B-; C-, D-. Because Q- or Y- or Z-, wherever we were, would no longer answer. The town was too small. Too large. Too dirty. Too provincial. The women were ugly. Worse, the women were faithful. What fabled town was that? Or, simply, he wished to go on. Movement is life, he said. We shall have enough stillness in death.

Of course, we stayed the longest the larger the place. In a city the Don's life fell quickly to the same routine. He rose fairly early in the morning, washed, breakfasted, dressed; rode for an hour; received visits from other idle gentlemen, or, more rarely, paid visits to them – but only if there was something to be had from such an outgoing; a name, a recommendation, a chance to see the lady of that house ... Other times, after a heavy night, he would slop around in his dressing-gown, reading Voltaire, the little monkey, or any others of that pack. Or he would work on his own writing. He left his notebook out once and I read the label pasted to the front; *A Refutation of Pascal*. It was like the priest of my childhood. Always with these clever men it is the refutation of one thing or another.

After a light luncheon he would most probably have arranged a meeting with some lady or other, whose husband was about his business. The husband was usually one whose acquaintance he had made so that he knew his whereabouts. Only rarely would he go to the lady's home; more often to some small house I had taken in the suburbs or a cheap apartment. In the case of urgency, a room in an inn or hotel. In all these rentings my name was used. I had a terrible reputation among those landlords.

At night, court life, or the next best thing the place afforded. The theatre. Opera. Music. If they were permitted, a mysterious meeting with his fellow Freemasons. Casino, if there was one. Brothel – there was always one; more than one. A long day.

Then, as I say, it would all come to an end. He would fuck the wrong wife. Or rather, the right wife, but of the wrong man. Get into a fight or duel or scandal. Wounding. Death. The tearful widow – who might be comforted, if there was time. The moaning man. Out of each such altercation my master stepped a little more tarnished. The Prince, the Count, the Mayor whose favourite he had become would turn against him. Tradesmen refuse us credit. The landlord appear in the doorway, twisting his hat in his hands, apologising, regretting ... But ... And we must travel on. Because, as the Don explained to me, he *was* interested at first in the new face each place presented; the doors and legs that opened before him – rather as a man of science opens an ant heap or turns over a stone and bends down to examine the life scurrying inside or beneath. But there came a time, he said, when he had discovered all the patterns they lived to, all the narrow channels and passages they ran in; when he had exhausted their conversation, their habits, their games and intrigues, their women . . . Time to move on.

Every place from which we departed – at dead of night usually – was left disturbed and knowing itself a little differently. Its old attachments no longer held. And so the Don's reputation, like a giant striding through the country, cast a long shadow, and our coming was known long before our arrival. The very appearance of his carriage in the streets took on the air of an entrance into a drama, the beginning of a fairy-tale. The whores flocked to him. The gamblers. The moneylenders. But at each new stop more doors shut against us. The Don had to entertain then at whatever home we had; against his inclination. And, because it is cheaper to eat others' food, and lie in their beds, a further drain on our finances. I found myself dipping into the savings I had made out of his past disbursements – for I was ever cautious with his money and skated over the household finances on as thin ice as possible. So, travelling up the backside of the country called France, I, as his go-between with women, his alerter to fresh opportunity, I became – oh, unknown to him – truly his pimp.

Meeting with servants in these strange towns, I searched out the wives of wealthy men who were unhappy, bored by their husbands and by the provincial lovers they took. I courted their maids, whispering in their ears that my master was the lustiest, gentlest, handsomest, most perfect gentleman-cum-fucker the world had ever known. That – for a consideration – I could put their mistresses in his way. That I could convey them discreetly to whatever meeting place they or the Don chose – with his superior knowledge in these matters . . . There are enough bored women in any town to be intrigued by such a proposition, I assure you.

The Don was willing to fall in with my suggestions. For now he seemed, more than ever, insatiable in his desires. If one woman, why not two, why not ten – They are food and wine, earth and air to me, he would say. Find me them. Find them. And so I would. His bed rocked like the cradle of the world.

If he was too ready; I was too greedy. I added a further twist to the screw. Hiring one of those low men who hang around girls and casinos, who are forever short of money and long of cock, I had this dandy represent me in a visit to the Don's current lady of virtue. Gaining entry to her on 'an errand of a personal nature', he intimated to her that all was known. That she had been observed proceeding to a private meeting with the notorious Don Giovanni, that in the interest of common morality he did not how the intelligence could be held back much longer from her husband – unless ... Unless he could stop a few mouths with gold. Or some little trinket if she had not access to cash ...

But someone will talk. Someone will always talk. This cheap fellow was over-greedy and was taken by the ears by the husband, who had a little more about him than the rest, and was made to disgorge his tale. I heard in a coffee-shop that the husband intended revenge. Frightened that my part in all this would come out, I tried to hurry the Don away that evening by pretending that the duns were about to seize us because of my not paying the household bills. The Don raged and railed at me that such things must be taken care of. Had he not given me money only last week? His good name was at stake. He adamantly refused to leave. What do you take me for? he bellowed. Of course, I reasoned to myself, the wife would never admit to paying for an introduction to the Don. But the husband now knew who her lover was.

The idiot found us that night and challenged my master to a duel on this matter of honour. The Don was forced to kill him in a wood the next morning. With the mist still hanging between the trees, and parrying the man's ineffectual, pathetic strokes, the Don despatched him cleanly through the heart. The man's wife took poison that same day and died.

The husband, though only a merchant, and therefore perhaps not worthy of his death in the Don's eyes, was popular in the town. The news of the tragedy and knowledge of the Don's part spread quickly round. We left this time in short order, stones banging against the sides of the coach as we rumbled away.

The Don was moody and ill-tempered. He had quite liked the fellow, he complained. Altogether the peculiar circumstances of our departure puzzled and depressed him. He did not care to be disliked.

We travelled on; our high adventures growing smaller and smaller as we ambled through these frowsty towns. His depression lingered. Was it now that the malady, or series of maladies, that plagued his life from then on, began? Up until that time, he had seemed to be almost miraculously vigorous, avoiding the poxes and claps that should have been his due. But whatever the cause, somewhere along the way the last of his youth was lost. His temper darkened. His appetites remained as strong, but as if they were a grim quest whose purpose and end I could not foresee. He seemed to harden, and for the first time an offhand brutality crept into his speech and manner.

He did not take to ageing.

One day – it would have been about six months after we had left that unfortunate business of the duel behind us – he called me into him with a great shout.

He was gazing with disgust at his hairbrush.

My God – what is this? he demanded.

The brush was thick with hair.

My hair is falling out. Good God, my hair is falling out! Look – His fingers scrabbled, searching the thick bush. Where has it come from? Is there a hole? He demanded. A gap?

He made me examine his scalp. At the crown a complete tuft of hair had come away. I said that it must be some poison in his food or bad wine he had drunk – I had seen the same thing in my village. I am not a bloody peasant, Leporello, he shouted angrily. What, what? Where is it? And his fingertips felt about the small bald patch as if frightened to be burnt. It is hardly noticeable, sir, I said. I combed the other hair back over this patch and assured him that one could not see the faintest trace . . . He looked at himself furiously in the mirror, tilting his head this way and that.

I will not grow old, he said. Not this way.

The next day a rash of spots appeared around his mouth. He would not go out.

When I suggested a doctor he became angry. But the hair continued to fall, and for the sake of his vanity he let me fetch the surgeon who tended the whorehouse in the town where we had lodged. The doctor, small, broad and jolly, was himself unfortunately completely bald under a lop-sided, slipping wig. He inspected the Don and asked him any number of strange questions which seemed to have nothing to do with hair. Then – had the gentleman ever had any form of the Pox?

The Don glared at him. He had got all that over with in his youth, he said coldly. Quite so, quite so, said the Frenchman. He produced from his bag a small phial of the sort in which they hold a saint's blood or tears. A thick, grey liquid. Three drops at each meal, he said.

It looks like goat's seed, said the Don. I am supposed to adulterate good wine with that?

If you wish to be well. It has worked wonders for my other gentlemen . . .

The Don would not take the medicine. It made him vomit, he said, though I saw no evidence he had tried it more than once at most. But he did rest up for a week. The rash cleared. His hair stopped falling. There, he said, it is all nonsense. He had got out of condition – a month of hard riding would beat his body back to health. And so it seemed to prove.

But his temper continued dark.

We had come to an estate owned by friends of his father. The family had removed to the capital for the winter – as the Don well knew. Only an old aunt was left in charge of the château. She was so charmed by the Don that she made him seigneur of the place until the owners should return. He had an enchanting young mistress for a while, a dancer whose company was in the town nearby. He had seemed perfectly happy with her until, one morning, he came down from his bedroom and sat glaring balefully at the ceiling. Is she never going? he said. Go up, Leporello. Tell her to go.

But sir . . . , I complained. (It was not my part. What was I to say to her?)

Tell her I have been called away. I am sick. Whatever you damned well please. Only get rid of her. Then he began a rant of how filthy these whores were – what did they want from him? He had given her a good fucking – the best she ever had. Now she just lay there, waiting his return, her breakfast, her little words of love – Well, damn her, he exploded.

I went up.

The door was half open. I hesitated, then knocked on the door.

Come in, she called. Don't be shy. I entered. Oh, she said. I thought it was Don Giovanni.

She looked quite divine. Like one of those women you see in the paintings; lying among the pillows, with only a sheet over her, so that you could see the line and beauty of her body – but so much more alive than any painting; her blue eyes shining, her face glowing in the bloom of youth.

I told her the Don had been summoned away urgently. That he had left his carriage at her disposal.

Ah – her face fell. She would get up at once of course. If you would not mind ... I withdrew modestly, eyeing with greed her gown and petticoats tumbled over the back of a chair, her stockings crazy-legged on the carpet.

While she dressed, I listened with pleasure to the rustlings and swishes and whispers of her clothes. I conducted her downstairs. As we came past the room where I had left the Don, his voice demanded loudly from inside, Has that bitch gone yet?

Oh, the shame and confusion that flooded her face on the instant. She halted as if struck. For an instant her eyes stared into mine; then dropped. I did not answer the Don. This way, madam, I said in a low voice.

In the courtyard, I called out the boy to harness the coach. The dancer stood, tiny enough, but now somehow reduced, wrapping her stole round her, this way, that; looking out blankly at the open country before the house, biting her lower lip. Take the young lady wherever she wishes to go, I said, feeling shame at the lack of honour in her going. She was a harmless girl. She mounted the step and hid herself in the corner of the seat so that I could not see her face. The boy whipped up, and they clattered away.

Now we must leave France – this accursed country, he called it. *It* was to blame for the ennui and depression that gripped him. *It* was wasting his life. He had influence in the courts of the Empire

– his name would count for something there. I was simply glad to be on the move again.

We drifted northwards and eastwards, passing from one small court to another. All these princes had their little clockwork armies, awash with 'generals'; a tough crew of Irish, English, Swiss renegades and mercenaries; near-gentlemen who drank hard and complained of the morals of the German women. That the women had too many, that was to say. The Don took to them. He would become a soldier once more; hadn't he fought the Turks as a young man? Philosophy was forgotten for the next brilliant summer and weeping autumn while the Don drilled, rode at the head of parades, hunted, shot with his new friends, had a succession of liaisons with married women – and declared himself at last more thoroughly bored than ever. As winter wrapped us in its cold fogs, we made our way southwards – in search of adventure; of something, *anything* of interest . . . So the years slip away.

So we ride in this coach, tugged through snow, towards the capital of the Empire, the city of V-, the driver shouting, Not far, not far now, sir; the Don's face scowling above his furs.

2

I'm looking into the square below. A cold spring morning. The clocks are striking ten. This city runs by the clock. It takes time to get used to their way of reckoning the hours. At home the church clock will ring one for sunset and five chimes for midnight. It makes sense to count from sunset and sunrise. Here the hours beat out, twelve to twelve, without meaning. The street-lights are put out at two strokes. At six, the streets are swept. Some time after that the rumble of carriages grows; the clack of horses' hooves and footsteps fill the air as the gentlemen arrive from the outer city, the workers from the new apartment houses. This is a city where men work for other men, and all work by the clock . . .

After an hour they are all in place. The streets send up the noise of lone carriages, men and women walking between the shops, stopping to talk and pass the day, all in a quiet, measured way. Even Turk and Greek – who in their own countries cheerfully slaughter one another – walk peaceably past each other in their bright or black gowns.

This life goes on until evening, when the roar of traffic swells again on its journey home. Lamps are lit in the streets. Here they take their pleasure as seriously as their work. But in its place – here everything has its place, and it is not in the street, but in the park, the concert hall, the opera. Carriages are forbidden to speed so that their noise and nuisance may be subdued. Uniformed policemen keep order, though everything is ordered. There are no beggars, but workhouses. Criminals and lunatics, as everywhere I suppose – but swept away from sight. Book and print shops; theatres and picture-galleries – but no ranting poets on street-corners, or street shows of puppets, or rude, vicious-faced Harlequins and pretty, black-browed Columbines. Instead, in every square the stout statue of some industrious man . . .

As there is in the centre of our square.

The morning rush has died. Gernsheim's print shop across the way has been open an hour. I turn away from the window, because I hear my master come into the room.

He has risen late again. His face is pale and drawn. He sits at the table and holds his head between his hands. Another 'bad-wine morning'. Not that he drinks to excess, but on and off all winter long he has suffered these blinding headaches, and at first he blamed the thin white wine they serve here. But I've suffered my fair share of hangovers and what he described was not one of those. There your head aches dully for an hour or so, then the pain lifts slowly away and you greet the morning like an old friend. No, his headaches, coming even when he left off drink, went on for hours. As if, he said, someone was splitting and splintering his skull. The only thing that could mollify the pain meanwhile was opium in water. That taken, he could rest, lying with a black cloth over his eyes, the attack muffled and put at arm's length, until it would suddenly withdraw and disappear as mysteriously as it had come.

I did not welcome his pain, but the sense of helplessness in his face gave me a queer pride in being able to minister to him, in being in charge of *him* for a while, instead of the usual way of things.

I mixed him a good strong draught. He sipped. When it began to take effect, he leaned back, rubbing his temples with his finger-tips, and said with gloomy humour, You'll make someone a good wife one of these days, Leporello.

We had been here all winter. The Don had volunteered his services to the Emperor's army, but the war which the Turks threatened had not broken yet. The Emperor put his mercenaries on half-pay; the Don and I lived quietly.

Well, quietly enough for the Don. Only I was allowed to see his sometime weakness; his complaints made little difference out-wardly. He kept up – as a matter of pride and duty – a steady stream of actresses and singers, with now and then a visit to one of the city brothels.

I kept a good house for him. House? Most of those who lived within the inner city walls took apartments, or single rooms, or shared a room. Behind the grand façades built over the coffee-shops and stables, furriers and cobblers, jewellers and cookshops, the tenements were full to bursting. Compared to the poor we lived well, in one of the best blocks, owned by a publisher and bookseller, an immensely wealthy man called Pabst. (You see, I do remember some names.) Pabst owned printers and binders, his own paper mills; the ground floor of our apartment house was taken up with his bookshop and warehouse.

That's how we had happened on this good place. Arriving in the city we had spent two months in small, flea-ridden inns. One day the Don went into Pabst's bookshop and was served by the owner himself. They became friends at once – which surprised me, for Pabst was a bachelor and had no wife to first attract the Don into his company. He was a Jew, and the Don always had the greatest respect for that people. They do not believe in the grey ghosts, he said. Though barred by his birth from the highest society, Pabst supplied most of its reading matter to the city. A Freethinker, he was interested by the Don's grandiloquent description of his *Refutation* – which I had seen him work at for maybe two days out of the last two months. Pabst was not to know that; he was most enthusiastic. He invited the Don to take the apartment above the shop – for a rent which, low enough, I do not think we ever paid. He even advanced him money against the promise of his book. As I understand is the way with writers, as soon as the Don received the cash he lost interest in working on his idea, and devoted his ingenuity to spending the money.

First, he purchased an entire new wardrobe – and I was able to step gratefully into his cast-offs again. We could not run to much more in the way of show, but the Don bought – did we ever pay for this either? – one of the carriages they call a *pirutsch*, from a high-class whore. The carriage was bright yellow; she had called it her Little Canary when it paraded in the parks, or between her assignations – but now she was to marry a baron and must put such frivolity away. The Don had it painted black, with his coat of arms picked out very small in blue and gold on the sides. Now it was discreet, unnoticeable at night, as sombre as if the doctor or bishop were calling.

With spring, his headaches eased, though he continued with opium to enable him to sleep. He doodled at his book for Pabst, went riding when the weather permitted, played billiards by the hour, and visited one of his two present mistresses on a strict rota. The liberality of the city, and of its emperor, appealed to him – though not at all to the great families he had thought to move among. They are all bloody tradesmen at heart, he complained. They berate the Jews for lending money; and build their empires on what they borrow.

For the most therefore, the Don lived in the *underpart* of the city. The highest we climbed was to the salon of the Countess of T-, who had left her husband and so was barred from the court. At her house the Don met an Englishman who had gone twice around the world. For what purpose I did not discover, as he seemed no wiser for it. But the Don was mightily impressed. Movement, he said again. Movement. It is the only way. To stay still is to die.

But we stayed, still; in the company of actors and actresses, of mercenaries who jangled medals on the uniforms of a dozen countries and none; of painters , coffee-house keepers, whores, musicians, and Pabst's stable of writers. I, who had mixed as an equal with the servants of princes and dukes, suffered a great fall, accepted familiarly by this crew, treated almost as an *equal*.

I was to fall further.

We could not afford a coachman. When the Don bought the carriage, he said, Leporello, you must drive.

I demurred. I said to him, How, sir, can I, known and dressed as your personal servant, appear as your coachman?

He stared at me in that puzzled way, surprised to find that I had feelings in the matter. In that case, he said coolly, you must wear a livery coat on the box and take it off when you get down.

I was insulted. At the least, I had always dressed as a second-hand gentleman. Was I now to be compelled to become less? And how, sir, I said, could I attend on you and your guests in the house, if it was known . . .

He waved his hand dismissively.

I will not do it, sir, I said.

His face hardened. Then I will get another servant who will, he roared.

Not so good as me, sir, I shouted back. They wouldn't put up with you.

He stormed out, his face black with anger. An hour later, he called me in to him. He was quite charming. After all my years of service, he must have been mad, he cooed. But, if he could not move about the city . . .

What else could I do? For the next few days I sat up on that box. Or rather, I skulked; a large hat pulled low, a greatcoat over my good clothes, its broad collar turned up to hide my face.

The merciful Gods took a hand. Only a week into my shameful occupation, the Don won 10,000 florins at *faro*. A huge sum then. I straightway announced that we could now afford a driver. The Don took my point, and we hired a young scoundrel.

We could have taken grander quarters, but the Don felt honour bound to repay some of Pabst's generosity and we stayed on. He was able though to rent another room in the city, where he could take his women. He did not tell me where it was. Lately he had become more secret in his affairs. I suspect he also wanted a bolthole where he could lie up during his attacks of pain, so as not to show his weakness to me. Certainly he would sometimes crawl back dead tired from an all-night tryst – whether with girl or opium nightmare, I could not tell.

He began to put on weight – a thing dreadful to him.

My God, I cannot be a *fat* lover, Leporello. He addressed the mirror, and my reflection standing behind his. A *fat* soldier!

Though in the past he had rehearsed to me the ideas of his hero Voltaire on the futility and idiocy of war, he had not abandoned his plan to enter the Emperor's service. Another point of honour – once embarked on a course he would not abandon it. There were endless bickerings between the Empire and the Turks, and skirmishes on the border, but no real battle. I think now that what the Don wanted was not war, but *movement*, distraction from the melancholy and pain he had lately to endure – that he put down to his body showing signs of age – some violent agitation of body and soul that would somehow take him back to his youth. And a gentleman must have some occupation. His book disappointed him. He could not get on with it, he complained. Not here. Not here. The only other work available for a gentleman is the lop-ping-off of heads. You could hardly expect him to go into trade.

As for me? I was settled. I had an understanding, as the English say, with a young woman, a seamstress who lived with her mother at the back of a very small shop in a very back street. When I was sure the Don was out for the night, I would let her into the apartment. I was attached to Lisa and she, I think, to me. We slept once in the master's bed. He must have left his magic there – my member stood like a pump handle all night. Dear Lisa . . . she only made me angry once. I had made love to her a fifth time as morning was breaking. I went down to the privy, and came back to find her fingering lovingly the Don's clothes hung in the closet, saying as I entered, Your master is a mightily handsome man, isn't he, Lepo – she couldn't wrap her pretty pointed tongue round the whole roll of my name – I have seen him riding in the park . . .

She made me unhappy for the whole day with this. When she came again we kept to my room.

But we got on well enough. I was thinking I might marry her even – God knows I was at the age when I should have been married. I pondered how, if it came to it, I should tell the Don; worrying both how he would take it – and, worse, if he would *take* Lisa. A young woman about the place – how could he resist? It would not be done to wrong or spite me. Merely, his right and duty. He would hand the *impressed* goods back, and expect me to take honour from the fact that he had stamped her worthy of service.

So we went on from day to day; which is the only way to use life up. But I was nibbled at the edges, as you might say, by my worrisome thoughts:

Could I marry in secret? – No.

Humbly beg my lord's assurance that he would not seduce my future wife? – Some hope.

Leave his service? I surprised myself by realising that this was the most impossible course of all. The truth was, my time with the Don had bitten so deep, it had unfitted me for any thought of a life of my own. I tell you: a servant is a barnacle; an extra hand; a piece of furniture to his master – they live off each other. I let things drift on, regrettably leading the girl further astray with my half promises; I flattered myself that this was how the Don would behave. Why shouldn't I?

But women can't let things alone. Lisa began to mutter that our engagement must be announced soon to the priest. That her mother was becoming insistent. Her good name … I should have dropped her then. There were plenty of others in that city, but I'm for one at a time. Why be at all that fuss?

I made up my mind. Almost. The only thing I would ask of the Don was his advice. I thought again over all my affairs, seated in a coffee-house across the way from the theatre where he was busy watching some opera or other. Probably by your Moser, or whatever you call him … We can afford to take her into the household, I whispered persuasively to the Don's ghost. Is she fair? Is she beautiful? came his shade's gloating reply. It was time to be gone. I got up and paid the bill. Outside, I dodged the carriages on the wide street and hopped up on the opposite pavement – into another part – the last part of our lives, if I had only known it.

For it is time to introduce Madame Schroeder; Frau Schroeder; Signora Schroeder. You have met her before.

In plays, the most shameless coincidences, the most amazing contrivances – sudden inheritances, ghosts, lost sons, true fathers – allow the players to meet and re-meet after years of separation, when the natural way of things would have flung and kept them far apart. But even life itself sometimes does not spurn the tricks the writers use. Or perhaps the spirits and demons of this world delight in picking us up and putting us down like so many toy soldiers, on any part of the map of our lives that they choose.

Here I was outside the theatre, waiting for the Don to come out in a few moments. Our carriage was at the steps; the boy on the box. I leaned into the dark coach, fiddling with something. The people were just beginning to turn out after the performance. A woman passed behind me, talking in court Italian, her voice clear and beautiful and rapid as water, though she spoke quietly. A voice I had last heard . . . I would swear . . . I recognised it instantly. I twisted out of the carriage. She was passing by, deep in conversation with a woman companion. It had been years, but that voice . . . It could be no one else.

Donna Sophia? I called.

She stopped and turned her face to me, enquiringly.

Donna Sophia – it is you? Oh, I was sure. You remember me. Leporello. In Pomodoro. The Abbess's. The young man who visited you? And afterwards, with my master in . . .

She stared at me as if I had popped out of a grave in her path, or a statue had spoken to her. She was dressed as a grand lady, and she acted the part. Her face, which for a moment had betrayed confusion, and perhaps fear, now returned to a calm, icy expression.

I am afraid I do not know you, sir, she said. I have never been in that city. And with that, she walked briskly away, her

252

companion throwing a curious glare of contempt and irritation over her shoulder at me.

The next instant the Don had come down the steps and stood at my side. Who the devil was that? he asked. Surely not a friend of yours? Before I could answer, I felt his hand on my back, pushing me forward. What are you waiting for? Follow them, my good fellow. Follow. Find out who she is – he commanded, in that suddenly urgent voice I knew so well.

Like a gun dog I was off at once, burrowing through the crowd, my experienced eye on the white shawl that now covered her hair. She hurried away under the lime trees. I glided from shadow to shadow. I am an expert at avoiding the light. The women turned the corner of the theatre building. A closed carriage awaited them; they got in, and started away.

It was no great difficulty at first to follow them in the press of traffic. When their carriage began to pick up speed, I broke into a trot, keeping an eye on the road. Luckily, I saw what I needed – a tradesman's cart coming up behind me. I waved the driver down. Two silver coins to follow the carriage ahead, I promised. He was a suspicious fellow, but with greedy eyes. He asked, Why? An affair of the heart, I said. He understood. At least, he understood money. Men of the world we sat together; the cart behind half-loaded with horse-dung. The carriage in front rolled sedately along.

We came through the city walls without let; gaining on the carriage which had been detained by the guard. We were in that part of the outer city where most of the villas had been built only in the past hundred years, since the last sack by the Turks. Going on a while through the streets, the carriage turned under an arch. I told the carter to pull up before we came level and got down, promising him another two pieces to wait for me and take me back.

I stole along the high outer wall and peeped round the gateway. A small courtyard lay through the arch. A largish house; the front door open, a maid holding a lantern as the two women entered. The carriage was parked to the side; the coachman just going in the servants' door. The women were inside. The front door closed.

I hadn't a clue where we were. If I was to find Sophia again, I had to have her name, and the address of this place. I tiptoed into the courtyard and hid myself in the corner where the gate pillar jutted from the wall. I might as well make myself comfortable. I sat down, my back against the wall and prepared to wait. It had turned chilly. The wind blew in the road outside. The moon shone onto the courtyard. In the house, the lantern's gleam went from the hall fanlight, wavering away into the house. Time dragged on. The light reappeared in an upstairs room. The slim figure of the maid came to the window and pulled the shutters to. More time. Her mistress was going to bed. I must allow time for the disrobing. To keep me warm I imagined each task. The dress pulled over her head. The petticoats. The stockings peeled down the white legs. The drawers drawn down. The nightgown sheathing the fine rounds of her hips.

I got to my feet. The last light had gone out. I must not rush. Wait. Wait. I was on service. One mistake can lose a battle.

I gave it a little longer. An owl hooted. I moved silently across the courtyard to the door through which their coachman had gone. I put my ear to it. Not a sound. I knocked softly.

I drew my figure up and stood off a pace from the door, guessing the maid would answer – the coachman would be too idle, as they all are – and not wishing to frighten her. I need not have worried.

Without a bolt being drawn, or a key turned, the door swung open. A whisper came out of the dark – Otto? You must be quiet . . .

Speaking just loudly enough to scare her, but not enough to waken anyone further in the house, I stepped forward and said, Madam, I am the servant of Don Giovanni di Tenario.

What? said the frightened voice inside.

The poor girl had evidently been expecting some bumpkin of a lover.

I was more than a substitute for *him*, whoever he was. I said, I am sorry to disappoint your ladyship. My master, Don Giovanni di Tenario.

Oh, what do you want? her poor voice wailed. Keep your voice down, *please*.

Certainly, my lady . . .

I am not the mistress. Please tell me your business and be gone.

Her lover must be expected any moment, I thought.

I gabbled on; My master has seen the beautiful lady, your mistress – a thousand apologies that I have confused you for her – but the mistake is surely understandable.

Yes? Yes? She pressed me to the point.

My master – it is not conventional, I know – he had me follow your mistress's carriage from the city tonight. I was to come to simply obtain her name and where she dwelt . . . I am sure you will understand . . .

Frau Schroeder. That's her name. Now will you go away?

She was in agony, poor thing.

At once – but the address of this house? There is no street name.

She hissed out the quarter, the street. Now go, she pleaded.

And your name, my sweet?

Go . . . She was in an ecstasy of embarrassment that her lover would come and find me there, or, worse, perhaps flee when he heard voices.

I will go, I said. But if my master gets to know your mistress, then I'll see you again . . . ?

Go . . . go . . . she moaned.

I did – and none too soon. I heard footsteps on the road outside. I just had time to gain my nook in the wall, when the steps stopped at the gateway, then came furtively on. A lanky young man tiptoed across the courtyard, making for the door. It opened silently before him. Frieda? came his hoarse nervous whisper. Otto? – her voice was scolding. Where have you been? Come in quickly. And be quiet. The mistress has only just . . . The door shut on them.

When I got back up the street the carter had gone. I had a long trudge back to town.

I did not tell the Don where the lady was, or *who* she was. I was not sure what her return might mean to us. It had been foolish of me to blurt out about the Abbess. Certainly that reminder of the past had made her afraid.

I told him that I had lost the carriage on the way, but that I knew the general quarter where the lady lived.

Then search her out, dear Leporello, he said impatiently. You know how. I am a busy man. Earn your wages.

He was brusque and energetic once more; his infirmities cast resolutely to one side, though they still nagged him. The war had broken out at last. Part of the Imperial Army was already engaged; in the city more men were being recruited and hastily trained. The Don wore the blue uniform of a colonel of cavalry – not, alas, the general he had hoped to be – there were far too many princes and counts and barons for that.

He made a fine figure again. He had lost weight; the grey in his hair was dyed out by me. He rode on a white mare in the Royal Park. Squads of men in long blue coats with white facings and gleaming brass buttons marched firmly towards each other, presented bayonets, snarled, and wheeled as firmly away. Guns boomed. White smoke drifted across the grass and up into the trees. Horses, unaccustomed yet to the noise of war, reared and squealed. Ladies watched from their carriages under the trees. Everyone agreed what a magnificent body of men we had. How the Turks would get a bloody nose and worse.

It wasn't my fight. I busied myself with more important matters. I went out to Sophia's house twice. The side entrance. By the end of my second visit I had displaced Otto in the maid Frieda's affections, and learned more about Sophia.

She was now Frau Schroeder, the widow of a merchant who had left her the house and a comfortable fortune. He had brought this wife back from his journeys south some years ago. No one knew quite what she was, said Frieda. They had lived quietly at first, keeping from society. Schroeder was the very picture of a doting husband, being much older than his wife. Later they had gone out a little more. Frau Schroeder had her own friends – good-for-nothings, said Frieda, who could be a straight-laced girl sometimes – filling the house with tobacco smoke, talking and playing music and dancing until the small hours. Long after the good husband had gone to bed. It was Frieda's view that he allowed a deal too much freedom to his wife. That the lady had allowed herself to go a great deal too far with a young fiddle player – a small dark pretty man, said Frieda contemptuously. She liked her men a little more robust did Frieda. Although she had to admit that she had never actually caught her mistress out, try as she might. But it was her opinion that the master had caught her in something and had died of a broken heart in consequence.

All this she told me as we lay in her narrow soft bed under the eaves on a fine morning when her mistress had gone out with her friend. There's another odd one, said Frieda. Then she said, Why do you want to know all this anyway? What about me ... and she reached down and vigorously began to demand my attention below again.

I could still feel the hard palms of her hands when I got back in the city. The master was out. Who should be waiting for me in the kitchen but Lisa? How did the Don live with this all the time?

Was she suspicious? She started in straightway. Have you told him yet? she demanded. What? That we are to be married? It is difficult. He has many duties. Duties? What about your duty? You have said we will marry. What if I miss my time this month? If he will not have you married you must leave him. A great lord, as you tell me he is, he'll make a settlement on you. That's the way of these noblemen. Yes, press him for a settlement. We can go into Mama's shop together.

Ever a practical girl, Lisa. I consoled her sufficiently to let me escape. I was not at all sure I wanted to join Lisa and her mama in their poky shop. Still and all, it was time I settled down. And I certainly didn't fancy going to the wars with the Don. A brave man, he would want to be in the thick of things. With me by his side. Knowing his luck, it would be me that got my head parted from my body. What good is war to a servant? It is an interruption to the daily round. An offence against domestic peace.

When the Don came back he was impatient to know what I had found out. I still did not know how much to tell him. He hated the past, he told me more than once. The past is for old men. Yes, it is.

257

The lady's name is Schroeder, I said. A widow. Artistic; no doubt sensitive. I did not paint a very enticing portrait.

In that case, he said, a letter was called for. Those women liked that sort of thing. Put coldly, it sounds calculating, but so many years' experience of women led him by habit to a certain line of conduct. Situations repeated themselves; he had been quickened by the sight of this woman, but that had happened a thousand times before. An element of weariness had crept up on him, or rather, wearisome sameness. He craved novelty, but even that repeated itself. I had tried to make this woman sound so ordinary, perhaps he scented some little mystery behind her. No doubt, like so many of his adventures, he reckoned it would come to a measure of success pretty rapidly, then the woman's secret plumbed, her reserve defeated, he could move on again.

Ah, my master should have been a great poet, or actor – no, not Ambrogetti – a famous general or statesman, but he was none of these things. He had one great gift – for *life*, for the charm, the brilliance of life. And that must be a constant display of fireworks, or a dark intrigue of passages and dangers leading into the night, to another pair of arms, another rendered body – or it was nothing. Even the most vivid of spirits can tire of fireworks.

There was an air of rote about the letter. He had written this one dozens of times, changing only the names of person and place. Tonight his eyes were tired, he had not the patience to write it himself, and dictated to me.

Madame, *no*, My Dearest Frau Schroeder (what an appalling language this is, he muttered), If you should find this letter impertinent I beg you to at once destroy it. I saw you last week at the Burgtheater – he spelled that out for me – and have since been utterly unable, and unwilling, to rid myself of that image of your beauty. I have taken the liberty of finding out your name. If you would allow me a private interview outside of the hours when you normally receive company then I might speak freely and without fear of compromising your good name. If you find me a bore, have me thrown out by all means. You may give your reply to the servant who bears this letter. He is my trusted companion.

Your fervent admirer,
Don Giovanni di Tenario

258

I arrived at the house the middle of the next morning. The Don had lent me his carriage. I was dressed in my best black coat and breeches.

The front door this time.

It was opened by my Frieda.

What are you doing? Are you mad? she said. She looked wildly back into the hallway.

I have a letter for Frau Schroeder, I announced, staring boldly into her eyes.

Is this a joke? She bit her lip. Go away, she said.

For Frau Schroeder. I held up the letter.

Give it to me. Then go. Go.

My instructions are to give it into her hand personally.

Who is it, Frieda?

A woman came out of a door into the hallway. I recognised her as Sophia's theatre companion. She looked coldly at me.

A letter, said Frieda. That's all.

For Frau Schroeder, I said.

The companion held out her hand.

Personal, I said. For the lady's hand only.

Come this way, she snapped.

Sophia was sitting in a small parlour, with the window open to a garden. She laid aside her book and stood up as we came in.

A postman, said the companion, who will not relinquish his mail.

How charming, said Sophia. Then she took me in fully. Why, you are the man who hailed me outside the theatre. Her face was puzzled, and annoyed.

The companion was as inquisitive as a weasel; her bright sharp eyes darted at me, at Sophia, sniffing blood.

She was to be disappointed. Sophia said, Regina, my dear, would you wait for me upstairs. I have some business with this gentleman.

Gentleman was one in the eye for Regina. She measured me up and down, and came to her own conclusions. Her mouth opened to speak. Closed. Spoke.

Gentleman? Of course – if you wish. I shall be close if you need me. With that she swished out.

My, but Sophia was beautiful. When I had seen her last she had been no more than a girl; now she was a fine-looking woman, her black hair drawn back from a long pale face, her mouth a straight bow, eyes large . . .

So, she said. What is it you want? If you have come to torment me with my past.

This was a great deal more dramatic an opening than I had thought to get. Her eyes were large and angry.

I have come to deliver a letter, I said.

Because you must know, she charged on, that I have long ago put all that unhappy time behind me. If you have some hope of taking advantage of knowledge you think you have of that time . . .

Donna Sophia – I would rather die. Do you not know me? I asked. With Don Giovanni?

She gazed steadfastly at me, then said: You were his man. Leopoldo . . .

Leporello, I said, and bowed.

After so many years, I had forgotten. I did not recognise you. How did you know me?

Your voice, Donna Sophia.

She could not decide whether to look vexed or pleased.

Then she said, But there – in the street – to bring up *that* place. The Abbess. Did *he* tell you? He swore never to tell.

He never did, signora. He would not do such a thing. It was I who told him of your plight in that place.

Her face reddened. She turned abruptly and went to the window. She stood looking out, her back to me. And how, pray, did you do that? she asked.

I told her that I was the young man who had been thrust into her dark cell one night. She would not remember that.

For a long time she was silent, then she said in a low voice, I remember. I thought you were a gentleman.

There is nothing I can do about that, signora, I said.

She turned and faced me. And last week, she said in a softer voice, I thought you were some blackguard who knew my past.

But you are not?

I swear not, my lady. We – the Don – would never have deserted you in that port except that he was fleeing for his life.

She came back and sat down. How strange. How strange, she said in a musing sort of way. Sit down, she commanded, and she rang a bell on the table beside her. We remained in silence until Frieda came in. Frieda gave me such a look. Her mistress told her to bring a glass of wine for the gentleman. The good, mind, she added.

When Frieda had gone, Sophia said, But why did the Don not come with you?

He does not know who you are, I said, with pride in my deception.

She bridled up. He didn't know me? she said.

No, no, I stuttered – he saw you from a distance only.

Then how did you find me?

Frieda came back. I took the wine glass gravely. She stared into my face as she straightened, as if asking, What's your game here, eh? Sophia again waited for her to go out of the room.

How *did* you find me?

I took the liberty of following your carriage, I said.

For the first time she laughed. What a pair of rogues you are, she said. Does your master send you often hot-foot after strange ladies?

No, no, Donna Sophia, I lied fervently, as I had learned to over the years. He did so admire her, I said, that he had to know where she lived in case he never saw her again.

And he gave you a letter for me? she asked.

I handed it over.

As she read, a smile came on her lips. Oh, but this is wonderful, she murmured. She laid it in her lap. She shook her head, still smiling. This note, she said – it is preposterous. It is that of a boy. Does he also make a habit of writing to ladies he has seen only at a distance? But her face was pleased now, charming in its new liveliness. I was forgotten. The go-between. Poor Leporello. I could have been half in love with her myself.

Take this reply ... She was as excited as a young girl, tripping over to the bureau, seizing paper and pen. Do not tell him who I am, she adjured me. Not who I really am . . .

So it was done. I took her reply back. The Don perused it once, twice, wrinkled his brow, pulled at his ear lobe, and put the letter in his pocket. Who was this? he asked.

The lady at the Burgtheater, I said.

He seemed tired. In the old days he would have been out of the house after a skirt as soon as I brought him news of it, but he had just broken with one mistress – the rumour was that she had dismissed him. Unthinkable.

I suppose I must go, he muttered.

You must, sir, I said warmly. She is very beautiful.

They are all very beautiful, he sighed.

But when he came back from her house the next night, he was in altogether brighter spirits.

An amazing thing, Leporello, he said. As if the years have fallen away. Do you not know who she is?

Frau Schroeder, sir, I said, straight-faced.

No, you dolt, who she really is?

No, sir.

So he told me, with great amusement, her name, and how unobservant I was. How poor my memory, but how I had done him a good turn nevertheless.

I suppose, sir, I said, that you picked up with her where you left off?

No, that's just the thing, dammit. His face was rueful. She won't have me, he said. She has heard all about me, she says. If I am to have her, I am to have no other. Out of the window with trollops and mistresses. No more midnight meetings; no more hot afternoons. I think she means marriage, no less. Marriage, my boy.

If he expected me to laugh, I did not. That night he sat on the side of his bed, quiet, watching me as I put away his clothes. He expected me I think to make one of those comically disparaging remarks about marriage that valets make in the plays. I did not oblige him. He retired, his face full of thoughts. No, leave the candle, he said, when I went to take it. Shall I mix you a draught, sir? I asked him. No, he wanted to think. But when I went into his room in the morning, the familiar brown smeared glass was by his bedside, the bottle had gone down, and he was still sleeping deeply.

From that time on he spent all his spare hours with Sophia. The very picture of the dutiful suitor. The first time I accompanied him there, he introduced me airily – You remember my man? Leporello? I do indeed, she said, and smiled, one conspirator to another. The companion, Regina, looked on stony-faced. Was she there as a chaperone? Even the Don would have difficulty making up a threesome with that one, I thought. When they dismissed me I took the opportunity of course of seeing Frieda. While they were engaged in their chaste courtship, I was pressing the maid against the kitchen wall.

Alas, I had little time for Lisa. I found I had lost my taste for her somewhat. When the Don was at Sophia's house and I at home, I told the boy to inform any callers that no one was at home. In the days that followed the boy came up with two notes from Lisa. The first he handed to me leeringly, hoping no doubt for some *buonamano* from me; he got the back of my hand on his ear. The second he tossed into my room and then fled down the stairs. I could barely read her scrawl, except to see that the first note was puzzled by my silence; the second mightily angry. Poor Lisa. I thought to keep her up my sleeve, in case the Don's pursuit of Sophia should falter and I had to lose Frieda. But the lovers went from strength to strength. I began to weigh the household of Frieda–Sophia in a better balance than Lisa–Mamma and the dark little shop. I should not have worried; the Don, as always, settled my fate.

One morning, on rising, he came out at last with the question.

What, Leporello, do you think of marriage?

I have not had any experience of that state, I said. I understand it suits for most people, less so for others.

Excellently put, he said. Because I think it is time we were settled. You too – you're well old enough.

I could say the same for you, sir, I said.

His eyes blazed. For a moment I expected a row. But then he smiled. A fair shot, he said. Well, I must tell you that I intend to marry Donna Sophia.

I busied myself, turning away from him.

Well? he barked. What have you to say of that?

Ah, sir, I faced him, and I swear that tears stood in my eyes. I was never better pleased at any news of yours, I said. She is a peach. A jewel . . .

Enough. I always knew you liked her well, he said. But he was most pleased. He got up and strode about the room. And you – you brought her to me – have you had no thoughts of marriage yourself? I have been a burdensome taskmaster . . .

No, no, I protested. But, I admitted that I had now and then entertained some such thought, but knew where my duty lay, and but for . . .

No buts. No buts, he exclaimed, slapping me on the shoulder. That little maid of Donna Sophia's. Ah, you see – I know all about it.

But sir . . . , I said.

Don't dissemble, he said. I know of her, I say. Of course you must, my dear. I will see Donna Sophia tomorrow. Without fail.

I did not mean, sir . . .

I don't think he heard me. He was so full of his own life once more. He rattled on: Perhaps this *quiet* life will suit me. Then we'll see, eh? Well, why not? he trumpeted. I've never been married. Yes, of course you must too, Leporello. Let us have a rash, an epidemic, a plague of marriages . . .

So, it fell out, like the end to a romance or fairy-tale, that he was reunited to a lost love; the servant married to his new mistress's maid. A double wedding, the Don insisted. Master and wife. Man and maid. What a witty conceit, the city gossiped. The weddings were to be made in the Cathedral, but the Archbishop refused the Don's grand plan, and Frieda and I were spliced in a side chapel by a priest with toothache, while out of our sight the choir sang orisons of joy over their bowed heads. But we emerged straight after the fine couple, and trod on the flowers flung down for them.

We all moved into a larger house, inside the city walls. Regina, the companion, stayed one whole week, and departed with cheeks flaming one morning – the Don standing out on the narrow balcony above the front door, his sword pointing into the air, roaring, Get out, get out, you bitch – like God commanding Eve to be gone from Paradise.

Sophia, when she returned later – for he had done whatever he had done while she was out – was at first upset at the loss of her friend, but friendship is nothing to love. And so we settled down together, as happy a household as you could wish. As happy as peas in a pod.

Only life is not like a novel. Not like a play.

And marriages, if made in Heaven, are broken in Hell.

3

You tell me all the legends have me as a clown. And this has all the necessaries for a farce – the rascally servant wed to the rough-tongued maid; the rake reformed, middle-aged, passions spent, bones aching, married to the rescued whore, who turns out a lady. Where could it go wrong?

For that was a *happy* house. The first, and last, I have been in. And so for the Don, I swear.

When he was away on his commission for the Emperor, Sophia was a darling, and I her favourite, oh I am sure. Her friend and confidant. She regarded me as the spirit that had brought her first and again to the Don. And Frieda seemed happy with my company, though I think sometimes that she regarded it as part of her employment to be expected to marry the new master's man. Women are most practical. Not that, like a lot of men fired by the constant congress suddenly available on first marrying, I did not spread my new joy about a little. Discreetly, of course – other men's wives, never single girls or widows. It was as if – I fooled myself, but what servant doesn't – I had taken on the mantle the Don had laid down. If *he* saw any other woman, I did not know about it.

On the contrary, he appeared to relish his new bride; her beauty, charm, the forthrightness and wit of her speech, the independence of her mind. Her friends – that easy-going mob of poets and musicians Frieda despised – became his friends. They were all male, but now felt free to bring their mistresses and even wives, so that all evening and half the night, music and conversation filled the house. I did not observe the Don making up to any of the women, and he was not jealous of any of the men on Sophia's account. How could he be? He regarded them with fond scorn as popinjays, amusing fellows, but compared to himself, why nothing, nothing at all.

So we were all a family, and I realised how much I had missed that feeling of belonging which had been snatched away from my childhood. Perhaps the Don felt the same. For he wrote, for the first time I had ever known, to his family home. He informed them proudly – I copied the letter for him – of his position in the Emperor's army. Of his new household. It would be weeks or months before he got his reply, but after the time the post should have taken at its fastest there and back, he grew impatient and angry. He was hurt by their silence. By the silence of his father. He wished him to be proud of his son.

How was the Don really faring? you ask. You say I have told you of his sickness, his moods – had they quite vanished? No. For all his ebullience, and the business of those days, and though he would admit of no weakness in front of Sophia, he did tell me that his infernal headaches had returned. He asked me to prepare a draught and lay a glass each night in the cupboard in his dressing-room – no doubt to keep it from Sophia's knowledge. Sometimes I found it still full; increasingly it was empty by morning.

For the rest our life went merrily on. How sweet to lie with my wife early in the morning, to wake with the sun sliding in the window, and to slide into the warm body beside me. To know that, behind the wall there, the master and his wife lie, enjoying the same sun, the same ecstasy. I got fatter and happier.

How, among all this, shall I introduce you to Tragedy? What could be more satisfying for the whey-faced moralists than to know that poor sinners come to grief. That is the way all moral tales end. Why should we have believed them? My master had cheated Hell once, given his legend the slip – why not continue to do just that ?

And my mistress, Donna Sophia, to make our happiness complete, announced that she was with child. Odd to think of my master, with all his knowledge of those *capotes anglaises*, condoms, French Caps, vinegar sponges; whirls, balls, douches, abortions and miscarriages, that he should turn out a father-to-be.

He warmed himself in her glow; the holy, inwardly-lit state of concern for her child and herself as the vessel in which it was being borne towards our world that shone in her face. He sent me a league out of the city to bring fresh milk from the dairy that supplied the palace. Frieda and the old cook we had taken prepared the most delicate and nourishing of foods for her. For the Don's son. Because they could not think that such a handsome man could produce any child but a son.

And the cook, despite her age, quick-moving, and with a lick of fire in her eyes such as these old women often have, appointed herself nurse to Sophia. Why not? She herself had produced four sons, who in turn had sired children without number or let, so that she made them sound like the start of the world. If such a woman as I am doesn't know about the bearing of ignorant men into the world, she said, who does? She followed Sophia about the house, forever chivvying her in what to wear, when to sit, when to stand, when to lie down. Bearing down on the Don too; that he must not tire his good lady, nor cause her concern – for she knew – Holy Mother of God, she knew – what creatures men are. And the Don took it in good part, and appeared before them all as the most attentive husband.

Sophia's belly rounded early – a sure sign, said the cook, of a boy.

In the kitchen they discussed all the other endless particulars that attend the condition – in my hearing because, being

Frieda's husband, I had become quite invisible to them. Their chief concern was Sophia's age. At thirty, the cook said, she herself had had all her four sons. To start now was a dangerous enterprise.

With autumn came the war that had been promised so long. The Don was called to his regiment. I was in the next room when I heard him tell Sophia that it would all be over before winter. That he was contracted to go. A matter of honour. And she said of course he must go.

It *is* a matter of honour, he growled to me that night. It is my part in this world. Was he to ponce off his wife forever? For her money had rented this house; she it was who gave him the money he then disbursed to me for the household. The servants soon get the hang of these things. I steeled myself to volunteer to go with him. Was I a coward? I was saved from knowing. The Don said that he knew I must want to go with him, but that it was my duty to stay behind. He was placing the house and Donna Sophia in my charge. It was small consolation, he knew. He hoped he did not impugn my honour . . . A strange thing, obscure to me, this honour in someone else's cause. No sir, it is a great enough honour you pay me, to look out for the mistress, I said. But who would look after him? He took my hands in his and squeezed them gently as he spoke, My friend, I *can* look after myself . . . We were like lovers parting. We are all fools at these times.

A few days later, we all gathered on the balcony to see the men go out of the city. He had arranged to bring his troops beneath our windows, as in the old days, he told me, a knight would pass from his own castle to the Crusades. I *did* feel a coward and less as we waited on that balcony; Sophia shawled against any autumn chill, Frieda one side of her, the cook the other. We waited, I hung back. Then they cheered and I joined in with a choke in my throat, hugging the shadow of the shutter that I might not be seen, as the riders jangled and clopped into the narrow street, the Don at their head. They were a brave sight, going to victory.

The city was quiet. No more boom of cannon or smoke in the park; no swaggering and jingling of troopers in the square. Winter had come. There was no news of victory. Snow fell. Prices went up. The poor went hungry as the poor always do. My fellow servants told me that their masters had begun to mutter against the generals, their cousins, waved off such a little time ago, and discussed replacements as they refilled their glasses.

In her room, her belly growing like a beautiful pear on a slender tree, Sophia had me tell her stories of the Don's adventures. When he was young. She always said it like that – *When he was young*, perhaps to distance those tales from herself and her life with him. She must have felt she was the last of his conquests; the one who had finally conquered.

So I told her fairy-tales. Of the Don waylaid by mischievous spirits in women's bodies. Of light-hearted affairs that came to no serious end. Of escapes, and dalliances, and plots to ensnare him. Oh, piffle, she laughed. I know him. He was not good at all. He will be good, but I know what he is like, Leporello. I *knew* what he was like. And I know that he has changed. But tell me the truth. Tell me about you two. How you met him. Tell me again . . .

And I would tell her, again and again, as I have told you. But, as an honest servant, not quite so honestly. I embroidered adventures, sewed together happenings years apart, making him the hero, the knight of his own life. And I his valiant squire – until she would laugh again and say, No, no – that's not how it was, and lead me into truth so that I gabbled and gave away too much. Which was still not enough for her. And once, when I had finished for the tenth time telling her how he had vowed to rescue her from the Abbess, how I had told him of her wretched plight, and he – for the tenth time – had said solemnly to me, Then we must help this poor girl, my boy – and thought for the tenth time I had gone too far – she said, Oh, Leporello, is that how it was, how it *truly* was? And for the first time she told me the story of how he had visited her in that place, which I had not known before.

It went like this.

It became clear to me, she began, that I could not spend the rest of my youth in that dark cell. Or be expelled from the house back to the streets with my reputation gone. I told the Abbess that I had reconsidered my position, but begged her to introduce me to life in that place in as gentle a manner as possible. My youth and innocence would be twice as attractive if dangled in front of her gentlemen for a little while. Very well, said the Abbess. She would give me two weeks in the public room. Men gathered there, not always to pick up a woman, but often just to talk, away from their wives and cares. She would say that I was her niece from the country, a most well-brought-up young lady – that, she said, should preserve me from their immediate advances. But then . . .

Then, she would select a gentleman for me herself. A man who understood such bashfulness. I would not be sorry, she assured me. And as soon as I knew what was what in that department, well – I would settle down to a comfortable life.

So I made small-talk, served food and wine, and watched the girls go out, and come back in again, as if nothing had happened to them. One or two had sympathy for me; the others regarded me as a fool. My day drew near.

I had had the mad idea that I could persuade some genial old widower to buy me out of the house; I would say that I was innocent, that I would make a good and honest wife, for the price of his visits he could have the same at home . . . But looking round those reptiles and rascals, I could not see one whose cunning face would fall for such a story, or any I could stomach as my liberator. I thought constantly of the young man – ah, yes, I did, Leporello – who had promised to help. But when I heard nothing further from him, from *you*, I thought him as faithless as the rest. Now came the evening on which the Abbess had pinned her hopes, and I feared to lose mine.

I was placed in one of the rooms and seated myself fearfully down on the bed.

The gentleman – the experienced gentleman – was brought in. The Abbess gave a coy smile to him; a hard stare at me. I had been expecting some repulsive old roué. This was – ah, but you know him, knew him – such a sturdy, handsome man. But at that moment he might have been the oldest and ugliest of them all.

He had heard a great deal about me, he said. He knows his duty only too well, I thought in despair.

Unlike the heroines of romance, I did not fall on my knees. I said, Sir, I know why you are here. But hear me first. I told him that I had been brought to this place by deceit. If he helped me to escape, he would be rewarded – I saw at once that I could not play on him the trick I had planned for some old fool. I even brought out a small knife I had hidden away and said that if I was touched, I would end his life first and then mine. I have a friend outside these walls who will protect me, I said.

He laughed at that. He did not come here to have his tripes out. Put up your weapon, he said, I know your friend. It was he who told me of your plight.

I interrupted her – He did not tell you your friend was his servant, then?

Why, no, Leporello, said Sophia, otherwise . . . And, oh, I should not tell you this . . . She blushed, her hands flew to cover her face, but she watched me between her fingers . . . He asked if my friend . . . he was most insistent . . . had harmed me in any way . . .

Harmed you? For a moment I did not know what she meant.

. . . Had taken *advantage* of me. Oh, dear. She laughed. Am I so wicked? Perhaps he would not have taken me out of that place if he had thought that . . . and nothing happened did it, Leporello? Except I fell asleep on your shoulder . . . Oh, I *am* sorry for laughing so, Leporello . . .

She was laughing merrily enough at her memory. And I thought bitterly also that the Don would never have lifted a finger for her if he believed she had lain with me. A knight cannot accept his squire's leavings.

What then? I said thickly.

Oh, you must know the rest. He told me that he was planning to leave the city soon. He promised to see what could be done for me. Until then he would instruct the Abbess that I was to be left alone. To be reserved for a special client. The Abbess knew that he was a friend of the Duke. No one would dare touch me. He would not desert me, he said. Oh, so very gently.

It was only after he had gone that I discovered his name.

The other girls were most jealous. They told me *terrible* tales of him. A couple of weeks passed. I had fallen into despair again, thinking that he too had deserted me. Then I was told to get ready to go with four of the other girls to Caesaretto. I could see no way out then – but of course there was.

He *did* keep his word. As you see.

She folded her hands on her belly.

As I would have kept mine, if I had been a gentleman, I said to myself. I realised again what I should have known as a good servant, that these two, Sophia and the Don, and all our masters and mistresses, live in a world truly above and beyond our own. In these talks with her I had been allowed to ascend the stair, but there were steps missing, an unbridgeable gap beyond. From then on my taste for these conversations quite cooled. I could not talk any longer with the same freedom to her, or enjoy the old warmth and familiarity.

I was the Don's servant, I reminded myself harshly. Play-acting entered into my solicitude for her. What was I now but the keeper for this house full of women? I should be at the war with my master; a soldier, a man.

I questioned, and doubted, my mistress's sweetness. Did everyone act out a part? That she could surround herself with her worthless friends while others had marched away. How come she had told me – a stranger – that tale in the brothel all those years ago? How had she – who so believed in what they call *love* – so conveniently contrived marriage to the wealthy merchant, Schroeder? What tales had she told to ensnare my master?

But I was always a poor hater. What seemed a lifetime of these dark thoughts was only a couple of weeks or so. How ridiculous these things become when we look back. Sophia summoned me to her one evening and asked me to sit down. I sat, with this new stiffness in my manner. She leaned forward in her chair, her hands pressed lightly together, inches away from mine, clasped firmly to my knees. She said, Leporello, have I offended you? We were so jolly. Now you go about sulkily all the time. If I have said anything to offend you – now tell me and I am sorry.

No, no, signora, and I tried to avoid her eyes, but was drawn back by her silence. If you could have seen how shining and beautiful her face appeared. I hesitated, then said, It is just that I feel I should be with my master. Heaven knows . . .

Ah, and he has left you in charge of us poor women? Well, do that, Leporello. It is his wish. There is no better man to do it. I know we both love the Don . . .

Ah, then I loved her again.

I knelt and kissed her hand. She gazed down at me with such puzzlement and affection I could weep to remember it. Oh come, Leporello, she cried, You are our dear squire. You must represent your lord.

Then I did. I swept about the house again in full happy pomp. I put in order all the duties I had neglected. I made the house buzz and stand to attention and whistle and sing to itself. We must be ready for the birth of the Don's son, for the return of the Don. The house must be proud.

When I remember how simple I was, how easily made happy.

The Don came back a week after the Christmas celebration. Not half as many as set out came back. Every church, every barn a *lazzaretto*, said the Don bitterly, full of the dead and dying. Not from wounds gallantly received, but dysenteries and cholera and plagues. The Russians, who had promised to fight alongside the Empire, had neglected to turn up for the war. What was left of the sick army, led by its counts and princes and Irish generals, had suffered rout after rout at the hands of the Turk. The returning army did not parade in triumph through the city. It arrived and dispersed almost invisibly, so that the only soldiers I saw appeared silently in the streets at dusk or just before dawn, some with the ghost of a dispirited swagger, but others hugging close to the walls as they hurried home.

The Don was in a poor way. I feared he had caught some fever in the midst of all that sickness and filth. The grey wires in his hair seemed to have multiplied twenty-fold; his eyes were sunken and dull above his cheekbones. That first night the women flocked about, to cosset and comfort him. But this only served to put him in a rage. I will not have all this, he bellowed. Leave me. Leave me. Frieda and the cook scuttled away. The Don said more gently, but with some effort to be so, Please, Sophia – leave me a while. Have the bed made up in my dressing-room. You must rest. Please go to bed. No, no, she would stay with him. Leporello will see to me, he said, and again told her to go to bed, with a testiness in his voice that he tried to hide but could not quite. She hesitated again, then bent over him and kissed him on the mouth. And this was to me somehow the most shocking thing I had ever seen, it was so private and tender. I turned away so as not to see them. You are sure you will be all right? she whispered to him. In the morning he would be fine, he said. Fine. But go now. She must rest . . .

When she had gone, closing the door softly to, he roused himself and strode in agitation about the room. He told me to bring him brandy. He was damned if he was going to feel like this all night, he muttered. He drank a large tumbler full of spirits and water, then had me refill it as he slumped back in a chair.

This war is a filthy, a shitty business . . . you have no idea, Leporello, he said.

I am sure you acquitted yourself nobly, sir, I said.

The one action he had taken part in, his regiment had been sent galloping the wrong way by some idiot general and had passed under the enemy guns. A hundred men, he said, were rendered into butcher's meat in a few seconds. Another hundred converted to cripples or blind beggars to dab along the streets. That was all he had seen of glory.

He sat in silence, looking into the fire. After a long time I dared to say, Won't you sleep now, sir?

He stirred in his chair, his eyes still on the flames. I do not care so much for my bed nowadays, he said.

I could think of nothing else to say for the moment. He waved a hand at me. You go. By all means, Leporello. You go.

But, sir . . . , I protested.

Go, he told me. Just go.

Reluctantly, I went to bed. Frieda was snoring softly. I lay

274

awake for a long time, straining my ears to catch any sound of the Don. At last I heard his steps pass my door. I heard his door shut, and I fell asleep.

A spring night.

The musicians and actors and poets had been banished now for weeks. The Don said that their music and chatter were not good for Sophia; but it was because he had no more taste for them. They were no longer invited; when they called I sent them packing. If they were lucky, that is. If not, they were likely to be met by the Don and treated to one of the terrible tempers which now blew up from nowhere. The house was quiet this night.

I sat in the kitchen. The master was out; at Herr Pabst's, he said. I was all set for an idle time; the women were upstairs. All at once, Frieda comes scurrying into the kitchen. I must go for the midwife at once. But she's nowhere near her time, I said, yawning.

Hurry, you fool, said Frieda, grabbing up linen.

The midwife was in bed. It took a good quarter-hour to rouse her and get her to the house, though she only lived a street away.

Frieda stood at the top of the stairs, watching for us. I ran up, carrying the midwife's carpet bag, the fat dame lumbering up behind. The door along the passageway was open and I heard Sophia gasp then cry out. Wait here, said Frieda to me, and hurried the midwife in. I edged along the passage. The voices in the bedroom were soft, yet urgent, enjoining Sophia to turn this way, lift that . . . then Sophia screamed and the shock of that sound struck through my body. She screamed again and again. I wanted to go from there. I could not stand to hear such evidence of agony. But I could not leave my position. A merciful quiet. The midwife came out, in her hands a large shallow bowl which she laid just outside the door. You, empty this, she cried. Fill it with fresh water. Be quick. The bowl was heavy, filled almost to the brim with blood whose warmth I could feel through the porcelain and again as it slopped, soaking through my sleeve.

When I brought the water back up, the cook opened the door to me. Sophia groaned and cried out, Oh, oh Holy Mother – what has he done to me?

Frieda, at the bedside, saw me, and reached up, rattling the bed-curtains together so I should not see her mistress. The cook took the water and shooed me out, saying in a low voice, You see what you men bring us to. You see?

I waited in the kitchen. The screams began again upstairs. I put my hands over my ears to shut them out, but they pierced through walls and bone. I poured out some wine, but could not taste it on my tongue, which had somehow dried and furred up. Should I go and find the Don? But what could he do? The house was feverish with something from which both he and I were excluded. They had not once asked for him. I drank some more wine. There was no sound from upstairs now. The clock tolled in the hall. I went to the foot of the stairs and listened.

Steps along the landing; Frieda leaned over the banister. Fetch a doctor, she called. Her voice was afraid.

What's wrong? I asked.

A doctor. A surgeon. Don't stand there.

Where am I to find a doctor? I said.

Fool! Her eyes blazed. Your mistress could die.

I was out on the street. Where was I to get a doctor? For a moment I panicked. I looked up at the house. Light shone dimly though the curtains of the mistress's room. She had suddenly become not Sophia, but a distant, threatened object, with women moving about her in ways I couldn't guess, but that somehow threatened us all. The house seemed to quiver in the darkness.

I ran to our neighbour, where I knew the steward. He spoke in alarm through the door, fearing robbers from my insistent knocking. His master was old; the house retired early. When he opened at last he was in his nightshirt. To my gabbled request, he answered, Yes, he knew Surgeon-, at -strasse. He shouted, Good health to your mistress, as I raced away.

The surgeon was at another house. I went there. Lights; the sound of a woman singing, the tinkling of a harpsichord. What did I want? No, the surgeon had gone. Did they know of another? The door slammed in my face.

The lamp on the wall flared in the wind. I heard Sophia's patient soft voice talking ... I ran here and there; to an inn, to another house where they knew the Don. They gave directions to two other medical men. Neither were at home. One at the theatre. Another – a wink – occupied elsewhere. I stood in a cold sweat in that street. Truly, I was a murdering fool. Then I saw that God had guided my steps to where I should have gone in the first place. A brothel my master had used before his marriage stood across the way.

Yes, said the maid, the doctor who saw to the girls was sure to be at home. He only worked in the mornings.

A kindly man, up reading at this hour, he hastened back with me.

The Don had returned before us. He stood at the top of the stairs, in shirt and breeches, his face wild. He spoke in a hoarse, urgent voice, Come up. Come up at once.

The babe – a son – was stillborn. Sophia died at noon the next day.

4

I despised them all, Leporello, except her. It is not enough for God that we are happy, but he must be repaid.

His voice was the only sound to break the silence of the upper part of the house on the day of the funeral, and this was his longest speech, apart from softly uttered requests or commands, since the deaths of a week before. Otherwise, silence. You felt that any normal converse, a laugh, a sigh even, would reverberate through the house, crack its walls, dissolve its stairs and windows; the whole place crumble and fall about our ears. So there was silence; to preserve us.

He stood at the window, black-suited, looking out at the fair blue day.

Do you know what I was doing, Leporello, the evening that your mistress lay dying? I was with a whore. I was sporting with a whore. A grand lady – but a whore. Now – what do I say to Heaven for that?

What could I say? I had no words then or now to know or think or describe or guess at what went on in his head. Words are the things we give to each other at such times, and they are never of any value. Death has no language. The only way we can cheat him is to leave some words like these. Oh do, if you read this, preserve us: Leporello and the Don and Sophia and the poor dead child, and the ridiculous Cavillosos and Ambrogetti the actor, the imps and dancers and the whores – they do not deserve to die. I am an old man – I do not expect many will outlast me. And when we are all washed away, who will care? The men and women of the future will have other heroes and fools. But if they forget us, forget utterly, they will lose the past, they will live only in the instant, in the terrible prisons of their bodies.

That is not enough.

Oh, my poor philosophy. It's not good to think about these things. It is God's task to arrange the world and for us to obey His will. Where would we be without God and the Holy Mother and all the angels ranged above us? If we ceased to believe would Paradise empty, the Tree wither, the Cherubim turn to stone? For the Don they had ceased to exist. Even now, in desolation, he did not turn to God.

At the window, he squared his shoulders, thrust his fists into his coat pockets, and turned to face me. His face was set; he looked ten years older. This is my first grief, Leporello. There will be no other, he said. He strode past me and went out of the room.

Looking back, it is from this day that I date his decline. Whether the malady that was to be his end already afflicted him I do not know; it came and went away and came again and why providence should make a man suffer at one time rather than another is a great mystery. But whenever it lifted, I noted that it always returned in slightly greater force, as if it had been an army recouping its strength, knowing what a formidable citadel had to be taken.

For weeks after the funeral the house moved around him silently; tiptoeing past his door. I was the only one allowed into his room – his old dressing-room, because he had ordered *their* bedroom sealed. He did not go out in company. He had glided, a stern ghost, through Sophia's acquaintance at the funeral. The house was closed to callers. At night he drugged himself to sleep, but still dreamed, waking me with calls that I hurried to answer – only to find him in deep, fretful slumber, sweating and turning like a feverish child. Whatever terrors they were he saw in sleep, he put them aside with day. Every morning he would have his horse brought out and ride for two or three hours in the parks that encircled the city. The rest of the day he spent in his room. One night, when he was unduly late down to dine, I knocked on his door. There was no answer. I opened the door quietly. He sat at his desk, or rather, crouched over it, his head bowed, his hands clamped in a great double fist on his forehead. On the floor in front of the desk were shards of paper he had torn and pushed over the edge.

I came in and knelt, beginning to gather them up.

What are you doing? his voice growled.

Your papers, sir, I said.

Who is that?

Leporello, sir, I said in surprise. I looked up to see that he had come round the desk and stood glowering above me.

His face was enraged. His mouth working, all at once he shouted, Get out. Get out. Grovelling like some worm.

As I scrambled to my feet he aimed a kick at me. I fled; his screams coursing me along the passage.

At the foot of the stairs the women had gathered, gaping upwards. The cook crossed herself. Frieda's fingers played at her collar. She said, What is the matter? What have you done?

The master is upset, I said sternly, gathering my tattered dignity together. It is his grief.

His grief, the cook echoed sagely in the irritating way of old people. He'll recover now, she said and paddled away to the kitchen.

An hour or more later his bell rang. I steeled myself going to the door. But if I was a coward, I was his servant too. The papers were still strewn across the floor. At first I did not know where he was. Then I saw his legs stretched out on the bed, the curtain hiding his body.

Quite calmly, he asked me to fetch him a basin of warm water with a spoonful of salt dissolved in it. And a soft, clean cloth. He must bathe his eyes. They were on fire.

When I got back, he sat on the edge of the bed and dabbed at his eyes, turning away from me. He was ashamed to let me see any sign of weakness in him. I asked if I should clear up the papers from the floor. Again quite calm, he assented. He did not seem to remember his rage at all. Whenever in the past he had lost his temper with me, for no real reason, he had always gone out of his way later to charm me back into a good mood – in a way that seemed to gently reprove me for making him angry in the first instance. There was no trace of this in him now.

That night, at his request, and for the first time, I made two draughts up. One in case he woke in the night, he explained. I was to leave the candle, but to screen it; to look directly at it hurt his eyes, but he no longer cared to wake into darkness.

This spell of illness lasted two or three more weeks. He said that it must be some fever he had picked up in the war. I did not remind him that his sleeplessness, his head pains, and the irritation in his eyes had plagued him before ever we came to this city.

It was now three months since Sophia's death. He never talked of it. Indeed he seemed to have come to a decision in himself to now renew his life. My master was, after all, a man of strong passions. Women were as necessary as food and wine are to you or me. As far as I knew, he took no new mistress, nor renewed links with any of the old. But he went out almost every night without saying where. I knew. He went to the whore-houses.

The fact was that I had lost half my occupation with him; as his scout for women, his arranger, his ponce, his go-between. All this

I had not missed during the short happy rule of Sophia over our fortunes; now, in this gloomy house, though summer stood outside, my own idleness, the knowledge that he had no need of my services, all chafed on me. Worse, the women soon discovered where he was going. The cook shook her head, but said it was a necessary thing for a man to seek women. Frieda was less forgiving. It is only now, all these years after, I see that she may have entertained some mad notion that the Don on the death of his wife might take her as his mistress, and she could not forgive his disregard. She said indignantly that he was a fine type, the poor mistress just gone, to act the libertine. It was not as if he was a young man either, she added venomously. And, though it was beneath his notice, I felt guilt at my own happy state and feared to make love to Frieda when he was in his room, in case he should hear us and it would remind him of his own loss. I began to fail my wife in the duties of marriage – a matter of great dishonour. And great discomfort too when her tongue lashed me, or she whispered in the kitchen to the cook. The old woman would snigger and look over at me, shaking her head. Did I imagine it or were my portions of food lessened, and put more dismissively before me? At least, I suppose, said Frieda, for all his faults, your master is a *man*.

Oh, unhappy state.

Suddenly, we all seemed to be splitting asunder. I longed for him to recover his health, his spirits, that we might set out on our travels in the old way; that we might be young again. There is nothing can replace youth; such wisdom as I have learned was not worth the price that had to be paid.

So, the Don must have women. That summer he worked his way through all the whorehouses. It was as if he could not stand to have the same woman twice. Odd tales came to me. There is nothing servants like more than to hear talk about others' masters, unless it is to tell tales on their own. It appeared, one told me, hearing it from the dinner table of his Count, that the Don would not always nowadays indulge in copulation, but would hide and watch through a peephole as the distinguished men of the city sported. But not too distinguished – because of the scandal if a grand name found out that he was being watched – unless of course, as sometimes is the case, he wanted to be seen at his task. For the most part the Don would watch merchants, lawyers, soldiers, scholars at work in the mines of Venus. He did not paddle himself as most of these watchers do, but simply placed himself on a chair, hands on his knees, put his eye to this *camera obscura*, and observed; his face expressionless. At other times, the legends said, his own appetite was insatiable. He would fuck two girls in a bed, turn and turn about for hours, until they were sore and exhausted, and he with his weapon still hard as a rock would call for another. That was to be expected of Don Giovanni. But not the tale I heard from a brothel servant. One of the maids had told him that she had listened outside of a room in the small hours and, thinking it empty, had opened the door. The room was dark. In the light from the corridor she saw the Don lying stretched, fully dressed, on the bed, his head on a black pillow, his face as pale as death. His eyes had opened and remained open, glittering, then slowly shut again . . . Frightened, she had closed the door again and hurried downstairs. There she learned that the Don had sent his girl away hours before, saying that he would pay for the room. Everyone was surprised, she said, that he should still be there . . .

Each night, before retiring, and against his return, I would lay by his bed what he called his Communion; a glass of wine blackened by opium and a thin piece of bread. This particular morning he must have come in about five. I had had too much to drink the night before so even the early sun did not wake me. Frieda had already got up. We no longer celebrated the dawn. It was the shouting from his room roused me. I must have forgotten his morning draught, but surely that should not have occasioned this bellowing? I hastened down the passage, pulling my breeches to as I went.

The Don stood in the middle of the room. He was dressed still in his court coat, everything, except his shoes. His face was scratched in three lines all down one side, the blood red and fresh. Leporello, he asked, staring at me, is that you?

Sir?

282

Of course it was me. The early sunlight poured straight in through his window.

Are the shutters open? he asked.

Why yes, sir, I replied.

And what time of day is it?

Why morning, a fine morning, sir, I said.

His eyes continued to stare at me. The damnedest thing, he said. I saw the sun come up. I bent to take off my shoes – and I cannot see. Why, man, I am blind. And he began to laugh; then he said, piteously, Am I to be led about now, like a zany?

No, sir. No, I said. I took his hand. He clutched mine strongly. Can you see nothing, sir? I asked.

He said he could see a little; shapes, movements; no more.

Now, sir, you must see a doctor, I said firmly, knowing his dislike of the creatures.

That will be rather difficult, my boy, he said gravely.

Go to Pabst, he instructed. He will know which of the charlatans will do me least harm. His clouded sight had begun to clear already, he said; but the *coup* had shaken him, I think.

I took the carriage to his old friend's house. Herr Pabst was delighted to see me, and distressed to hear my news of the Don, though their acquaintance had dropped away when the Don shut himself up. Now, he was all kindness. He must come back with me at once. I told him the Don would only refuse company, especially of his friends, while he was ill. He does not like to be seen so indisposed, I said. But I added that my master had assured me he was recovering and when that was completed, well, then . . . Very well, said Pabst – but I'll not be put off forever, mind. He gave me a letter to take to the new Hospital. They are the finest men of their kind in the continent, Pabst said, and, making me promise to keep him informed of the Don's progress, I came away. A rare thing, a good man.

The doctor visited the next day. Professor Nebel. Which means 'fog' in their awful tongue.

You are well named, sir, said the Don.

Eh? said the doctor, who didn't look like a man built for humour. What is this, sir? he demanded. Your man says you have lost and recovered your sight in the space of a day. That is most strange. I never heard of such a thing.

Leporello, said the Don, the man you have brought me is a fool. He sat behind his desk, perfectly composed, as if interviewing the doctor for the post of footman. Show him out, if you please. There is money in a purse by the front door.

But, sir, I remonstrated, your eyes.

Am I to be treated like this? said Nebel.

My eyes are better, Leporello, said the Don, ignoring the doctor.

What is it you want of me? asked Nebel.

At least let him take a look, sir, I said.

The doctor had not swept out insulted; like all of them his mouth had been wetted by the mention of gold. Do you, or do you not wish an examination? he huffed.

Oh, very well. Come, earn your fee, sir, said the Don. He had composed himself into a state of high good humour.

And miraculously – a prodigy of strength, my master – his sight did appear to have returned almost wholly. Almost.

Nebel took a white wand and a black wand from his coat pockets, and a thin silver chain on which hung a polished stone. He dangled the stone in front of my master's face and asked him to follow it with his eyes as he swung it slowly to and fro. And truly my master's eyes followed perfectly the swinging stone. Then the doctor, in an impatient, peevish way, pranced in front of him with the wands; bringing first the black, then the white near to this eye, then to the other, asking the Don to cover one eye, then the other; moving them back and forth, and stepping forward and back and asking the Don at each position what he saw. At all of which the Don answered levelly, and as if he were amused, watching a stage play. But I saw that not all of his answers were correct, that he fumbled and tossed aside the wrong answer, asking for the *trick* to be repeated, wishing to make it appear that it was the doctor who had made a mistake.

But Nebel did his job.

He looked more closely into my master's eyes, bidding him

turn his face to the window. And here, despite himself, the Don winced and screwed up his eyes at the light.

Ah, that hurts, eh? said Nebel. And had the Don had other pains and for how long? Had he ever fainted? Numbness? Fever? Did he sleep? Dream? – pressing his fingers on the Don's temples, feeling his hands, his pulse, behind his ears . . . all the while the Don submitting with less and less amusement, answering the questions in a resentful tone.

At the end of his inspection, Nebel pronounced his verdict coldly. Your eyes are impaired, sir, he said. You must take great care. You must stay indoors in a darkened room. I would tell you to bind them in a black cloth until they are improved but I can see you are not a man to abide by good advice. You must rest and not exert yourself if you wish to be wholly well. I shall prescribe a course of treatments and medicines.

But what, the Don interrupted, was the *cause* of this malaise?

Who can tell? The doctor shrugged his shoulders. A fever of the brain. An inflammation of the nerves. A minor apoplexy. A deeper-rooted infection perhaps. He would write out a list of herbs from which a decoction should be made up. We will see how your condition answers to that.

Yes, yes, said the Don. I am better already. You work miracles, my good sir. My servant will pay you.

If you wish to be well, sir, that is your concern. You asked for my advice . . .

I took the doctor downstairs and paid him from the purse we kept for tradesmen and waited while he wrote out the list of things I must obtain.

You are an intelligent man? Nebel asked, frowning at me. You can read? I nodded. Then make sure that you follow the instructions and administer these to him. He settled his hat on his head.

But, what, sir, I said boldly, is wrong with the Don?

My dear fellow, he growled, I shall have to wait and see. Has he been poxed before?

Pox, sir?

The French Pox. The Neapolitan Pox. The Great Pox. The *syphilis*, dunderhead.

Into my head came pictures of men rotting down to dungheaps, their noses melting like wax, their bodies covered in ulcers and chancres, pus oozing from their sores.

Oh no, sir, I said vehemently. Nothing of that. I would have seen.

It may not be. If it is – well … He waved a hand impatiently in the air. I have seen these signs in men of his age before, he said. He will get better. He will get worse. Each time a little less better; a little worse. The intervals will grow shorter – until. Who knows? He shrugged. He may live one year. Ten. I may be mistaken. Good day.

So the drugs were sent for and made up. With a wry face the Don tried, then abandoned them. He kept to his room for a few days, then found the regime intolerable and insisted on riding again. But I knew by the sounds at night that his sleep was still disturbed; from the tightness of his face that headaches troubled him. The bottle holding the tincture of opium needed renewal more often. Nebel's nostrums remained untouched. The Don sent a message to the good doctor that he would not require his services further. When I asked him timidly one day if he was quite recovered; he replied, I see, I ride; I eat, I drink; I fuck – what more can a man do?

But things he had ceased to do: to read, to write; to seek the company of his equals. I kept as good a house as I could for him, but my heart no longer was in this place of unhappy memory. My wife had become a shrew; the cook slovenly; the boy insolent. The ship was beginning to leak.

Time for a change. To move. Had not the Don said movement was life; to remain still to die? For God's sake let us move.

What moved us was this letter. I take it from among his papers:

My dearest brother,
I have your address from the letter sent to Papa last year. I had grieved that you never wrote to us. To me. I found your few letters among Papa's papers. They were unopened. It is sad that he would not allow me to see them.

I must tell you the terrible news that our father is dead. Three days ago he came back from riding, and complained of pains in his chest. The next morning I sent Tartini to Papa's room to rouse him, as he had not come down at his usual hour. Tartini returned with the palest of faces and informed me that our poor Papa lay calmly in Death.

Dear brother, by the time this reaches you all ceremonies will be over. You are now master of the estates. The lawyers will inform you of all the details. Please do return as soon as ever you may. You cannot know how much I have missed you. In the latest letter you sent I learned of your marriage and send my sisterly love to your wife, who must, from what you say of her, be a true companion to your life. To her I extend welcome and love over the great distance that separates us. May it be lessened day by day.

God send you good speed.

Your loving sister, Eugenia

So that is that, said the Don without emotion. He said to leave him, but then called me back. Make preparations for our journey, he said.

We were going south.

5

Under the seats of our new large travelling coach were cupboards stuffed with bed linen, clothes, wine, salted meats, the Don's books – though he never read in them now – plate, cutlery, waterproofs, a medicine chest; our gold: all the necessaries we should need on the long journey and which we would not get on the way. On the inside walls hung pistols, the Don's sword, a cutlass, an axe, a purse for bribes. On the outside back a great chest contained our second-best outfits and a sufficiency of trinkets and bottles and coins that the customs might filch, so that perhaps they would not pry into the cupboards inside. Another purse was hidden upon me, for the tolls in which the roads of the Empire abound; the post-houses where we changed horses; to pay inn-keepers and ostlers and chambermaids – all those whose hands are endlessly extended to travellers. A packet of passports, that grew with each *lascia passare* and *fede* and certificate of health that had to be got from each town and shown at the next, without which it was impossible to progress from one to another, or even from a town's border to its worst inn's lousiest bed. And for each of these papers a little something must pass from my hand to the dirty gold-ribboned hand of one of those army of clerks and customs men and police who guard so zealously their fellow citizens from honest men: sequins, soldi, lire, francs, marks, grosses, testoons, crowns, ducats and a dozen other coins, all acceptable silver and gold. Even though it was obvious by our carriage that here a great man was travelling, without me the Don would have been robbed a thousand times over.

But we were moving, going forward. This was *life* once more, and the Don put up with all discomforts without complaining. When we set out he had told me he was selling the house; would I accompany him? he asked. If I wished to remain he would settle a good sum on me – but he was going home. Did I wish to remain in this city . . . ? He would not beg me. But, sir, I said. How can you travel alone? A gentleman without a servant. Sort out your affairs then, he said. Decide what you wish to do. Your wife . . . ? I do not know how long you will have to remain parted. If at any time you wish to return . . . Of course I would go with him. My parting from Frieda was eased with money and the getting of a good place for her at Herr Pabst's – though she complained of having to go work at 'that old Jew's'. I swore I would return soon. She shed no tears. A most business-like girl. In both our hearts, I think, there was relief, not sorrow, at this parting. I remember thinking she would not be long in finding consolation.

We travelled for the best part of September. We rolled south day after day. When we got among the mountains it seemed we should never get out. It was too cold to sleep in our coach. We went from one verminous smoky inn to the next, sleeping, or not, in those wooden cots that resemble nothing so much as coffins as your body sinks into the mattress; seeing forever far-off snow-capped peaks that barely shifted all day as our wheels ground on; ascending into the foothills of snow, where the Don put on a pair of smoked green spectacles to protect his eyes from the glare; descending again into tree-filled valleys and stony gorges that were gloomy on the brightest of days. At last we left the last customs post of the Empire, the hideous mountains fell behind and we got down onto the warm broad plains. After almost four weeks, entering a terraced valley of yellow corn and green vines, he announced that we were but two days from his home.

An end in view, he stirred himself and gazed raptly out of the window as if to urge forward his first glimpse of Tenario. His spirit was infectious and I too began to feel a lively apprehension of our journey's end. Do you know that set of cards that children play with? There are forty-eight cards and each shows a scene of land and rivers and skies. The land undulates, trees rise up, rivers wind, and no matter in what order you deal the cards their edges always match in the most perfect fashion; horizon meets horizon, water flows into water, road meets road. The children shuffle and lay the cards out in a line, making a new landscape each time; and as they put each card down, they must pretend they are on a journey, and make up a story about the people and places on the cards; a different journey every time, a different story. And so, as we went on, a multitude of sights were dealt up each day against the tall card-shaped windows of the coach: a farmer riding his mule; an obelisk at the roadside; a barge on a distant river; an ancient, ruined castle on a hillside; a clump of wild olives; cattle standing, their front hooves in a pond; a ship in full sail on an estuary; three soldiers, bayonets fixed on their muskets, whistling and shouting at girls showing their legs naked to the thighs in a rice field; two cavalrymen, cantering the other way from us, with pikes raised and helmets gleaming; a flight of birds rising from an island in a river; a village with a mushroom-roofed church; a mysterious stone tower standing on its own; the empty plain; travelling folk – a rogue in a blue coat with a sack over his shoulder, three children, a dog; a cart bearing a body wrapped in a dirty shroud; nothing; nothing; a line of poplars before a tumbledown farm; a bear at the roadside, resting on its haunches, with no one in sight, a chain around its neck, fastened to a stake in the ground – as if it had escaped from the forest and set its mark here;

a man gnawing a hunk of bread, his eyes burning; a red and yellow quartered kite high on a long string pulled by a boy running through dry grass – all past, all gone, we cannot stop for any of you, our rattling coach said; we shall never see you again, even if we return this way. Every time a different journey; a different tale.

The last morning of our journey, as if he could now taste his home in the air, the Don began to tell me of his childhood there.

Every night, Leporello, he began, we carry Death forward over a dark stream, then drown him in light. That is what Man is, a ferryman; an assassin. You wonder that I detest the hours of darkness. All my life as a man I have had to fill them with something. Now it is detestable dreams and sweats and sickness. But women – ah. What after all are women, but life? Life itself. Even in the churches it is a woman who holds sway over people's hearts. Not that stretched, tortured man on his cross.

I crossed myself.

But when you are a child, Leporello, there is no Death, no God, no looking forward or back. There is only day and night; each morning shines like the dead waking to Paradise.

For some, sir . . .

Ay. Ay – don't interrupt me, he said gently. Night comes down then like a blessing on what we have done that day, a command to rest and wait the next resurrection. The days are not numbered. The hours have no appointments. There are no hours. The trees shimmer in summer and shiver in winter. The seasons are immeasurably long. The land about you stretches each way to Eternity. The house itself is an inexhaustible combination of rooms and possibilities. This is the room where at a certain hour each day my father meets his steward. But at all other times it is my world and everything therein is mine; his books filled with mysterious figures, his scraps of bills, his pens, ink, sand, the white portraits on the wall – for *my* visits they are the library of an archangel; the records of Heaven.

It is a big house, sir? I said witlessly. I slept beside a stove. My father was killed in the square. None of this last I said to him. I envied him this house of childhood.

Let me tell you, he said. My house is set on a hill, Leporello. It is a white house. We will see it from miles off. Our family has been there for centuries, since my ancestors returned from the Crusades. They had – fortunately for them – better fortune from their wars. Their old castle is embedded in the walls of the present villa. The trees they planted shade it. The vines they strung give us wine and the fields they marked out give us bread. We pull our water from the same river. Well, not the same river. As Parmenides would say – you can't step in the same river twice. My father – a model landlord; fair and firm. He used no cruelty or usury to bind his tenants to him. Every year at spring, he gave a feast for them – as I must. They will come up with their faces washed, their hair brushed, dressed in their good shirts and waistcoats and skirts and petticoats and each head of a family will bow before me, while I sit like Zeus in my father's high-backed chair.

My father taught me to ride and swim, to shoot with bow and gun, to fence. An Englishman who came to stay taught me, or tried to, how to *box*. He stood in front of me with fists raised so . . . I laughed. I had to tell him scornfully that no gentleman would fight like that. Not the commonest peasant in a brawl. We prefer the knife or sword, I told him – infinitely more civilised and decisive weapons. The Englishman called me a barbarian. The English consider everyone but themselves to be barbarians. God – in their country . . . We must go there, Leporello. Yes, I will take you there. You will not believe how the English live – their food, their climate. No wine. You will think you have gone to the Moon. Their women are fair. But *civilised*? One night when I had been allowed to stay up, they were talking of music and my mother asked the Englishman if he would give us a taste of English song. *Certamente*, Ma'am, he said. He stood up, bowed to my father and mother, my sister and me, pulled back his shoulders, thrust out his chest – and let out the most awful howl. And this went on and on, for verse after verse of words only a cow could understand. My mother and father looked on gravely and when at last he was done, they clapped most politely and said, How delightful. And my mother said, You must be exhausted after that, Mr Butcher –

whatever his name, that suits him – for she was terrified he would begin another rant.

Ever afterwards, whenever I was alone with my mother, she would settle herself solemnly down, hands clasped in her lap, and say, Come, *Giovannaccio mio*, give us the English song. And I would compose myself into the attitude of the Butcher and proceed to bellow out as much unintelligible rubbish as I could.

The Don laughed at the memory, but as often when we laugh at the past, it makes us the moment afterwards serious in the contemplation of what has been lost. So it was with him. He was silent for a few moments, then carried on in a gentle tone.

Ah, but she sang beautifully herself, Mamma. She taught me to read and write, to speak and walk with grace; to draw. What a poet was – though poets are no more, I fear. Do you remember that one in . . . ? How music was made. What Song the Sirens sang – that is what women teach us.

As for the rest of my education; that was completed in the attic under the roof. I had my tiny bedroom there, next to the maids. From my earliest years I was petted and spoiled by those delicious creatures. They kissed me and tousled my hair, and I used to creep into their bed – which amused them very much, for they slept two in the one bed and often woke to find me curled between them; a cherub between two goddesses. For I was a pretty child, Leporello. And these were young enough, and old enough, thirteen or fourteen years old and changed every year or so. My mother came to hear of it and scolded me gently and told me that I must not bother the girls; they had their work to do; I was the son of their master. It was not seemly. Of course I obeyed. For a time. After a decent and lonely break of at least two nights, I resumed my trips to the maids. Ten, eleven – I was awakened very early to other delights than the mere warm proximity of their soft bodies, my dear. The inevitable thing . . . It is after all a common occurrence. I got used to going with one or the other most nights. I thought nothing of it. One day, months after my first experience, my father called me to his business room. He looked me up and down – there was not so much to see in those days. Is it true? he demanded. I was at a loss to know what he meant. Then he told

292

me that one of the servant girls was expecting a child. In tears she had stated that she had known no one, no one. The only male ever in her bed had been the little master and he could not have done such a thing, could he? I rule out a second Virgin Birth, said my father. Did you do this, do that? To all of which I had to confess that I had done *this*, and *that*. Well, well, I must say I think he was secretly proud of his son's early prowess. My mother said nothing to me, but I was moved from the attic to a room next to theirs. At a price, a husband was found for the girl. I must say that it still rankles with me that I made such little physical impression on my first conquest that she did not even know what I had done. Still, she was a very plump girl.

Oh, and for my further protection, another bed was placed in my room, to be occupied by a tutor they had engaged. A rather unfortunate arrangement, as it turned out. I was a charming boy. The poor young man was smitten with me. He was dismissed by my mother, and fled before my father could kill him.

We are near now; very near, he said looking out again.

We were rolling along a road, skirting a hill, the road enclosed on both sides by a thick line of trees, giving every now and then a view of a lush valley below. We went on a little, with the Don gazing intently out. When the trees closed again, he turned back.

Was this a good idea? he murmured.

Idea, sir? I said.

To return home. Why do we not just go on and on? Forever? His voice, which had been so matter-of-fact and cynical, seemed now dreamy. I thought he was tired by the journey. I was certainly. I knew from what he had said earlier that he wanted very much to see his home; to play the lord, to rest and get back his strength. Then we might set out again . . . To take his mind off such thoughts, I said, What happened to you then, sir?

Then? he said, puzzled.

In your youth?

Ah, my youth. That is a long while ago, eh, Leporello. I was sent away to school. A dreary seminary in B-. There I learned Latin and Greek; Rhetoric and Philosophy, among the other clods and rascals who were well-born sons. I learned also to make my way out at night. There were the daughters of the city after all – too young for the convent and the marriage bed. I was asked to leave that school. And another. I ran away at sixteen; I was a soldier at seventeen. At that age you are happy to slice men in half. I returned home but could no longer settle. I did not go back again. Not until . . . until my mother died. I would write to her from wherever I was. Letters to amuse her, full of my travels, my adventures – not all of my adventures. There I argued with my father. He suddenly seemed an old man to me. I did not know what grief was. I was the charming prodigal come home. Ah, how they all made so much of me; my sister asking longingly about all I had done and seen out there in the world; the servants spoiling me; the village girls rolling their eyes. But my father was embittered. What have you become? he said. You are nothing; neither soldier, nor scholar; not a man of business, nor any responsibility. I was a coxcomb, a cocksure adventurer, a libertine – all the things he had been in his own youth. We quarrelled terribly. I left two days after the funeral, vowing never to return. He shouted after me that I would starve. That it was well that our line should end with me. It may. It may – though even then I suppose down in the valley somewhere my bastard walks about . . .

There, sir, I cried. For the trees had ended, and I saw across the green and yellow valley a house set on a hill, as he had told me. Sir, is that your house? And we both looked out of the valley-side window as the country dealt up its last card; the house on the hill shining white through the cedars; its whiteness, shiningness promising a new beginning.

PART IV

The Table Of Demons

1

It should have ended there. But you must have all. What started as the story of my life has become the story of the Don. How could it be anything else? Who would read the memoirs of a servant except those interested in his master? And such a master whose fame lives in legends and operas and plays – so you tell me. Before we start to tell tales and make up stories it is necessary that we live; I am an old man and all old men are haunted by the ghosts of their younger selves. The Don became a ghost before he died. How should I feel now, by telling this, except that I am killing him over again?

For I could have stopped this anywhere, couldn't I? With the Don's escape from the mock flames of Hell. The ship sailing from the real flames of Pomodoro. I could have had him fall gallantly in the war against the Turks. Or told of his triumphal return to settle with Sophia and her child – both miraculously preserved. A second child. A third. The Don, hero, reformed rake, good father, to come to Tenario as its lord and to rule, a grand wise ancient patriarch, to the end of his considerable days. But, no – I have to condemn him to rot within, to lose his powers, his mind, by way of this foul disease. And you wish to hear me tell all this because it comforts lesser men to know how a great man is brought down.

So we arrived at Tenario. The Don had the coach stopped short as we approached and had me help him on with his splendid blue and gold coat – we were in shirt sleeves for the heat – he brushed his hair back, whitened his teeth with powder before he would allow us to proceed. They must have seen the coach coming from a way off, because when we crossed the valley and pulled up the winding poplar-lined drive to the villa and through its gates, standing in front of the house was a line of servants and on the steps to the house a small woman in a black dress, her hands clasped in front of her. This was his sister, Eugenia. We rolled to a halt at the foot of the steps, the servants bowed and lifted their hats, and the women servants looked with hot eyes at the coach door – the Don clambered down and advanced up the steps. The faint sweet smile on her mouth that had broadened in welcoming joy, faltered and faded. Brother . . . ? she said. After all, she had not seen him for fifteen years. He had left here a fine young man, and returned . . . as he was – grey, worn, still a fine figure, but . . .

But if ever there was a setting for Paradise it was that; though the valley fields below were plucked, the yellow newly-turned earth was rich and glowing in the sun. Tall thick woods covered the hill behind the house and across the valley only the church's tower peeped above the lush foliage.

It was easy to see what he had seen as a boy. In the next few weeks, though the year waned, he walked often on the terrace, in a plain white silk shirt and a waistcoat and breeches, his face and arms tanned; only the dark green spectacles he wore against the sun hinting of his illness.

I wondered at his sister, Eugenia. She was a year younger than the Don; she had never married. She was slim, small, and dressed ten years behind the city. She showed their kinship by her fine brow and eyes, but she was no beauty. Her lips were thin, as if sucking on a coin. She smiled rarely. There was altogether something recessive and solitary about her. She walked in the veranda overlooking the valley as if its pillars were there for her to hide amongst. At first, if I was in a room with the Don, she would hang back shyly in the doorway. May I come in, brother? And she would gaze at me in mock puzzlement, a sort of, What, are you here again? look, flicking her eyes away when I stared boldly back. For the Don it was clear she had great love and concern. If she had been shocked at his appearance when he got down from the coach, she was now determined to show that he was her beloved brother, the master here, and here to stay. He hid his illness from her – masters and brothers can have no weaknesses. The irritation in his eyes, he told her, was due to a powder discharge near his face in the war. His reason for wishing to be alone was that he was engaged on a great work of scholarship. He must have a room separate from others because he worked sometimes at night. Leporello must have a room nearby, because I was his man. His sister smiled graciously at each request and hurried away to make the arrangements he wanted. She was full of concern for him; full of suggestions for his well being. Which the Don at first found flattering and charming – but I saw when he became irritated and bored by her. I am an ignoble fellow like the rest of you. He was my charge, after all.

The servants were led by his father's old steward, Tartini. How I hated this fellow. There is nowhere like a little paradise settling into winter to find out hatreds. Tartini jealously guarded the business of the estate from me, closeting himself with the Don for long periods while I seethed, equally jealously, in my room. The servants had all been with the family for five hundred years it seemed; I could not even roam the house idly without engaging their glares of contempt, whispered comments, and sniggers. And I the most senior amongst them – or should have been. I was not happy. Things had not worked out as I had foreseen. The Don took his duties seriously. I found myself bored for the first time, unwanted it seemed except as the Don's doser – I had brought a good supply of the opium with us, and Nebel's drugs, which the Don still refused to take. Did he know what ailed him? He must have suspected. I watched him avidly for outward signs. What else was there for me to do? What good is a dresser when the master goes nowhere, a pimp where there are no whores to get; a body servant when there is another nearer to him to attend to all his wants? I had grown used to cities, and to travel and adventure between them. In the city of V- there had been the comforts, however tarnished by use and custom, of my wife; the company of the charming Sophia. That was all gone. My one hope was that rest, and cool, fresh surroundings – getting cooler by the day now – would restore my master's health sufficiently for us to resume our travels in the spring. Otherwise ... for the first time I began to think of leaving him. There were people here to tend him, if not as well as I could. Was I a nursemaid? I was out of place here. Out of my place. I stood outside his room one night, about to knock, to ask forlornly if he required anything further that evening. A clockwork footman. The door was an inch ajar, I heard his sister's voice.

Your man, Leporello, he does not seem happy, she was saying. And went on to say that she would find him work to occupy his idle hours if her brother so wished.

He is my manservant, said the Don with surprise.

Brother, you needed a manservant perhaps in *society* – she caught the word and dangled it in her mouth like a cat with a spider. Here, he is a sore thumb, she said. He walks about half the day, dressed in gentleman's clothing. He wanders into the kitchen and upsets Maria and Theresa (God bring me back Marta and Placida!).

He tries to interfere in Tartini's duties. He has such airs ...

My dear, said the Don, all servants are like that in the cities. They ape their masters. (I hated him for that.) Besides, he is a good man. (I loved him for this.) And Tartini will not last forever.

So he is to be your next steward then? said Eugenia.

He would make an excellent one, Eugenia. (So I would, so I would.) You do not understand, Eugenia. Leporello has been my true companion. (Ah, how my heart swelled again.)

On your travels. In the past. You are the head of our family now, dear Giovanni. I cannot do what is needed. If you wish to keep your friend ...

He is not my friend, he is my servant, the Don snapped.

It was time to go. I retreated from the door, then re-approached, with stern, officious steps and knocked loudly.

Yes? What do you want? he demanded as I came in.

Eugenia, seated on a stool, looked down and picked at her skirt.

Only to see if you wanted anything, sir.

No. Go away, he barked.

You see, I heard Eugenia say softly.

How was I to regain his favour? I was mortified. Again I thought of leaving. I would find another master, as my father had advised. When I thought of what I had done for the Don. Of the gullible servants I had lied to, cajoled, seduced on his behalf. Of the nights he had slipped past me into darkened houses, while I held the door, so that he might meet some daughter or wife. Of the whispers from a hundred bedchambers while I kept guard outside. The grand ladies I had guided to their rendezvous, who had pressed money into my hand and smiled upon me when leaving those rented rooms. The angry husbands I had faced down. The pale girls who had come to our lodgings demanding to know tearfully why, oh why the Don would not see them any more. The miscarriages procured. The flights, fights, escapes, concealments arranged. I lay on my bed and they whirled before my mind; the virgins, wives, husbands, madams, whores; apothecaries, abortionists, moneylenders, all appeared before me, and said sweetly or harshly, Why, Leporello, do you stand this? He is a wastrel, a philanderer, a rogue, a brawler, a murderer – they all brought their accusations and laid them before me. Oh, and I condemned him too. It was pitch dark outside the window, and darker in my mind. I sat up and looked about the little room. I was near thirty and what did I have to show for my life? A couple of suits hung on the door, a small bag of coins, much depleted, hidden beneath a loose floorboard; a few shirts, a wife five hundred leagues away who I had not missed since we came here. Was I to go back to her? To seek service in that city? To set up in some little inn or shop and grow old with Frieda and a half-dozen children and a querulous old mother she would produce, like a conjurer, from the country? Why, no. I was a man of spirit, wasn't I? Had not the Don educated me in the ways of the world, so that now I was not to be satisfied with anything less? The Don had grown cold to me. His ugly, whey-faced, spinster sister had turned him against me. She was a witch, a bitch.

I drank some wine. It was cold and lay on my stomach like a toad. It was a long time before I slept. When I did I dreamed of the days before the Don. The groves of the Cavilloso estate had become somehow entwined with the pillars of the temple where Signor Cavilloso found me. He came from between the trees, a smile on his fat face and I knew, though I could not see, that Eleonora spied on me from an upper window. Cavilloso took my hand; his was terribly cold. The sea, he said. It is a long time since we sailed together, my boy. Only I was not a boy, but a man of my present age. Then we were in his house which turned by magic to the palace of Caesaretto. It was day and full of light, and richly-dressed people strolled about and ignored us as we passed like ghosts from room to room. Cavilloso spouted nonsense interminably in my ear and clutched my hand. He is near, he said, and straightway vanished, and I was in the palace alone. At once it was night. I could see the stars above and the moonlight slithered in front of me, withdrawing before my steps, leading me on, from one tall room to another. The palace was not half-built but had fallen into ruin. I did not want to go on, but somehow Cavilloso was at my side once more, though I could only sense his presence. He was pushing me in some mysterious way towards a pair of great doors. I don't want to go, I shouted. Because I knew something terrible waited behind those doors. But he was pulling and pushing me. You must, he said. Go on, it is your life. I was at the doors. My hand was raised to knock. My whole arm was raised, but seized by terror I could not either bring myself to strike or to lower it again. Knock, said his voice. Knock. Your life is behind the door.

Dreams summon life, it seems. I struggled to wake. The dream fled. There *was* a knocking on my door. I stumbled across the dark room and opened. Eugenia stood in the corridor, dressed in a robe, clutching it together with one hand, the other holding a candle. Her voice was frightened. Don Giovanni must see you, she said. He insists. I feared the worst, not for him, but for myself. This was the impetuous way he did things. This was the end of our association. I was to be pensioned off. She had done her work. I followed her down the passage, cursing inwardly the thin form that went before me.

The Don did not want me. He needed me. Eugenia's candle spilled light into the room. The Don stood, erect, pale-faced; his good coat above his night shirt, his ankles and feet bare. I almost laughed at the odd combination.

That is all, Eugenia. He spoke with obvious effort.

Brother? she said.

No. Leave us. Please go back to bed. I am sorry I roused you. His words came thickly.

She set down the candle on the table by the door. His own light burned behind the screen. She stood, holding the door handle. Is there nothing I can do for you? she asked.

Leporello knows. Leporello knows what to do.

She still hesitated in the doorway. I came forward to my master, my back to her.

You are sure . . . ? she began again.

No. Please – he said harshly. Then his voice softened. Please *go*. I heard her step; the door closed reluctantly on us.

The Don sat down heavily on the edge of the bed. He clasped his head between his hands as if it was a great weight he was trying to support. When at last he raised his face slowly it was a deadly white. The pain was worse than ever, he said. The opium answered only in part. I must prepare him a dose. Much larger than before, then perhaps he could sleep. He ground his teeth in pain. I made him a very strong dose, and stirred into it some of the herbs Nebel had prescribed. God in heaven, what is this? he said, but gulped it greedily down, then resumed his attitude, head in hands. Again, he muttered. It is too much, I protested. Again, he roared. I gave him another, weaker dose. The pain must have been easing, for he sipped at this, then put it aside with disgust.

He lay down on the bed in his court coat. I stood about, listening to his breathing ease. I was suffered to stand beside the door for another half-hour I think – I heard the clock downstairs boom out, and a few minutes after that the church clock rang across the valley the hour of three. I judged he was asleep and eased the door handle down to leave.

Stay, Leporello. His voice was drowsy, but came steadier. The candle will need replacing soon, he said. I do not care for the dark. You may sit.

Sir. I sat in his high-backed armchair.

Are you comfortable there? He raised himself on his elbow and turned to look at me. His face was flushed and sweat stood on his brow.

He lay back. Pull these about me, will you, he said. The blankets were disarrayed. When I had pulled them over him, I sat again and listened to him breathe. It was cold in that room, the fire had withered away. There was a fallen blanket peeping out from beneath the bed. I pulled it towards me stealthily and wrapped myself in it.

What are you doing? came his voice. I had thought he was asleep, but he sounded perfectly awake.

Settling myself, sir, that is all, I replied.

There was a long silence. Then he said, I do not sleep well. I never did. There are dreams . . .

Dreams, sir? I said as cheerily as I could. What is there to fear from dreams?

I did not say I was *afraid*, he said. They disturb me.

I knew a woman who could tell you the meaning of every dream . . . , I began.

I'm sure you did, he said. I would not bore the good lady with mine.

But what do you dream, sir? I asked.

I entertain the past, he said. It reminds me I am no longer young. There are others.

Sir?

. . . and when I wake, exhausted from their ministrations, I become tetchy and ill-tempered and cause a great deal of trouble to everyone, don't I?

Why no, sir, I lied half-heartedly.

When I am like that you must forgive me, he said.

It is not in my gift to forgive you, sir, I said.

You sound like a bloody priest, Leporello. I am sorry. No. That's why I asked for you this evening. I will not appear weak before a woman. My sister is . . . my sister. Now, read to me, my dear fellow. Your potion is working to make me drowsy. Put good thoughts into my head to rest on if I should fall asleep.

There was a small pile of books on the table by my chair. I picked them up awkwardly and held their titles to the weak light from the candle. These are all in French, sir, I said. I have never read a French book.

Nonsense. You speak French. Open one anywhere. Just read.

304

I began, not comprehending more than one word in ten.

My God, what a barbarous jingle. What is that? said the Don.

Diderot, sir, I said.

O, Diderot. My poor Diderot.

Shall I go on, sir? I asked.

I don't think I could stand any more. He re-settled himself under the blankets. Tell me a story, he said. Tell me again about you and the priest's housekeeper. Tell me *your* wicked youth, Leporello.

So I began the story of Giulietta and the priest and how kind she had been and how I had run away and joined the bandits and how they had not been bad men at all, except by accident, and how they did not deserve ... when I heard his breathing change again and he slept.

The rumours that the house servants had passed down to the valley flew back full-fledged as tales of the mad Don. The wizard. The recluse. Letters from his neighbours of five leagues away, inviting themselves for a visit, went unanswered. We might have been as alone as a ship on the sea.

Winter came down. Winter without, and within the house. Morning meal. Evening meal. Bright day. Dull day. The wind biting up the valley. Snow on the far hills; the sun travelling low. Not as bitter as the winters I remembered from my own village, but made greyer and more leaden by the slow hours that pass in an isolated house. I caught his sister looking at me in a new way. Whatever vision of life she had entertained for her brother and herself it was clear that she regarded me as an interloper, perhaps a threat. I meant something to the Don, had some place in his life, in his past – what that was she could not know, but she was puzzled by my present part and looked for ways to release whatever hold I had over the Don. But I was in the saddle again, and determined to ride at least some way with my master before relinquishing him to home and sister and this dreary life.

To ride. One bright December morning the Don called me and told me to get two horses saddled. I will be pent up no longer, he

said. A man could die living like this. When he came out to the
yard his skin was yellow and drawn. His sister hurried after him
with a fur wrap – he was dressed for summer. No, he snapped.
What am I, an invalid? When I was a boy I rode in my shirt in this
season. He pulled himself up into the saddle and cantered on
ahead, waving me to follow him.

I followed dutifully, not daring to speak to him. He sat erect
and showed no sign of discomfort. I thanked God that it was a
still, mild day. At last my horse edged almost level with his.

I have got into a rut, that's the truth of it, Leporello, he said at
length.

Whatever you say, sir, I said cheerfully.

I have been ill and let it prey upon my mind.

You have not been well, sir, I said gravely.

We rode into the valley. The fields were bare and resting, or
here and there sown with spring wheat; the valley dotted with
the small farms of his tenants. Smoke hung up from their chim-
neys. On one roof a late stork stood one-legged, gazing south. A
child's voice shouted from the middle of a field as we passed. The
Don raised his hand in salute. Each farm stood in the centre of its
own land, with a grove of poplars or cypresses at its side; lines of
trees, of hawthorns, or those stone markers they call *confini*
marked off one neighbour's land from the other. All this the Don
pointed out. He told me who lived in each one; his family name,
that this one had a son who was an idiot, that one was marked by
the beauty of his daughters. We came to a pool fringed with bare
trees. He pulled to. As a boy I used to bathe here, he said. The girls
would watch from behind those bushes there. He looked down
at his hands. How pale we have grown in that damned house,
Leporello. My hands are as thin as a bird's. What have I come to?
Wait until spring. We shall come down here every day and brown
ourselves and pull the girls in with us. What do you say?

Aye, sir, I said. It is a pity there are no women here now.

You are a fool, he said without looking at me and rode on.

An old man walked up the road towards us, bent under a pile
of firewood. He halted as we trotted up, and bowed so low that I
thought the wood might tumble over his head. He showed his

face and said gruffly, May Our Lady bless you and your father's house, Don Giovanni.

You know me? said the Don.

You are Don Louis's son. You are our lord, said the old man, squinting shrewdly up. The Don tossed him a coin for his goodness and we rode on.

You see, said the Don, delighted, You see – they know me. I have not been here for God knows how many years and that old man knows his master.

We came through a wood and on its other side was a tumbledown farm. I don't know whose place this is, said the Don. What a hole. In the middle of the yard a dog scratched single-mindedly for a flea. A girl with a basket of washing balanced on her head and supported by one hand stepped from the side of the house and over a low wall, to go down to the river. She affected not to see us, but I knew too well that sly sideways flick of the eyes these country girls use to take in everything.

Signorina, the Don called. A moment.

She put down the basket and looked at us, from behind the wall.

The Don steered his horse to the wall. To which family do you belong? he asked.

Tosi, my lord, she replied.

To peasants all men on horseback are lords.

The Don raised his eyebrows as if the name meant something special to him. Your own given name, child? he asked.

Lucia, lord.

And who else lives here. Your father? Mother?

My mother and my sister, lord.

The Don smiled. Your mother's first name, my dear?

Rosetta, sir. The girl blushed to name her own mother.

Tosi, the Don murmured.

Lucia, a voice rang out. Who are those men?

A woman, fine looking, bearing on her hip a little boy who looked old enough to walk, but well satisfied to be carried, had come out of the house. She was about my own age, I guessed, and well preserved for a farm woman. I called back, This is my master,

Don Giovanni. Your master too. The woman said nothing but stared at us. The Don nudged his horse the few steps across to her and looked down. Do you know me? he asked, smiling.

I saw you as a young man, signore. Many years ago.

His smile faded. You are? he said shortly.

Paola.

Your sister? He pointed to the girl at the wall.

She is my sister, said the woman. She shouted to the girl, Go about your business, Lucia. With a little shrug of the shoulders, the girl picked up the basket and went on her way down to the river. The child shifted himself more comfortably on the woman's arm, his thumb in his mouth, gazing wide-eyed at the Don. The Don leaned in the saddle and chucked the child under the chin. The woman did not move but stared, with no change in her expression, at my master.

Then another voice wheezed out of the doorway. What is it, Paola. Who's there? An immensely fat, short woman ambled into the light. Old – I would have said about fifty – it is hard to tell. The mamma of the house, no doubt of it.

Rosetta? said the Don softly. *Rosetta*? Then he began to laugh. And laugh. Not good-naturedly as one does meeting some friend after many years, but a mad, galloping laugh, that went on and on, though he tried to stifle it, with, I am sorry, I am sorry, gurgling out of him at intervals. His horse moved restlessly. This mad laughter still spluttering from his mouth, with, No, it cannot be. Excuse. Excuse, he backed his bucking horse, turned, and cantered out of the yard and on to the road again, his head shaking from side to side. I stared down at the women. My master, I began to say, but could think of nothing else to say to them, except, Excuse, excuse, in feeble imitation. I set off after him.

He made a fast pace, and it was all I could do to keep him in sight. When I got back a boy was brushing his horse down. Tartini was in the yard. Where is my master? I asked him. You mean the Don? he said, as if my master was someone else entirely. He is gone inside, said Tartini and turned his back, to shout at the boy.

I found my master in his bedroom. Sitting on the stool in front of the long looking glass, still in his muddy boots, he was staring at himself. In the mirror, he saw me enter. Without taking his eyes from his image, he said, Come here, Leporello. No, no – behind me.

I appeared in the mirror over his shoulder.

That girl we saw – the young girl. How old would you say she was?

Oh, thirteen, perhaps fourteen, sir.

Did you see how beautiful she was? Like a flower.

Yes, I did. Was I to procure her for him? He had never fancied such young buds before. More madness.

And her sister – how old was she?

Perhaps twenty-seven, eight. A little older, sir.

And that grotesque dumpling, that mountain of lard that came from the house. How old?

I laughed. Oh, I could not say, sir. She could be fifty – or more.

Her name is Rosetta Tosi. His eyes held mine in the mirror. I thought I remembered, he said. She is the maid who bore my child. When I was little more than a child. Tosi was the man she was married off to. So the woman with the boy – what was her name . . . ?

Paola, sir, I said. If I remember.

Yes, Paola. That is my daughter, and the boy my grandchild. They are surly peasants who live in a farm which has not been worked properly in years. They are the lowest thing I have seen on all our proud estate. And their blood is mine. Now here, look here. What do you see?

He stroked his finger across his forehead.

I did not answer.

Lines, furrows, he said. And here, here too, Time's plough has been busy. His finger traced the deep lines in his cheeks and from the base of his strong nose to the corners of his mouth. What does this tell us of *lineage*, he said bitterly. Of nobility. I am an old man. Suddenly. An old man.

Nothing I ever heard struck me with such sadness. I had never thought to hear such a thing from this man. I wanted to cry out – My lord, let's get away from this place. Fly, enjoy our travels once more. The world awaits us . . .

He grimaced at the mirror.

What a pair of ugly mugs we are, he said quietly. You're losing your hair too.

He stood up then. He had come to some sort of decision.

He put his arm round my shoulders and smiled wanly at our reflections. His fingers clenched on my shoulder. I shall not leave this place, Leporello. You have been my faithful companion. You must remain so. Call your wife down here if you wish. You must be happy.

I am a great man now, he said to the mirror. I am the lord of this estate; of perhaps two hundred souls. I have been an infant for forty years, Leporello. Now I shall be a man; their kind father.

I thought for a moment that he was joking, but his face was set as he looked deep into his reflection.

You must take a gift to the Tosi family, he said. I will not have them living like that. The whole valley knows of their connection with my house. Take gold from the chest.

How much, sir? I asked.

Fifty – no, forty pieces. That will do. Give it to Paola. If she *is* mine, I wish her to have it. Not the mother. I do not want her gratitude. Say to Paola that it is a pension for her father, Tosi. I want no one to say that I neglect my duty.

Duty – there was a new word from his lips.

But, that evening, when he decided we were to answer the letters from his neighbours, the task put him in a bad mood. He shuffled through the pages impatiently. Here, he said, passing them over. Read them to me.

They wished to renew their acquaintance with the Don. They had been friends of his father. They expressed their deepest sadness at the news of the death. They had heard of the new Don's illness. They hoped he was quite recovered.

I will not have them here, Leporello. They are such bores. Their conversation would kill me. Write to them, Leporello. Tell them I am unable to receive visitors at the moment. Invite them to the spring feast. That must be done.

Will you dictate then, sir, I said, taking up a pen.

What? No – you write. Damn it, you know my thoughts by now. You write the letters.

Write to whom? Eugenia said from the doorway. She had let herself into the room silently. Are you answering the Baron?

Yes, yes. Baron B–; Count C–. Nuisances, the Don said.

They are all good people, brother. They attended our father's funeral, she said quietly. They extended their help when there was no other at hand.

You mean by that my absence? His face coloured up.

I sat at the bureau, pen in hand, staring down at the paper; the good servant.

Brother and sister stared at each other. Then she turned to me. What are you doing, Leporello? I rose and bowed to her. The Don has asked me to answer the letters, I said.

A servant to answer our letters? I had thought that was my task. She laughed; it was not an action to which she seemed accustomed.

Leporello, go. I'll call for you later, said the Don.

I went smartly, bowing meekly again to the lady as I passed. I listened with pleasure outside the door to the sound of their raised voices. Why do we revel in these petty victories; harbouring for half a century, like a warm stone in a cold bed, the memory of dissension sowed; slights returned, the tiny rifts driven between our governors?

But she had won. When I took his draught in later that night, I asked if he wanted his letters written now. But the candles on the bureau were out; the surface was bare.

No, no, Leporello, not now, he said irritably.

Then I will do them in the morning for you, sir, I said.

That will not be necessary. My sister has written the replies. He stared at me boldly as if waiting for me to say something else. I did not, but handed him his glass and left him.

I was angry at his defeat, and the fall in my position once more. I went to my room muttering, you are taking root, sir. She has you by the balls. And me too. Well, we'll see. What am I, your bloody nursemaid?

In the morning he was in a bad mood. He had slept badly. His headache was worse than ever. He was stiff, he complained, from the ride the day before. I had to remind him of the gift he had promised to the Tosi farm. How much did I say? he demanded. When I told him, he reduced it to thirty pieces and gave them to me grudgingly. That is all they get from me, mind, he said, as if the gift had been my idea. So much for duty.

I rode down that afternoon. It was another fine day for winter. When I got to the farm the yard was empty. Hearing my horse, Paola came to the door. The little boy clung to her skirts. Another boy, aged about seven, looked from inside. There was no sign of the sister or the mother.

I dismounted and went up to her. She was a strange, surly creature. She did not move. I began to deliver a fine, high-faluting speech. I was on a mission from the Don. To honour the service of her father to the estate, the Don had seen fit to grant him this pension. I held up the bag of gold coins. She turned and went into the house without saying a word. She left the door open and I supposed I was to enter. The inside was one large bare-stone walled room. A smoking fire. Two beds set into the wall, with a short ladder to the upper one. A bench. Two chairs. A table. Pots and pans hung about. I had forgotten how it was to live like this. I put the money on the table and began to repeat my speech. She detached the younger child and told the older one to take him out to the yard to play. She closed the door on them. I heard their shrill voices immediately start to gabble and argue in the nonsensical way of children. The dog began to bark.

She went to the table and weighed the bag in her hand. This is for my father? she asked in her harsh voice.

Why yes, I said. The rancid smell and smokiness of the room, with the only light from its oiled paper window, this fine, upright, proud-faced woman looking me straight in the face . . .

Then I suppose I must pay you for it, she said. She went to the lower bed, pulled back the coverlet and got in. As simple as that. The children shrieked outside. The dog squealed and scampered. She climbed into the bed. Get in then, she said. What was I to do? Fascinated, excited, I stood over her – then jumped in beside her. She hoiked up her skirts, revealing her black bush. After all, I had

312

not had a woman for ages. I clambered onto her. She gripped me firmly. Her eyes were hard and staring as I got into her. I thrust – oh, the ecstasy of that reeking bed – but only for a few seconds before I spent. She twisted at once from under me and stood up, straightening her skirts. She went over to the door and opened it. She shouted to the children in dialect so fast that I could not follow her words. Then she turned to me, fumbling to put myself to rights on the edge of the bed.

There, she said. That is what you wanted eh? Her face was quite without expression.

The two boys stood looking in at me as if I was a captured bear. Or a little red-haired fox.

That's what you all want, isn't it? she said. Tell your master, the Don, to send his servant and his gold again, if he wants to. Tell him *his* great father had me when I was young. We are proud of our family. I brushed past her at the door, I swear with a silly grin on my face.

She pushed the children in. The door banged behind them. And I rode back, my shrunken tail between my legs.

A sour place, Paradise. I should have left then.

2

Whatever demons possessed the Don would lay low for weeks at a time before renewing their attacks. In that dreadful winter, they began to undermine him. Spikes were driven into his spine, so that he must lie and groan on his bed for hours at a time. When they have finished with their red-hot needles in his spine, they let him rise and walk, his face grey, on the terrace. And when he walks, they decide in their humour to tie and twist the sinews and muscles in his legs, causing him suddenly to jerk, or to run a few constricted steps like a hobbled pony. But even demons must rest. They would go away to whatever part of the Don housed them and converse among themselves about where next to attack him. When they tire of physical tortures, they sport with his mind.

What of Eugenia, and the rest of the house? Is this all invisible to them? The Don could not bear for anyone but myself to see him ill, but it was sometimes beyond even his control to hide his pain from his sister. A fever from the marshes where he camped in the war, he told her. It is nothing, it passes. He bore himself bravely. Only I was allowed to minister to him.

So it was, that one night, he with a sort of ague-like pain playing all over his body like fire, sent me running to my room for a fresh draught. I had not been in there all evening, but a candle burned on the table. It had been lit by Eugenia. She was waiting for me, like a tiger in a cave.

Now, my brother's man, she said in a cold, sneering voice. What ails my brother? You know. My servants have seen you mixing potions. I have seen the glasses by his bedside. Are you poisoning him, little gentleman, or what? She advanced on me, her finger stabbing into my chest.

Madam, I am not his physician, I said.

What are you then? she demanded. What are *you*? The Don's *personal* man? The *valet*? Something tortures him. When he came, I could see the change in him. Since then he has become worse. Is it you? What is it?

I was deeply wounded. I cared for the Don. I had shared more of his life than this woman ever could know. I opened my mouth for my stout defence – when there came a great shout of, Leporello. *Leporello*, from along the passage.

Oh, see her face blanch then, her eyes flash hatred at me. She rushes from the room, I follow.

When we come in, the Don stands in his night shirt by the bed. There. What do you see there? His question trembles in the air. He points to the corner into which the candle casts its light. There. It was there, his voice trembles.

What is there, brother? Eugenia asks, bewildered. She does not look into the corner; her eyes search his face.

He crouched, says the Don. Watching till I slept. Then he came. But who? wails Eugenia. Who is it that comes? Where is he? Here, my lord? I cross to the corner. Here?

Yes, the Don whispers. Do not wake him again.

Here? I say. And here? I kneel – though I was scared too, knowing what spirits get into houses at night. So with fear I lowered my hands into the corner, expecting what? – an animal? Warmth? Fur? A man? The feeling of *something*? To my immense relief, I felt nothing. I passed my hands in the empty air, and felt pride that I had shown such bravery in his service. It is gone, sir, I said. There is nothing here any more.

The Don looked in slow bewilderment from me to Eugenia, then back to the dreadful corner once more.

It was, he whispered. He visited me.

What, brother? said Eugenia, bewildered.

But this was a matter between men. I helped him back to bed. His body had been as hot as Hell, but now was quite cool. He lay down and closed his eyes, turning away from me. I heaped furs on him. I checked that the shutters were sealed and the heavy drapes drawn against the night. It is all closed, sir, I assured him. No one can come in. He did not answer. I ignored Eugenia, who stood at her brother's bedside, pawing softly at his coverings, her hands light and nervous. I could not think what went on in her head. Why should I care? This was the Don's world. And mine. She stood back at last. We waited in silence. I do not think he slept, and neither of us wished to be the first to move.

You may go now, she said at last.

I will stay, I said.

You will go when I say.

So I did. She stayed. A long time after, she came to my room. I expected her.

She demanded to see the medicines I had been giving to the Don. With ill-grace I opened the cupboard. There was one full bottle left. Nothing but opium in suspension, I said. And these? Herbs from a doctor in V-. This? A phial of mercury – never given.

She plucked out her skirt in front and stowed the medicines there.

I shall take these, she said. We shall see how he goes on without your ministrations.

Yes, we shall, I said bitterly.

The Don woke late, rested, but uneasy. What did he say last night? He remembered a dream. It was not pleasant.

I was . . . Was my sister here? he enquired casually. By setting his wanderings as a dream he cast about for confirmation or denial of his acts; he was like a drunkard trying to discover in a roundabout way if he had disgraced himself the night before.

Your sister came in a brief time, while you slept, sir, I said.

But he was uneasy. She saw me?

Only while you slept, sir, I said; his witness.

No – that is not how it was, he said solemnly. He broke out, My God, Leporello, have I got to live like this forever?

Not forever, sir, I said brightly, but he did not hear me.

I live like an invalid, he said. I cannot go in the sun, for it sears my eyes. I haven't had a woman for God knows how long. What's worse, I haven't wanted one. I will not have this. I must get well, Leporello. Come, fetch me water and salt to bathe my eyes. Open the shutters. Let's have the sun. Today I shall work on my papers. Tomorrow we go out and ride again and *live*. My sister wants to swaddle me up like a babe. Let somebody else give her babies. She would eat them.

He went to the bureau and began to pull out and shoot drawers to again, turning over papers impatiently. Where is it, Leporello? My book, where is it?

Sir? I said.

My manuscript. My answer. My work, he shouted. You are my servant, you should know where these things are.

I did not. There were the few letters we had brought with us. Otherwise I had packed all his things and knew of everything he had. I said I did not know. There were only those bits and pieces he had prepared for Herr Pabst. He had torn them up at V-.

So where are the pieces, numbskull? He remembered now, I am sure – and because of his remembrance he had to rage.

I don't know, sir, I said.

So how can I work? he waved his hand contemptuously at me, at the bureau. I can't work then, is that it? I can't work. I can't sit. I can't stand. I can't ride. I can't see in the light – shut the damn windows again. I can't fuck. What am I to do, then, Leporello? Die?

316

No, sir, I said stupidly.

Christ. Your Christ. Make me a drink, he said. Your stupidity has made my head ache again.

I told him his sister had taken the bottles.

What? He controlled himself barely. What a warrior you are, Leporello, he said. Then, in a tight voice, he asked me to bring Donna Eugenia to his room.

I came back through the gloomy house with Eugenia in front, twisting and turning on her heels as if a cockroach pursued her and she narrowly missed treading on it as a piece of sport.

When she entered his room, the Don said, in a light teasing way, but with an undertow of concern – My medicine, Eugenia. Leporello here tells me that you have *seized* my medicine.

It is what is making you ill, my dear. Her expression was pitying, yet stern. (Oh God who looks down on us, why do you let these farces play?) I am certain of it, she continued in her self-righteous way. I have observed you. Larger and larger doses – and all the time your temper, your condition, your nightmares have grown worse.

It-takes-away-my-pain, he said deliberately, pressing his teeth together. He was white as a ghost.

And gives you mad sights, she said, and makes you too weak to go out and your eyes feeble. If you have not the strength to do without your servant's nostrums ...

I have the strength for anything, madam, he bellowed. Leave me. Both of you. I can do without you. Without medicine. Go!

Now we shall see, said Eugenia sweeping past me in the passage.

Now we shall, I said.

The dreary day processed. I stayed in my room out of the way.

The Don had his meal sent up to him. When I knocked on his door in the evening he roared me away. No one came near that end of the house. It was with a heavy heart that I went to bed that night, lying awake a long time, wondering how the Don fared. I dozed off, and drifted in and out of sleep, cat-napping – when a new sound woke me. It sounded at first like a cat shut up some-where, scrabbling and mewling to be free. I got up and padded out into the cold passage. The noise stopped, then came again, sharper and more piercing.

I went back into my room. My fingers fumbled with the tinder. I took the lit candle along to the Don's door. There was another sound from inside; of something bumped rhythmically on the floor. I opened the door. Naked, the Don knelt, thrashing his head down, up, one side, then the other, as if trying to strike out his brains on the carpet. The high, mewing sound came from his mouth.

As I stood, terrified at this sight, Eugenia arrived at my side. She stood for a second irresolutely, then ran and knelt beside him, her hand hovering above the nodding, whimpering head. A convulsion ran through his body. Another and another. He jerked on the floor like a fish out of water.

His opium, madam, I shouted. Get it. She hesitated. Now, I shouted again. He is mad with pain.

Some stay of his agony must have been granted to the Don, for though his legs continued to twitch, his curved contorted body and his head were still. He lifted his eyes to me. Oh, the shame and pitiable disgrace in his eyes. What terrible quirk in our natures, pulls our nerves awry at these times, pulling the muscles of my face into an involuntary smile?

Eugenia came running back with the bottle. I snatched it from her. Some wine in a glass, half-full, I ordered. A moment, sir. I was afraid though to touch him. I held the bottle in front of his face, as a talisman of succour. His teeth were bared, clamped shut together; his breath hissed between. All at once his body straight-ened, his hand shot out and seized the bottle. No, no, sir, I cried. It must be diluted. But now he has the cork out and the brown syrup is running over his clenched teeth and down his chin. That's all I saw for a few moments; his other hand swung round and sent me reeling with a mighty blow on the ear. There were other servants in the room then; a dark confused mêlée round the thrashing limbs of the Don. They are holding him down and two of the stable boys have forced his jaws apart and Eugenia is pouring wine down his throat. Their huge shadows sway on the wall, as he threshes about, roaring and cursing filthily. Eugenia dances in front of his agony from foot to foot, as if dying to relieve herself ... His limbs grew slack. They dared to get up from him. I covered the Don's modesty and they bore him to the bed.

He may do damage to himself in this state, said Eugenia coolly. Bind him with sheets to the frame.

So they trussed him like a wild horse and his noble head sank like a stone into the pillows. He had had enough of a dose to kill a horse. But it took more than that to kill Don Giovanni – the Gods would not be so kind.

The yard hands stood in a little bunch, regarding their trussed master. One of them laughed. Tartini shooed them from the room. It was not my job.

When he came back, Eugenia instructed him to stay with the Don for a little while until she returned. Then she would watch him. Have someone clear this mess before I come back, she said. There was a splattering of vomit on the carpet. The opium bottle had broken and its contents filled the room with a heavy odour. She ordered the window opened. Her brother might suffocate in here.

Donna Eugenia, I began. It is my duty ...

Come with me, she said.

She took me downstairs and into the old Don's business room. Now, I must tell her the exact nature of the Don's illness. I do not know, madam. I told her what Nebel the surgeon had said to me in V-; how the illness – if it was indeed what he thought, and he could not be certain – progressed in leaps and bounds, with lulls when he would appear better, but those periods shortening.

But what is it? she demanded.

Truthfully, I said, I do not know. The surgeon said ...

Yes?

That he may have the pox. He could not be sure. That it takes men in many ways. It is a cunning disease.

She stepped forward and slapped me on the cheek. My brother *poxed*. Poxed? What do you mean? She looked half-mad. What have you done with him? She said. Poxed – that is a thing for the gutter. For people of the gutter. You come to my house and use the language of the gutter. Why then, sir, are you not poxed also? What do you mean?

I only know what I am told, I said sullenly.

She stared wildly at me. It crossed my mind that if the Don was dying, I was in her power. At that moment she would have gladly had me hanged.

And these spirits you give him – opium, whatever? This Nebel prescribed those? That is the cure?

For the pain, madam, I said. For the pain.

I must give her whatever else I had. She would administer it to the Don. There would be an end to this. If I had harmed him . . .

Madam, I said, you took the last bottle, and that was spilled.

She rang for Tartini and asked him to bring down the broken bottle. Was that a look of satisfaction he threw me as he received his instructions?

He brought it to her. Most had been lost. There was enough, I told her, for perhaps two good measures. He had been taking a larger and larger dose of late.

Then we need more of this?

A lot more, in my opinion.

You know the requirements? What to ask for? she demanded.

It is my duty to tend to him also, madam. I said.

She did not want to let me go – but she could not trust any of the country buffoons, and not spare Tartini. She gave me money to buy whatever was needed. I must ride to the nearest city of B-, and there bring back the drugs required. And the most renowned doctor.

I took the best horse, after the Don's own, and rode out early that morning. It was a cold but clear day. Spring would be here soon, thanks be to God. The house on its hill fell behind and then was swallowed by the hills I came into. I needed no map; there was only one road. My horse drummed along, I breathed in deeply the fresh morning air. Did I get to thinking that here I was, with a good horse, a suit of the Don's clothes, gold in my pocket – that

I could go anywhere I wished? Or return to a sick man's house, full of the stenches and horrors all that brings in train? To a house of people who mistrusted and hated me? Who could want all that?

And these thoughts chased wickedly though my mind even as I entered the city; in the apothecary's shop, as he weighed out the powders; as he gave me directions to a physician's house; as I got the doctor's promise that he would follow in a few days. All this time I thought of freedom. It wasn't much of a city, but there were women walking about, and wine shops, and such a feeling of health and briskness after Tenario. I had grown too used to that dull, sad life. I could have instructed the apothecary to send a rider to the Don's estate, asked him to arrange for the doctor – and I myself jig merrily off to a new life where your master does not writhe on the floor and punch you on the ear and where the only prospect is sickness and death for him and then – what fate for me?

So I got on the horse and turned his head back to Tenario and the punches on the head and the hatred of Tartini and the distrust of Eugenia, because you must do what you have promised your soul and the souls of others.

The Don is rested. The drug takes away his pain. When the doctor comes the Don refuses to see him, saying he is well now. I said to him, Sir, do you wish to go on like this forever? Quite well today. Tomorrow? And all this time the doctor downstairs, listening gravely to Eugenia's version of her brother's condition.

The Don relented. So this doctor made his examination and let a dozen ounces of blood. He instructed me in the dry-cupping of the Don's spine, to relieve the pressure of blood on the brain. This doctor left. Others were summoned in his wake. The next pooh-poohed the cupping, and said more blood must be let. Another recommended hot salt baths. The next, plain baths, cold. The Don's body, already a battlefield, became the ground for contention between these learned men. And all the time the Don, in their presence, retained, or affected, an air of dry ironical comment:

Will this mumbo-jumbo really cure, my good sir? Would they please leave him a little blood so that he might still walk and talk. Leeches, cups, lancets, hung on him; surrounded; advanced, glinting, towards him.

Other visitors came – also intent on blood. These were representatives of the moneylenders and mortgagers he had used so liberally on our travels; promising this estate in return for life. Eugenia saw to them. The Don remained in his room when these gentlemen called. Bad news travels faster than the wind ... They were paid in full as far as could be. Estate and Don limped, blanched and bled, into the early spring. There was no question of ruin, you understand; the bankers will not let a gentleman fall. It was simply that the ancient heritage leaked away into others' hands; invisible hands that worked as busily over the Don as the soft hands of his doctors. I came upon him once, when he thought himself alone, after one of these black-coated men had called – doctor or banker, who knows? – beating his forehead on the shutters, moaning, God, God – why can I not be in Hell now?

Is he to be stripped of everything? Not yet. Not yet.

A supreme piece of brave acting; always well dressed, shaved, perfumed, if possible standing erect in the centre of his room, he convinced at least some of his physicians that he was indeed getting better. I see now that this was for his sister's sake. It tortured him to know that she had seen him brought so low. He had resolved there would be no repetition. Well, you may force the body; but the ills of the mind are not so biddable; madness descended on him unawares. He ordered the long cheval glass removed from his room, complaining that he could see himself moving in it while he lay in bed. Indeed he did see himself – he confided to me that while he lay in near darkness the mirror showed him himself; young, handsome, walking in daylight in the depths of the glass.

One morning in March, he insisted on resuming his walks on the terrace. I tried not to play his keeper as we went along towards the end that overlooked the valley. His walk was a strange, jerky movement, pulling his left leg to him, as if it remembered it had been left behind. To try and correct this he brought down a cane, which he would flourish and point with, to distract attention from his limp. But his eyes were better today, he said. I can see with my old clarity, he remarked, it is simply that my body twists me aside from what I would look at. He gazed down at the farms. My estate, he murmured. My patrimony. My people. And the bankers'.

I looked down at the valley and could only see the whore, Paola, as if the whole basin made up her face, scornfully staring up at me.

The newly warm air invigorated his body perhaps a little, but not so his mind. When he came back from his walk one afternoon, after saying testily that he did not require my company, he told me quite calmly that he had seen himself walking through the olive trees. That this other Don was an equally calm, grave-faced young fellow. He had not recognised him at first, and raised his hand in salute. That the other had not replied, but stopped on the edge of the wood, looked across at him, smiled, then turned back among the trees, without sign or word. How he had thought for a moment of following him. But who knows where I should lead myself, he said, forcing a joke out of it.

Now I must sleep in his room. To make room for my bed his travelling trunk, the battered reminder and repository of our days, was moved to my room. My bed was put in the corner where his monster had lurked. I put a crucifix on that spot and crossed myself each night before trying to sleep. After a huge draught the Don would sleep, while I kept watch, on his command. When I heard his breathing change, I would allow myself to relax, to start to doze, but like an animal, always aware of every twitch and murmur from his curtained bed. In the small hours he woke, sweating, from the heaviest dose, sometimes with a yelp like another animal, one not yet created. I would struggle up and pad to his bed, with another prepared beaker of liquid, presenting it to his trembling hands, his devouring mouth.

Sometimes, drugged, he tells me his dreams.

I am standing, Leporello, in a room which is dark and yet not dark – the lighting of these particular displays affords no distinction between our waking light and dark. A lady lies in bed. The sheets are drawn up to her neck by her little fists. She gazes raptly at me, her eyes bright, mouth mischievous. I advance towards her. But the next moment I am out of there and at some ball. The lady is at my elbow, plucking my coat, asking me to turn this way and that and please to look at her. As in a game of blind-man's buff I twist this way and that, trying to catch sight of her, but always she swings just away. I grow angry and shout – though you can hear nothing truly in these dreams; the words hang about the air. The people at the ball begin to titter and laugh. There are the most vulgar, lewd faces about me; their fingers at my clothes, plucking at the cloth, pinching my flesh, and all the time whispering the most loathsome and vile insults. A rumour rises among them, passed from one to another, He is coming. *He* is coming. And there, again, myself, the young Don, swaggers through the parting, adoring crowd.

Golden mirrors reflect his magnificent progress. He comes towards me. Now the mob are turning me, turning me round. My clothes slip from me like water. My young self says, Bring in the Don's lover. And this creature is suddenly before me. She is a grossly fat dwarf, her flesh grey, her breasts wrinkled, flat, flapping; her head a loathsome imbecile's. She squats like a spider and presents her behind and waddles backwards on all fours. And I am pressed forward while her passage gapes and gapes to receive me, her eyes twist round ... Then he, from the rear, *uses* me ... And, good God, I am grateful, Leporello. Grateful.

Another dream, of war. He lies among the fallen. He is still alive though pinned down somehow, surrounded by the groans of his comrades. The dead display the most horrible signs of decay and the only way he can help them, to restore them to life, is to suck the black fluids of their rotting limbs, to lick the little worms tenderly from their faces ...

And another, where he is a boy. He is walking up a steep path. The bright sparkling sea is below. His father calls him from above. But the cliff top is empty. On the sea a ship, from which a voice hails him. And this ship, as he looks down, he sees is made of flesh, the ropes of sinews, the pulsing heart and viscera the deck, the cables disgusting entrails, the sails of skin. Then he is on board . . .

But are there no happy dreams, my lord? I say. These are terrible things.

They are not the most terrible, he says. They happen later in the dreams. Of those I cannot tell.

What, sir, I say, what could be worse than these?

I eat. I enjoy. I dwell, he said.

3

To eat. To enjoy. To dwell. The Saint's day, the Day of the Feast was here.

Replies had come long ago from the neighbouring estates. They would be delighted to attend the ancient festival. They remembered the days of the old Don, of *his* father. They will also, I thought, be pleased to see how true the stories of the Don's madness are, to cast an eye over the dying estate; to see where their benefit might lie in his misfortunes, how they could swallow him up whole after partaking of his wine and food. The Don might despise them, but I knew how cunning these country cousins are.

That morning I had not seen him look so well for a long time. He was full of the day. Today he would be prince in his own domain. Go about your art, he commanded me. I rouged his cheeks and whitened his teeth. I brushed his hair black with powder. At noon, I laid out his finest clothes, sprinkling them with scent as he put them on. We erected a king, not a prince. He got up decisively before I had finished, and demanded to see himself. I had to take him along to his sister's room, where the long glass had been put. Luckily it was turned from the window and cast only a mellow light back on him. He twisted anxiously before the glass, with, Do you think this coat, this shirt, this handkerchief, this stock – quite the thing? I assured him, Yes, yes, all was perfect. He called for his cane and walked up and down in front of the mirror, until he was convinced that his limp was barely noticeable. Is everything . . . ? Yes, my lord. Perfect. We went down.

The rooms below had been decorated with flowers. Every surface was polished, floors swept, rugs beaten; all was fragrant and clean. Tartini bowed from a doorway. The Don flourished his cane in response. Eugenia came from another door. Brother, you are sure you are well? she asked. She was in a cream gown with flowers embroidered across her bosom. Face powdered – why, she looked almost pretty. I had had nothing since my encounter with Paola. Well? Well enough, the Don thundered. Lead on, Leporello, to the kitchen. There was a reckless good humour about him, as if he had resolved to shake off, for this day at least, his dreadful condition.

Outside, coming from the short covered colonnade along the side of the house into the enclosed yard, he looked about with satisfaction. The long tables where the guests would feast were set out end to end. The stablehands were dragging out benches. They averted their eyes from the Don's eager gaze. He mounted the steps to the kitchen heavily. As I followed, I looked back and saw Eugenia watching us from deep within the shadowed colonnade.

A babble of voices came from the open kitchen door. They stopped as we entered. No, no – go on, shouted the Don, swinging in. Where is the *bollito*? he demanded. They buried their heads over their tasks in silence. They have heard I am mad, said the Don loudly. Now they have the pleasure to see I am not. Girl, come here, he beckoned to a little slip of a village girl helping with the preparations. She came to the Devil. Guide me, he said gently.

We passed among tables laden with dishes and plates; of chopped rabbit, cheeses, pastries; through the smells of garlic and hot sauces, fishguts spilled into a bucket; offal and fruit and oil, basil and roasting pork; pepper, orange, and chestnut; and the fresh sweet odour of baking bread.

As we crossed the kitchen, led by the little girl, those we passed began to talk again in whispers. They had fed on the notion of the mad Don through the thin winter; few of them had seen him since he had come back – but he was their master, and madness is not caught from such. He leaned forward on his cane. He had put on weight since the doctors had gone, and from idleness. His face was without that beautiful play of charm and joy that used to grace it, but here, as he moved through the tables, he was charming and graceful, calling here and there the name of one he recognised from the old days. So that one woman called, God bless your lordship, and some ventured to smile, as he moved limping among them.

Then we were at the huge pot over the fire. Lit early that morning before the sun came up to have it bubbling now. The Don called for a spoon to taste the *bollito*. With no more than a tongue's tip in it, he pronounced it good. Very good. Though not as they used to make it when he was a boy. Nothing is ever as good as when we taste it young. But good, good, he bellowed to them. He hobbled back and as we left the hubbub rose again. I heard later that one of the old mothers threw the spoon he had used into the fire, in case of demons. And none of the women would taste the stew. They would have tipped it away and fled from that kitchen if they knew what true demons lurked in my master's head. Out on the steps, he said, Good people, Leporello. Good people. This was his day and he was determined to enjoy it.

In the yard the village musicians had arrived and stood talking in a group round Tartini.

Gentlemen, the Don called. You are welcome. Don't wait for our guests. Strike up. Give them wine, Tartini. Tartini bowed, and the musicians did the same.

We made our way out of the yard and round to the front of the house. No music followed us. My father, the Don said, always greeted his people from there. He pointed his stick to the gates. Eugenia watched us from one of the lower front windows. Overhead the sky was a brilliant blue, with a few white clouds hung low beyond Tenario's church tower.

We moved slowly down the gravelled approach, between lemon trees in newly washed pots, down to the open gates.

Apollo and Diana. The Don named the statues that stood just outside and each side of the gates. A naked woman, one hand on one breast, the other between her legs. A strapping young chap, a cloth round his loins; helmet. This was the first time I had been close to them. Like me, my father was a pagan, he said. They are very old. They have stood here a long time. Perhaps they will join us. Give us strength. The statues looked blindly over the valley.

The poplared avenue fell curving into the valley. Along the sweep where the trees finished and the bare road took up I could see the first of the Don's guests moving upwards on foot. Bright clothes flamed on the road, flickering red and yellow and white as they came to the first of the trees. Others were leaving the little farms, each with its spread handkerchief of fields and feathery trees, making their way carefully across each other's boundaries of stones and brooks, until they met on the narrow road that followed the river. And, tiny as a thimble, on the hill road, the way we had first come to this place, rolled the first coach bearing gentry. Those who reckoned themselves my master's equals.

Music came, thin and jaunty, over the house. The sun was hot at its spring height. We stood and awaited his guests.

Will they spare me? the Don asked suddenly.

Sir? I said, surprised.

Nothing. No, he said with great force. Here I shall stand. It is my duty.

The confidence in his face had drained away. He was again pale.

The sun is very bright, sir, I said. Perhaps you should not ... Shall I fetch your hat at least?

My sword. That is it. Where is my sword? He slapped the side of his coat. You have taken my sword, you wretch, he shouted.

I'll fetch it, sir. At once. This was the first time for weeks he had been so well; I did not wish to do anything to upset him. And your hat. Hat and sword. Hat and sword, I repeated ridiculously as I ran to the house.

There was no sign of Eugenia. I ran to his room and back down; sword in one hand, broad-brimmed hat in the other. But at the bottom of the drive the gateway was empty.

328

Turning to look back at the house, I saw him at some distance toiling slowly but steadily across the terraced garden. I shouted to him, but he did not hear me and kept going up, until he disappeared behind a high bay hedge.

The families were arriving. I heard their chatter in the avenue. They came round the last corner. I hid the sword and hat behind the statue of Apollo. I drew myself up. I cut a fine sight – in my eyes, if not theirs. They halted a little way off the gates, their numbers growing all the time; women in black dresses, girls in white, their hair threaded with spring flowers; the men wore red and yellow and blue blouses, embroidered waistcoats; their boots gleamed. They stood, regarding me with suspicion. A delegation of two tall young men flanking an elder came forward.

The old man, with a head like a bull with a springing crop of white-yellow curls, gave me a curt bow; a mere formality, not a sign of any respect.

You are the Don's man, he said. Not a question, but a statement.

Where is the Don? said one of the young men. He had red hair and bulging eyes, as if he had a fire in his head.

They are bringing the statue of the saint from the village, said the other young man. What he looked like I can't for the life of me remember.

Come in, sirs. Be welcome, I said, with as much jollity as I could muster. From the valley I heard the low beating of a drum.

We cannot enter on your say-so, said the old man bluntly. We cannot enter without the Don's blessing. He must greet the statue.

I am sure . . . , I began grandly.

Are you the boss now? fiery eyes asked. We just told you – we cannot go in before the statue. Without the Don's words. The growing crowd pressed up to us. They fell to discussing my ignorance and stupidity and appearance as if I was not there. The old man waved them to silence. Pardon, he said, with no apology in his voice. You are a stranger here.

All will be done in the proper manner, I shouted to the assembly. Compose yourselves . . .

All at once their expressions changed; scorn dissolving to that sly respect peasants show their betters. I congratulated myself on my natural authority. But they were not looking at me, but past me to where Eugenia and Tartini were coming down the drive. Eugenia walked by me without a word.

The old man bowed so low I thought his head would touch the earth.

Signor Laschi, it is a year since we met, said Eugenia as he kissed her hand. Too long an absence. I have to tell you that the Don is unwell. He has asked that I represent him today.

The old man's face puzzled this out for a moment. But it is always the Don, he said at last.

She smiled. I do know the words my father used, she said sweetly. We shall wait for the statue, then go up to the house.

He backed away bowing and consulted with the other men. It was clear they were not happy that a woman should perform the rite.

I edged to her side. My master? The Don . . . , I began. But I did not exist for her. She stepped away from me and addressed the crowd. Come, while we wait for our saint, you will take wine. Tartini, you and Leporello (my name plucked out and held aloft with tongs) fetch down some wine for these good folk.

Reduced to stablehand or footman by her tone, I was to take orders from the steward. Tartini's mean little eyes, swimming in their watery mustard, registered his pleasure. As we went back, I saw that the white shutters on the Don's window had been closed.

We got up to the courtyard. I halted. Come on, said Tartini.

Fetch your own wine, old man, I said. My duty lies with my master.

His face twisted. Get moving, you little bum crawler, he said. You had an order from our mistress.

If there were enough of your body to give the maggots a good feed, I'd kill you for that, I said, as cool as ever the Don would have been.

The wine, he screeched as I left him.

Stick it up your arse, I said.

So two gentlemen's gentlemen conversed in a courtyard, on a hill, in a bowl of the world, under the April sky, as if they were any more than ants in the hand of God. It is a very long time ago – and the memory still pushes the angry blood along my veins.

The musicians sat against the wall, drinking, lazily absorbed in our debate. Play, I shouted. Play. Your friends are coming.

Inside, the house was silent and cool. Going up the stairs, with the fear just settling in my stomach that I had burned my boats with Tartini, and the prospect of God alone knew what lying in front of me, I heard the band strike up, because, after all, they too were cowards on this earth, and were not certain who had just ordered them to play.

Their strains weakened as I mounted into the house; were shut off in mid-bray as the lined door shut behind me on the passage that led to the private rooms.

I listened a moment at his door, heard nothing, and knocked.

Yes? his voice was testy and low.

Leporello, sir, I announced and went in.

The Don sat in the chair against the window, the sunlight striping across his body through the shutters.

It is cold, he complained. Let the sun in.

Your eyes, sir? They will not trouble you?

Open the shutters, he commanded. Bring me the spectacles.

He stirred like a salamander when the warm sun struck across him. I brought the green spectacles. He took them but made no effort to put them on.

Is there anything I can get you, sir? I asked.

I had to come back here, he said. I could not ... My father must look down on me and weep. I could not face them.

The spectacles dangled in his hand. His body sank inside his crumpled clothes.

Today, I thought I would be well, he said. His eyes stared straight at the bright sky outside. And then he said, Do you know that I entertain in this room? Women. In that bed. I wake in my own filth, my milt. Like a frog.

He gripped the arms of the chair and pulled himself upright. Sophia came to me once. He spoke on in this level, cold, dreamy way. My child too. My child appeared. He spoke to me. A grave little soul.

I looked round the bright room, as if willing them to appear for his sake.

What – I want to ask you, Leporello – what is going on? What precisely is going on with me?

It . . . it's your fever, sir, I stammered. The war . . .

I know what fever is, he said. I'm as cold as a corpse. Feel. Feel my hand.

I held back. How can you feel your master's hand?

Don't fondle me, he bellowed. Grasp it. Tell me what you find.

It is warm, sir, I assured him. But it was cold. As if a cold dew came from it. He clutched me with great strength. There, he said. He crushed my hand. Does that hurt?

N..no, sir, I gasped.

He let go. And left the stain of his cold still on my palm.

What else then? You think that I am mad?

I made no answer.

Madness. That would be an answer, he said. Were you ever in an asylum, little Leporello? Do you know how they whirl you and soak you and bleed and beat you? Oh, even the grandest of gentlemen. We are all equal there. What do you think, eh? Do I belong there?

Your fever, sir. It was all I could think to say.

These things return. They go away, I said.

They do? Go to the window, he said in almost his old authoritative way. Tell me what you see. I can hear them.

The throb of the drum was much nearer now. I looked out.

They are bringing the statue of the saint up the hill, I said. As they were. The gaudily painted figure, borne aloft on a stretcher on the shoulders of four men, swayed between the trees, disappeared, bobbed out again. I watched, hearing only his breathing and the drum.

It is at the gates, my lord, I announced.

I stood at the window, not caring to turn round.

My father was there every year to welcome the saint of Tenario, he said in that terrible new, calm voice.

I gazed on. Eugenia in her cream gown. Tartini in his cow-shit suit. A priest in white and silver. The drummer in his quartered blouse, beating slow. The statue. Villagers and farmers behind – and the coach we had seen on the hillside, the sun flashing off its roof among the poplars.

Do you know why I left the gate? the Don continued. I was afraid. I have tried never to be afraid of anything in my life. It is a glorious trophy, life. What is there to be afraid of in it? But when you left me and I stood alone and looked down into that valley, the valley of my childhood and youth, standing to greet my neighbours and all those reckoned to be mine, my property – the tenants, the girls I fucked who are grown women now, my bastards, each tree and grove and pool – all I could see creeping up the hill was their giant worm. The birds jabbered in the trees. The wind crackled like fire in the new leaves. The sun had set the whole valley on fire ...

I still did not turn.

So I sent Eugenia to say I was not well. She did not even argue with me. Or beg me to present myself. He was silent again, then said. What do you see?

The procession, sir, nothing more.

Just the procession, sir, I repeated when he did not answer. They are nearing the yard. Going out of sight. A coach is coming. Nothing more. Spurred by his silence at last I looked round. I raised my hand in a tentative movement to gain his attention and realised that though his eyes stared fixedly at the window, he could not see at all.

Not quite true. He could see the window as a milky oblong, myself as a shimmering black shape; like a snake on a fan, as he said. He had no choice but to admit his blindness to me. He swore me to keep his secret. Such attacks had occurred before, and after the first, which I knew about, he had managed to conceal them. They passed in a few minutes usually. This one had come on when he had got back up to the house. He had reached this room. But his sister had come in directly. He had stumbled into the chair, saying he felt faint. To his shame, he had shouted at her to leave him, to send Leporello to him. Only Leporello ...

(Ah, good, dear, true Leporello . . .)

How can I face them like this, he cried dreadfully.

With my help, sir, I said quietly. What was I thinking of?

He was a sick man. But without him I was nothing. I would be adrift in the world. So servants use their masters.

A few minutes, he said. A few minutes. You are right. What was I thinking of? I shall be well in a moment.

He sat for no more than that, then rose, a little shakily, but on his feet.

Prepare me, he said. I will go down and be with my people.

I prepare him. Asking him as I do so – is he quite well? Should he not rest? And all the time his temper and wounded spirit rising in him. As I intended.

Will he take his spectacles?

God – No!

He takes a few turns round the room, limping.

His cane?

Again – a thunderous No!

Let us go down.

The feast was in full swing. The Baron B- and the Count of C- have brought an unmarried daughter apiece to see the handsome Don – a marriage may well be politic now, they think, because the Don would be glad of any settlement however small, and by all accounts he was not long for this world, and there was the chance of the whole estate of Tenario . . .

The tables had been pushed back. From the niche in the wall where they had reverently placed him, the saint overlooked the dancers. Their steps stamped the last of winter into the first dust. The sun hung a foot over the house, westering. The Baron and the Count and their veiled daughters and hard-faced wives and the grannies and granddads who had not drunk enough yet to forget their age and dance and the children too young to dance sat on the benches along the wall and watched youth and middle age whirl before them.

And what did the unmarried daughters make of the man they

had come to see? The wicked son of the old Don, the terrible ravisher and seducer, came from between the pillars of the colonnade, myself tactfully, as if by accident, guiding him by the elbow. Still a handsome man by any score; but grey-headed, his face heavy and severe; the figure of legend thick-set, the muscles of his arms swollen to fat and bulging out his coat. For the first time I saw him with others' eyes and for the first time pitied him.

There was no respectful slackening of the music when he appeared, rather the piper pumped his elbow deeper into his bellows and puffed out his cheeks like balloons; the fiddler's elbow flew faster. The dancers swirled and capered, their eyes flickering over the Don, then fastening again on their partners; their efforts redoubled as if to show how he had insulted them by his absence. That they had no need of him.

Eugenia came to his side. Her face was angry. The yard had become a common riot, she said. Brother . . . Then, with a venomous glance at me, she whispered fiercely in his ear. His eyes blinked once. I caught Tartini by the arm, and pointed out to the yard.

Why this insolence to our master? I hissed.

They are upset because he did not come to greet them. That he saw fit to send his servant, he said.

And why your insolence? I demanded. Bring a chair for our master. Or do you want me to tell him how you milk the estate? A vicious and lucky guess, as I saw by the change in his face.

Two of the boys brought out a heavy, carved chair. As the Don went to sit, he swayed. A momentary faintness, I thought. But he seemed to recover at once, straightened his back and sat, a king above his people.

When the dance ended, Eugenia looked at him expectantly. When nothing was forthcoming, she called out, Well done. Wine for the good people of Tenario.

Some murmured their thanks. More inspected the Don, with scorn on their faces. This was the first time many of them had seen their master since his return. They had heard much of him while he had been away. Their faces said. Is this the great Don Giovanni? The scourge of women. The terror of men?

Come, join our dancing, Don Giovanni, one of them called. But he only smiled benignly and waved a hand in a polite gesture of regret. The men round the one who had shouted out laughed derisively. The Don must have thought this part of the general merriment, for he only smiled gently again. The Baron B- and Count C- led their wives and daughters in to present them to the Don. Their effusive greetings, the presents they put at his feet when he failed to reach out his hands for them, all seemed to go for naught. They came away with faces puzzled by his bland weary manner, empty smile, the few vague words which were his only answers to their enquiries as to his health, their health. There were to be no marriage plans laid that day, it seemed. Their journeys had been wasted.

The dancing began again. The Don asked for his chair to be moved back; the light was too bright, he could not see the dancers. The late afternoon sun now shone straight into the colonnade. He sat back in the shadows, at a farther remove from the company, until it seemed that by and by he was forgotten by them. Only the declining rays reached to him – until the sun sank below the outer yard wall; the white of the house turned to honey, then to rose.

When the Tenario bell rang the sunset hour and the yard was full of warm grey shadows, the first torches were lit, the tables dragged together into the middle of the yard, benches carried to them. Dishes and plates and flagons poured down from the kitchen in a never-ending stream, and the villagers seethed at the sides of the table like the banks of a swift river. And all this time, through the visits of his honoured guests, the dancing, I stood behind the Don's chair and he said not a single word to me.

Something had happened to him. I did not know what, but this latest, benign, simple Don was more terrible in its way than ever as a roaring madman. Eugenia came to him. It was time for him to preside over the feast, she said. When he did not respond, she repeated herself, as if to a refractory child. He got up slowly. He stumbled on the shallow steps into the yard, but then seemed to compose himself. My hand hovered at his elbow, but he walked straight-backed with hardly a sign of his limp to the head of the table, the boys bringing his chair down behind.

At the far end, in the other place of honour, the statue of the saint had been placed on a chair. The painted mouth given a faint smirk by the torchlight, right hand raised in a blessing; its huge black ringed eyes stared down the table at the Don.

God and the saint alone knew what the Don saw. On his right hand sat Eugenia. On his left, the priest of Tenario. The priest rose hastily and bowed to the Don. The Don ignored him. The priest hesitated, murmured a few words of holy apology, and lowered himself down again. Priests must be polite to their lords. No sign of Paola or any of her family. Silence reigned. They all waited for the Don to do something. But he did nothing but sit, his hands resting on the table. His sister looked expectantly at him. The priest fingered his cross with one hand, his crotch with the other. Then the old man I had seen at the gate stood up abruptly. He spoke in a loud, grating voice: Before the meal can be taken the Don must say the words. Forgive me, signore, for speaking so bluntly. It is a long time since you were among us. It was your father's custom to welcome us and the new spring. It must be yours too. With a brief bow to the Don he sat down as abruptly as he had risen.

The Don remained seated.

You must speak, brother, I heard Eugenia whisper to him.

He rose then. His face, empty of expression, seemed rested, younger; but weakened too, as if his strength had drawn off somewhere inside to fight other battles.

My friends, he began, and forthwith stopped. They gazed at him.

My friends, you are welcome, he began again. My father . . . his speech halted again. Then his words flowed on. I welcome your saint. A wooden man. Old Marinari carved him in my childhood. I remember because from the same wood he made me a tiny chariot . . . His voice drifted away, he screwed up his eyes to peer over their heads to the sky.

. . . Monsieur Voltaire has the god Priapus say that he was carved from a fig tree, the carpenter did not know whether to make a god or a bench, so he made a god. I could not travel in my chariot; the saint cannot walk or talk, locked in his wood – His words were dammed again; trickled free – You will have heard of the momentous events in America, in France. Everywhere men are aflame, flickering. They rise ... flicker ... rise. Who is to say whether we live or die, whether our motions, our travels about the world, our breaths ... He stopped dead then, in their dead silence. Men flame, he said. His mouth worked but no more words came. He sat down. He talked quietly to himself. It seems, I heard him say, that there has been a confusion in the lighting of the heavens. That diamonds, linen, grooves, emperors, journeys to come, still to be done. To flame ... He raised his head suddenly and said in a thick, slurred voice, Go on – go on with your feast, good citizens.

He slumped in the chair, his eyes gazing down at his hands. All were silent.

Eugenia stood up and said in a cool clear voice, The Don is ill. Go on. As he told you. Tartini. You – Leporello – your assistance.

When my hand went under his arm to lift him, the Don looked suddenly up. There were tears in his eyes. We helped him across the yard, with no word from the tables. Once through the house door I was shocked to hear the babble that instantly broke out; the delight of gossip in misfortune.

We put the master into his bed. Eugenia, with an odd harshness, said, You will stay and watch over your master, Leporello. Someone must oversee the feast. I will have the girl bring you a light. She took one more look at the Don, then she turned and walked firmly from the room. He lay with his back to me, facing the wall. As I stood, irresolute, he spoke in a low voice: Has she gone?

Yes, my lord, I replied.

He did not turn, or say another word.

When I came down the church clock rang the mid of night. Twice it had chimed since the revellers had left, sullenly bearing their saint away under the dark poplars. Ordinarily, the kitchen girl who brought me the light had said, these feasts lasted well into the night, the dancing began again after the meal, there was licence and fumbling and husbands to be got in the dark outside the yard – but not tonight.

338

I let myself out into the garden. My master above was sleeping deeply; too deeply. I had yielded my duty to Eugenia, and left her sitting, tense and watchful, watching her brother with a stern, helpless face.

I went down two of the grass terraces. I peed against a tree and, buttoning, gazed up at the house. All dark, quiet, folding its horror inside itself. I wandered on to the gravel approach, walking slowly and sadly between the scenting trees. Something was amiss at the gates.

As I came up I saw that the head of the statue the Don had called Apollo had been knocked off, the Don's sword inserted down the hollow neck, his hat placed at a jaunty angle on the hilt.

And seeing this desecration tears came to my eyes at last. Oh, let us ride, my lord, I whispered into the night. Let us ride once more. You and I. Go. Move. You say that movement is life . . .

And in my mind he comes from between the trees, speedy and silent as he used to escape from a tryst. He says to me, Quick, Leporello, the horses. Or they will surely have me. My sword? Hat? I gesture to the statue. He leaps lithely onto the plinth and plucks sword and hat away. From the bushes I lead out the miraculously provided horses. You are a wonder, my boy, he exclaims. But quick now, or they will take us. Let's ride. He twists up in the saddle and his mount rears for joy.

Then we are on horseback and streaming across the plain of Caesaretto; then in a coach; another and another, all the time moving, moving, through houses and women, locks and virgins, seas and widows, trees and trumpets, husbands, strumpets, cold smoking dawns and hot nights and all the time the faces of smiling women and girls call on us to stop, stop, just once, just once more, dear sirs, as we dash on through rivers and windows, walls and woods, beds, chamberpots; skirts up, money down . . .

Ride for your life, Leporello, he shouts in triumph, and bugger Hell and Heaven . . .

All was silent. I clambered up the broken statue and retrieved his belongings. Down in the valley a single tiny torch flame crossed from one darkness to another. I got down awkwardly and walked slowly back up to the house, to my duty, to my master.